Western
Voices

Western Voices

125 YEARS OF COLORADO WRITING

Colorado Historical Society

Edited by
Steve Grinstead and Ben Fogelberg

Fulcrum Publishing
Golden, Colorado

Library of Congress Cataloging-in-Publication Data
Western voices : 125 years of Colorado writing / Colorado Historical Society ; edited by Steve Grinstead and Ben Fogelberg.
    p. cm.
  ISBN 1-55591-531-0 (alk. paper)
  1. Colorado—History. 2. Colorado—Description and travel. 3. Colorado—Biography. I. Grinstead, Steve. II. Fogelberg, Ben. III. Colorado Historical Society.
  F776.5.W475 2004
  978.8—dc22   2004013717

Printed in the United States of America
0 9 8 7 6 5 4 3 2 1

Editorial: Katie Raymond, Faith Marcovecchio
Design: Cover by Nancy Duncan-Cashman, Interior by Patty Maher

On the cover: The young reader on the cover was photographed in 1882 or 1883 at the Frank Kuykendall studio in Maysville, Colorado. He surrounds himself with props taken straight out of western lore: a six-shooter, a poker deck, a sturdy pair of boots, a generous supply of beer, a lit stogie (with a second cigar at the ready), and a spittoon. Clichés by today's standards, perhaps, but the photographer took this image when the American West was still in its infancy. Just a few years earlier, and only three years after achieving statehood, Coloradans foresaw the state's historical riches and founded the Colorado Historical Society to chronicle the West as it was truly becoming—its people, its paraphernalia, and, most of all, its stories.

Colorado Historical Society publications are available for purchase at the Colorado History Museum Store (1300 Broadway, Denver, Colorado, 80203) and at the Society's regional museums. Or, join the Society and receive publications as a benefit of membership; for information, call (303) 866-3678 or visit us on the Web at www.coloradohistory.org.

Generous assistance for this publication was provided by the Colorado Historical Foundation, with funding provided in part by the Josephine H. Miles Fund and the A. E. Reynolds manuscript fund.

Fulcrum Publishing
16100 Table Mountain Parkway, Suite 300
Golden, Colorado 80403
(800) 992-2908 • (303) 277-1623
www.fulcrum-books.com

Contents

Foreword

Ever since the region's first inhabitants chiseled petroglyphs and scratched pictographs on canyon walls, westerners have celebrated and recorded their history. Foremost among Colorado institutions to collect, preserve, exhibit, and publish has been the 125-year-old Colorado Historical Society.

The Society's publications have thrived on contributions not just from card-carrying historians but from any and all interested writers. Those contributions have ranged from the work of students thrilled at their first publication, to reflections by the state's movers and shakers, to the reminiscences of the earliest settlers to put down roots.

One Society founder, *Rocky Mountain News* editor William N. Byers, was the state's leading booster and a man of encyclopedic interests. Newspaper stories, of course, are the first draft of much history. But journalists often do the *final* draft too, with books that make first-rate history. Such is the case with two best-selling authors included here, Clark Secrest and Richard A. Kreck. Some of this book's authors—Helen Hunt Jackson, Louis L'Amour, David Lavender, and Pulitzer Prize–winner Wallace Stegner—have achieved national literary acclaim. The voices of such prominent historians as Quintard Taylor and Patricia Nelson Limerick are heard here as well.

Other authors, such as LeRoy R. Hafen, Steve Leonard, Duane Smith, and myself, have made teaching and writing Colorado history their life's work. Hafen deserves a pedestal as the Society's first professional historian, armed with a University of California at Berkeley Ph.D. Arriving by Model T from California in 1924, he turned *The Colorado Magazine* into a gold mine for researchers and writers. Since 1923 that wonderful journal has published thousands of documented articles. It is *the* place to begin exploring Colorado people, places, and things. The magazine and its predecessor, the Sons of Colorado's *The Trail*, and its successors, *Colorado Heritage* and the Society's scholarly journals, provide a twelve-foot shelf from which the pieces in this anthology were selected. This celebration of the Colorado Historical Society's founding in 1879 offers a tiny but tantalizing sampling of the Society's productions.

Maxine Benson, another of the Society's historians, followed Hafen, Agnes Wright Spring, and Harry Kelsey as editor of *The Colorado Magazine*; she produced for that magazine's farewell issue a centennial history of the Society, and she provides one of this book's outstanding selections. David F. Halaas and, most recently, Modupe Labode have subsequently filled the chief historian's chair and also contributed to this book.

Today, *Colorado Heritage*, the Society's glossy popular-history magazine, is by far the best way to keep abreast of both new research and general-interest tales of Colorado's past. *Heritage* has been inventive in dealing with not only past but also current events of historic proportions, such as the Columbine High School massacre and the great blizzard of 2003.

Society publications director David N. Wetzel expedited this volume—edited by Steve Grinstead, current editor of *Colorado Heritage*, and Ben Fogelberg, editor of the monthly *Colorado History NOW* newsletter. They offer it to you, dear reader, in honor of the Colorado Historical Society's 125th anniversary. This anthology, like the Society itself, strives to reach beyond the mythical West to bring you the people of Colorado's past and their stories—the tragic as well as the celebratory.

This past grows ever richer and ever more relevant as we face a future with ups and downs just as deep as Colorado's canyons and as high as its peaks.

—*Thomas J. Noel*

Preface

Shortly after he was hired as editor of *Colorado Heritage* magazine in 1990, Clark Secrest bought a complete set of its longtime predecessor, *The Colorado Magazine*, from a rare-book dealer. Then he began to read it, cover to cover—from the first magazine, published in November 1923, to the last, published in 1980. Reading nights and weekends (when he was not busy writing a major book on vice, crime, and prostitution in Denver), he spent the bulk of his eleven years at the Society digesting something like 1,350 articles spread across thousands of pages. Thus, when he says, "The old *Colorado Magazine* is a state treasure," he speaks with authority.

The person most responsible for this treasure is LeRoy R. Hafen, the influential first editor of The Colorado Magazine, the Society's first state historian, and one of its most important curators. Hafen brought all three of these responsibilities to bear on The *Colorado Magazine*'s legacy, for he scoured the state in search of newspapers and other valuable documents; researched and wrote prodigiously (publishing some fifty articles in The Colorado Magazine alone); and sought out pioneer reminiscences, primary historical accounts, and—most important of all—new authors. Nor did he worry about specialties and professional academic degrees, for among the magazine's 850 contributors can be found lawyers, doctors, educators, philanthropists, poets, ranchers, anthropologists, and philosophers. Forty of these, not counting Hafen, had three or more articles to their credit over the life of the magazine.

When Hafen retired in 1954, after a thirty-year tenure, Agnes Wright Spring took over the magazine's editorship. Like Hafen, Spring performed other valuable services for the Society while editor—primarily, directing the education program—and she was a highly respected researcher and writer. The only person to hold the position of state historian for two states (Colorado and Wyoming, at different times), Spring pursued the same practices and favored the same kinds of subjects as

Hafen—a balance of firsthand accounts with secondary historical writing, and an emphasis on traditional subjects such as mining, ranching, forts, the gold rush era, and individual, social, and community life in nineteenth-century Colorado.

By the time Spring retired in 1963, however, a fundamental change had taken place in the history profession, and the magazine reflected that change. Graduate education boomed in the postwar years, "publish or perish" became a driving force in academic life, and teacher-historians like the University of Colorado's Robert G. Athearn encouraged their best graduate students to publish early and often—particularly in *The Colorado Magazine*. As a result, the magazine became more the province of scholars, and new emerging subjects vied for space with the old—among them politics, studies of ethnic life, historiography, historic preservation, women, architecture, and twentieth-century issues.

But if its articles were slightly more academic, the magazine also became more appealing in its format and design, featuring bold cover illustrations and generous photographs and artwork inside. Its new editor, Harry E. Kelsey Jr. planned this change with designer William Marshall, the Society's executive director, and for nearly two decades *The Colorado Magazine* combined excellent scholarship with a more popular look. In addition, the Society launched a monthly four-panel newsletter, *Mountain and Plain History Notes*, which led off with a historical cover story that raised it above the aspirations of most newsletters. During his three-year tenure, Kelsey received his Ph.D. from the University of Denver, and in 1969 the Society, in cooperation with Pruett Publishing, issued his revised dissertation as one of its first full-length books, *Frontier Capitalist: The Life of John Evans*.

Maxine Benson, who received her Ph.D. in history at the University of Colorado in 1968, took over as the magazine's editor in 1966, when Kelsey resigned to become state historian of the Michigan Historical Commission. Like her predecessors, Benson was appointed Colorado state historian, and she served as editor of *The Colorado Magazine* until 1971, when she took a year's leave of absence to accept an editorial fellowship with the Joseph Henry Papers at the Smithsonian Institution. During that time, Virginia McConnell Simmons served as the magazine's acting editor. When Benson returned to the Society as curator of documentary resources, the editor's mantle fell to Cathryne Johnson in 1973. The occasion of her return was particularly apt, since the magazine had just turned fifty, and a special anniversary issue brought together the reminiscences of its four guiding editors—LeRoy R. Hafen, Agnes Wright Spring, Harry Kelsey Jr., and Maxine Benson.

During the next four years, momentous changes took place in the Society, and these led to the end of *The Colorado Magazine* and its era. Construction of a new home for the Colorado Historical Society caused unexpected repercussions for all programs and activities—including the magazine—and the appointment of a new president, Barbara Sudler, in 1979 posed an opportunity to go in new directions. Already, under Cathryne Johnson, the Society had squeezed two books out of the magazine series—*Bent's Old Fort*, which is still in demand, and *The Colorado Book of the Dead: The Prehistoric Era*, a study of Colorado's early cultures by archaeologist Bruce Rippeteau.

To address Barbara Sudler's plan for a broad-based membership-building magazine, Johnson (and Maxine Benson, who continued to serve as advisory editor) developed an ambitious three-part program consisting of a popular historical magazine, *Colorado Heritage*, a monograph series, and a monthly newspaper of eight to twelve pages replacing *Mountain and Plain History Notes*. The final issue of *The Colorado Magazine*, a concise history of the Colorado Historical Society by its last state historian, Maxine Benson, appeared as a single volume for the year 1980.

The new program, which began that year, is still in effect almost twenty-five years later—except for one significant modification. Rather than simply adding a separate monograph series, the Society adopted a dual-purpose program consisting of *Colorado Heritage* and a set of scholarly volumes that could accommodate a collection of articles (in a single, continuing journal) or, from time to time, a historical monograph. Called *Essays and Monographs in Colorado History* (now simply *Colorado History*), the series more closely resembles the old *Colorado Magazine* in its fuller documentation, outside manuscript review, and appeal to a more focused audience of historians, students, and history buffs. Meanwhile, *Colorado Heritage* remains the Society's popular flagship publication, appealing to a broader audience with well-researched but generally shorter, well-illustrated articles on inherently interesting topics written with the general reader in mind.

Today, slightly more than eighty years after *The Colorado Magazine* first appeared, it's fair to say that more readers of the Society's publications— and more *kinds* of readers—are learning more about Colorado history, in general and in depth, than ever before. During the past quarter century, by itself or in cooperation with regional publishers, the Society has produced a biography of Denver's first significant architect, Robert Roeschlaub; an evocative word-and-picture study of childhood in early Colorado; a massive two-volume work on the history of Leadville; and an inside look into the world of the Cheyenne Dog Soldiers based on the drawings of Indian warrior-artists. In addition, *Colorado History NOW*, a new incarnation of the Society's first newspaper of 1981, offers fresh monthly cover stories on people and events in Colorado history, as did the old *Mountain and Plain History Notes*. Its content also reflects its readers keen and active interest in historic preservation. And in the Society's newest publishing venture—unforeseen in 1981—the Society brings history and biography to young students on its Web site, as well as book reviews, bibliographies, and an updated list of new Colorado books for historians and mature students.

The credit for this sizable, if not vast, accumulation of Colorado history goes, of course, to the authors who have contributed to the Society's magazines, journals, newsletters, and newspapers over the years—some of them anonymous, which usually means "staff-written." But an equal measure of credit goes to its editors. Earlier editors include *Colorado Heritage* magazine's Judith Gamble, whose enthusiasm for linking the past to the present led her to the San Luis Valley for a photo-essay on Hispanic textiles, through Denver's park system, and on an intermittent walking excursion along Denver's Highline Canal to provide a firsthand look at that 120-year-old engineering marvel. The redoubtable Clark Secrest, who followed Gamble as *Heritage's* editor, not only gave the magazine a decisively reader-friendly tone and edgy character but also left a significant legacy in preparing, over ten yearly issues, a broad, colorful view of the last century in a boxed volume called *Twentieth-Century Colorado: A Decade-by-Decade History*.

Among the current editors are Steve Grinstead, who originated the idea for *Western Voices: 125 Years of Colorado Writing*; Ben Fogelberg, who joined Grinstead in judiciously making the selections; and Larry Borowsky, a graduate of the University of California at Berkeley, who began as a publications department intern in 1990 and carried on a serious (and accomplished) flirtation with the Society as a freelance writer and editor until finally becoming wedded to the editorship of the *Colorado History* series.

All these—my editorial forebears and colleagues—I thank for their commitment to the authors, to the Society, and to Colorado history. And since my colleagues understand my penchant for databases, tables, and charts, I hope to recognize others, apart from my own name, in the following list as having made a considerable contribution to the program. Finally, however, a good deal of thanks—for the publications program and for this book—goes to the Society's presidents since I have been editor and publications director. They have all made their own mark, and a beneficial one, on the program: Barbara Sudler (1979–89), James E. Hartmann (1990–96), and the Society's current president, Georgianna Contiguglia.

—*David N. Wetzel*
April 2004

Colorado Historical Society Publication Editors, 1923–2004

The Colorado Magazine
LeRoy R. Hafen, 1925–54*
Agnes Wright Spring, 1954–63
Harry E. Kelsey Jr., 1964–66
Maxine Benson, 1966–71
Virginia McConnell Simmons (acting editor), 1971–72
Cathryne Johnson, 1973–80

Mountain and Plain History Notes
Harry E. Kelsey Jr., 1964–66
Maxine Benson, 1966–71
Virginia McConnell Simmons, 1971–72
Cathryne Johnson, 1973–80

Colorado Heritage
Cathryne Johnson, 1981–82
David N. Wetzel, 1983–86
Judith L. Gamble, 1986–89

Clark Secrest, 1990–2001
Larry Borowsky, 2001
Steve Grinstead, 2002–present

Colorado History series**
Cathryne Johnson, 1981–82
David N. Wetzel, 1983–96
Steve Grinstead, 1997–2002
Larry Borowsky, 2002–present

Colorado History NOW
Cathryne Johnson, 1981–82
Alicia Fields, 1983–86
Margaret "Peg" Ekstrand, 1986–97
Dianna Litvak, 1997
Clark Secrest, 1997–98
Ariana Harner, 1998–2000
Ben Fogelberg, 2001–present

*Before Hafen assumed editorship of the magazine in January 1925, the responsibility rotated among the Society's curators. Hafen's name did not appear on the masthead, however, until 1928.
**Originally *Monograph Series*, then *Essays and Monographs in Colorado History*
***Originally *Colorado Heritage News*, then *Colorado History News*

Acknowledgments

Culling the selections in this volume from more than a thousand candidates and piecing them into a cohesive whole was no small task, and the editors relied on the wisdom and efforts of many in making the book happen. We would like to thank our editorial review committee—Maxine Benson, David Fridtjof Halaas, and Stephen J. Leonard—for their knowledge and their insights in reviewing the essays. Former *Colorado Heritage* editor Clark Secrest provided valuable up-front input regarding his personal favorites from past issues of *Heritage* and *The Colorado Magazine*. Colorado Historical Society chief historian Modupe Labode offered thoughtful feedback, studied opinions, and an always timely sense of humor (her trademarks) along the way. Our trusted advisor and patient boss, David N. Wetzel, supported this project from its inception and did some nice detective work in tracking down copyright holders for permissions.

Eric Paddock, the Society's curator of photography, steered us to the image that became a unanimous choice for the book's cover. Associate curator of photography Judy Steiner helped us find many of the other photographs for the selections. We extend a personal thank you to our coworker Susan Romansky for her scanning assistance and for patiently sharing her computer equipment with us. Interns Diyn Logan and Amy Zimmer helped out greatly by carefully cleaning up scanned text for a few of the essays. And, as always, we could never have done it without the hardworking librarians of the Society's Stephen H. Hart Library—Rebecca Lintz, Barbara Dey, Karyl Klein, and Ruba Sadi—and the equally hardworking photo studio crew—Jay Di Lorenzo and Michael "Spydr" Wren—who helped us with the illustrations.

We feel fortunate to have worked with Robert Baron of Fulcrum Publishing, and we appreciate all of the talent at Fulcrum. Finally, we thank Colorado Historical Society president Georgianna Contiguglia, former director of interpretive services Martha Dyckes, and, again, publications director David Wetzel for their support of this project.

—*SG and BF*

Editors' note: Any text that we or the editorial review committee have added to the selections in this volume—in the form of new endnotes, footnotes, epilogues, or otherwise—is indicated in italics. Title and date of the original Colorado Historical Society publication in which each essay appeared is given following the text. In the few instances where we have changed the title of a piece, the original title appears at the end of the essay as well.

I n 1853, eighteen-year-old Ferdinand Heinrich Gustav Hilgard arrived in the United States from Germany. He learned English, took a series of jobs, and was soon a newspaper correspondent, having changed his name to "Henry Villard." With the onset of the gold rush into today's Colorado, the young journalist—who had already earned a reputation through his coverage of the Lincoln-Douglas debates—joined the throngs of prospectors, entrepreneurs, and fellow reporters venturing westward. He hopped a coach and rode across Kansas into Denver, the line's western terminus and the reputed hub of gold activity. With a journalist's keen eye for observation, he recorded what he saw.

Villard penned a series of eight accounts, sending them home from Denver, in Kansas Territory, to his paper in "the States," the Cincinnati *Daily Commercial*. His first was dated May 17, 1859. Less than a month earlier, William N. Byers had founded Denver's first newspaper—the *Rocky Mountain News*—after he too had come to the gold regions from the Midwest. But in contrast to the rosy picture of the gold prospects that Byers and other local boosters painted, Villard's reports offered up a steady dose of reality to his readers back in Ohio.

LeRoy R. Hafen, longtime historian, curator, and editor at the Colorado Historical Society, reprinted this, Villard's first report, in 1931 when the Society acquired a copy of Villard's series. Following his return to Ohio in the fall of 1859, Villard had published a fuller account of his travels under the title *The Past and Present of the Pike's Peak Gold Regions*. With contributions by Hafen, the volume was reprinted in 1932.

After a career as a Civil War correspondent, Villard married the daughter of abolitionist William Lloyd Garrison. (The couple's son Oswald went on to become editor of *The Nation* and a prominent pacifist.) Henry Villard embarked on railroad-building ventures and amassed a fortune, eventually serving as president of the Northern Pacific Railroad and manager of the *New York Evening Post*. He died in 1900, and his two-volume autobiography was published four years later.

1

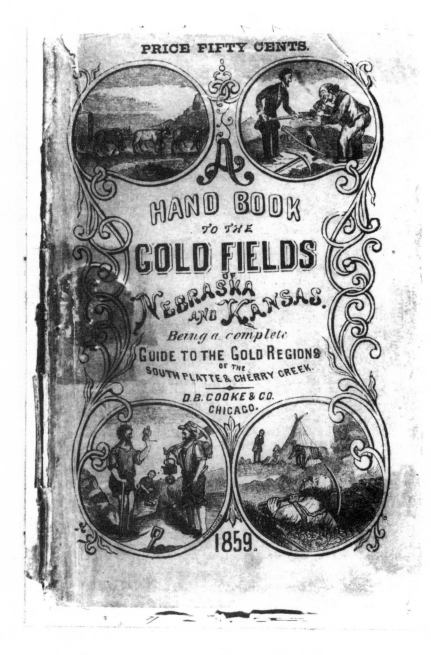

PRICE FIFTY CENTS.

A
HAND BOOK
TO THE
GOLD FIELDS
OF
NEBRASKA AND KANSAS.

Being a complete
GUIDE TO THE GOLD REGIONS
OF THE
SOUTH PLATTE & CHERRY CREEK.

D. B. COOKE & CO.
CHICAGO.

1859.

To the Pike's Peak Country in 1859 and Cannibalism on the Smoky Hill Route

—Henry Villard

It was some four weeks ago that I entrusted my bodily self to one of the coaches of the Leavenworth and Pike's Peak Express Company, and bid farewell for some months to the pleasures as well as vexations of civilized life. The prospect of being freed once more from the drudgery and mechanism of a reportorial existence was so elevating to me that it was with feelings of impatience that I had awaited the day of my launch upon the broad prairies of the Far West. And when the driver's whip gave forth its first cracking, and the wheels commenced to revolve, no "liquid signs of weakness" coursed down my cheeks, but I felt as though I was to burst into a shout of delight at the severance of the ties that had, up to that moment, prevented me from enjoying the invigorating freshness of border life.

From Leavenworth to Junction City the route of the Express Company follows the old military road to Fort Riley. It leads over undulating prairies that occasionally change into hilly elevations; are traversed by many streams of water, and combinedly form landscapes whose claims to beauty are as well founded as that of any other section of the West. Many towns are springing up on the banks of the various creeks that course across the country toward the Kaw River, among which Easton on the Stranger, Ozawkee on the Ozawkee, and Manhattan on the Big Blue, and Junction City, a short distance from the Republican, are the most prominent. The high, well timbered bluffs of the Kaw River began to serve as a background to the scenery as we approached Manhattan, and heightened its attractions to a considerable extent.

3

A short distance this side of Fort Riley we came upon the ruins of Pawnee and Riley cities, consisting of two or three store-houses on both banks of the Kaw, which were considered but a few years ago as the beginning of surely great cities. It was here that Gov. Reeder wanted to locate the state capital, for the purpose of subserving the land interest he owned in this vicinity. But in this, as is well known, he signally failed, and the aforementioned edifices will stand as monuments of a speculation that overleaped itself.

Fort Riley is the best built military post I have seen upon my extensive travels through the West. Officers' quarters, sutlers' establishments, stables, etc., all have an appearance of solidity and cleanliness which differ greatly, and pleasingly to the eye, from the rudely constructed cabins of which the towns we had passed consisted.

At Junction City, which is a combination of about two dozen frame and log houses, which derives its name from being at the Junction of the Kaw and Republican rivers, and is situated 140 miles west of Leavenworth, I fell in with some officers from the Fort who were celebrating their Easter Sunday in a manner that was truly military, but by no means in conformity with the sacredness of the day. Wicked as you know me to be, I was easily induced to join in their peculiar mode of observance, and had what I thought the very last spree for some time to come, for the thorough enjoyment of which the laying over of the coaches till next morning gave me ample opportunity.

During my stay at Junction City I paid a visit to the "Sentinel" office, the most westerly located newspaper establishment of eastern Kansas. Its office is a most original institution. It serves the purposes of a printing house, law office, land agency, and tailor shop, and the followers of these different avocations appear to live, and sometimes to starve together in unbroken harmony.

From Leavenworth to Junction City, which represents Station No. 7, the express route is in the very best working order. I came through in 22 riding hours, which is better time than even the oldest stage lines are able to make, and fared as well on the way as though I was making a pleasure excursion along a highway of eastern travel.

After leaving Junction City we at once entered upon the unmodified wilderness of the seemingly endless prairies that intervene between the waters of the Missouri and the eastern slope of the Rocky Mountains. Having no company but a speechless mailbag, the first few days of my journey were rather dull and found me in anything but good humor. The arrivals at the different stations, however, the meeting of numberless trains of emigrants, with which I never failed to have a chat, the sight of herds of buffalo, antelopes, and other game, the frequent intercourse with roaming bands of aborigines of various tribes, soon contributed to the diversification of the trip, and every sensation of mental weariness disappeared entirely. ...

From Junction City to [Denver City] the route is divided into four divisions of five stations each, so that Denver City figures as Station No. 27. The distance between the several stations averages 25 miles. Care has been taken to locate the stations on creeks, in order to furnish the necessary supply of food and water. From 18 to 24 mules, under the charge of a station-keeper, his assistant, and four drivers, are kept at each of them, to furnish relays for the coaches from the East as well as the West. From two to three stages are made a day by the latter. Passengers obtain three meals a day and plenty of sleep in tents, which will soon give way to log and frame houses.

The road is an excellent one. It was surveyed expressly for the Company by a party of engineers of large experience on the plains. Water, grass, and timber, the indispensable necessities of the navigators of the former, are plentiful throughout with the exception of the valley of the Republican, the extremely sandy character of which renders it destitute of timber. For the 125 miles that the road follows its course, grass and water is, however, ample. The existence of grass on the sandy desert I ascribe to the strong pregnation with alkali and plentiful natural irrigation of the river valley.

It is a very common notion to suppose that the country between the Missouri and Rocky Mountains is a dead level, without the slightest undulations of the surface. Although I did not fully entertain that opinion, I yet supposed to find few ups and downs. I was, however, surprised to find myself riding over a succession of steadily rising, rolling prairies, the altitude of which often approached that of respectable hills. Ravines intervene between most ridges, revealing the washing of transient courses of water. When reaching the divide between the waters of the Republican and those of the South Platte, the traveler finds himself several thousand feet above the level of the ocean.

Many objects of interest will be discovered by those that will follow the route of the Express Company. Among these I would mention extensive beds of iron ore between stations 8 and 9; a curious elevation with a rocky cap, between 13 and 14; hundreds of prairie dog villages and plenty of game all along the road; the sudden sinking of the Republican between 21 and 22 into a dry bed of sand, under which it continues its course subterraneously to its sources; beautiful pine groves from 24 up to 27, and last, but not least, a full aspect of the veritable snow-browed Pikes Peak, which becomes already visible at station 13—a distance of 100 miles. It first looks like a cloud, but, as one comes nearer, assumes clearer and greater dimensions, and when arriving on the last ridge before running down into the Cherry Creek valley, its eastern front is completely revealed to the eye, together with a long chain of peaks, partly covered with snow and partly with pine, and extending in a northward direction as far as Long's Peak. I have seen the Alps of Switzerland and Tyrol, the Pyrenees and Appenines, yet their attractions appear to dwindle into nothing when compared with the at once grotesque and sublime beauty of the mountain scenery upon which my eyes feasted before descending into the valley above referred to.

After striking the Santa Fe tract the road appears as well traveled as any country road in Ohio, and enables the different kind of vehicles to make good speed for the common point of destination.

Denver City and Auraria

My expectations as to the outward appearance of these two towns, which, as it is undoubtedly well known by your readers, are situated immediately opposite to each other, on both banks and right at the mouth of Cherry Creek and the South Platte, not being very high flung, I felt no disappointment when the clusters of log cabins, intermixed at intervals with frame structures and Indian lodges, rose upon my vision. Were it not for the beauty of the location and the surrounding country, these two much talked of towns would, indeed, be sorry places. Each of them numbers from 100 to 150 structures of the already described kind, at least one-half of which are, however, at the present moment either half finished or vacated. They are, almost without exception, floor, ceiling, windowless. Lumber is so very high ($100 per 1,000 feet) that but few can afford the luxury of a regular floor. The absence of the ceiling is explained by the same reason, and the window glass has reached this quarter of the world in but insignificant quantities. In its stead canvas is used, which renders it necessary to keep the doors open during daytime

6

in order to procure a sufficiency of light. Canvas and dirt are generally used for roofing purposes.

Both Denver City and Auraria are regularly laid out. Rectangular streets and squares form their respective areas. The former place is located partly on a bluff-like ridge, extending from the right bank of Cherry Creek in a northeasterly direction, and partly in the bottom bordered by the same ridge. The site of Auraria, on the contrary, consists of nothing but bottomland. The western city boundary is the South Platte, the eastern Cherry Creek. The former runs towards the latter in a northeastern direction, thereby giving the northern part of the city area an angular appearance.

Both towns contain a number of one-horse stores, the aggregate stocks of which would hardly fill a third-class Western Row grocery; one or two abortive hotels, whose guests are obliged to repose on the bare ground; a number of whiskey dens that strongly indicate a precocity, as far as the spiritual wants of the inhabitants are concerned; and the inevitable appendages of border towns in the shape of legal, medical, and land offices. In one of my succeeding letters I will endeavor to give you the results of my peepings into the inner life of these original localities. For the present I shall confine myself to generalities.

The population of the towns is made up of elements of the most heterogeneous character. Indians of several tribes, Mexicans, mountaineers in buckskin, gold-hunters in flannel, blacklegs with stove-pipes, can be seen about here. The number of actual residents has, however, become greatly reduced, in consequence of causes that I will mention hereafter.

The most attractive feature in this and adjoining town is the beautiful mountain scenery, which one has constantly in view. When the eye becomes weary with the wretched appearance of the improvements in both towns, it needs but turn upon the towering peaks, their eternal snows and dark green pine dress, and new life will at once be felt. From Cherry Creek to the foot of the mountains, it is but a few miles of a mountain tour, is spoken of by all as paying for the journey across the plains alone.

The Immigration

When I left the Missouri River at least ten thousand had already left and were about leaving from the various river towns for this reputed Eldorado. I supposed myself justified in the belief that upon arriving here

I could find many thousands of people breathing in and about these two towns. But on the day I made my advent I am satisfied there were not over five hundred individuals to be found within the limits of both places. On the one hand, the gold washing on Cherry Creek—which I am strongly inclined to believe was never carried on except in the letters of some interested newspaper correspondents—was no longer thought of, and everybody that had the means to go had struck for the mountains; and on the other, a good many gold-hunters that had arrived here with the expectation of making an instantaneous plunge into a rich harvest out of the Cherry Creek, easily found themselves most refreshingly mistaken, had become chopfallen and taken the back track towards the States after a stay of but a few days. I am reliably informed that several hundred of that class have become guilty of such folly, and also that they succeeded in producing a panic among those that they met on their way back moving hitherwards, in consequence of which thousands are returning without having seen the "elephant."

Much misery has been and is experienced by many in crossing the plains, and upon coming here. The hand-cart and footing gentry had and have to pass through indescribable sufferings. Most of them started with an entirely insufficient stock of provisions, and if not starved before arriving, found themselves without the least particle of food upon coming in sight of the land and water of hope. As money is also a scarce article among most of them, starvation is their lot, from which to escape they resort to all possible means. Every morning the rapidly articulating voice of a backwoods auctioneer may be heard exerting his eloquence to the utmost in the attempt to find buyers for articles of outfit belonging to fundless gold-hunters. Whole and tattered garments, picks, shovels, hand-carts, etc., can be bought in any quantities, at mere nominal prices. Thus I was offered a good steel pick and shovel for twenty-five cents this morning. A hand-cart was sold in my presence for thirty-five cents. As a general thing everything, with the exception of provisions, can be bought at half the money it would cost in the States. A number are building skiffs to go down the Platte, which is at present very high and swift, in consequence of the melting of the mountain snows. This is, however, a rather perilous undertaking. A good many poor devils that landed here without anything either to eat or sell, are at present hanging about the doors of those who are better provided with the necessaries of life, begging in the most pitiful terms for something to subsist on.

What it takes to live on in this section of the country you may conceive an idea of when I tell you that bacon sells at 50 to 75 cents a pound, coffee and sugar at 50c, flour at from 15c to 18c, New Mexico onions 25c apiece, molasses $5 per gallon, and everything else in proportion. Fresh meat, however, particularly game, is cheaper here than in the States. Any quantity of antelope, mountain sheep, and elk can be bought from white and copper-skinned hunters at very reasonable rates. The provisions now here have mostly been brought from New Mexico. Some domestic animals, such as a few grunters and majestic Shanghais, have also been imported from that latitude. Several milch cows have lately arrived from the States.

To give your readers an idea of what gold-hunters have been subjected to while crossing the great plains, I subjoin the following blood-congealing narrative of the adventures of two individuals. The statement of Mr. Blue is authenticated by Mr. B. D. Williams, the Superintendent of the Leavenworth and Pike's Peak Express Company, who went back where the Indians had found him and found and buried whatever was left of the body of the brother that died last.

Statement of Daniel Blue, late of Clyde Township, Whiteside Co., Ill., made on the 12th day of May, 1859, at the office of the Leavenworth and Pike's Peak Express Company, in the city of Denver.

On the 22nd day of February last I left my home in company with my two brothers, Alexander Blue and Charles Blue, two other residents of the same county, John Campbell and Thomas Stevenson, for the Pike's Peak gold regions. We arrived at and left Kansas City on the 6th of March, taking the Smoky Hill route. In the neighborhood of Topeka we fell in with nine others, also bound for Western Kansas. The company had one horse, which belonged to the original Blue party, and was to carry their provisions. The rest were footmen, carrying their provisions on their backs. We journeyed together for 16 or 17 days on said Smoky Hill route. Myself and eight others then continued our journey, while the rest remained behind for the purpose of hunting buffalo. Three or four days elapsed after the separation, when we lost our packhorse. Our stock of provisions was then very much reduced, and we packed whatever we had left and pushed onward. After having traveled eight more days, two other members of the company left us. Upon their leaving our provisions became exhausted, and for ten days we laid still, endeavoring to kill a sufficient amount of game for our subsistence. A few hares, ravens, and other small game was, however, all that came within our reach. Our only firearm was a shotgun, all other arms having been thrown away in consequence of the weakness of their owners. At about the same time three others parted with us, with the intention of making for the nearest settlement for the purpose of securing relief to the remaining ones— leaving but the three brothers Blue and one man by the name of Soleg, from Cleveland, Ohio—all of the party being very weak and nearly exhausted. After a short effort to continue our journey we were again compelled to lay up, and the next day Soleg died from exhaustion and want of food. Before he breathed his last, he authorized and requested us to make use of his mortal remains in the way of nourishment. We, from necessity, did so, although it went very hard against our feelings. We lived on his body for about eight days. We then were, as I afterwards learned, on Beaver Creek, which empties into the Bijou, one of the tributaries of the South Platte, and about 75 miles east of Denver City. After the consumption of Soleg's body, Alexander, my eldest brother, died, and, at his own last request, we used a portion of his body as food on the spot, and with the balance resumed our journey towards the gold regions. We succeeded in traveling but ten miles, when my youngest brother, Charles, gave out, and we were obliged to stop. For ten days we subsisted on what remained of our brother's body, when Charles expired from the same causes as the others. I also consumed the greater portion of his remains, when I was found by an Arapahoe Indian, and carried to his lodge, treated with great kindness, and a day and a half thereafter (that is, on Wednesday, the 4th day of May) brought to the encampment of the Leavenworth and Pike's Peak Express Company's train, en route for Denver City, under the charge of Mr. Superintendent B. D. Williams, where I was received and taken care of, and left at station 25 to recover sufficient strength for the continuation of my journey. By direction of Mr. Williams, the second coaches that came along took me up and brought me safely to this point free of charge.

The above statement I make freely, voluntarily, and without compulsion. Knowing that it will reach the eye of the public at large, I wish to give expression to the sincere gratitude I entertain towards the employees of the L. and P. P. Express Company in general, and Mr. Williams in special, for the truly humane treatment received at their hands.

DANIEL BLUE.

Denver City, May 12, 1859.
Subscribed in the presence of J. Heywood, Sacramento, Cal.;
Wm. T. Carlyle, Saline County, Mo.;
M. K. Lane, Leavenworth City, K. T.;
Jo. M. Fox, Gen'l Agent L. & P. P. Ex. Co.

Mr. Blue came up to this place on the same coaches that I did. He looked like a skeleton, and could hardly use his limbs, and his sight was impaired.

The Gold Prospects

In opening this chapter—probably the most interesting to your readers—I will say that I shall not presume to express any ultimate opinion as to the true character of the gold washing of this country. I shall perform the part of a faithful reporter of what I have seen (not heard) and nothing further. I am aware of the responsibility of my position, and shall convey no information to the readers of the *Commercial* that I know not to rest on facts.

In the first place, I wish to remark that in calling this the Pike's Peak gold region a vast radical misnomer is made use of. From here to that much-mentioned glacier the distance comes not much short of seventy miles, and in but a single locality between the two points gold washing is carried on. Whatever digging and washing is now going on is north of this place, and the mines that are reported to be best paying are some thirty miles off in the same direction.

On Cherry Creek, as already stated, nothing in the way of washing is going on at present. It does not pay. Any shovel full of sand on the bottom between the South Platte and Cherry Creek will give one the color, but the most diminutive substance of gold, and the idea of turning those all but invisible particles to account has been abandoned. On the South Platte, about six miles south of this, a company from Georgia has dug a ditch; is busily at work, and doing well. I visited their claim myself, and found them doing well. They take out dust at the rate of from $5 to $7 per day each, six individuals.

All other mining operations are at present taking place at the head-waters of the northwestern tributaries of the South Platte in the mountains. Of the various diggings along and in the latter I know but by hearsay, and will, therefore, speak of such of their yieldings as have come within my immediate observation. In a few days I shall start upon a mountain tour, for the purpose of a personal inspection of them, and lay the result in due season before your readers.

The Leavenworth and Pike's Peak Express Company has shipped during the last week about a thousand dollars worth of scale gold. It was bought from a number of individuals that had brought it mostly from the mountains.

Wm. Fisher, a merchant from Denver City, has in his possession three hundred dollars worth of dust (seen by me) which he had received in different quantities in exchange for goods. Similar amounts are in the hands of three more tradesmen.

Yesterday morning I assisted Mr. Joe Heywood, formerly a well known Cincinnatian, but now of California, who came here on a prospecting tour, in weighing six ounces of scale gold which he bought of two men who had taken it out of Plum Creek in six days.

Mr. Gregory came down from the north fork of Vasquez Creek with thirty-seven dollars worth of gold dust, which he had washed out of forty pans of sand. He also had several specimens of quartz and shot gold, the result of his explorations at various points.

In strolling over town in the course of the same day I saw dust varying from 18 to 62 dollars worth, all of which had arrived from the mountains for the purpose of buying a new stock of provisions. The quantities appear insignificant when compared with the discoveries in California. But this smallness can be easily explained, first by the fact that the mountains have become accessible but two or three weeks ago, and that from the inability of most miners, on account of a want of means, to lay in a supply of provisions for any considerable length of time, which circumstance renders their return to town, after a few days' work, imperative.

From all appearances it is, however, clear that this summer will have to be devoted almost entirely to prospecting, the result of which will finally settle the question of the paying character of milling operations in this latitude. Great depression of mind prevailed here at the time I arrived, with regard to the diggings. The favorable returns of the last few days have, however, brightened up the countenances of all, and a general rush for the mountains is imminent.

Various Items of News

The loose state of society and the large influx of lawless individuals has already made resort to the lynch law necessary in this part of the country. About four weeks since a German by the name of John Stuffer, formerly of Louisville, was suspended by the neck for the murder of his brother-in-law.

On the morning of Sunday last, Judge Lynch again convened his Court, for the purpose of trying an alleged horse thief. The whole town had turned out to witness the spectacle, which was truly an original one. The meeting was called to order, and a President and Secretary elected. A jury was then summoned by these officers; a prosecutor and counsel for the defense appointed, and the trial proceeded with. The evidence not being sufficient to convict, the accused was acquitted although six stolen animals had been found in his possession. He received warning to leave the town at once, which he did. He returned, however, in the course of the evening, was caught once more and swung up, for the purpose of frightening him, when he confessed the theft, and revealed the existence of a regularly organized band of thieves. He gave the names and whereabouts of his confederates, and regulators are now after them.

Some ten days ago thousands of Indians were encamped all along Cherry Creek. These were the peaceable Keota and Arapahoes, and the warlike Cheyennes, Apaches, and Comanches. Since then most of them have, however, started for a buffalo hunt. No depredations were committed, except by the Apaches, who drove off 150 head of cattle. Mr. Davidson, the special correspondent of the *New York Tribune* and *St. Louis Democrat*, became tired of the country after a six weeks' exploration of the same, and undertook to go down the Platte in a skiff, on his way home. But thirty miles east of this, his means of river navigation was wrecked, and he and his companions very narrowly escaped drowning. All of his property, valued at over $1,000, and including some valuable mineral and botanical collections he had made on his tours through the mountains, were lost. He returned to this place, whence he embarked eastward in the express coaches on Sunday morning last.

Excerpted from "To the Pike's Peak Country in 1859 and Cannibalism on the Smoky Hill Route," *The Colorado Magazine*, November 1931

S eventeen years after Henry Villard wrote his cautionary report of the gold prospects around Denver, Helen Hunt Jackson penned her own set of Colorado observations for the *Atlantic Monthly*. The two writers' styles could hardly be more dissimilar.

In contrast to Villard's fairly direct reportorial style, Jackson revels in the mountains' beauty and delights in the locals she happens upon in her travels. In "Our New Road," the result is an adoring look at Cheyenne Mountain, near Colorado Springs, and a classic piece of early Colorado nature writing. (Colorado became a state the same year—1876—that the piece was published.) From sweeping vistas to the tiniest facets of flora and geology, Jackson didn't miss a detail in her sketch of a carriage ride up the mountain's newly opened toll road.

A native of Massachusetts and a published poet, Jackson had come to Colorado on the advice of her doctor, who suggested a season in the West as a cure for her ill health. She stayed, writing more than a dozen novels while living in Colorado Springs. She earned praise for her depictions of hardworking settlers, and she developed a passion for drawing attention to atrocities against native peoples, most notably the Sand Creek Massacre of 1864. After her death in 1885, she was buried, at her request, on Cheyenne Mountain. Her remains were later moved to a cemetery in Colorado Springs.

Today, Cheyenne Mountain is not what it used to be—to put it mildly. The interior of Helen Hunt Jackson's favorite mountain has been hollowed out, and it houses a massive and heavily guarded subterranean military base. Inside Cheyenne Mountain is the Cheyenne Mountain Air Force Station, where more than a thousand people work within fifteen buildings linked by a network of passageways. There, space command units monitor a global network of data from satellites and other sources worldwide.

It's a far cry from Jackson's toll road.

Our New Road

—Helen Hunt Jackson

What a new singer or a new play is to the city man, a new road is to the man of the wilderness. I fancy the parallel might be drawn out and amplified, much to the exaltation of the new road, if the man of the wilderness chose to boast, and if people were sensible enough to value pleasures as they do other fabrics, by their wear. It would be cruel, however, to make the city man discontented. Poor fellow! He is joined to his idols of stone, buried alive above them now, and soon he will be buried dead below them. Let him alone! It is no part of my purpose in this paper to enter the lists in defence of my joys, or to make an attack upon his. It is merely to describe our new road; and my pronoun "our" is by no means a narrow one,—it is a big plural, taking in some four thousand souls, all the dwellers in the town of Colorado Springs and its near neighborhood.

The "new road" is up and across Cheyenne Mountain. Cheyenne Mountain is the southernmost peak of the grand range which lies six miles west of our town. Only those who dwell at the feet of great mountain ranges know how like a wall they look, what sense of fortified security they give; people who come for a day, to gaze and pass by, or even people who stay and paint the hills' portraits, know very little. A mountain has as much personality as a man; you do not know one any more than you know the other until you have summered and wintered him. You love one, and are profoundly indifferent to another, just as it is with your feeling towards your neighbors; and it is often as hard to give good and sufficient reason for your preference in the one case as in the other. But no lover of Cheyenne was ever at loss to give reasons for his love. The mountain is so unique in its grandeur and dignity that one must be blind and stolid indeed not to feel its influence.

As I said, it is the southernmost peak of the range lying west of Colorado Springs. This is as if I said it is the southern bastion of our western wall. It is only two or three thousand feet above the town (the town be it remembered, lies six thousand feet above the sea). Pike's Peak, a few miles farther north, in the same range, is nearly twice as high; so it is not by reason of height that Cheyenne is so grand. Pausing now, with my pen in my hand, I look out of my south window at its majestic front, and despair of being loyal to the truth I would like to tell of this mountain. Is it that its eastern outline, from the summit down to the plain, is one slow, steady, in-curving slope, broken only by two rises of dark timber-lands, which

Helen Hunt Jackson
(Courtesy of the Colorado Springs Pioneers Museum)

round like billows; and that this exquisite hollowing curve is for ever outlined against the southern sky: Is it that the heavily cut and jagged top joins this eastern slope at a sharp angle, and stretches away to the northwest in broken lines as rugged and strong as the eastern slope is graceful and harmonious; and that the two lines together make a perpetual, vast triangulation on the sky? Is it that when white clouds in our heavens at noon journey south, they always seem to catch on its eastern slope, and hang and flutter there, or nestle down in an island-like bank reaching halfway up the mountain? Is it that the dawn always strikes it some moments earlier than it reaches the rest of the range, turning it glowing red from plains to sky, like a great illumined cathedral? Is it that the setting sun also loves it, and flings back mysterious broken prisms of light on its furrowed western slopes, long after the other peaks are black and grim? Is it that it holds canyons where one can climb, among fir-trees and roses and clematis and columbine and blue-bells and ferns and mosses, to wild pools and cascades in which snow-fed brooks tumble and leap? These questions are only like the random answers of one suddenly hard pressed for the explanation of a mystery which has long since ceased to be a mystery to him,— ceased to be a mystery not because it has been fathomed, but because it has become familiar and dear. No lover of Cheyenne but will say that Cheyenne is better than all these; that no one of all these is quite truly and sufficiently told; and I myself in the telling feel like one stammering in a language but half learned, the great mountain all the while looking down on me in serene and compassionate silence. At this moment, it looks like a gigantic mountain of crystals, purple and white. Every smallest ridge slope fronting to the east or south is of a red purple, like the purple of a Catawba grape over-ripe; every smallest ridge slope to the north or west is white like the white of alabaster, and soft with the softness of snow. The plains are a dear, pale yellow, and the spot where the slope melts into the level, and the purpose melts into the yellow, is a triumph of shape and color from which men who paint might well turn away sorrowful.

Knowing well, as I do, just where among these crystalline ridges our new road winds, I yet look up incredulous at the sharp precipices and ledges. But it is there, bless it!—our new uplifter, revealer, healer, nearer link of approach to a nearer sky! The workmen know it as the road over to Bear creek valley, and they think they have built it for purposes of traffic, and for bringing down railroad ties; it is a toll-road, and the toll-gatherer takes minute reckoning of all he can see passing his door. But I think there will always be a traffic which the workmen will not suspect, and a viewless company which will elude the toll-gatherer, on this new road of ours.

It was on one of our tropical midwinter days that I first climbed it. A mile southward from the town, then a sharp turn to the west, fronting the mountains as directly as if our road must be going to pierce their sides, across brooks where the ice was so thick that our horses' hoofs and our wheels crunched slowly through, up steep banks on which there were frozen glares of solid ice, and across open levels where the thin snow lay in a fine tracery around every separate grass-stalk,—one, two, three miles of this, and we were at the base of the mountain, and saw the new road, a faint brown track winding up the yellow slope and disappearing among the pines.

As we turned into the road, we saw, on our right, two ranch-men leaning, in the Sunday attitude, against a fence, and smoking. As we passed, one of them took his pipe from his mouth and said nonchalantly, "S'pose ye *know* this ere's a toll-road." The emphasis on the word "know" conveyed so much that we laughed in his face. Clever monosyllable, it stood for a whole paragraph.

"Oh, yes," we said, "we know it. It's worth fifty cents, isn't it, to get high up on Cheyenne Mountain?"

"Well, yes," he replied, reflectively, "'spose 'tis. It's a mighty good road, anyhow. Found blossom rock up there yesterday," he added, with the odd, furtive, gleaming expression which I have so often seen in the eyes of men who spoke of a possible or probable mine; "true blossom rock. The assayer, he was up, an' he says it's the real mineral, no mistake," he continued, and there seemed a fine and unconscious scorn in the way he fingered the dingy and torn paper half dollar with which he had paid for the right to drive over what might be chambers of silver and gold.

"Blossom rock," I said, "why 'blossom'?" To call this particular surface mineral the flower of the silver root lying below, is a strange fancy, surely; it seems a needlessly poverty-stricken device for Nature's realms to borrow names from each other.

A few rods' steep climb, and we have left the foot-hill and are absolutely on the mountain. The road tacks as sharply as a ship in a gale; we are facing north instead of south, and are already on a ledge so high that we have a sense of looking over as well as of looking off. The plains have even now the pale pink flush which only distance gives, and our town, though it is only four miles away, looks already like a handful of yellow and white pebbles on a sand beach, so suddenly and so high are we lifted above it. We are not only on the mountain, we are among the rocks,—towering rocks of bright red sandstone, thick-grown in spaces with vivid yellow-green lichen. They are almost terrible, in spite of their beauty of color,—so high, so straight, so many-pointed are they. The curves of the road would seem to be more properly called loops, so narrow are they, so closely do they hug the sharp projections round which they turn and wind and turn and wind. One is tempted to say that the road has lassoed the mountain and caught it, like a conquered Titan, in a tangle of coils. At every inner angle of the curves is a wide turn-out, where we wait to give the horses breath, and to watch if there be anyone coming down. Round the outer angles we go at a slow pace, praying that there may be no one just the other side. When we face northward, the mountain shuts off all sun and we are in cold shadow; the instant we double the outer point of the ridge and face southward, we are in full sunshine; thus we alternate from twilight to high noon, and from high noon to twilight, in a swift and bewildering succession. On our right, we look down into chasms bristling with sharp rocks and pointed tops of fir-trees; on our left the mountain-side rises, now abruptly like a wall, now in sloping tiers. After a mile of these steep ascents, we come out on a very promontory of precipices. Here we turn the flank of the mountain, and a great vista to the west and north opens up before us, peak rising above peak, with softer hills crowding in between; below us, canyon after canyon, ridge after ridge, a perfect net-work of ins and outs and ups and downs, and our little brown thread of a road swinging along at easy levels above it all. There is no more hard climbing. There are even down slopes on which the horses trot, in the shade of high pine-trees on either hand, now and then coming upon a spot where the ridge has widened sufficiently for the trees to dispose themselves in a more leisurely and assured fashion, like a lowland grove, instead of clinging at a slant on steep sides, as they are for the most part driven to do; now and then coming out on opens, where a canyon lies bare and yawning, like a great gash in the mountain's side, its slopes of fine red or yellow gravelly sand seeming to be in a perpetual slide from top to bottom,—only held in place by bowlders here and there, which stick out like grotesque heads of rivets with which the hill had been mended. Here we find the kinnikinnick in its perfection, enormous mats of it lying compact, glossy, green and claret-tinted, as if enamelled, on the yellow sand. Painters have thought it worth while to paint over and over again some rare face or spot whose beauty perpetually eluded their grasp and refused to be transferred to canvas. Why should I not be equally patient and loyal to this exquisite vine, of which I have again and again, and always vainly, tried to say what it is like, and how beautiful is the mantle it flings over bare and stony places?

Imagine that a garden-border of box should lay itself down and behave like a blackberry vine,—run, and scramble, and overlap, and send myriads of long tendrils out in all directions,—and you have a picture of the shape, the set of the leaf, the thick matting of the branches, and the utter unrestrainedness of a root of kinnikinnick. Add to this the shine of the leaf of the myrtle, the green of green grass in June, and the claret-red of the blackberryvine in November, and you will have a picture of its lustrousness and its colors. The solid centres of the mats are green; the young tendrils run out more and more vivid red to their tips. In June it is fragrant with clusters of small pink and white bells, much like the huckleberry blossom. In December it is gay with berries as red as the berries of the holly. Neither midsummer heat nor midwinter cold can tarnish the sheen nor shrivel the fulness of its leaf. It has such vitality that no barrenness, no drought, deters it; in fact, it is more luxuriant on the bare, gravelly slopes of which I was just now speaking, than I have ever seen it elsewhere. Yet its roots seem to take slight hold of the soil. You may easily, by a little care in loosening the tendrils, pull up solid mats five to seven feet long. Fancy these at Christmas, in one's house. I look up, as I write, at one upon my own wall. It has a stem an inch in diameter, gnarled and twisted like an old cedar,—the delight of an artistic eye, the surprise and scorn of the Philistine, to whom it looks merely like fire-wood. From this gnarled bough bursts a great growth of luxuriant green branches, each branch claret-red at its tips and vivid green at its centre. It has hung as a crown of late dower over the head of my Beatrice Cenci for two months, and not a leaf has fallen. It will hang there unchanged until June, if I choose. This virtue is partly its own, partly the spell of the wonderful dryness of our Colorado air, in which all things do as Mrs. Stowe says New Englanders do when they are old,—"dry up a little and then last."

Still running westward along the north side of the mountain, the road follows the ridge lines of the huge, furrow-like canyons which cleave the mountain from its base to its summit. These make a series of triangles piercing the solid mass; and we zigzag up one side, round the sharp inner corner, and down the other side, round the outer point, and then up and down just such another triangle,—and so on, for miles. The sight of these great gorges is grand: a thousand feet down to their bottom on the one hand, and a thousand feet up to their top on the other. Looking forward or back across them, we see the line of our road like a narrow ledge on the precipice; a carriage on it looks as if it had been let down by ropes from the top. Soon we come to great tracts of pines and firs, growing scantily at incredible angles on these steep slopes; many trees have been cut, and are lying about on the ground, as if giants had been playing jackstraws, and had gone away leaving their game unfinished. They call these trees "timber;" that is "corpse" for a tree. A reverent sadness always steals on my thoughts when I see a dead tree lying where the axe slew it. The road winds farther and farther into a labyrinth of mountain fastnesses; gradually these become clear to the eye, a certain order and system in their succession. The great Cheyenne Canyon stretches like a partially hewn pathway between the mountain we are on and the rest of the range lying to the north of it. This northward wall is rocky, seamed, and furrowed; bare, water-worn cliffs, hundreds of feet high, alternate with intervals of pine forest, which look black and solid in the shade, but in full sunlight are seen to be sparse, so that even from the other side of the canyon you may watch every tree's double of black shadow thrown on the ground below, making a great rafter-work floor, as it were, from which the trees seem to rise like columns. Above this stretch away endless tiers of peaks and round hills, more than one can count, because at each step some of them sink out of sight and new ones crop up. Some are snow-topped; some have a dark, serrated line of firs over their summits; some look like mere masses of bowlders and crags, their upper lines standing clear out against the sky, like the jagged top of a ruined wall. On all the slopes leading down into the canyons are rows of pines, like besiegers climbing up; and on most of the upper connecting ridges lies a fine white line of snow, like a silver thread knitting peak to peak. From all the outer points of these gorges, as we look back to the east, we have exquisite glimpses of the plains, framed always in a triangle made by sloping canyon walls. I doubt if it would be possible to render one of these triangle pictures as we get them from between these intersecting and overlapping walls. A yucca plant, ten inches high, may happen to come into the near foreground, so that it helps to frame them; and yet their upper horizon line is miles and miles away. I have never seen so marvellous a blending of the far and the near as they give.

Still the road winds and winds, and the sense of remoteness grows stronger and stronger. The silence of the wilderness, what is there like it? The silence of the loneliest ruin is silence only because time has hushed the sounds with which the ruin was once alive. This is silence like that in which the world lay pregnant before time began.

Just as this grand, significant silence was beginning to make us silent, too, we came suddenly upon a little open where the wilderness was wilderness no longer. One man had tamed it. On our right hand stood his forge, on our left his house. Both forge and house were of a novel sort; nowhere but in the heart of the Rocky Mountains would they have been called by such names. The forge consisted of a small pine-tree, a slender post some four feet distant from it, a pile of stones and gravel, a log, and a pair of bellows. The house was perhaps eight feet high; the walls reached up one third that height: first, three logs, then, two planks; there the wall ended. One front post was a pine-tree, the other a rough cedar stump; from the ridgepole hung a sail-cloth roof which did not meet the walls; very airy must be the blacksmith's house on a cold night, in spite of the southeast winds being kept off by a huge bowlder twenty feet high. On one side stood an old dead cedar-tree with crooked arms, like some marine monster; one of the arms was the blacksmith's pantry, and there hung his dinners for a week or more, a big haunch of venison. A tomtit, not much larger than a humming-bird, was feasting on it by snatches. The tiny creature flew from the topmost branch of the tree down to the venison, took a bite, and was back again safe on the upper bough in far less time than I take to write his name; less than a second a trip he took, I think; never once did he pause for a second bite, never once rest on a lower branch: he fairly seemed to buzz in the air, so fast he flew up and down.

"So you board the tomtit, do you?" we said to the blacksmith, who stood near by, piling boughs on a big fire.

"Yes; he's so little I can afford to keep him," replied the blacksmith, with a quiet twinkle in his eye and the cheery tone of a good heart in his voice: "he jest about lives in that tree, an' there's generally suthin' there for him."

It was a spot to win a man's love, the spot the blacksmith had chosen for his temporary home, the little open had so sheltered and sheltering a look: to the south, east, north, mountain walls; to the west a vista, a suggestion of outlet, and a great friendliness of pine-trees. Two small brooks ran across the clearing. A thick line of bare, gray cotton-woods marked them now; in the summer they would be bowers of green, and the little bridges across them would be hid in thickets of foliage. The upper line of the southern mountain wall stood out against the sky in bold and fantastic shapes, endlessly suggestive. That rocks not hewn by men's hands should have such similitudes is marvellous. I have seen photographs of ruins in Edom and Palmyra which seem to be almost reproductions of these rocky summit outlines of some of our Colorado peaks.

A half-mile farther on we came upon the camp of the men who were building the road. "Camp" is an elastic word. In this case, it meant merely a small pine grove, two big fires, and some piles of blankets. Here the road ceased. As we halted, three dogs came bounding towards us, barking most furiously. One of them stopped suddenly, gave one searching look at me, put her tail between her legs, and with a pitiful yelp of terror turned and fled. I walked slowly after her; she would look back over her shoulder, turn, make one or two lunges at me, barking shrilly, then with the same yelp of terror run swiftly away; at last she grew brave enough to keep her face toward me, but continually backed away, alternating her bark of defiance with her yelp of terror in a way which was irresistibly ludicrous. We were utterly perplexed by her behavior until her master, as soon as he could speak for laughing, explained it.

"Yer see, that'ere dog's never seen a woman afore. She was reared in the woods, an' I hain't never took her nowheres, an' thet's jest the fact on't; she dunno what to make of a woman."

It grew droller and droller. The other dogs were our good friends at once, leaped about us, snuffed us, and licked our hands as we spoke to them. Poor Bowser hung back and barked furiously with warning and menace whenever I patted one of the other dogs, but if I took a step nearer her she howled and fled in the most abject way.

Two men were baking bread, and there seemed a good-natured rivalry between them.

"I've got a leetle too much soda in it," said one, as I peered curiously into his big bake-kettle, lifting the cover, "but his'n's all burnt on the top," with a contemptuous cock of his eye towards his fellow-baker. It is said to be very good, this impromptu bread, baked in a shapeless lump in an iron kettle, with coals underneath and coals on the lid above. It did not look so, however. I think I should choose the ovens of civilization.

23

The owner of my canine foe was a man some fifty-five or sixty years old. He had a striking face, a clear, blue-gray eye, with a rare mixture of decision and sentiment in it, a patriarchal gray beard, and a sensitive mouth. He wore a gray hat, broader-brimmed even than a Quaker's, and it added both picturesqueness and dignity to his appearance. His voice was so low, his intonation so good, that the uncultured speech seemed strangely out of place on his lips. He had lived in the woods "nigh eight year," sometimes in one part of the Territory, sometimes in another. He had been miner, hunter, farmer, and now road-builder. A very little talk with men of this sort usually draws from them some unexpected revelations of the motives or the incidents of their career. A long lonely life produces in the average mind a strange mixture of the taciturn and the confidential. The man of the wilderness will journey by your side whole days in silence; then, of a sudden, he will speak to you of matters which it would be, for you, utterly impossible to mention to a stranger. We soon learned the secret of this man's life in the woods. Nine years ago his wife had died. That broke up his farm home, and after that "all places seemed jest alike" to him, and "somehow" he "kinder took to the woods." What an unconscious tribute there is in that phrase to nature's power as a beneficent healer.

"There was another reason, too," he added. "My wife, she died o' consumption, hereditary, an' them two boys'd ha' gone the same way ef I hadn't kep' 'em out-o'-doors," pointing to two stalwart young men perhaps eighteen and twenty. "They hain't slep' under a roof for eight year, an' now they're as strong an' hearty as you'd wish to see." They were, indeed, and they may thank their father's wisdom for it.

Just beyond this camp was a cabin of fir boughs. Who that has not seen can conceive of the fragrant loveliness of a small house built entirely of fir boughs? It adds to the spice and the green and the airy lightness and the shelter of the pine-tree a something of the compactness and deftness and woven beauty of a bird's nest. I never weary of looking at it, outside and in: outside, each half-confined twig lifting its cross of soft, plumy ends and stirring a little in the wind, as it used to do when it grew on the tree; inside, the countless glints of blue sky showing through the boughs, as when one lies on his back under a low pine-tree and looks up. This cabin has only three sides built of boughs. The fourth is a high bowlder, which slants away at just the right angle to make a fire-place, The stone is of a soft, friable kind, and the fire has slowly eaten its way in, now and then cracking off a huge slice, until there is quite a fine "open Franklin" for the cabin. It draws well when the wind is in the right direction, as I can testify, for I have made fires in it. If the wind is from the east, it smokes, but I never heard of an open Franklin that did not.

The coming down over our new road is so unlike the going up that the very road seems changed. The beautiful triangular pictures of the distant plains are constantly before our eye, widening at each turn, and growing more and more distinct at each lower level we reach. The blue line of the divide in the northern horizon looks always like a solid line of blue. By what process a stretch of green timber land turns into a wall of lapis lazuli, does the science of optics teach?

It is nearly sunset as we descend. The plains look boundless. Their color is a soft mingling of pink and yellow and gray; each smallest hollow alike seem dimples on the smooth expanse. Here and there patches of ploughed land add their clear browns with a fine effect of dark mosaics on the light surface.

As we pass the bare slopes where the kinnikinnick is richest and greenest, we load our carriage with its lovely, shining mats. Below, on the soft pink plains, is a grave we love. It lies in the shade of great pines, on a low hill to the west of the town. Surely, never did a little colony find ready to its hand a lovelier burial-place than this.

Long ago there must have been watercourses among these low hills, else these pines could never have grown so high and strong. The watercourses are dried now, and only barren sands lie around the roots of the great trees, but still they live and flourish, as green in December as in June, and the wind in their branches chants endless chants above the graves.

This grave that we love lies, with four pines guarding it closely, on a westward slope which holds the very last rays of the setting sun. We look up from it to the glorious, snowtopped peaks which pierce the sky, and the way seems very short over which our friend has gone. The little mound is kept green with the faithful kinnikinnick vines, and we bring them, now, from the highest slopes which our new road reaches, on the mountain our friend so loved.

From *Westward to a High Mountain: The Colorado Writings of Helen Hunt Jackson,* edited by Mark I. West, 1994

If a picture is worth a thousand words, several good photographs might be worth an act of Congress. Though William Henry Jackson's 1874 photographs of a southwestern Colorado cliff dwelling did not lead directly to the government's creation of Mesa Verde National Park, the images called attention to the ancient structures and set the stage for their preservation.

Jackson learned the photographer's craft in New York and Vermont portrait studios. After the Civil War, he moved west, working odd jobs in Utah, California, and elsewhere before opening a portrait studio in Omaha, Nebraska. Unchallenged by portraiture, Jackson focused his lenses on the western frontier while his brother managed the store. Ferdinand V. Hayden, director of the U.S. Geological and Geographical Survey of the Territories, noticed Jackson's photographs of landscapes and American Indians in 1869. Like all government surveyors, Hayden hired photographers to document his expeditions. First-rate photographs accurately portrayed the West's landforms, resources, and native people. Government surveyors like Hayden, John Wesley Powell, and Clarence King also used photographs to lobby Congress for additional funding.

Jackson spent seven summers with Hayden's survey crews. Three of the expeditions focused on the central Rocky Mountains in Colorado. While photographing the San Juan Mountains in southwestern Colorado Territory in 1874, Jackson met Tom Cooper, an old friend from Omaha who regaled him with stories about ancient ruins. Cooper had been mining the La Plata Canyon with John Moss, a self-styled "captain" and leader of a group of prospectors from California. Jackson and New York reporter Ernest Ingersoll jumped at the chance to see the place.

Jackson's reminiscence, written in 1924 and based partly on his survey report, tells the story of how he and his party "discovered" and photographed what came to be called Two-Story House. Two years later, Jackson collaborated with Hayden Survey geologist William Holmes on a scale model of the ruins for Philadelphia's Centennial Exposition. The diorama won a bronze medal and increased the impact of Jackson's photographs, articles, and reports on the American public's imagination.

Of course, native peoples have known about Two-Story House—which lies just outside Mesa Verde National Park's boundaries in the Ute Mountain Tribal Park—and the other cliff dwellings for centuries. And Spanish explorers and traders found ancient ruins in the region as early as 1765. But Jackson, by photographing the Ancient Puebloan sites, was the first to publicize their existence to a mass audience.

Two Story House, from a series of stereoscope images made and published by William Henry Jackson when he worked in Denver

First Official Visit to the Cliff Dwellings

—*William Henry Jackson*

The Photographic Division was outfitted as a separate unit of the U.S. Geological Survey of 1874, the same as the year before, and, in starting out from Denver the 21st of July, was instructed by Dr. Hayden to proceed first to Middle Park via Berthoud Pass and then to work south, crossing the head of the Arkansas to the San Luis Valley and thence to the San Juan Mountain region. Our itinerary had been talked over and changed many times before our plans took definite shape, the underlying purpose being that we should traverse some portion of the territory of the other divisions of the Survey. Wilson had been assigned the southern or San Juan region and, on account of its reputed wonderful mountain scenery, I was expected to cooperate more fully with him and make this the main objective of my season's work. The near half century that has passed since then has obscured my memory as to some details, but I am very certain there was no intention to go south of Baker's Park into the San Juan basin until we met Cooper and his outfit near the head of the Rio Grande on his way into that country.

Having worked over most of the territory assigned to us we finally reached the Rio Grande on our way into the heart of the "San Juan" via Cunningham Pass. On the 27th of August we camped early in the day at Jennison's (Chemiso) Ranch, as it was too late to make the Pass that day, and also to do some photographing in the neighborhood. Another and equally potent inducement to stop was the opportunity to get a good square meal served by the rather attractive young hostess of the ranch, as we were almost out of "grub" and no more to be had until we reached Howardsville.

While we were unpacking, a burro pack train came along and went into camp near by. As they passed us there was much hilarity over the very comical appearance of one of the party, who was astride a very small burro, with another one of the party following behind with a club with which he was belaboring the little jack to keep him up with the train. On our return to camp from our photographing later in the day this same man had come over to visit us. A mutual recognition followed our meeting as I remembered him as a fellow townsman in Omaha when I was in business there a few years previously. With all of us grouped around a rousing big fire after supper we talked long into the night, Tom Cooper explaining that he was one of a small party of miners working some placers over on the La Plata, that he had been out of supplies and was now on his return to their camp. As he appeared to be well acquainted with this part of the country, we "pumped" him for all the information he could impart. As he was naturally a loquacious individual, he had a great deal to say, and, understanding in a general way the object of our expedition, urged us by all means to come over to the La Plata and he would undertake to show us something worth while.

It was generally known that many old ruins were scattered all over the southwest, from the Rio Grande to the Colorado, but Cooper maintained that around the Mesa Verde, only a short distance from their camp, were cliff dwellings and other ruins more remarkable than any yet discovered. All this interested us so much that, before we "turned in" that night, we had decided to follow him over to his camp as soon as we could outfit for the trip.

Cooper had not traveled over the country where the most important of these ruins were to be found but had his information largely from John Moss and his associates. Moss, he explained, was the high "muck-a-muck" or "hi-yas-ti-yee" of the La Plata region, who, through his personal influence with the Indians, had secured immunity from trouble not only for his own operations but also for others traveling through the country.

A few days later, after dividing our party in Baker's Park and traveling light, just Mr. Ingersoll and myself with the two packers, we were on our way to the La Plata. Soon after leaving Animas Park we overtook and passed Cooper's outfit and a few miles farther on were very much surprised by the appearance of Moss himself coming up from behind on a jog trot with the evident purpose of overtaking us. Riding along together until we reached camp, cordial relations were established very soon, and, with a good deal of preliminary information, he promised us his co-operation, and possibly his company, in our further operations.

Moss at this time appeared to be about thirty-five, of slender, wiry, figure, rather good looking, with long dark hair falling over his shoulders, and as careless in his dress as any prospector or miner. Quiet and reserved in speech and manner generally, he warmed up to good natured cordiality on closer acquaintance, and, as we found out later, was a very agreeable camp companion. Jogging along together over the trail, he described in a general way what we might find, the natural features of the country and the difficulties to be met with. He also had a good deal to say about a recent treaty with the Southern Utes, by which new boundary lines had been established excluding them from the mountain regions, very much to their dissatisfaction, not only on account of the loss of their hunting grounds, but also because of the failure of the government so far to make some promised awards. As one of the consequences they were frequently ordering all white men off their former reservation, and, while there was but little actual hostility, there was a good deal of uncertainty and apprehension. Moss explained that when he first came into this country he had made a treaty of his own with the principal chiefs, and, by the payment of a liberal annuity in sheep and some other things, had secured their good will and freedom from molestation in their mining operations.

The camp was located on the La Plata where it emerged from Babcock Mountain, and was, in truth, a camp only; a few mall tents and some brush "wickiups" afforded all the protection they had provided for themselves up to this time. Their mining operations consisted of a ditch line, partially completed, running out on a bench extending down the La Plata some two or three miles and supposed to contain enough free gold to pay for working it. I believe this was afterwards found unprofitable and the work abandoned. Both Ingersoll and myself were donated generous shares on the "bar," but it didn't mean anything to us in dividends. They were a jolly lot of old timers, mostly from California and the Southwest generally. Their operations were financed by San Francisco capitalists and engineered by Moss as their representative. Just at this time, however, they were all very much worked up over an election that was about to come off. A new county, or township, perhaps, had been formed from the newly acquired territory and officers were to be elected. I do not remember any of the details as to who or what was to be voted for, except that Moss was one of the candidates, and that he had promised to go with us as guide and counselor as soon as this election was over. To help matters along all our party voted with the miners, there being no residence requirements, and as soon as this formality was over we started off the packers on the first stage of our journey. The rest of us waited until

Moss closed the polls and then, with Cooper as the sixth member of our party, we made a rapid ride over to Merrit's Ranch on the Mancos, where we all put up for the night. Merrit was one of Moss' outfit who had taken up a claim on the Mancos, built a log house and was experimenting in gardening. Just now he was bewailing the loss of some of his vegetables by an early frost; his hardier crops had turned out very well, however.

So far, I have drawn largely upon memory in relating the incidents that directed my attention to archaeological, instead of scenic, photography on this San Juan expedition. I intended leaving the story at this point, but, in looking over my old notes again in an effort to revive recollection of almost forgotten details, I find some descriptions of personal experiences that, I think, will bear repeating.

"Sept. 9th to 15th, inclusive, was occupied with the investigation of the Cliff ruins, all of which is set forth fully in the Bulletin of the U.S. Geological Surveys, Vol. 1, 1874–75. The following notes will omit the details of these investigations, and will mention only a few incidents in the day to day happenings of, to us, a very eventful week.

"I have already mentioned, in my daily notes, the composition of our party up to the time we reached the La Plata camp, but I will bring the different members together again, at Merritt's Ranch, as made up for this occasion, all eagerly expectant as to possible discoveries, and alert with the spice of adventure because of the uncertain temper of the more unruly Indians who frequent these remote canyons. When we started out this bright and bracing September morning we had as guide and mentor Capt. John Moss, a small wiry man of about thirty-five, as hardy and tough as an Indian, quiet, reserved and even tempered, help-ful and resourceful in all that pertains to life in the open—his knowledge of the country and of its little bands of aborigines was of great service in many ways. Cooper came with us, not that he will be of much help, but because of former friendship and that he was the means of bringing us to the La Plata camp and the acquaintance of John Moss. He was an easy going chap, somewhat indolent and content to follow along with the packs—very loquacious and full of wonderful stories concerning himself—supplying most of the amusement in the banter around the camp fire after the day's work was over. Ingersol and myself with the two packers, represented the Survey. We had three pack mules, 'Mexico' carrying the photographic outfit—a little rat of a mule but a good climber, and could jog along at a lively pace without unduly shaking up the bottles and plates. 'Muggins' and 'Kitty' carried the 'grub' and blankets, and as both were reduced to bare necessities, their packs were light and they could be pushed along as fast as we cared to ride. Steve and Bob with their packs kept close to the trail most of the time, while the rest of us were roaming all over, investigating every indication of possible ruins that came to our notice; and when photographing was decided upon, 'Mexico' would be dropped out, unpacked, tent set up, and the views made while the others jogged along until we overtook them again.

"Our first discovery of a Cliff House that came up to our expectations was made late in the evening of the first day out from Merrit's. We had finished our evening meal of bacon, fresh baked bread and coffee and were standing around the sage brush fire enjoying its genial warmth, with the contented and good natured mood that usually follows a good supper after a day of hard work, and were in a humor to be merry. Looking up at the walls of the canyon that towered above us some 800 to 1,000 feet we commenced bantering Steve, who was a big heavy fellow, about the possibility of having to help carry the boxes up to the top to photograph some ruins up there—with no thought that any were in sight. He asked Moss to point out the particular ruin we had in view; the Captain indicated the highest part of the wall at random. 'Yes,' said Steve, 'I can see it,' and sure enough, on closer observation, there was something that looked like a house sandwiched between the strata of the sandstones very near the top. Forgetting the fatigue of the day's work, all hands started out at once to investigate. The first part of the ascent was easy enough, but the upper portion was a perpendicular wall of some 200 feet, and half way up, the cave-like shelf, on which was the little house. Before we had reached the foot of this last cliff only Ingersoll and I remained, the others having seen all they cared for, realizing they would have to do it all over in the morning. It was growing dark, but I wanted to see all there was of it, in order to plan my work for the next day, and Ingersoll remained with me. We were 'stumped' for a while in making the last hundred feet, but with the aid of an old dead tree and the remains of some ancient foot holds, we finally reached the bench or platform on which was perched, like a swallow's nest, the 'Two Story House' of our first photograph. From this height we had a glorious view over the surrounding canyon walls, while far below our camp fire glimmered in the deepening shadows like a far away little red star.

"As everyone took a hand in the camp work we were generally off on the trail quite early, not later than sun up, each morning, and were able to make fast time and good distances, despite the many diversions to investigate and photograph, but on the fourth morning out, on the head of the McElmo, we got a late start, with a long ride ahead, where it would have been much better to have made the greater part of it in the cooler hours of early morning. It was all owing to the wanderings of our animals. Generally they were tired enough to remain near camp when there was water or any kind of feed. If likely to wander, we hobbled, or staked out, the one or more that were leaders. Whenever we could trust them, however, we preferred to do so, for it was but a scanty picking they got at the best, and we liked to give them all freedom possible. So this morning at Pegasus Spring, with the prospect before us of a long ride under a hot desert sun, we had breakfast dispatched before sunrise, and while the rest of us packed up, Steve went out to bring up the stock which was supposed to be following the strip of moisture and scanty grass in the bed of the wash below us. Our work was soon done, but no mules appeared. Finally after an hour's impatient waiting, we saw Steve coming up in the far distance, accompanied by an Indian but without the animals. Cap. and I ran down to meet them; Steve reported that he had been unable to find any of the band, but the Indian, who said he was the father of the 'Captain of the Weemenuches,' was of the opinion that our man did not know how to follow trail, and that our animals had left this valley and gone up a left-hand branch leading back to the mountains. Moss understood Ute

33

well enough to get all the information we wanted, and also, that there was a small band of Indians camped below. Perhaps they had something to do with the disappearance of the stock in the hope that some stragglers might be picked up later, but we accepted his protestations of good faith and sent him up to our camp, while Cap. and I struck out at once to pick up the trail. A mile below we found where it turned off to the right. High up on the top of the mesas we heard Indians calling, or signaling one another, in the long drawn out highly pitched key peculiar to them, but what it all meant we did not know. Keeping up a jog trot, or run, as fast as our wind and endurance permitted, we finally came out on a low divide where we met a couple of young bucks mounted and loaded down with skins. They were on their way to the Navaho country and intended stopping at the spring where we were camped. If we did not succeed in finding our stock they would assist us after they had had a rest. We trotted on, however, keeping up a stiff pace, passing the five mile spring, and then coming to a big bend in the trail, I followed around while Capt. cut across, and there, where we met, at the foot of the last hill leading up the Mancos divide, we found the animals all grouped together under a tree, whisking their tails in contented indolence. Mounting bare back, with lariat ropes for bridles, we took a bee line for camp, and pushing them along at a stiff pace, were back to the spring by ten o'clock. Found the camp full of Indians, all mounted, the Captain himself among them, a venerable, gray headed, old man. Most of the others, with the exception of the one we met with Steve, were young bucks bound for the Navaho country. Were all quietly good natured and did but little begging. The old Captain wanted to know what we were doing down here, and when our business was explained to him by Moss, all of them laughed most hilariously, not comprehending what there could be in these old stone heaps to be of such interest.

"It was intended to reach the western limit of our explorations this day, on the banks of the Hovenweep, so we had a long drive before us, under an exceedingly hot sun blazing down into the dry and barren wash of the McElmo. We pushed right through on the double quick, deferring all photographic work until our return, but investigating and noting everything of interest as we traveled along. We made only one stop, and that for water, late in the afternoon, at a point where we left the McElmo to cut across the mesas to the Hovenweep. Water was expected to be found here, but the bed of the wash seemed perfectly dry, as it had been all day since leaving the spring. Water we must have, so we got busy and with a shovel that we had with us, dug down in the sand to about four feet, when water began to trickle slowly through, but the sand caved in so fast we could not get much of a pool. After a drink around ourselves, we filled our hats, a cup full at a time, and gave our animals a taste at least. They stood around whimpering in eager expectancy, and apparently appreciated our efforts to help them.

"On the return trip from the Hovenweep, we were three days getting back to the La Plata. It was a busy time with a good deal of photographing and some digging about the ruins. On the way from Pegasus Spring to the Mancos, Ingersoll got interested in some fossils and fell behind some distance. When he came out on the broad open divide between the Dolores and the San Juan, he failed to pick up our trail and went off on another that led over into Lost Canyon. He was lost for good nearly all night, but by taking the back track managed to rejoin us at Merrit's soon after sun rise.

"Remained long enough at the Mancos to make some negatives of the ranch house and then 'lit out' for the La Plata at top speed, getting there just in time for dinner before dark. The miners have all moved down from the upper camp, and are just starting a new one for the winter, the ditch having been brought down to this point.

"Sept. 16th, off for Baker's Park again, after a very cordial leave-taking all around. Made many plans for the continuation of our work next year. Found Animas Park almost entirely deserted and farms abandoned because of the 'Indian scare.' Took this opportunity to load up with fruit and vegetables, as our supplies were at the vanishing point."

The Colorado Magazine, Vol. 1, No. 4, 1924

"I do not consider myself a notable editor or a fine writer," LeRoy Hafen wrote in 1973. He was wrong on both counts.

Hafen joined the Colorado Historical Society's staff in 1924 after completing undergraduate and graduate studies in his native Utah and a Ph.D. at the University of California at Berkeley. As the state historian, Hafen edited the Society's first regular publication, *The Colorado Magazine*. Under his direction, the magazine gained a reputation for its exemplary primary sources and cutting-edge scholarship. He also traveled throughout the state collecting artifacts, diaries, letters, maps, old newspapers, and, most of all, stories.

Those stories reached the public by way of Hafen's pen. He wrote forty-eight articles in *The Colorado Magazine* and almost as many books during his thirty-year career. Most of his writings deal with westerners on the move: mountain men, gold seekers, Mormon pioneers bound for Zion, explorers, and Overland Mail carriers.

Unlike his subjects, Hafen stayed put. Soon after he came to Colorado, members of the Ku Klux Klan learned about his Mormon background and tried to oust him. Hafen withstood their pressure, only to face another challenge during the Great Depression. In 1933 the state legislature cut the Society's appropriation by 36 percent. Enduring a large pay cut, Hafen remained at his job and established a public history work relief program—the first of its kind in the nation—using Civil Works Administration funds.

"Fraeb's Last Fight" exemplifies Hafen's narrative style. He gave the facts and got out of their way—as if he wanted to set the stage and then, as all good historians do, let his subjects do the talking.

Fraeb's Last Fight

—LeRoy R. Hafen

Henry Fraeb, partner in the famous Rocky Mountain Fur Company and subsequently proprietor of Fort Jackson on the South Platte River, was a leader of mountain men during the most active days of the fur trade in the central Rockies. Northern Colorado was his chosen field; here he clung with great persistence, and here he was to make his last fight.

Fraeb, whose name was usually rendered "Frapp" by his trapper companions, was a German from St. Louis, Missouri. Of his early life nothing has yet come to light, nor can we tell the year of his first entry into the fur trade of the far West. He is mentioned as a leader of independent trappers in 1829,[1] and he soon comes into more definite prominence as one of the five men who on August 4, 1830, bought out Smith, Jackson, and (William) Sublette for $30,000 and organized the Rocky Mountain Fur Company.[2] His partners in this venture were Thomas Fitzpatrick, Milton G. Sublette, Jim Bridger, and Jean Baptiste Gervais. All were seasoned fur men and had been closely associated for a number of years. In three seasons the Rocky Mountain Fur Company was to send 210 packs of beaver skins to market (a pack was about 80 skins), which would pay its indebtedness and leave the partners with their outfit in the clear.[3]

During the season of 1830–31, Fraeb and Gervais took their party of men into northern Colorado, trapping in Middle Park and vicinity. Upon returning to the summer rendezvous on Green River, southwestern Wyoming, they met the other brigade leaders, but found that Fitzpatrick, who had gone back to the states for supplies and trade goods for the company, had not yet come in. Blankets were worn out, ammunition nearly exhausted, knives and traps were scarce and tobacco and whiskey were gone.

---

1 Frances F. Victor, *The River of the West*, 57.
2 The document exhibiting this transfer is in the Sublette Collection of the Missouri Historical Society at St. Louis. N. J. Wyeth says, in his *Correspondence and Journals*, 74, that the transfer price was $30,000. A note for $16,000 was accepted as part payment. H. C. Dale, *The Ashley-Smith Explorations*, 288.
3 Wyeth, op cit., 74.

Everyone grew restless. At last Fraeb, who, like many other trappers, had picked up some of the superstitions of the Indian, sought out a medicine man of the Crows, to get prophetic wisdom. Being a true professional man, the Crow oracle required a generous fee, of the value of a horse or two, before he could make medicine. With this requisite provided, the ceremony began and after several nights of singing, dancing, violent contortions, and the beating of drums, the exhausted medicine man fell asleep. When he awoke he announced that "Broken Hand" (Fitzpatrick) was not dead but was on the wrong road. Thus encouraged, Fraeb determined to find him, and taking a few companions set out forthwith.[4] The long-absent partner was found and brought to the rendezvous.

The years 1832 and 1833 found Fraeb with his party of trappers again in the Colorado Rockies. While in South Park, Mr. Guthrie, one of the trappers, was killed by lightning. The men had gathered in Fraeb's lodge and Guthrie was leaning against one of the lodge poles when the lightning struck. "Frapp rushed out of the lodge partly bewildered himself by the shock," says Joe Meek, "and under the impression that Guthrie had been shot. Frapp was a German, and spoke English somewhat imperfectly. In the excitement of the moment he shouted out, 'Py Gott, who did shoot Guttery?' 'G— a'Mighty, I expect; He's firing into camp,' drawled out Hawkins, whose ready wit was very disregardful of sacred names and subjects."[5]

After the rendezvous of 1833 Fraeb took twenty men and with "Old Bill" Williams as guide went down the Green River to trap.[6] Meek reports meeting the party as far south as Bill Williams Fork of the Colorado, in present Arizona.[7] Though far afield, as these trapping parties were wont to go, they managed to return to the regular summer gathering place.

In the early thirties, competition had become very keen in the fur trade of the far West. The great American Fur Company, founded by John Jacob Astor and backed by his genius and financial resources, was winning the field from Fraeb and his partners. In addition, there was competition from the companies of Bonneville, Wyeth, Gant & Blackwell, Bent & St. Vrain, and lesser independent organizations, not to mention the powerful

---

[4] Victor, op cit., 99–101.

[5] Ibid., 158. Mrs. Victor or Meek makes out the year of this incident as 1834, but in a letter written by Thomas Fitzpatrick from Hams Fork of Green River, November 13, 1833, he says: "Mr. Gutheru was killed last fall by lightening and Biggs since supplied his place."—Sublette Mss., Missouri Historical Society.

[6] Fitzpatrick's letter of November 13, 1833, cited above.

[7] Victor, op cit., 152–53.

Hudson's Bay Company of Great Britain. The country was overrun with trappers, and the beaver streams were being depleted of furs. In addition there had been introduced in the style centers of London and New York the silk hat, which was beginning to replace the beaver hat and thus further to reduce the market and the price of beaver skins.

At the summer rendezvous of 1834 the Rocky Mountain Fur Company was dissolved.[8] Fraeb received for his interest "forty head of horse beast, forty beaver traps, eight guns, and one thousand dollars' worth of merchandise."[9] During the two following years he most probably continued as an independent fur man.

Fraeb was wedded to the frontier; he could not return permanently to the settlements. Accordingly, he decided to turn to the buffalo robe trade and try it as a substitute for or supplement to the beaver skin business. He formed a partnership with another old-time trader, Peter A. Sarpy, and in the spring of 1837 they obtained a stock of trade goods from Pratte, Chouteau & Co. of St. Louis, brought them out to the South Platte, and established Fort Jackson. This trading post—located on the east bank of the South Platte near the present town of Ione, Colorado—began competition with its near neighbors, Forts Lupton, Vasquez, and St. Vrain. After two seasons of trade Fraeb and Sarpy sold their fort and goods to Bent and St. Vrain, who were already operating Fort Bent on the Arkansas and Fort St. Vrain on the South Platte.

In 1840 Fraeb and Jim Bridger formed a partnership and with thirty men set out, presumably, to trade and trap on the waters of the Columbia River.[10] But their old-time haunts seemed more alluring and soon they were again in the valley of the Green River, Wyoming. Here they established a trading post in 1841.[11] While Bridger was at the post, Fraeb led a party of trappers toward northern Colorado to "make meat" and get furs. On the Green River, in July, he met the first overland emigrants bound for California (the

---

[8] The articles of dissolution are reproduced in H. M. Chittenden, *The American Fur Trade of the Far West*, 1864.

[9] Ibid., 304.

[10] Letter of W. L. Sublette to Sir William D. Stewart, September, 1842—Sublette Mss. Missouri Historical Society. It is probable that Louis Vasquez was in the partnership also. Basil Clement, who went up the Missouri River in 1840 and to Fort Laramie with Louis Vasquez in the spring of 1841, was in the Fraeb fight and speaks of the "three partners." See the South Dakota Historical Collections, XI, 282, 288, 291. We know that Vasquez was Bridger's partner at Fort Bridger after Fraeb's death.

[11] The location of the post is uncertain. Stansbury, who got his account from Bridger in 1850, says (in his *Exploration and Survey of the Valley of the Great Salt Lake*, etc., 240) that Fraeb's fight occurred while Bridger was erecting his "trading-post on Green River." Basil Clement, an employee of Fraeb and Bridger at the time, after telling of the fight, says (So. Dak. His. Coll. XI, 291): "Bridger was not with us in the fight, he was at Fort Bridger on the Black Fork." If this is true it would place the founding of Fort Bridger two years earlier than the generally accepted date. W. L. Sublette, in writing to W. D. Stewart in September, 1842 (op cit.), says that Fraeb was killed "whilst out making meat from the fort."

Bartleson party) and the Catholic missionaries headed for Oregon, all being guided by his old-time partner, Thomas Fitzpatrick.[12]

In the valley of the Little Snake, a branch of the Yampa River, Fraeb with his white hunters and Snake Indian allies were menaced by a large party of Cheyennes, Arapahoes, and Sioux. A pitched battle occurred in late August, 1841. A number of brief mentions of this fight have appeared in historical writings, but heretofore no good detailed or first hand accounts have been available. From Jim Baker, the picturesque Colorado pioneer, who had come out with the Bartleson party of emigrants and joined Fraeb's party at Green River, we get some interesting details. To an interviewer in 1886 Baker told the story:

> "Shortly after I came out here the second time we were camped on the very creek where I live now—Snake River we called it then—and there we had a lively fight with a party of about 500 Sioux, Cheyennes, and Arapahoes. The Arapahoes didn't do much fighting, but they urged the others on. There were twenty-three in our party, and I can give you the names of every one of them. Old Frappe was in command. The Indians made about forty charges on us, coming up to within ten or fifteen paces of us every time. Their object was to draw our fire, but old Frappe kept shouting, 'Don't shoot till you're sure. One at a time.' And so some of us kept loaded all the time. We made breastworks of our horses and hid behind stumps. Old Frappe was killed, and he was the ugliest looking dead man I ever saw, and I have seen a good many. His face was all covered with blood, and he had rotten front teeth and a horrible grin. When he was killed he never fell, but sat braced up against the stump, a sight to behold. Well, when the fight was over there were about a hundred dead Injuns. There were three of our party killed."[13]

A few years before his death Jim Baker gave to a Superintendent of Schools some additional data on the battle and its exact location: "It was the hardest battle I was ever in. It was not on that mountain [Battle Mountain], but down in the valley at the mouth of Battle Creek at its junction with the

---

[12] Father De Smet reports that Fraeb had just returned from California.—H. M. Chittenden and A. T. Richardson, *Life, Letters and Travels of Father Pierre-Jean De Smet,* etc., I, 300. This has not been verified. John Bidwell, of the emigrant party, says that Fraeb's party purchased a supply of trade whiskey from the emigrants.—*The Century Illustrated Monthly Magazine,* XLI (New Series, XIX), 119.

[13] *Denver Tribune-Republican,* July 10, 1886.

Snake. I can show you some of the rifle pits there yet. The whites with their allies, the Snakes, were fortified at that point. Many of the whites had married squaws of that tribe. Before the battle began they sent their squaws to a mountain south, at a point of safety, and where they could watch the progress of the battle. The battlefield is in Routt County, less than a half mile from the Wyoming line. Their enemy, two tribes, Cheyennes and Arapahoes, came down Battle Creek and made the attack. Some were armed with rifles and some with bows and arrows. At that time they were scarcely out of the stone age. Would pay a good price for a barrel hoop to convert into knives and daggers. They fought all day, and no sooner did the enemy retreat up the creek than the whites and Snakes retreated to the mountain where the squaws were. From this circumstance that mountain has since been known as Squaw Mountain. Battle Mountain, Battle Creek, and Battle Lake, at the source of Battle Creek, took their names from this hard fought battle." [14]

The losses sustained by the enemy Indians could not be determined, for the Indians usually carry off their killed and wounded. Even in the reports of white losses there is some variance. The earliest accounts report the death of Fraeb and four of his men. [15]

The Colorado Magazine, May 1930

---

[14] *Steamboat Pilot* (Steamboat Springs, Colorado), March 2, 1904.

[15] Rufus Sage was told by mountain men in September, 1841, that Fraeb and four of his men were killed. Two years later he visited the site of the engagement. See his *Rocky Mountain Life*, 52, 286. Sage says the enemy lost fifteen or twenty killed but drove off eighty head of horses. J. C. Frémont was told of the fight by Bridger and others in 1842. He reports that the enemy "Indians lost eight or ten warriors, and the whites had their leader and four men killed."—*Report of an Exploring Expedition*, etc., 40. Frémont passed the site of the battle on his return from California in 1844. W. L. Sublette in his letter of September, 1842, to Stewart (op cit.) says that Fraeb and three others were killed.

Capt. Howard Stansbury, guided near the site of the battle by Jim Bridger in 1850, was told of the fight by Fraeb's partner. Stansbury reports (in his *Exploration and Survey of the Valley of the Great Salt Lake*, etc., 239) a preliminary fight and then the main attack about ten days later. Fraeb "had but forty men; but they instantly 'forted' in the corral attached to the trading post and stood on their defense. The assault lasted from noon until sundown, the Indians charging the picket several times with great bravery, but they were finally repulsed with the loss of forty men. Frappe himself was killed, with seven or eight of his people."

Basil Clement, who was in the fight, gives the following report in the *So. Dak. His. Coll.*, XI, 291: "We had a fight with the Sioux and Cheyennes there [on Little Snake River]. Old Frappe (Henry Fraeb) was killed there, he was one of the three partners. We went there (from Black's Creek) on a buffalo hunt to make jerked meat. We got meat of the Sioux and Cheyennes, with 47 men. After we had plenty of meat they made a dash for us. We defended ourselves. That was in the morning about 8 o'clock. This was about July, some time early in the July. We fought them from the morning about 8 o'clock till dark. They killed ten of our men, and killed 110 head of horses that belonged to us; and of the 45 head of horses alive, there was only five not wounded. All that we had to protect us was dead horses. We made a fort of them. The next morning we fired guns and showed fight, for them to come out, but they wouldn't come. Then we made a cache and put dried meat into it. This was my first year with Bridger. Bridger was not with us in the fight; he was at Fort Bridger on the Black Fork." The statements of Clement were obtained by Charles E. Deland in 1899 and 1909. Mr. Clement was born Jan. 7, 1824, and died Nov. 23, 1910.

A lbert Sanford's dedication to history nearly cost him his life. In 1935 officials planned to mark the fifty-ninth anniversary of Colorado's statehood with a twenty-one-gun salute on the capitol building's grounds. To the delight of a cheering audience, national guardsmen fired the first shot from a territorial-period cannon. Sanford, the state historical society's seventy-two-year-old acting curator of archaeology, had personally supervised the antique's restoration. He walked toward it, unaware that an officer was about to give the signal to fire the second shot from a modern artillery piece. The cannon fired its salute cartridge of black powder and wadding just as Sanford passed in front of it. The blast knocked him to the ground and blew his hat fifty feet away. Police rushed him to a hospital, where doctors removed bits of paper and clothing from his burnt flesh.

Exactly fifty-nine years before, a barefoot, teenaged Albert Sanford displayed a budding sense of history by attending Colorado's first statehood celebration. Born at Denver's Camp Weld to parents who met and married on the trail during the 1859 gold rush, he had already earned the title of "pioneer." One year after Colorado's admission to the Union, he accepted an invitation to vacation with Colorado's fourth territorial governor, Alexander Hunt, and his sons Bert and Bruce, in the San Luis Valley. The trip left such an impression on his young mind that he would be able to recall vivid details for *The Colorado Magazine* more than fifty-five years later.

Returning home, Sanford continued school, became one of Denver's first high school graduates, and earned a mining diploma from Denver University. In 1884, he went back to the San Luis Valley, where he farmed and ranched until 1893. He ran an assay office in Denver for the next twenty years.

Sanford joined the State Historical and Natural History Society of Colorado (as it was called then) in 1924, where he assumed, according to the Society's news bulletin, "the special duty of collecting the pioneer stories." He served as assistant curator of history, specializing in territorial and mining history, until 1939. During that time he wrote thirteen articles for *The Colorado Magazine*. He also contributed a chapter on "Organization and Development of Colorado Territory" to the *History of Colorado*, a book that remains invaluable as a general reference.

Though Sanford never fully recovered from the accidental cannonade, he continued to collect and write stories, mark historic sites, and recall his days as a pioneer and true son of Colorado.

Recollections of a Trip
to the San Luis Valley in 1877

—Albert B. Sanford

Early in June, 1877, the writer "passed" from the "Third Reader Room" to the "Fourth Reader Room" of the old West Denver Public School at Eleventh and Lawrence streets. Howard F. Crooker and "Billy" Crowley, still living in Denver, were members of the same class and were included in this scholarly advancement. Bert and Bruce, sons of Alexander Cameron Hunt, Colorado's fourth Territorial Governor and one of the incorporators of the Denver and Rio Grande railroad, were also fellow pupils but had left early in the spring to join their father at the end of the railroad track that had just been completed over Veta Pass. Governor Hunt was in charge of the surveys and construction of the road from Walsenburg west to the Rio Grande and beyond into the San Juan country.

A few days after the close of school the Governor sent me an invitation to visit his boys and promised me a good time fishing and hunting. He enclosed a round trip pass and requested me to advise him of the time of my departure. After a brief family council and upon my promise to observe certain rules of conduct, permission was granted.

A day of general preparation followed and the next morning I was at the depot at the foot of Eleventh street fully an hour before the time for departure of the train. In addition to my first jointed fishing rod and supply of lines, flies, and hooks, I had been provided with a personal expense fund. My "roll" consisted of fractional paper currency of ten, twenty-five, and fifty-cent denominations, besides some silver coin.

I had witnessed the laying of every mile of Denver & Rio Grande track as far as Littleton, had "dead headed" on work trains and been to Palmer Lake on a Sunday School picnic, but this was my initial experience on traveling first class. At Castle Rock, we sidetracked for an incoming

43

freight train. It was late and I went up ahead to inspect "Montezuma," the first locomotive used by the D. & R. G., to watch the engineer "oil round" and to renew an acquaintance begun that morning at the depot when I told him of my destination and, incidentally, of riding on a pass from Governor Hunt.

"Here she comes, sonny: better cut back and get aboard—or: say, how would you like to ride with us to the Divide? Climb up there on the fireman's side." "Sonny" climbed.

As we took the main track, my engineer friend told me I might blow the whistle and ring the bell as we approached stations and road crossings. I was to watch him for the signal. He shook his head and frowned a little when I blew for a cattle guard but I thought he must have overlooked this precaution. I will always remember that twenty-mile ride in the cab of "Montezuma" and regretted leaving it and my good friend, the engineer, as we stopped at Palmer Lake[1] and I resumed my place in the coach.

It was near dark when we reached the end of the track, then at Wagon Creek, where Orman & Crook, contractors, had huge tents for housing and feeding hundreds of men and others for sheltering scores of horses and mules. Bert and Bruce, dressed in regulation buckskin suits, greeted me in choicest Spanish and led the way to a cook tent for supper. Later we drove down Sangre de Cristo creek seven or eight miles to Governor Hunt's headquarters where Garland City had been surveyed and some buildings commenced.

The Denver & Rio Grande Railroad's Locomotive No. 1, the "Montezuma"

Aside from the happy experience on the locomotive, nothing seems to have impressed me more that day than Governor Hunt's greeting as I was unloaded at his tent door and shown to my bunk in a corner of that large canvas structure. He inquired about the school, smiled when told of my reaching the "fourth reader room," and remarked that his boys' school days were probably over and they would likely be associated with him as the road was extended into the San Juan country. He told me of a proposed trip with the boys, along the railroad survey to the Rio Grande and south to Guadalupe (present Conejos) where we were to visit Major Lafayette Head, then Lieutenant Governor of Colorado, and fish somewhere along Conejos River.

Plans for leaving early next morning were delayed by the escape of our broncho team from the corral, and at sun up we were off for a horse hunt. With lunch, canteen of water, halters, tin pail, and small bag of oats, we took up the horses' trail that led into the low piñon-covered hills lying at the base of Sierra Blanca. Every glade was searched without success until mid-afternoon, when we climbed a particularly high point before abandoning our efforts for the day. From here the southern and southwestern portion of the San Luis Valley spread before us. It was my first view of this inland empire. Bert handed me a high-power fieldglass and pointed out Fort Garland[2] several miles away. The flag floating from its staff on the parade ground and a troop of cavalry approaching from the south were clear and distinct. To the west and northwest, I traced the course of the Rio Grande from Del Norte to near the center of the valley, by a long dark line of cottonwoods. Beyond, were prominent peaks of the San Juan Range and southwest, San Antonio, the big round mountain just over the line in New Mexico.

Viewing of this wonderful, entrancing landscape was interrupted by Bert's reaching for the glass. After a moment he announced the discovery of the strays a half mile below, standing in the shade of a big yellow pine. Little trouble was experienced in attracting the horses as we shook the pail partly filled with oats and both were soon wearing halters and quietly following us to camp. After walking some distance, I suggested that we take turns riding, but was informed that while both animals were perfectly broken to harness, so far no one had ever succeeded in riding them. However, if I cared to try either one, I had permission. With this information, walking looked exceedingly good to me and no further mention of the matter was made.

45

That night we dined with the Governor and a few members of his engineering staff. I listened to much detail of the selection of the next terminal on the river and of the probability of its being a permanent town and railroad division point. Surveys and plats had recently been completed for the Governor's inspection and I learned he had already named the town Alamosa.

Our outfit was brought to headquarters early next morning. There was an almost new platform spring wagon with complete camp equipment and a "mess box" generously loaded with good things to eat from the commissary. Bert had a Winchester repeating rifle, Bruce and I carried shot guns. My fishing tackle looked modest compared with the rods and reels the other boys sported. With a few parting instructions and a hearty goodbye from the Governor, we were off.

In an hour we reached Fort Garland, then garrisoned by two troops of Negro cavalry[3] and under command of Lieut. Cook, who showed us over the entire post and entertained us for a while in his quarters—the same Kit Carson occupied during his administration there in 1866–67.

In late afternoon, and after a hot and dusty ride of twenty-four miles along the survey,[4] we reached Hunt's cabin on the east bank of the Rio

The first steamboat on the upper Rio Grande River, at Alamosa. Governor Hunt's sons equipped their boat with a small upright steam boiler and engine. In the boat are (left to right): unknown, Bert Hunt, Bruce Hunt.

Grande. This had been built for the convenience of himself and survey-ors and at that time was in charge of two of his trusted men. A ferry had been established that would easily carry two teams and wagons. It was operated by a two-inch rope anchored to either side. This was provided with heavy pulleys, which could be so arranged that the force of the current carried the boat across. As I remember, the river was from four to five hundred feet wide and from six to eight feet deep.

A large rowboat had been especially built in the Denver shops and equipped with a sail. One morning this was loaded on the running gears of a freight wagon and the men hauled us with guns and fishing tackle about eight miles up the river and launched the boat. They cautioned us about certain bends where the current was treacherous, promised us a good supper, and returned to camp. Bert at once assumed authority as "captain," Bruce and I promised obedience to his orders and the voyage began.

In those days the Rio Grande had no diversion of its flow excepting a few small ditches that served meadows along its banks and the greater part of this water returned immediately to the stream. Few sections of the river were much over a quarter of a mile in a straight course and many large bends of a half mile or more curved back to within a few hundred yards from [the] starting point of the curve.

Fondest expectations were more than realized that day. We landed frequently and caught all the trout we could possibly use. All along the river's course were old channels filled with back water where we crept in on flocks of young teal and blue wing mallards. Long-legged herons tempted a shot as they rose from sand bars and soared to nests in the tall *alamos* (cottonwoods) along the shore. A number of times when the breeze was favorable, we hoisted sail and reversed our course for a mile or so. This was another first experience of its kind to me and was real sport. The sun was dropping below the La Garita Hills when we tied in at the cabin. With the many big bends of the stream and our sailings we had covered more than twenty miles on the river.

Another morning we were ferried to the west side and an hour or more spent in going over the site of the new town where blocks and streets were plainly marked by stakes and the railroad depot site and other rights-of-way laid out. This was all that existed at that time of what is now one of the most prosperous young cities of Colorado.

We discovered a rather dim road pointing south which we followed to the border of the vegas, then covered with overflow from Rock and

Alamosa Creeks and extending easterly to the river. Skirting this, we worked on through sagebrush and finally located a traveled road near what is now La Jara, as I remember, and that afternoon pulled into the Guadalupe plaza, the home of Major Head,[5] where we were heartily welcomed by that noted soldier and pioneer. The major's home was a long, low adobe building with porch extending the entire length and shaded by numerous cottonwoods. The main living rooms were filled with most interesting furnishings of Mexican and Indian workmanship. The floors were carpeted with Navajo and native Mexican blankets and rugs.

Head had come to the Conejos River region in 1854 and was one of the first permanent settlers with the Mexican people who came up from New Mexico. He had married a Spanish-American woman. At that time the Indians made frequent attacks on the Mexicans and robbed them of much stock and provisions. To protect these pioneer settlers of the San Luis Valley the Government had established Fort Massachusetts in 1852. This was located six miles north of Fort Garland, built in 1858.

Head enjoyed the respect of both Mexicans and Indians and the Ute chiefs were favorably influenced by his honesty and regard for his promises. He was appointed Indian agent by the Government and served for a number of years. He was a member of the commission that went to Washington in 1868 at the time large portions of Indian lands within Colorado limits were ceded to the white men. He had served in the New Mexico legislature and was a member of Colorado's constitutional convention. I recall his asking many questions as to the progress of the Denver & Rio Grande construction and was enthusiastic over plans for the main line to follow the Rio Grande to El Paso.[6] He owned and operated a flour mill at Guadalupe that was run by water power. The millstones were of native formation taken from nearby hills. An especial courtesy was shown us in visiting the Catholic church "Our Lady of Guadalupe." This structure was made of sun-dried adobe brick and at that time had been standing about twenty years. Reluctantly, we left our friendly host and the comforts and delights of his home for a particular section of the Conejos River some ten or twelve miles below, where Head told of deep holes where some big native trout had been recently taken.

Our camp was opposite a flat top mountain[7] whose base bordered the stream and was sheltered by many large cottonwoods. Our first day's fishing was so successful that it was agreed that the next would be devoted to getting a shipment for Martin Welch's Bon Ton restaurant in Denver, where the boys had a standing order for mountain trout. With an early start, our catch amounted to over a hundred pounds by mid-afternoon and that night the lot was dressed and hung to dry and cool. It was shortly after daybreak next morning that we had our mess box packed with fish and grass alternating, and began the return trip.

Following the Conejos to near its mouth, we crossed the Rio Grande at Stewart's Ferry, traveled east and north to the Trinchera, where a brief visit was made with Tom Tobin, noted scout and friend of Kit Carson.[8]

At nightfall, we pulled into Garland City[9] where, during our absence, many large buildings had been commenced to house the freight for shipment by ox and mule teams to the then new gold and silver towns of Ouray, Lake City, and Silverton, besides many other camps that had sprung up in the San Juan Triangle. Wagon Creek had been moved bodily with its contractors' outfits, shacks, and tents devoted to saloons and dance halls. Already acres of space were occupied by great piles of merchandise, mining machinery, and building material, which was covered with tarpaulin for protection against weathering. Surrounding the center of town were corrals and stables for the use of freighters and stagecoach companies, all where but a very few weeks before had been an undisturbed area of sagebrush and greasewood. Probably the files of the Engineering Department of the Denver & Rio Grande Western railroad hold surveys and other data on Garland City that, in its brief existence, was the liveliest of all temporary railroad terminals in Colorado. If there is anything to attract particular attention to the site now, it is a noticeable difference in the size of the sage and greasewood that returned to its own within two or three years after the place was abandoned. One may easily kick up pieces of dishes, old wagon irons, bottles with varied colors developed by suns of many years.

The morning following our return I was on the train headed for Denver. Bert and Bruce waved a goodbye from an improvised platform and I replied, "Adios mi amigos." At La Veta we stopped some distance from the depot. A Mexican murderer[10] was still hanging from a telegraph pole where a mob had strung him up the night before.

We were late reaching Denver that night but Dad met me to help with my outfit and a fine mess of trout that had been well iced at Garland and proved to be in perfect condition on arrival. I could hardly eat or sleep until I had related my outstanding experiences and told of the wonderful charm the sunny San Luis Valley had for me—a charm that has not lessened but intensified as the years have come and gone.

Last September I stood on the east end of the railroad bridge at Alamosa, within twenty rods from the ground occupied by Hunt's cabin and about the same distance from where the rope ferry was operated. Over at the base of Sierra Blanca, I noted a prominent hill that was, without much doubt, my first viewpoint of the valley that afternoon over fifty-five years before. The experiences I have recorded left impressions that remain with me and seem strangely vivid and clear as I live them over again in this effort to tell the story.

The Colorado Magazine, September 1933

Endnotes

1 Palmer Lake is not, as many suppose, an artificial construction but is a natural basin fed by springs. Accompanying the report of Col. Dodge who passed this way in 1835, is a map showing the lake to be the source of Plum Creek. In pioneer days it was called "Divide Lake."

2 *Fort Garland has been preserved and is operated as a public museum by the Colorado Historical Society.*

3 *Ninth Cavalry Buffalo Soldiers served at Fort Garland from early spring 1876 to September 1879.*

4 On this road and some seven or eight miles east of the river we stopped at Washington Springs. The strange part of the place was the water, cold and clear, that issued from the top of a mound at least ten feet above the surrounding area. No doubt the water came from a crevice in the shale formation that underlies the whole valley and below which strata of artesian water now flows from a thousand wells. The springs were named after Washington Wallace, who had a ranch there in early times.

5 *Lafayette Head.*

6 Until final agreement between the Santa Fe and the D.&R.G. railroads followed the "Railroad War" in 1879, the D.&R.G. planned for the main line to follow the river to El Paso and Hunt had made a reconnaissance of the proposed route.

7 Many years afterward, and during an examination of the site of Pike's stockade, I was convinced that our camp in 1877 was near the spot that has been locally declared the actual site of Pike's fortress.

8 *Thomas Tate Tobin was a well-known mountain man and Army scout. The frontiersman is remembered most for tracking and killing two of the three serial killers known as the "bloody Espinosas" in 1863.*

9 There was "a gentlemen's agreement" between the railroad officials and the builders of the larger warehouses, hotels, and other structures, that the terminal was to remain at least a year. Accordingly, many of these buildings were constructed in a way that permitted taking them down without much loss and shipping in sections to Alamosa. The first train to cross the Rio Grande at that point was on July 6, 1878.

10 At that time, Charles D. Hayt, afterward a member of the Supreme Court of Colorado for twelve years, was a young attorney practicing at La Veta. He followed the railroad to Alamosa where he located permanently. During my residence there from '84 to '94 the Judge and I frequently discussed local history. At one time I told of my first trip into the Valley and of the Mexican lynching. Of this he said, "Yes, I well remember that incident for the court had appointed me to defend the accused. I was in my office that night preparing for trial when the mob relieved me of further duty by hanging my client."

The 1893 bankruptcy of the Philadelphia & Reading Railroad started a national panic that turned a three-year case of economic malaise into a bona fide depression. In Colorado, the crisis worsened when Congress tried to cure the ailing monetary system by repealing the Sherman Silver Purchase Act. Silver, the state's primary export, became almost worthless overnight. Roughly half of Colorado's mines shut down. Thousands of unemployed miners left homes in Leadville, Aspen, Georgetown, and the San Juan districts and headed for a booming gold camp called Cripple Creek that seemed immune to the troubles. Emil Pfeiffer, a bank accountant turned gold-seeker, joined them.

Pfeiffer moved to Altman, one of several new towns near Pikes Peak that materialized in and around the Cripple Creek Mining District during the mass migration. Straddling an alpine saddle between Bull Hill and Bull Cliff, the village commanded a fine view encompassing several of the district's largest mines. This strategic location guaranteed its role as a union command center in the inevitable confrontation between miners and mine owners.

Blessed with a labor surplus, many of the owners tried to lengthen working shifts without increasing wages. John Calderwood, a Scotsman representing the Western Federation of Miners, organized two-thirds of the district's laborers. Their battle cry was "an eight-hour day for three dollars' pay." When the union called a strike, the owners called the El Paso County sheriff to intervene on their behalf. The war, Pfeiffer noted, was on.

Rarely mentioned by labor historians, the strike brought prestige to the Western Federation of Miners. Forty-two years later, Pfeiffer wrote down his memories of the "Battle of Bull Hill" for *The Colorado Magazine*. Articles of this type filled the publication in the 1930s. Editor LeRoy Hafen knew that aging Coloradans, the men and women who shaped the state's pioneer period, were ready to tell their stories.

Some of those stories found second homes in popular history books. Marshall Sprague probably used Pfeiffer's article to flesh out portions of *Money Mountain: The Story of Cripple Creek Gold*. Sprague understood that personal reminiscences, especially those written long after the events they describe, can be one-sided. After all, people forget details and tend to remember the good things. But Pfeiffer's reminiscence remains a historian's gold mine.

The Kingdom of Bull Hill

—Emil W. Pfeiffer

The Cripple Creek mining district, located in the western portion of El Paso County, came into prominence just after the panic of 1893. The silver mining camps were dead and the miners looked to the new camp as a life-saver and flocked into it from the older localities. The population of the entire district, both towns and hillsides, increased rapidly, as did the mining activity also. The Victor, Isabella, Pharmacist, Zenobia, and Free Coinage were some of the prominent mines on Bull Hill, although there were many more of lesser magnitude.

The town of Altman was platted in the summer of 1893. It was about three miles from Cripple Creek and up hill more than 1,000 feet, its elevation being 10,700 feet. It was nine miles in an air line from the top of Pikes Peak. A population of some 1,200 was served by stores, boarding houses, post office, a livery stable, and five saloons.

The first "Miners Union" of the district was organized there that summer, a branch of the Western Federation of Miners. The mines were working eight-hour shifts, with one-half hour for lunch on the company's time; the pay was $3.00 per day. Some mines were working three shifts, day shift, night shift, and "graveyard" shift, as it was called; thus it was possible to employ more men and get out more ore.

The first sign of trouble came in August, 1893, when the then superintendent of the Isabella Gold Mining Company, at the shaft of the Buena Vista mine, had notices posted to the effect that after September 1st the hours of the shift would be ten, nine for work and one for lunch, but with no increase in pay.[1] Trouble came to the "super" without delay. He came to the mine daily from Cripple Creek in a horse-drawn cart. On the morning of the day when the order was to become effective, as he approached the mine, he was surrounded by the incensed miners and addressed in most vehement language. He very unwisely tried to bluff his

52

way out of a very intense situation. Not until a loud voice was heard saying, "Bring on that can of tar," did he realize his predicament. He was pulled out of his cart and threatened with violence if he did not rescind the order. After a few minutes of talk he decided to comply and I am sure he posted the notice at once and without the knowledge of the owner.

"If at first you don't succeed, try, try again," was the motto this "super" seemed to follow, for he finally succeeded in getting all the owners of the large mines into an agreement to put the ten-hour shift into effect. So on January 20, 1894, notices were posted at all the mines. The following day, as usual, he drove from Cripple Creek in his horse-drawn cart, a deputy sheriff on horseback preceding him, and another deputy sheriff on horseback following behind. He was just passing the "Dougherty Boarding House" when he was met by a crowd and stopped; another crowd of men in the rear cut off his retreat; his two guards were also captured.

He was dragged from his cart and subjected to rough treatment. He was walked down backward by two husky fellows to the wagon road in Grassy Gulch; then down the road toward the old Spinney Mill, all the time being told that he was to be hanged at the mill. Upon arriving there, however, the gang relented. He was forced, nevertheless, to kneel down in the road and take an oath that he would never return to the district unless invited by the miners themselves. The horse and cart were returned to him, an escort was provided, and he was set out on his way down the old Cheyenne Canon road to Colorado Springs.

Following this event, about February 1, 1894, the "Kingdom of Bull Hill" was born. An army was recruited, picket lines were established and patrolled by squads of men selected by the officer of the day; no one was allowed to enter or leave without a proper pass, the result being that we were without the confines of the United States. We were a band of outlaws; the mines were closed; a few watchmen were permitted to remain on the properties, but the owners were not allowed to work them. The war was on.

At this time in my story it is proper to say that the Governor of the state was Davis H. Waite, a Populist, who had been elected in 1892, was a well-known advocate of union labor, and no doubt a friend of the striking miners.

The mine owners appealed to the authorities of El Paso County to take steps to restore possession to them of their properties. To this end the County Sheriff organized a "posse" to the number of 1,200. In the course of events the Sheriff had his force encamped near the town of Gillett, about four miles from Altman. Meanwhile, a force of one hundred

detectives were employed in Denver to attempt to regain the possession of the mines—it was said they would bring plenty of arms and a cannon.

The miners appeared to be well entrenched in their stronghold, with guns and a fair supply of ammunition, also a "Johnny wagon." This was a wagon rigged with an electric battery, spools of wire, and a supply of dynamite to be used as occasion arose.

The roads and trails were planted with charges of explosives ready to be set off. It was said that a cannon mounted on the bluffs above the Victor Mine was part of the equipment. This, however, was not true. It was only a bluff, the artillery being a round log dressed up for the part. A big timber was fashioned into a bow gun, grooved in the center so that a beer bottle filled with nails and other missiles could be projected quite a distance, in case the fighting was close. Steam was kept up at the Pharmacist Mine to be used in blowing the whistle for signals, also as an alarm. When an alarm was sounded all men responded, the team was hitched to the "Johnny wagon" and off they went to investigate. It was a virtual state of siege for a while during the months. With much bad weather, snow and, as spring came on, rain, the pickets suffered, but they stuck to their posts.

Let me here digress to personal affairs. When the strike was called I was working on a mine and living in Altman. At the same time, with others, I was trying to make a "stake" in a lease on a mine. We had a good lease on a property which we lost by reason of the trouble and the owners afterward took out two million dollars! One of the partners had been a cadet at West Point.[2] During his fourth year he was dismissed for his part in hazing a fellow student. He drifted west and became a good miner. We became such close friends that he was taken into our home as one of the family. He came from a fine southern family. Because of his West Point training he was selected to be general of the "army." He mapped out the territory and laid out the plan of a defensive campaign. Owing to his wise counsel to the men no property damage resulted, with one exception, to which reference will be made later. He was opposed to any destruction, although he had a hard time in restraining many of the so-called "fire eaters" and extreme radicals.[3] With his knowledge of military affairs and law, during the hostilities, he effected an exchange of prisoners with the authorities of El Paso County. This, he said, was a recognition of the rights of belligerency and was his greatest triumph.

From the beginning affairs began to get to a stage when there must be a final "show-down." Each side of the controversy was becoming desperate. The month of May was a most trying one, with its heavy snows and rains, and the men on picket duty began to complain. Also it was difficult to obtain food and other necessities. The railroad from Florence to Victor had just been completed and a train bearing detectives from Denver was en route.[4] They were reported to be well armed and had on board a cannon. Then arose the most acute situation of the war.

The "general" decided it was time to make a demonstration of force and, as such, it was to be one of terror. As the train approached slowly on a curve in sight of Victor the shafthouse of the Strong Mine was blown into the air. The train halted, then backed down to a station called Wilbur. At the blown up mine two men were trapped. They were taken as prisoners to Altman, held a time, and then exchanged for three prisoners held in jail in Colorado Springs.

After the train with the detectives aboard was stopped at Wilbur the miners planned to capture the whole outfit. A locomotive and cars were manned and the raid was on. The men were so eager to accomplish their purpose that in their enthusiasm their approach was too noisy and they were discovered. A battle ensued, resulting in the death of a deputy sheriff who had been one of the guards of the offending superintendent, and three miners were captured.[5] The attacking forces were compelled to retreat, but the detectives made no further effort to renew the combat and returned to Denver. Hell began to pop. The El Paso County "posse" began preparations to take Bull Hill. Governor Waite came on the hill and gave the men a talk. He had ordered out the state militia and after some tense days General Brooks and his troops marched into Altman.

Were they welcome? I'll say they were! They received a royal welcome from the men, even though they did bring along the sheriff, who had warrants for the arrest of some four hundred miners. A few of the miners gave up and were taken to Colorado Springs to jail. Had not the troops intervened just at that time between the El Paso forces and the miners I am of the opinion there would have been much blood shed.

After a number of conferences between the Governor and representatives of the miners and the mine owners, the trouble was settled. Eight hours' work with the lunch time of one-half hour on the men's time was the result of the compromise.

Many outrageous things happened during this "war." One of them occurred at Colorado Springs when the Adjutant General of the State was taken from his hotel and was tarred and feathered. Old Tom Tarnsney did not deserve such treatment. By whom and by whose orders? Thus endeth my story of "The Kingdom of Bull Hill." Altman is now extinct.

The Colorado Magazine, September 1935

Endnotes

1 *Bradford Locke.*

2 Junius J. Johnson. He afterwards became a major with the Arkansas Volunteers in the Spanish-American War and died at Anniston, Alabama, in 1898.

3 *Jack Smith and a gang of toughs.*

4 *The detectives were ex-policemen and ex-firemen from Denver itching for revenge after a losing confrontation with pro-union Governor Davis Waite at City Hall.*

5 *Other sources reported that two men were killed and five miners were captured.*

V isitors to Dinosaur National Monument in the northwest corner
of Colorado know Echo Park as the picturesque site of a
campground, prehistoric petroglyphs, Whispering Cave, and a
series of hiking trails. Whitewater rafters and kayakers know well the
stretch of narrow river canyon that U-turns around the massive
Steamboat Rock; the canyon's sheer sandstone walls create the striking
echo effect that gives the adjacent park its name. But fewer are those
who know the story behind Echo Park's alternate name—"Pat's Hole"—
and the hermit who made the park his solitary home.

Edgar C. McMechen weaves the tale of the loner Pat Lynch and
his mysterious life story. In doing so, McMechen relies on the memories,
firsthand accounts, and correspondence of the few people who met
Lynch, either in passing or as his neighbors in this remote valley—a
valley long known as a hideout for cattle rustlers, tax evaders, and
sundry other outlaws. As McMechen writes, the notorious Butch
Cassidy was not the only fugitive to use the treacherous "horse-thief
trail" that led through Pat's Hole from Hole-in-the-Wall, Wyoming, nor
was explorer John Wesley Powell the only traveler to tangle with this
stretch of the Green River.

When he wrote the piece, McMechen was the newly appointed
curator of archaeology and ethnology at the Colorado Historical
Society. In such capacity, he served as the longtime backup to LeRoy R.
Hafen, the Society's peripatetic director, curator, and historian. During
the 1930s and 1940s, McMechen contributed eighteen articles and
many book reviews to *The Colorado Magazine*. He later served as curator
of the State Museum, a post he held into the early 1950s.

The Hermit of Pat's Hole

—Edgar C. McMechen

A t the confluence of Yampa River with Green River in northwestern
Colorado lies Pat's Hole, one of the most spectacular topographical
spots in the intermountain West. The little park, formed by erosion of
the rivers, is surrounded by high, vertical sandstone walls. Here Green
River reverses its course, flowing in opposite directions on either side
of a mile-long wall of rock which rises approximately eight hundred
feet above the valley floor. The Green enters from the north through
Lodore Canyon, wheels, and exits to the north and west through
Whirlpool Canyon. The glorious Yampa Canyon, with its gray, red,
pink, or saffron walls, extends to the eastward for fifty-eight miles.

Human associations in this remote locality have been few, but
intensely romantic; and none more so than the story of Pat Lynch, the
remarkable Irish-born hermit after whom Pat's Hole has been named.
While Pat did not appear upon the scene until thirty years after the close
of the fur-trapping era, that typical trapper terminology, "Hole," seems
particularly appropriate because General W. H. Ashley and his daring
trappers were the first white men to have seen the retreat.

On May 8, 1825, Ashley and six of his men, navigating skin boats,
entered what is now known as Lodore Canyon. They descended that same
day to the mouth of the Yampa, to which Ashley gave the name Mary's
River. His diary leaves no doubt as to the identity of the spot. His description of Pat's Hole, the first ever penned, fits the locality perfectly: "Mary's
River is one hundred yards wide, has a rapid current, and from every appearance, [is] very much confined between lofty mountains. A valley about two
hundred yards wide extends one mile below the confluence of these rivers,
then the mountain again on that side advances to the water's edge."[1]

The next reference to Pat's Hole appears in the Powell report that
details his first trip through the Colorado River Canyon in 1869, when

he named the various canyons, rocks, and rapids encountered during the trip. This nomenclature still is retained, except in the case of Pat's Hole, which Powell called Echo Park. The first Powell Expedition reached the Yampa on June 17, 1869.[2] The name, Echo Park, followed normally the naming of Echo Rock, the monolithic stone wall previously mentioned, sometimes called locally, "Steamboat Rock." The Powell name for this cliff, because of its aptitude and historical association, seems preferable.

Major Powell devoted considerable attention to Echo Park, particularly to the extraordinary echo here. He described the main features of the park in great detail, mentioning a land entrance down a lateral trail through a side canyon which, he stated, had been made by Indian hunters "who come down here in certain seasons to kill mountain sheep." The park was inaccessible elsewhere, according to Powell, the inference of course being that he meant by land. In this, as will be shown, he was mistaken.

Major Powell's description of the echo is almost lyrical:

> Standing opposite the rock, our words are repeated with startling clearness, but in a soft, mellow tone, that transforms them into magic music. Scarcely can you believe it is the echo of your own voice. In some places two or three echoes come back; in other places they repeat themselves, passing back and forth across the river between this rock and the eastern wall.
>
> To hear these repeated echoes well you must shout. Some of the party aver that ten or twelve repetitions can be heard. To me they seem to rapidly diminish and merge by multiplicity, like telegraph poles on an outstretched plain. I have observed the same phenomenon once before in the cliffs near Long's Peak, and am pleased to meet with it again.[3]

Frederick S. Dellenbaugh, who accompanied Powell on a later expedition, confirmed the statement that a sentence of ten words is repeated by the echo, and asserted: "Such an echo in Europe would be worth a fortune."[4]

Local reports among those who knew Pat Lynch intimately, as well as a reference by Ellsworth L. Kolb, indicate that Pat first appeared in northwestern Colorado at the time of the Powell expeditions, although which expedition is not certain.

The Kolb brothers reached Pat's Hole on their photographic trip through the Colorado River Canyon on October 2, 1911. Pat was not home at the time, but they found his little ranch of about twenty-five acres on the left side of the river. There were a few peach trees, a small garden, and two small shacks in a state of dilapidation, the doors off their hinges and leaning against the building.[5] The trail to the top of the mesa or tableland south of the Hole was plainly marked. The Kolb party ascended this and called at the Chew ranch house on Pool Creek. While there a very old, bearded man rode in on a horse which he had broken himself—bareback—without assistance. He was then on his way to the post office, miles away, to draw his pension for service in the Civil War.

Pat Lynch lived for some forty-eight years at the junction of the Green and Yampa Rivers.

> He was Pat Lynch [continues Ellsworth Kolb], the owner of the
> little ranch by the river. He was a real old-timer, having been in
> Brown's Park when Major Powell was surveying that section of
> the country. He told us that he had been hired to get some
> meat for the party, and had killed five mountain sheep. He was
> so old that he scarcely knew what he was talking about, rambling
> from one subject to another; and would have us listening with
> impatience to hear the end of some wonderful tale of the early
> days when he would suddenly switch off on to an entirely
> different subject, leaving the first unfinished.[6]

Kolb makes the statement, as hearsay, that Pat would place a spring
or trap gun in his houses at the river, "ready to greet any prying marauder."
This, however, is at variance with the accounts of others who knew Pat.
Universally they have described him as a harmless, gentle old man.

The man credited with having known Pat Lynch best is Fray Baker,
formerly a resident of Elk Springs, Moffat County, at whose home Pat
died in February of 1917 after an illness of two or three weeks. Also,
from W. S. Baker of Lily Park come certain facts of Pat's life.[7] These are
briefed below.

Pat Lynch settled first at the present Chew ranch on Pool Creek
above the Hole. When the Chews filed on the land, Pat moved from the
open cave that he had occupied into the depths of the Hole. He left a
few trifling possessions in the vacated cave. These never have been
disturbed by the Chews, a Mormon family.

Pat possessed a wonderful memory and was quite loquacious. He was
fond of relating his experiences and would ramble along, laughing
frequently during his narration. He was very deaf and paid little
attention to comments. He was interested in history and took several
papers and magazines, among them the *New York World*, *Collier's Weekly*,
and the *Literary Digest*.

An article printed in the *Craig Empire*, February 28, 1917, four days
after Pat's death, states that Pat was born in Ireland. He took service on
a sailing vessel when he was fourteen years old; was shipwrecked on the
coast of Africa and captured by a native tribe. Pat remained with this
tribe for two to four years, according to stories told by him to various
persons, and rose to a place of importance with the natives. An English
sailing vessel then rescued him and took him to India.

Upon coming to America Pat joined the United States Navy under the name James Cooper, at the time of the Civil War. Pat often told of an incident during a naval battle when a "time" bomb was thrown upon the deck; and that, in seizing it to throw it overboard, he was badly wounded. He was rendered unfit for active service, and the wounds continued to suppurate, but he succeeded in enlisting in the Union Army under his own name. He drew a pension for this service. Pat's age at death is given as ninety-eight years and ten months.

When the war closed Pat was in Georgia. He went to Missouri and, for a short time, lived in a cave near Cane Hill in Polk County. He told Baker that he had left a knife there, after inscribing his name on the cave wall. If this record is still extant it probably will prove to be a sailing vessel, as this seems to have been his identification mark. He drew many ships upon the rocks of Yampa Canyon.

After engaging in the Indian wars of the plains Pat came to Denver, and then drifted to Brown's Park, then the haunt of a few derelict fur traders and meat hunters. He made a trip to California to secure some horses but ended by returning to Colorado for them. A popular legend in Moffat County is that Pat first appeared riding a fine blue-roan stallion of Arab extraction, and that for many years wild blue-roans were common in the Brown's Park region.[8] Baker states that Pat owned a marked bible, said his prayers by his bed, and called Protestants "devil scallas."

Another interesting account of Pat's history, habits, and peculiarities is contained in a letter to Mrs. Ada Jones, Craig, Colorado, written January 15, 1919, by F. C. Barnes, who knew the old hermit intimately.

> Old Pat Lynch was quite a character [wrote Barnes]. He was a soldier in the Civil War, and also in the Indian War. After the Indian War he drifted down along Green River until he came to the mouth of Bear River,[9] which is known far and wide as Pat's Hole, although Pat called it Echo Park. Old Pat lived here nineteen years under a ledge of rock. Then, for several years, he had four forks, set up and covered with willows. No sides to the shed. This was all the house he had until just a few years before he died. The cowboys built him a cabin. The wall around Pat's Hole is so high and straight that the sun never shines in there six

months out of the year. He had beaver and deer as tame as cattle and hogs. He never killed any of them. He lived just like a coyote. If he found a dead horse he would take a quarter or a half and make jerky out of it. This is the kind of meat he always kept on hand. I have known him to take a drowned horse out of the river and make jerky out of it. He had jerky and bread cached all over the mountains. I have been riding with him on different trips. He would stop and study for a minute, then turn to one side and go to a rock or cleft and get some meat and bread. The meat was always jerky and the bread looked like it might have been cooked a year or more. The last three years of his life he lived with W. R. Baker in Lily Park.

The tales of Pat's friendship with wild animals are widespread in northwestern Colorado. During the winter of 1904 the Moffat Railroad sent a surveying party under Paul Blount, locating engineer, through Yampa Canyon on the ice. The spring break-up of the ice jam in the canyon caught the party near Pat's Hole, and the surveyors went into camp close to Pat's cabin. Pat spent many nights regaling his visitors with his tales. Richard L. Hughes of 1350 Sherman Street, Denver, was a member of this party and, in a recent interview with the author, confirmed the story of the blue horses, many of which were roaming the country at the time. One of Pat's stories, told to Mr. Hughes, related to a pet mountain lion. Pat claimed to have tamed this creature which, he said, frequently brought a dead deer and left it at his cabin. He would call this animal with a peculiar, plaintive wail, and the lion would answer from high in the cliffs. The identical story was told the author by Carey Barber of Maybell, who was born in the country and knew Pat well.

"Pat claimed that the lion would come out upon a high cliff and scream in answer to his yell," said Mr. Barber, "and old Pat would say 'That sound is sweeter than any Jenny Lind ever sang.'" Old residents of the Brown's Park country still call this cliff the Jenny Lind Rock.

Mr. Barber is authority for the statement that Pat had his private horse-brand, called the "Ox-Shoe" brand. It was formed by two half-shoes (split because of the cloven hoof) in position, i.e., as they are placed upon an ox's hoof.

Pat had two blood-curdling stories he would relate when the mood seized him. One was that he had killed a man in Pittsburgh and had come West to escape punishment; the other, he had killed his mother. That Pat had some connection with the sea seems probable from two facts. He was elaborately tattooed, and he continuously drew pictures of sailing vessels. In Hardin's Hole, located in the depths of Yampa Canyon between Pat's Hole and Lily Park, is a large cave. Local settlers have a legend that two of the women captives taken by the Ute Indians in the Meeker Massacre of 1879 were hidden here while United States troops were searching for them. The records of this event make it extremely improbable that the women were ever near Yampa River, but the cave received its name, "Indian Cave," from this legend. [10] Farrington R. Carpenter, state revenue director and an authority upon northwestern Colorado history, states that there is the outline of a sailing vessel on a wall of this cave, which is attributed to Pat.

In the Powell narrative reference is made to the solitary land entrance to Pat's Hole. As indicated at the beginning of this article, there was another trail into the Hole, with which is connected much of the romantic background of the region.

This trail began in the cedars, high upon the southern shoulder of Douglas Mountain, overlooking Pat's Hole to the southwest. It may still be plainly traced down abrupt limestone cliffs to the upper end of a box canyon. Here, a vertical drop of three or four feet led to a huge table-rock. A second drop of the same distance, at right-angle, landed a horse and rider upon a narrow shelf, which followed around the side of the canyon wall, finally emerging on Green River about half a mile above the mouth of the Yampa. This was the famous horse-thief trail, which came from Hole-in-the-Wall, Wyoming, through Butch Cassidy's hangout at Powder Springs, Brown's Park, Pat's Hole, and up through Pool Creek into Utah. Some twenty years ago cattlemen of Brown's Park destroyed the table rock connection with dynamite.

For many years, until the rustlers were driven from this section of the country, stolen horses and cattle were run out of Brown's Park over this frightful route. Many a pack-horse, pushed off to the table-rock, lost balance and crashed upon the rocks two hundred feet below. The boneyard is still there. Cattle, less temperamental, fared better.

During Pat's day this trail saw considerable use, but Pat's loquacity never led him to talk about the phantom riders' trips over the horse-thief trail. No one remembered trail herds seen in strange locations in those days, and Pat followed the general custom. Hence, he died peacefully in bed, instead of floating down Green River.

Thus ends the saga of Pat Lynch, perhaps the West's most extraordinary hermit. Years hence, when tourists arrive in this desolate and solitary valley, now included in a national monument,[11] to test the unequalled echo of the great rock, not the least of their interest will center upon Pat Lynch, whose eccentricities have imparted to his life story all the glamour of legend.

The Colorado Magazine, May 1942

Endnotes

[1] H. C. Dale, *The Ashley-Smith Explorations and the Discovery of a Central Route to the Pacific* (Cleveland, 1918), 146.

[2] J. W. Powell, *Explorations of the Colorado River of the West and Its Tributaries, 1869–1872* (Washington, 1875), 30.

[3] Ibid., 32–33.

[4] F. S. Dellenbaugh, *The Romance of the Colorado River*, 256.

[5] E. L. Kolb, *Through the Grand Canyon from Wyoming to Mexico*, 72.

[6] Ibid., 75.

[7] From notes given by W. S. Baker and transmitted to E. C. McMechen in 1933. State Historical Society Records.

[8] Carey Barber, Maybell. Interview with E. C. McMechen in 1933.

[9] The Yampa is called the Bear above Craig. The two names for one river have frequently caused confusion.

[10] *The Meeker Massacre was an uprising of Utes at the White River Agency (at today's town of Meeker, southeast of Dinosaur National Monument) in response to agent Nathan Meeker's aggressive efforts to "reform" the Indians' ways of life. Meeker and eleven other men were killed in the battle, and the Utes took hostage Meeker's wife, his daughter, and another woman and her two children; the hostages were later released.*

[11] *Founded in 1915 and expanded in 1938, Dinosaur National Monument contains one of the world's largest concentrations of Jurassic-era dinosaur fossils. Paleontologist Earl Douglass discovered the first of the fossils in 1909.*

M uriel Sibell Wolle looked at history with the eye of an artist. Born in Brooklyn in 1898, Wolle earned degrees in advertising and costume design from the New York School of Fine and Applied Arts, along with a diploma in art education from New York University. She came to Colorado in 1926, and on a Fourth of July outing she passed through the picturesque mining town of Central City. The experience changed her life. "As the result of one ride," she writes, "I dedicated myself to recording pictorially the mining towns of the state before they disappeared, or before those which are still active were 'restored' past all semblance of their past glory; and almost without knowing it, I was deep in history."

She went back to New York, set about finding a teaching position in the West, and returned the next year to the University of Colorado art department. She taught there for more than forty years, earning an English degree as well.

During the five decades she spent in Colorado, Wolle tirelessly explored its back roads and jeep trails, seeking out and sketching hundreds of crumbling mining camps. Back in the studio, she translated her sketches into rugged and vibrant watercolors, fleshing out the details from memory. Today the Denver Public Library holds some 2,000 of these works of art.

In the process of creating the images, Wolle wrote profiles of these "ghost towns" as well—profiles that showed as keen an eye for historical detail and local color as her paintings did. Her meticulous research and her skills at interviewing old-timers lent her essays the authority and readability of only the best historical writing. She adapted the essays into authoritative volumes; her *Stampede to Timberline* has been reprinted more than a dozen times and is still a trusted source for anyone exploring, via armchair or scholar's desk, the mining camps of the Colorado mountains. In a sense, *Stampede* is a record of two eras—the early mining period itself and the years from the 1920s to the 1940s, before Interstate 70, before the skiing boom, before gambling.

Wolle visited Irwin, just west of Crested Butte in Gunnison National Forest, in 1941 and again in 1946. Today, travelers over Kebler Pass know Irwin as little more than a cemetery with a scant few graves still visible. In this 1947 essay and the images that accompany it, Wolle paints a picture of Irwin's past—and of its decay into a true ghost town as nature reclaimed it.

66

Irwin, a Ghost Town of the Elk Mountains

—Muriel Sibell Wolle

An old photograph and a mine inspector's question sent me looking for Irwin. The photograph showed a booming mining camp with more than one business street, hundreds of buildings, and a white church with a steeple. The town was laid out in a sloping valley surrounded by timbered hills with a backdrop of snowy peaks. I asked the name of the town and found it was Irwin.

Later that summer I met a mine inspector. "Have you been to Irwin?" he asked. "It was a big camp with lots of buildings. You should see it," he added. "The boom started in the winter and trees for cabins were cut at the snow line. In the spring the stumps were found to be ten feet high."

The idea of ten-foot stumps was exciting, so I went hunting for the place. The last stretch of road was rough and washed out and when I should have been at the site of the town there were no signs of it. The road had by now become a stream-bed. Where was Irwin? Suddenly in front of me, on either side of the gully and at regular intervals although overgrown with weeds, were water hydrants, rusty but erect. So this WAS Irwin and the gully was the main street.

In 1879, when a man named Fisher drove a team up the valley there was no town and no one had found the rich ore deposits which lay in the immediate vicinity. Fisher's wagon got stuck in mud and so grateful was he for the help given him by a man named Mace who came to his aid that he promised his benefactor that he "would locate him in on any mining location that he found." A few days later Fisher located two claims, the Forest Queen and the Ruby Chief, both destined to be big producers. The Forest Queen he gave to Mace, keeping the Ruby Chief for himself.

About the same time Dick Irwin and other men who had made a strike in the vicinity packed several tons of ruby silver ore on burros and sent it to Alamosa and the railroad, 200 miles away, to be shipped to Denver to be smelted. Then winter set in and the prospect holes were abandoned, but in Denver word got about that rich ore had been found in the Elk Mountains and by spring the news had spread from the Atlantic to the Pacific.

Not only had ore been found at the Forest Queen and Forest King mines, but the Sylvanite near Gothic Mountain showed vast quantities of native silver and the Augusta in the same neighborhood promised rich returns. As soon as weather permitted, therefore, prospectors from all over the country began stamping to the new silver region.

The camp was called Irwin after the Hon. Richard Irwin, one of the original discoverers of silver in the region and a member of the first Colorado Legislature. As more paying mines were found more men scrambled over the passes and floundered through the deep snow to reach the incredible camp before all the choice locations were staked out.

A townsite was platted, lots were sold, and tents and cabins erected. In no time the place grew to amazing proportions and squeezed out or annexed its adjacent rivals—Ruby and White Cloud.

Everyone was waiting for the snow to melt. Prospectors plunged over the mountains but supplies had "to wait until they could be packed over the range." Dick Irwin hired an ox-team to haul supplies from Gunnison to the snow line at King's Ranch, a few miles below Irwin, the trip taking six days. By the spring of 1880 "tons of goods were dumped at the foot of the long grade below Irwin waiting for the snow to go." Many of these supplies were perishable and were desperately needed by the miners in the new camp. There was no flour nor bacon for sale, and lumber was extremely scarce. Finally those who had ordered the supplies "employed packers at 10 cents a pound to bring the produce in, on their backs, by traveling on the snow crust in the early morning. The packers would start about three o'clock and arrive in camp about five carrying 100–200 pounds on their backs and earning from $10–$20 each trip."

The snow was still twenty feet deep in spots. Clearing the ground for a cabin was like digging a cellar. There was no sawmill and builders contracted for sets of house logs as soon as they were cut. Carpenters were paid $10 a day. Lots were selling at $10–$25, only to be resold for fabulous sums. In the original platting of the city a lot was set aside for the newspaper office and another for the church. J. E. Phillips claimed the newspaper lot and began shovelling snow so as to clear the ground for his office. Before he had finished shovelling he was offered $1,000 for the lot for a grocery site.

Everyone was building. Before long Main Street ran a mile up the gulch and was filled with a "seething mass of people." At the peak of the boom, between 1880 and 1882, there were 5,000 people milling about the town and even the winter population was over 2,500. Bands played in front of the theatre; a snowshoe run was laid out[1]; a post office was opened and a telegraph service established. Five daily stages ran all summer from Gunnison via Crested Butte. Twenty-three saloons with every kind of gambling device ran full tilt. "Irwin had everything a modern city of 3,000–5,000 people could have and all in the space of six months." Everyone had money and spent it freely.

Irwin's first newspaper, the Elk Mountain Pilot, got off to a good start in spite of almost insurmountable difficulties. The editor, J. E. Phillips, shipped his hand press direct from Rosita to Alamosa, the freight for-warding point for Irwin, in March 1880. From there it was freighted by ox-team to the foot of the long hill three miles from Irwin, where the press and everything else was dumped out. Phillips and his companions held a meeting in the snow, resolving to cross the range as soon as snow-shoes could be made. When these were ready "the printing material was distributed among the men, when with type in pockets, part of the hand press under each arm, and cases of paper strapped to their backs the jour-ney across the great mountain range began. The ascent was made, many times at an angle of 45 degrees, and the descent commenced, the typos gliding gracefully down on their snowshoes over an unknown depth of snow." Arrived in Irwin, Phillips set up the press in a log cabin and print-ed the first issue of the Elk Mountain Pilot on June 17, 1880. "The first six copies sold for $158"; later copies sold for normal prices.

Under the able guidance of J. E. Phillips the Pilot ran successfully for four years and only closed down when "Irwin was getting down to a whisper." When Gunnison County demanded taxes, it was the Pilot that led the campaign to resist payment on the basis that Irwin was not in the county but was laid out "within the boundaries of the Ute reservation and therefore could not record its plat nor register the sale of lots." The

[1] Snowshoe was the term for a ski in the parlance of the day.

town's location on the eastern edge of the Ute territory caused some apprehension in the early days. A company of so-called Minute Men were ready for any emergency. Capt. U. M. Curtis, the United States interpreter for the Utes, stayed in camp during 1880 to see that no trouble occurred, but by mutual agreement Indians and miners let each other pretty much alone, and even when Irwin became a booming camp Indian clashes were unknown.

The mines of Irwin carried "brittle wire, ruby horn, and native silver with arsenical iron." The most important mines were the Forest Queen, the Ruby Chief, the Bullion King, Venango, Chiquita, Hopewell, and Lead Chief, although before the summer of 1881 there were as many as 25 shipping or treating ores.

Beyond the town and across Lake Brennard were Ruby and Purple Peaks, on whose slopes were located the Ruby Chief and Ruby King mines. The Forest Queen, at the lower end of town, was worked perhaps longer than any of the other mines, employing 100 men at one time and 30 men as late as 1891. In 1900 it was unwatered and continued to produce until 1932, when it was assessed at $1,000 and advertised for sale at $40.45, yet at one time the owner had refused $1,000,000 for it. Today there is some work being done in the mine for it still contains valuable ore. In fact none of the mines were worked out, but low-grade ore and increased costs of extraction made them unprofitable.

Irwin at the height of its boom, 1881–82

The long winters and the deep blankets of snow which shrouded everything greatly hampered production. A story is told of a man who snowshoed to the camp to get some information about the Hidden Treasure mine. When he reached the spot where the mine should have been he "saw a deep hole in the snow where there were signs of habitation. He tossed down a snowball. There was an answering 'hello'."

"What place is this?" he asked.

"The Ruby Camp Post Office."

"Can you tell me where there is a mine called the Hidden Treasure?"

"Yes, right across the way under about 70 feet of snow."

"Huh," he remarked, "It's certainly been well named," and he returned to Gunnison.

In its day Irwin was visited by all kinds of people, including Wild Bill Hickok, Bill Nuttall of vaudeville fame, Theodore Roosevelt, Governor Routt, and General Grant. Grant's visit caused the greatest excitement, the "town being all agog about how to entertain its distinguished guests." Irwin had no regular band but "they loaded a kettle and a base [sic] drum into a spring wagon, pulled by two little mules ... and he drove up through town to the Ruby Chief" mine ahead of the general and his party.

All the miners who owned horses brought up the rear in a whooping, shooting cavalcade to add flourish to the affair. At the Ruby Chief some fine specimens of ore were laid out for the guests' inspection and a trip through the mine was arranged. Later Grant was entertained at the exclusive Irwin Club, the only place outside of a saloon where members could meet friends or discuss business. Despite the lusty life of the camp there were relatively few violent deaths as compared with other places but "deadly snowslides took a liberal toll of lives every winter." In 1891 a snowslide at the Bullion King buried four persons. The body of one woman was brought into Crested Butte on a sled made of snowshoes and drawn by nine men. Another of the victims was found alive after having been buried four hours.

When a cemetery was contemplated it was found impossible to dig in the rocky soil of the camp and a site near the road to Ruby-Anthracite (or Floresta as it was called later) was selected. "The first man died with his boots on, killed by exploding dynamite." A coffin was made but as there was no parson to officiate, J. E. Phillips, who had the only prayer book in camp, was prevailed upon to read the burial service.

Later, when Bishop Spalding visited the camp and conducted service in a tent, the Phillips prayer book was pressed into use again. The tent in

Muriel Sibell Wolle, *School House, Irwin.*
(Courtesy of the Denver Public Library, Western History Collection)

which the bishop spoke had been prepared for the event. Fresh sawdust had been spread on the dirt floor and candles arranged around the box which served as a pulpit. The tent was so close to the gambling hall that all during the service the "clinking of chips and the voice of the dance hall caller could be heard singing out 'honor to your partners, allemande left, ladies and gents waltz to the bar'." The proprietor refused to stop play during the time of the meeting but he announced to his customers, "You fellows, plug up the kitty and give the bishop the benefit of the next play," with the result that a hat full of silver was collected.

Crofutt's *Gripsack Guide* of 1881 devotes several paragraphs to Irwin and describes it as a city containing "a great number of stores of all kinds, one stamp mill, one large sampling works, six sawmills, one bank, three churches (Episcopal, Methodist, and Presbyterian), one theatre, many hotels, chief of which is the Elk Mountain House, a brass band and one weekly newspaper, the *Pilot*." In spite of all these necessities the town had no dairy as feed for cattle was very expensive and there was no place to graze cows. A herd was located east of Crested Butte and milk and butter were delivered at regular intervals. "Instead of skimming off the cream to make butter and selling the inhabitants of Irwin skimmed milk, the dealers hit upon a novel plan of leaving the cream on the milk and by the time they had chugged and jolted over the rough road, 10 miles, they had a lump of butter in each milk can and thus had fresh milk and butter to sell to their patrons."

By 1883 the town was so well established that it had several streets lined with frame buildings and marked with iron street signs, a schoolhouse, and a waterworks. The water from Lake Brennard (now Lake Irwin) was piped several hundred feet through the hill at the upper end of Main Street and then through town, to supply a series of water hydrants which had been installed. Yet by the end of that very year no ore was being shipped and but few miners were employed in the mines. "One by one people were leaving and it began to look as if the place was fast drifting into a ghost town." By 1884 it was virtually deserted and by 1925 "the only thing left were Sam Metzler's water plugs up and down the gulch." For years the place lay dormant with only occasional mining being done.

In 1946 I visited Irwin again. The water hydrants were still there, but fewer of them and they leaned drunkenly. Climbing up to the Forest Queen mine, I looked back toward the lake and the Ruby Chief. There lay Irwin below me, flattened piles of lumber marking the site of many of its buildings, especially along Main Street. The log schoolhouse up near the lake stood roofless, with big trees growing inside it; terraces marked the location of many private homes and stores, from which even the timber was gone, and caving foundations or a hollow in the ground indicated where the building had stood. The ground was marshy and carpeted with dog tooth violets. The only sounds were the rustle of wind, the whistle of marmots, and the gurgle of water which rushed harmlessly down what had been the main thoroughfare.

The Colorado Magazine, January 1947

lready in his late eighties, in 1945 A. R. Ross published his first of seven reminiscences for *The Colorado Magazine*. His father, a Civil War veteran, had worked in the 1870s on an early train crew and settled his family on a homestead by the South Platte River near the town of Evans. Their closest neighbor lived seven miles away.

Evans began as a rail stop but the town dwindled once the line reached Denver. Its resurgence came in 1871 with the arrival of a colony organized by the St. Louis–Western Company out of Illinois and led by a Reformed Presbyterian minister. The colony was one of several such cooperative agricultural settlements founded throughout the region. Evans never rivaled the success of the adjacent Union Colony at Greeley, but it did offer one thing the Union Colony didn't: saloons. Thus, Evans sometimes drew the Union Colony's less abstinent colonists into its environs.

The teenaged Ross signed on as a rider for area cattle operations, an occupation he often writes about in his recollections of life on the plains of northeastern Colorado. In the following piece, he recalls another fond memory: his admiration for a particularly good hunting dog.

Hunting Antelope with Dogs

—A. R. Ross

I came to Colorado with my parents in 1871 when it was a territory and a frontier country in every sense of the word. I took Horace Greeley's advice and grew up with the country. We were members of the St. Louis Western Colony which settled the town of Evans which was the county seat of Weld at that time. My father, W. D. Ross, after being discharged from the Army, joined this group which was composed of many Civil War veterans. The Homestead Law had just been passed, and father immediately filed on a quarter section of land in the "Big Bend" district a few miles south of Evans, then an open cattle range—the Big Bend referring to the bend of the Platte River west of Evans.

I was a lad just entering teen age at the time. There were five of us in the family and we all moved out on the claim in the spring of 1872 and were the pioneer settlers on homesteads in that section. Our nearest neighbors were at Ft. St. Vrain some seven miles west on the Platte River.

I was appalled at the vastness of the new country and thrilled by the adventures it presented. We were able to see objects at so great a distance in comparison to my native state of Illinois. Game was plentiful, especially antelope. No license was required to hunt any kind of game and no limit to the number you were allowed to kill.

Antelope traveled in droves and in the winter months came down to the settlements to feed at the settlers' straw stacks. I had designs on them when I first saw them and had an idea that they could be caught by dogs, even if they were considered the fastest animals on foot in America; and if such a sport could be developed, it would be thrilling.

I began looking for dogs that I thought would be suitable for such hunting. I secured two greyhounds that looked good to me and was anxious to try out their speed behind a bunch of antelope. I had been taking extra care of my horse and had been feeding the dogs regularly in my preparation for a chase.

Finally "H-day" came when the short grass was covered with a deep fall of snow and the antelope began to drift down to the settlements. In looking over the snow-covered prairie, I decided they would be around our ranch by noon, but before that time they were in the fields. I called the dogs and they came bounding toward me. They looked ready and fit for the run, and as I rode out they followed close behind the horse. Time and time again I ordered them back in order to get closer to the antelope before they started to run. When the dogs sighted them, I gave a sharp command, "Go get them." They started quickly showing some speed but did not close in on the antelope as fast as I had expected. I ran my horse much too fast in order to encourage them, and we went for miles before we caught one. By the time we had gotten three we were all exhausted. The dogs lay flat on the ground and began eating snow, and my horse was breathing very hard as he stood with sweat dripping off his sides to the ground. The antelope were glad to stop and had only gone a short distance away and turned and stood there curiously watching us. Their lolling tongues clearly told of the energy they had used to keep away from the dogs. They were exhausted and with very little more effort, and with a fresh horse and dogs, I could have driven the remaining ones of the bunch to the ranch and put them in the corral.

At this point, other hunters who were attracted by the barking of my dogs rode up with fresh horses and shepherd dogs and took up the chase of the helpless animals which looked cruel and unsportsmanlike to me.

I was left on the snow-covered prairie with three antelope to transfer to the home ranch with one tired horse to do it. My dogs should have been hauled home after such a run. I took the back trail to gather up the antelope. I carried one across my saddle in front of me and tied two to my faithful horse's tail. They gave me no trouble for they slipped over the snow easily.

Our hunt was a success in a way, but it was a record of endurance instead of speed, and the kind of hunting one could not call a high type of sport. I still hoped to find a dog fast enough to catch an antelope within one-half to three-quarters of a mile. I had decided on the way home that I would not go out hunting again under the same conditions.

The following day one of the dogs died because he had become overheated on the strenuous run and I was compelled to give up hunting for a while at least.

Some time later a neighbor, who had heard of my losing the hunting dog, offered me a pup about three months old. He told me he had been selling them for a good price but this was the last of the litter, and he would cost me nothing. He was a cross between a hound and a shepherd dog. I thanked him kindly, picked up the tiny ball of flesh and fur and carried him away in my arms wondering if this little mite would some day be able to catch an antelope.

I watched his development day by day and as the months passed had some hope for a spectacular antelope hunt some time in the future. By the time he was one year old, he had developed into a wonderful looking dog, not as tall and slim as a hound but heavily muscled on all four legs with shorter nose and coupling. He carried himself proudly alert and was quick to know my wishes. He showed some affection for everyone he met and was fond of children.

Another winter had come and once more antelope were drifting down into the settlements. It was hunting season again. I told my folks I was taking the pup out for a run, and they thought it unwise at his age, but I promised I would keep him from running too far. I rode away in high spirits to see my fuzzy pup take his first run. When we got fairly close to a bunch of antelope, I got off my horse, called the dog to me and pointed out the bunch of antelope as I held his head between my knees. He quickly sighted the animals and was eager to go. "Now, Tige," I said, "I want one of them, go get it!" and made a motion with my hand. He jumped from between my knees like a shot from a gun and by the time I had mounted he had them on the run. I rode fast to be near, if he caught one, to see how he performed. I was near enough to see him make a spring and catch one high up on the hock and set back. The antelope landed flat on its side and the dog jumped across its body and caught it by the throat. The antelope never got on its feet again for he cut its throat as well as I could have done it myself. He didn't need any help. He whined and started after the bunch. I called him to me, patted him on the head, and cried, "Glory be, you are the dog I've been looking for. Where did you learn to do that trick?" He looked up at me and then at the retreating band of antelope anxious for the go-ahead sign to catch another. If he had been able to talk, he would have told me it was no trick but was his nature and that, perhaps, he also was a descendant of a stag hound that caught and destroyed their catch as well. Tige caught the first antelope he ever saw and proved to me that he needed no extra training, and caused my fondest hopes and dreams of a spectacular hunt to be realized. His work was done quickly and silently. He never barked as a fox hound would, but saved that energy to increase his speed. My fuzzy pup had demonstrated that a dog can catch and kill an antelope without his master's help, thus also saving him the disagreeable sight of looking in the eyes of the timid and terrified animal. I looked down at the fallen antelope at my feet and then at my faithful dog as if I were in a dream. All of this had happened so quickly I could not realize it was true. In less than 30 minutes from the time Tige started to run, I came up to where he stood beside the dead antelope with its throat cut and ready to be loaded on my horse without any help from me. As I stood in this daze, my dog, who had noticed something strange about me, roused me from my dream by raising on his hind legs and placing his paws on my chest. He licked my face and hands showing that he understood my surprise and thrill. If you are the proud owner of a dog, no move of yours escapes his watchful eye. You are his world. He seemed to be as happy as I about the catch as he trotted along beside the horse on our way home, looking up now and then to see that the antelope was riding safely in front of me in the saddle.

My folks were certainly surprised when I rode up to the ranch with an antelope, no sweat on my horse, and the dog as fresh as when he left. As time went on Tige was allowed to catch more antelope until he had gotten as many as nine on one run. He was always ready to catch more and his method was always the same: he threw them and neatly cut their throats. After each catch he looked back at the hunter for further orders. A wave of the hand and he would be off after another.

People from nearby towns came to borrow Tige, who was willing to go with the other hunters and catch and kill as many as they wanted and be brought back showing little fatigue.

No one ever came to the Ross Ranch in the winter months and went home empty handed if he liked antelope for we always kept a supply of them hanging hog-dressed in the yard between the cottonwood trees as a "help-yourself" offering to the neighbors. Coming home early one morning after being out at a New Year's party, I noticed a bunch of antelope in front of the house. I had been out all night and we had more meat than we needed so I was not interested in a chase just then, and was hoping my brother, Jim, with whom I bunked, would not see them and want to take a run. Jim was getting up to do the chores as I dropped into bed. He soon came running back and told me about the antelope. "Yes," I said, "I saw them. We don't want them." He replied, "I'm going to take the dog and you follow up with the mules and the sled." He was off without waiting

78

for me to answer. I raised up in bed, looked out of the window and saw the dog catch the first antelope, throw it, cut its throat, and look back at Jim who waved his hand toward the bunch, which was the go-ahead sign. Jim kept him going until I thought he must intend to catch them all. Tige was always ahead and caught and killed antelope as long as the signal was given him. When we came up to the dog, we found him standing over the last antelope looking after the retreating bunch anxious to catch another.

We loaded the last one killed on the sled first and followed the trail back through the snow for the others. We found each one as the dog had left it, no sign of a struggle, dead where he had thrown it. Our sled load of antelope numbered nine and the dog had done it all in a chase of about a mile and a half.

During his entire life, Tige insisted on being with me when I rode the range. Nothing and no one could detain him for he always broke away and followed me. That very faithfulness and devotion to me was the cause of his untimely death, but that is another story and a sad one on which I do not care to dwell.

A man may shake you by the hand
And wish you to the devil,
But when a good dog wags his tail,
You are sure he is on the level.

The Colorado Magazine, July 1947

J ohn Wesley Powell—a disabled Civil War veteran, ethnologist, and geographer—gained national fame after he led a scientific expedition down the Green and Colorado Rivers and through the Grand Canyon in 1869. Wallace Stegner, a writer known more for his fiction, earned a place among the best historians of the American West by writing Powell's biography in 1954.

In *Beyond the Hundredth Meridian: John Wesley Powell and the Second Opening of the West*, Stegner presented readers with what he later called "pure adventure story." He devoted nearly a third of the book to Powell's first trip through the Grand Canyon, describing how the one-armed scientist filled in one of the last "great blank spaces" on the U.S. map while speeding down the Colorado River on an armchair bolted to the deck of a twenty-one-foot wooden boat. The rest of the book tells how Powell tried to use data he gathered on that trip and on subsequent surveys to reconcile American land-use policies with western geography and climate.

In 1949 Colorado Historical Society historian and editor LeRoy Hafen found a 1902 letter written by Jack Sumner to *The Denver Post* (the Society still has the original letter). Sumner, a prominent but disgruntled member of Powell's first Colorado River expedition, criticized Powell's leadership abilities and professional integrity. Hafen asked Stegner to comment on the letter for *The Colorado Magazine*.

Stegner's balanced response gives today's reader a glimpse of the sources and methods he employed to write *Beyond the Hundredth Meridian*. It also shows how he used sound research tools to create complex, realistic western characters in fictional works such as *Joe Hill*, *Angle of Repose* (Pulitzer Prize, 1972), and *The Spectator Bird* (National Book Award, 1977).

Stegner founded the Creative Writing Program at Stanford University in 1946. He taught at the University of Wisconsin and Harvard University as well. He died in 1993.

Jack Sumner
and John Wesley Powell

—*Wallace Stegner*

Jack Sumner, the author of the letter reprinted below, was Major J. W. Powell's principal assistant on the expedition which first explored the canyons of the Green and Colorado Rivers in 1869—perhaps the last great exploration within the continental United States. The letter, printed with minor editing by *The Denver Post* in October, 1902, represents the earliest form of charges which were later assembled in elaborate detail in R. B. Stanton's *Colorado River Controversies*, 1929, and which were apparently corroborated by the testimony of Billy Hawkins, the cook of the expedition, first published in Bass's *Adventures in the Canyons of the Colorado* in 1920.

A full treatment of the controversy over Powell would run to many pages and would bring in considerations far outside the scope of this note. It is enough here to remark that Stanton did not have quite all the evidence, and that his two principal sources are not as unfailingly reliable as they might have been. It is clear too from Stanton's correspondence with both Sumner and Hawkins that he encouraged criticism of Powell by leading questions, and evidently corrected not only Sumner's grammar and syntax but some of his most crucial misinformation, such as the story of the $50,000 Congressional appropriation, while writing the story up. And since Sumner's grudge seems to have been based to some extent on this misinformation, the credibility of the whole story is weakened, though not necessarily destroyed.

Deviations from fact or from other accounts of the expedition are considered in detail in the notes below. The documents relevant in checking Sumner's letter include Sumner's own journal (incomplete); Powell's journal (also incomplete); Powell's published *Report on the*

Exploration of the Colorado River of the West (so mixed with records of the 1871 expedition as to be unreliable); letters sent out from the river by O. G. Howland to the *Rocky Mountain News* and by Powell to the *Chicago Tribune*; a letter from Andy Hall to his brother, written from the Uintah Agency; certain correspondence of Robert Brewster Stanton preserved in the New York Public Library; the letter books of the Powell Survey in the National Archives in Washington; and two versions of Sumner's side of the question as it has come down in the Sumner family, one an interview with Sumner's son and the other an interview with his nephew. There are also the Hawkins and Sumner statements, each in two versions. Most of these documents have been reprinted recently in the *Utah Historical Quarterly*, volume xv.

John Wesley Powell with a member of the Paiute Indian tribe near the Virgin River, Utah. Powell lost his right arm during the Civil War.
(Courtesy of the U.S. Department of the Interior Geological Survey)

Here follows Sumner's letter, apparently the first published indication that the Powell expedition had had trouble not of the river's making,
and the first gun in a continuing campaign bent on demonstrating that
Powell was an incompetent and autocratic leader, that he withheld from
his men not only public credit for their achievement but even their actual
pay, and that he rode Bill Dunn and the Howland brothers so hard that
he eventually drove them off the river and to their deaths at the hands of
the Shewits Indians on the lonely plateau south of St. George, Utah. The
original of the manuscript letter written by Sumner is in the library of the
State Historical Society of Colorado. We reproduce it as written.

Camp in Henry Mts., Utah, Oct. 13/02

Editor Denver Post
Denver Colorado

Dear Sir
In your issue Sept. 24th 1902 I note your notice of the death
of Maj J W Powell which contains many errors, and as I have
seen several accounts of the explorations of the Colorado
River, all more or less misleading, as I hapened to be a member
of that expedition, I am requested by others to write you this,
which you can consign to the waste basket or publish as you
see fit. In the fall of 1867 Maj Powell came to my camp at the
hot Sulphur Springs Middle Park where I was trading with the
Utes. He brought letters from Denver parties[1] requesting me
to extend courtesies. I took him a two week trip through the
Park and killed some fine specimen of natural history for him.
He seems to have got struck on me for some foolish reason or
no reason at [all], and wanted me to go with him to the Bad
lands of Dacotah on a geological trip.[2] I objected to that
program and offered the Colorado River Program. [H]e
argued that it was impossible as three Govt expeditions had
failed. After several windy fights around the camp fire I finaly

[1] William N. Byers, publisher of the *Rocky Mountain News*, and Sumner's brother-in-law.
[2] Powell's original intention had been to include the Dakota badlands in his 1867 trip; he gave up
the notion because of the uprising of the Sioux. It seems credible, though Powell nowhere corroborates the notion, that Sumner may have given him the first suggestion for the river exploration.

outwinded him and it was arranged that he was to furnish half
the outfit and I the other half.[3] We were to start the following
spring. He left me in Nov 67 and went to Washington.[4] I
staid in the park that winter and collected specimens for the
Smithsonian Institute. During the Winter Session of 67–68 an
appropriation of fifty thousand dollars was passed through the
influence of Senetor Trumbul of Ill and placed in the Hands
of Proff. J W Powell for the exploration of the Colorado
River of the West.[5] In May or June[6] 68 he appeared on the
scene at Berthoud Pass with a gang of 25 or 30 college students,
good enough in their way, but about as fit for roughing it as
Hades is for a Powder House. After fooling away the summer
in which we done nothing worthy of note, unless the assent
of Longs Peak could be so called,[7] the outfit pulled out from
Hot Springs for White River. After several Mishaps we
camped on the ground made historical by the Meker
Massacre.[8] By this time the Body Guard of students had
dwindled down to two. After various incidents creditable and
otherwise we left our winter camp for Fort Bridger, Howland,
Dunn and myself remaining behin[d] for three weeks to look

[3] Sumner was not hired, note. He was a partner in the expedition or rather, his group and Powell's joined forces. The purpose of Sumner and his friends, aside from the sheer adventure, was certainly to some extent at least the fabled gold in the gravel bars. For a sample of the kind of speculation common in these years about the unknown canyons, see William Gilpin, *The Mission of the North American People*, 47.

[4] The *Rocky Mountain News* of Nov. 6, 1867, reported as follows: "Major J. W. Powell left for the east this morning. He will return to the territory next spring to prosecute his scientific labors, and will go down the Grand to its junction with the Colorado River." No mention is made of an exploration of the Green or of the Colorado below the junction. Sumner's statement that the river expedition was to start in the spring of 1868 seems dubious; Powell's own reports to the Illinois State Normal University do not mention any such plan. The party in fact spent the whole season of 1868 along the Grand, White, and Yampa, and in several overland trips to the upper Green.

[5] This $50,000 appropriation, which was one of Sumner's chief causes for discontent, did not exist. Powell had no government help whatsoever for the river expedition of 1869 except the right to draw supplies for twelve men from any western army post, and to turn in certain parts of the routine ration for cash; he thus turned in much of the meat ration for cash with which he hired hunters to supply the party with fresh meat. The exploration of the Colorado was conducted on an incredibly slim budget, supplied principally by Illinois State Normal, The Industrial University of Illinois, and the Illinois Natural History Society, of which Powell was secretary. The Smithsonian contributed a little, mainly in instruments, and the railroads provided free transportation for men, supplies, and boats. Powell enumerated the sponsors of his expedition in a letter to the *Chicago Tribune*, May 22, 1869.

[6] Actually the end of July.

[7] In company with Byers and several of his own company, including Sumner, Powell made the first ascent of Longs Peak on August 23, 1868.

[8] The spot, a few miles west of Meeker, is still known as Powell's Hole, or Powell Bottoms.

up the country Bordering Bear, Snake and vermillion Rivers, which was done and Report handed to him at Green River Wyoming.

After he had sold the pack and saddle stock, he went to Chicago and had the boats built from plans which I drew in our winter camp on White River.[9] I awaited the Boats and the Proff. at Green River, Wyoming. May 24th 1869 the Expedition pulled out into the swift current of Green River and Hell commenced and kept up for 111 days. Through a misunderstanding of signal (If given at all)[10] one of the boats was lost in a rapid eight miles below Browns park, the Howland Brothes and Frank Goodman escaping by a scratch. We made thought without furthr mishaps and landed at mouth of Uinta River where Goodman left us and went to the trading Post some 35 miles from the mouth of Uinta River. He admited that his curiosuty was satisfied. Maj Powell went up with him to try and repenish supplies lost in the wreck. He Reported prices to high; and only brought a meager mess. July 6th 69 we left camp at mouth of Uinta and struck out into the unknown, with parting salute from some utes. "Heap dam fool; water catch em." At the junction of Green and Grand River we overhauld our supplies and found we had 250 lbs of Roten Flour and probale 75 lbs of bacon for Nine Men. Not a nice state to be in and there was some cussing of the Commander Uinta parsimony or economy, call it as you like. I call it stupidity in such a case.[11] After a wild Dangerous trip of 700 miles through continuous canon mared

---

[9] An uncorroborated claim which appears unlikely. The design of the boats, which turned out to be singularly sound, was of the greatest importance to the expedition. Though Sumner had grown up on the Cedar River in Iowa and may have known boats to some extent, Powell before the war had gone by boat down the Illinois, the Ohio, and the Mississippi on natural history expeditions, and as a scientist and a military engineer he was far better qualified than Sumner to design boats for use on the Colorado.

[10] The wreck at Disaster Falls was the beginning of trouble in the party, and put them on short rations. Powell may have blamed O. G. Howland for not following his signal, but that a signal was given by Powell is attested by Bradley's journal, and Howland's own letter to the *Rocky Mountain News* says: "About one o'clock the signal boat signals at the foot of a very bad rapid to go ashore: boats nearly full of water—two were made fast, but owing to not understanding the signal, the crew of the 'No Name' failed very effectually, owing in the main, to having so much water aboard as to make her nearly or quite unmanageable." Later Sumner directly blamed the wreck on Powell's failure to signal. It is impossible to check the incident in Powell's or Sumner's journals since the earlier parts of both were lost when the party split at Separation Rapid.

[11] The plain fact is that Powell had so little money that he could not afford many supplies.

Powell's boat with his chair attached, Grand Canyon, 1872.
(Courtesy of the U.S. Department of the Interior Geological Survey)

by disgraceful squables Between Commander and two of the
men which would not look well in Print coming from me. Powell
did not manage the Running of the boats after a hundred miles
below Green and Grand River. We finaly made the mouth of the
Rio Virgin in S.W. Utah where J. W. Powell and his brother
Wa[l]ter H. Powel left us and went to Salt Lake, leaving Andrew
Hall, George Bradley and W. R. Hawkins with me. I took nessary
instruments and went on to Fort Mojave A.T. where I drew 4
month supplies and was treated vey kindly by Cononel Tracy the
post comander. Hall and I then went on down the river till we
come in sight of the head of the Gulf of California, Hawkins
staying at Ehrenburg A.T. as the work was finished. [12]

When Proff Powell left us at the mouth of the Virgin
Rive[r] he gave me 100 dollars in green backs worth then on

---

[12] The work was finished before Powell left the river. Though Sumner, here and elsewhere, takes
credit for being one of the two to go clear to the river's mouth, there was no scientific reason for
Powell's doing so, and Sumner's taking "necessary instruments" is pure nonsense. The river had
been traversed both upstream and down from the foot of the Grand Wash Cliffs by Lieutenant
Ives and by a Mormon party under Jacob Hamblin and Anson Call, in 1857 and 1865.

the Coast 75.00 to Hall he gave the great sum of 20 dollars to Bradley a pleasant smile and a volume of thanks. None of us had a better suit than overalls and a Cotton Shirt. Where did this fifty thousand go to, and how did he pay and to who did he pay out of his own Means, as stated in the papers. I paid out of my own pocket more than a thousand dollars and nearly two years time and Recd neither money nor credit to this day for it.[13] Personaly I care not but seems to me that thirty three years is a long time to wait for some recognition of the services of the men. Fremont give credit to all of his men. Powell give credit to none. As to his being the only one ever making the trip there is a mistake.

The first Expedition that left Green River in May 69 consisted of ten men all told with 4 boats: they were J. W. Powell, Walter Powell, Senica Howland, O. G. Howland, Wm Dunn, Wm Hawkins, Andrew Hall, Frank Goodman, and Jack Sumner. I believe they all dead now but Hawkins who lives in Eden, Graham Co. A.T. and myself. The Howland Brothers and Dunn left the Main Party eighty miles

[13] This matter of the unpaid wages (or the unshared and mythical appropriation) seems to lie at the root of both Sumner's and Hawkins' enmity. Yet Sumner's grudge could not have been born at once for he was prevented only by heavy snows from going down the river again with the second Powell Expedition in 1871. And Hawkins, who complains that he never got the money for his traps and pack animals and never got any pay either, was hired for several years after the river trip by Powell's surveying parties in south-central Utah, and in the middle seventies was still writing letters to Powell in Washington, addressed to "My dear old friend," and full of the friendliest sentiments. For some reason, both Sumner and Hawkins grew bitter in later years, and their stories grew bitter with them. It seems impossible now to come at the true facts of the agreement between Powell and Sumner's mountain men. He evidently hired some of them as hunters, and none but Hawkins and Sumner ever complained of being cheated. Sumner says he paid out a thousand dollars; elsewhere he says he paid all the expenses of the winter camp at Meeker. But if, as he says, he and Powell were to share the expenses, Powell's contribution of rations for the entire river trip, boats, instruments, equipment, and a small amount of cash ought to have evened the account. Viewed in that light, his distribution of a few dollars to the men at the Virgin was a generous sharing of his last resources. At least one of the men, Bradley, was strictly a volunteer: Powell got him released from army duty in order to go along. As to the failure to give credit to the men, there is a difference of opinion possible. In no part of his *Report* does Powell go out of his way to praise his men, but he never fails to record their heroisms (including Sumner's), and he scrupulously refuses to lay blame either upon Frank Goodman, who quit the expedition at the Uinta, or on the Howlands and Dunn, who deserted at Separation Rapid. Sumner's own journal is harder on them than Powell ever was. "They left us," Sumner wrote, "to go it or swamp." What Sumner might have said with the greatest truth is that Powell never gave adequate credit to, or even mentioned the names of, or the existence of, the members of his second river party. In the interest of telling a good story he fused the second expedition with the first in his *Report* and did a very real injustice to his men. But Sumner and the first party had no such legitimate complaint.

above the Virgin. In trying to make some Mormon settlement they were killed by Indians. Bradley died in San Diego, California Result of an accident. Hall was murdered in Arizona while defending U.S. Mail which he was carrying. In 73 or 74 there was a second expedition called Powells Exploring Expedition, But in Reality under the command of Capt. Dutton.[14] They did not go through all of the canon, But had their boats hawled around the Grand Canon and launched below Danger line.[15] I get this information from A. L. Storr of Milford, Utah, who done the Hawling. In 89 I think Frank Brown of Denver started to make a Rail Road Survey from Grand Junction to tide water but having more courage than discretion himself and two men were drowned. [T]he following winter Mr. Robert B. Stanton reorganized the expedition and made the trip with twelve men with the slight accident of one man Braking a leg. The Trip can be made now by going in midwinter when the water is at its lowest stage. Supplies can be got a comparatively short stage and there is no danger from Indians.

But dont go unless you are a Reasonable good boatman and have lots of caution and Plenty of Nerve to go with it. But if you do go you will See Grand works of Geology and feel like Dante as he came up from below.

I could write much more but Prefer to let some one ask for it first. Much information can be obtained from W. R. Hawkins, Eden, Graham Co., Arizona. [H]e is a rough Frontiersman and will give the facts, and will give much more than I have writen.

Wal[t]er H. Graves did not belong or go with the first expedition he probably did have something to do with the 73 affair.[16]

---

[14] An error. Powell's second river voyage was planned in 1870 and conducted through the field seasons of 1871 and 1872. Captain Dutton's expeditions in the high plateaus of Utah and in the Grand Canyon district were made under Powell's direction, but several years later, and did not go down any part of the river.

[15] Sumner's original misinformation is here compounded by his desire to minimize Powell. The second expedition went through the entire series of canyons as far as Kanab Wash. Sumner's mistake may have originated in the fact that in 1871 the boats were cached at the mouth of the Paria, and the trip renewed from that point the next spring.

[16] Walter H. Graves did not have a part in either river expedition. He was briefly a member of Powell's party in 1870, when routes for supplies were being explored down to the river.

The first part of this communication you can get verified by calling on Mr. Wm. N. Byers of your City as he is well acquainted with the facts.

As I have more acquaintance with the pick and shovel than the pen and Know the Hammer Better than the Pencil, you will probably get disgusted with this and fire the whole Busnes into the waste basket.

Jack Sumner

Hanksville, Utah

Stanton's elaborately documented attack on Major Powell is built primarily on the evidence of Sumner and Hawkins. Yet Hawkins, as I have shown, apparently never thought of attacking Powell for years after the expedition, and was in his employ and on the most cordial terms with him. His account of the troubles, too, is weakened by the grossest self-inflation and exaggeration. It is the only account which corroborates Sumner; Bradley's unpublished journal, which Stanton knew but did not use, does not hesitate to criticize Powell sharply for other things, but finds no fault with his leadership and does not even hint of the mutinous squabbling attested by Sumner and Hawkins.

It will be clear from the annotated letter above that Sumner, though a brave man and a big factor in the success of the expedition, could be grievously misinformed, and could also nurse a grudge. If it is permissible to speculate, in the absence of convincing evidence, I should guess that his grudge dated from the time when he found Powell something of a national hero for his exploit, and himself still a prospector and hunter; and especially from the time when he heard of a Congressional appropriation and got the mistaken notion that Powell had had government support for the 1869 expedition and had held out on the men. By 1907, when Stanton got his detailed story, he had been disabused of that notion, but by that time the grudge was imbedded and had been passed on as part of the family legend. Hawkins could easily have been led into an exaggerated statement of the case by Sumner, who seems to have corresponded with him, and by Stanton, whose letters asking information are loaded with leading and provocative questions begging for anti-Powell answers.

That there was trouble within the party there is no doubt, and it should surprise no one that there was. Every difficult and dangerous expedition has some of the same. The river equivalent of cabin fever is easy to acquire a half mile down in the earth, on a furious river that is forever freakish and forever dangerous, with alternating heat and cold, with mosquitoes and joint-wrenching labor on the portages and no guarantee that within the next half mile the river would not go over falls impossible to run or portage. Moreover, Powell had been an army officer; his men, with one or two exceptions, were undisciplined mountain men and hunters. They expected—and this is of great importance—that they would be able to pan the bars all the way down, and perhaps clean up or locate rich placers. The wreck of the *No Name* with large quantities of their food forced them to cut their intended ten-months' run down to four. Powell, the scientist and explorer, got at least part of what he went for; the boatmen got nothing but the ride.

And yet that was not Powell's fault. He was running on a shoestring, and he shared what he had with them at the end. But it is noticeable that on his next trip he did not take a single mountain man along; he took scientists and students, and he had no disciplinary troubles. He was the same leader he had been in 1869, but he had different and more amenable followers.

Sumner's grudge has been pointed out and his story discounted by L. W. Keplinger, who was a member of the 1868 party. It was a grudge that grew with years, and the story Sumner told grew more circumstantial and more damaging as he told it over. This version, close to the source and unedited, was undoubtedly what Sumner himself believed to be true, but its errors and its bias render it, and the case later built on it, open to considerable skepticism.

The Colorado Magazine, January 1949

B efore the dust settled at Ground Zero in lower Manhattan, the Pentagon, and western Pennsylvania, journalists declared the September 11, 2001, terrorist attacks "the worst U.S. tragedy since Pearl Harbor." A nation blessed with decades of peace on its own soil had turned to the only measuring stick for grief that it possessed. In a universal display of sympathy and respect, museums and other historical organizations everywhere—including the Colorado Historical Society—asked people to commit their reactions to paper. Those thoughts and prayers are now as much a part of our national heritage as the World War II diaries and letters in family scrapbooks and public archives.

Clara May Morse, a mother of two sons who died at Pearl Harbor, kept one of those diaries. For the occasion of the fiftieth anniversary of Japan's surprise attack, *Colorado Heritage* editor Clark Secrest wrote an introduction to the journal and excerpted entries spanning thirteen years of her life. At that time, her words offered a personal, heartrending glimpse of irreconcilable grief and loss. In post–9/11 America, her thoughts—especially the haunting words she composed on December 7, 1954—jump off the page like prophecy.

Pearl Harbor and
One Mother's Heartbreak

—Clara May Morse

December 1991 will mark the fiftieth anniversary of Japan's unexpected attack on Pearl Harbor. Japanese aircraft destroyed or disabled twenty-one vessels at Pearl Harbor; five battleships quickly sank. One of those was the USS *Arizona*, which carried 1,177 shipmates to their deaths, and there the men remain entombed even today. Thirty-five sets of brothers were aboard; thirty-four of them perished, including Norman Roi Morse and Francis Jerome Morse, ages twenty and twenty-two respectively. The Morse brothers were born in Lamar, Colorado, and were reared there and in Denver, attending East High School. Their father, Roy, died in a 1930 accident. Attesting that there was little future for "fatherless" boys, their mother, Clara May Dyer Morse, "after a period of decision," signed papers allowing her sons to enlist in the Navy and to serve together aboard the *Arizona*.[1]

Norman and Francis had been extraordinarily close to their mother, who as the result of Pearl Harbor was tortured by abject and inconsolable grief for the rest of her life. She often stated that her existence ended on December 7, 1941. During the most severe periods of her melancholy she was virtually decimated, talking to the boys' pictures on the wall, speaking to them through her diary, and assuring them that she would join them soon. Seemingly with few close friends to offer comfort, Clara Morse's dark and unremitting bereavement was interrupted only by an occasional motion picture, or through her intense dedication as a Red Cross nurse's aide attending to servicemen in veterans hospitals coast to coast. (At age forty-seven and deadened with loneliness, she even considered adopting an infant from one of the hospitals in which she served.) In these military environments she was able to substitute the servicemen under her care for her deceased sons; indeed, when she observed any military man in strife, she was eager to help. Her pain, almost paralyzing at times, was particularly severe on her sons' birthdays and on each succeeding December 7.

Often with long lapses between entries, Clara Morse consigned her overwhelming sorrow to a small notebook inscribed

> To My Sons
> When my dear sons were home for the last time, July 1941, they asked me to write a memory book, things I remembered, So here is the way it turned out. God help me and keep my dear ones untill [sic] I can ship over with them.
>
> Mother

Following her 1982 death in San Diego, Clara Morse's papers came to the Colorado Historical Society, which has applied to the Department of the Navy for the Pearl Harbor Commemorative Medal to be issued posthumously to the Morse brothers.[2] Excerpts from the Morse diary are published here, a demonstration of the insurmountable calamity which the Pearl Harbor attack wreaked on one mother, and the courage with which she survived.

Clara Morse heard of the bombings on her home radio and immediately wrote a letter to each of her sons, postmarked December 8, 1941. The letters were returned to her marked "Unclaimed"; she retained them but never reopened them, placing them instead with her personal papers. The letters finally were opened in 1990 at the Colorado Historical Society, of which she was a life member. They read in part:

> My own Dear Son: I heard all, and am almost beside myself. However I am sure our U.S.S. fleet can handle it, God bless our men and officers of the fleet, help them to keep up and going. Francis I am alright only worried about my dear boys. Have you seen Norman. ...
>
> My own dear son: I have sat here by my radio and I know what has happened. ... Will write again soon. Good bye now.

Her diary continues the story:

Dec. 7th, 1941

Sunday. I'll never sing before breakfast again, for this is what I did this morning even when my dear sons were giving their lives I was singing. But then it's only a part of the cruelty of things. ... Oho the horror of this Sunday.

Christmas Day 1941

Oho God how can I ever go on without my dear ones. Every one of them has been killed, only me left.

Francis Morse, at left, and brother, Norman, from
a snapshot taken by their mother, Clara May, the final
time she saw them, in California, July 1941.

Feb. 2, 1942
I left dear old California [her temporary home to be near her sons when they had shore liberty] for Newport News, Virginia. While there I was in the Portsmouth Va. Hospital, also visited U.S. Naval Ward No. 13teen a number of times, always taking magazines, candy, cig., and when the two boxes of candy which I sent to my two dear sons for Christmas was returned, and lots of books returned, I took them to Chaplain [B. F.] Huske who gave them to the boys in Ward 13teen. One of the boys a Marine named Harry Mills wrote me a beautiful letter. ... I am so glad their shipmates could have it, my heart is Broken, But I must go on.

June 5th, 1942
I went to Fitzsimons Government Hospital [Denver] for my physical [for nurse's training]. I hear over the radio that our Boys are knocking the —— [her dashes] out of the Japs in the Pacific, wish my own two sons could have been spared so that they could have taken part in the clean up, but it was not to be.

July 12, 1942
I have not written anything in this Book. ... My heart is too [undecipherable]. Grief is about to smother me. I must fight 24 hours a day to keep going. I must keep busy every day. How I do dread both Saturdays and Sundays. [She attended nurse's aide classes on weekdays.] I hope I do make the grade, as one derives a certain satisfaction from being able to do for others.[3]

July 19, 1942
Today is my dear Norman's birthday. God how I feel I am so broken up, he never had any life. Again I say it is not fair. I am no better inside, I'll never be happy, never again. I just want to help others all I can while I'm waiting for the call to go to my loved ones where ever they are. I am living on borrowed time.

July 21, 1942

After Pearl Harbor my life was over, or this is the way I felt. But because of good friends and a very strong will, and always the thought before me that my dear sons expected me to carry on ... I just keep fighting the longing to stop here and go to them, but there is work to do, and I must not give up. Maybe I can help other mothers who have suffered loss. ... Time to dress now in my dear little Red Cross uniform, how I love it. ... How I do wish Norman and Francis could see mother now. [She took her nurse's aide training at Denver's St. Anthony Hospital, graduating into the Red Cross Nurse's Corps No. 5 on August 10, 1942.] How I do like my work. Always hate to leave the hospital. The Red Cross is a haven of rest, and blessing, to all people.

August 25, 1942

Then maybe it is better this way ...

Aug. 26, 1942

Well I've tried to never hate anybody, or peoples. But it is not within reason not to hate a people who [were] so inhuman as the Japs. I say right here I do hate the ones who are responsible for my own dear sons death and thousands of others with every fiber in me. ... I am so weary of everything, but of course I must try to keep it to myself, for others sake. ... Nothing [can compare] with my great sacrifice, nothing can hurt me now, as I ceased to feel and live December 7th, 1941. People don't know how well off they are, while they still have their loved ones. I am so completely crushed.

November 22, 1942

Today is my dear Francis['s] birthday, he is 23 years old, and I worked $5^1/2$ hrs at the Hospital in his memory. Aho I am so miserable, nothing left for me now except hard work. There is a dear baby at the Hospital for adoption, but I am afraid something would happen to it if I should take it. Would love to have it. Tonight, I am thinking of my dear children and they are with me at all times.

July 19, 1943

My Norman's birthday, how I miss you dear one. Norman this is our own little page, but I pray I'll be with you before I write in this again. You just wait for mother, you and Francis and your father and some day we will understand. Good night.

July 19, 1944

Today [is] my Norman's 23rd birthday. God have mercy on us all, I am dying each day, a torture. No one can ever know except we who have to go through it. Jesus suffered too, why not we? I went over to Ocean Side [California] today to be alone with my memories, no one cares for our griefs. No one here even knows it was your birthday, dear one. But we know. God bless and keep you wherever you are. And you too my Francis. Remember how we used to save pennies to go to a show and dinner on our birthdays?

March 26, 1945

Camp Butner General Hospital [North Carolina]. I love my work. Our boys are the most courageous group I've ever seen. We have lots of fun talking, they tell me all about their folk, and what they would like to do when they are out of service. Love to do things for our Boys. God bless them and the little wives, pour souls. I wish some folk could see the looks on their faces when they meet here in the Hospital Ward.

July 19, 1945

Army General Hospital Camp Butner, N.C. My Babies Birthday, how I miss you. More and more. Norman where are you. My heart is broken in a thousand ways. I am trying to carry on with my work with the poor soldiers who have returned, and each time I help my boys I think of how I was denied the privilege of helping my own loved ones.

Thanksgiving, November 22nd, 1945

Instead of saying I am not grateful on this day, I am going to say thank you God for loaning them, even for so brief a stay. I have had so much. Nothing can ever take away our memories.

Nov. 22, 1946

My God Francis I can't stand it very much longer. You are away
since 1941, and you never had a chance. Did you die in vain?
And here I am back in this place [Long Beach, California] where
I last saw you. I keep running away from everything. Every
where I go the pain gets worse. You dear ones are up here on
the wall looking down on me, smiling as you always did.

Undated

Once, while waiting for a bus from Portsmouth Va over to
Newport News, I saw the [bus] agent abusing a sailor who had a
few drinks. So I went right down to the [newspaper] and wrote
an article in the Sunday paper. In Long Beach one rainy afternoon I stopped into Mannings Coffee Shop. Two sailors were
there, seated at the counter and counting their change trying to
figure out if they had enough to get coffee and doughnuts and a

Clara May Morse in her beloved Red Cross uniform

show. You guessed it, I paid for theirs, and told them to go on to the show. Down in Flag Staff [*sic*] Ariz I bought 4 dinners for a soldier, two sailors and a civilian. In Washington DC later I gave up my seat on the bus to Norfolk to a soldier. Once on the bus leaving the capital city I sat with a fine soldier, he worked with an Army chaplain. After he insisted on sharing his lunch with me his wife had made for him, I presented a little pocket flash-light to him, he was very pleased.

Dec. 7, 1946
Five long years since you went away, all three of you ([husband] Roy left this world 1930), and after carrying on for four years or more I'm tired and ready to quit. I don't want to go on. Well I simply must pull myself together and carry on. God bless you all and keep you, it's nearly 17 years since you Roy went away, and five years since you Francis and Norman went away. ... The whole world has gone wild, or else I look at it this way. What a dull life yet I've had a good full life, thank you God for loaning them for even a short time. Good night, Dear Ones.

July 19th 47
[To Norman] You were a good son and as your commander wrote in a letter I have, a credit to your mother, your country and your ship. The *Arizona* is gone with you, completely destroyed. No I don't think so. What a ship the *Arizona* was. I have visited aboard her so proudly. Yes pals, you will live on. [On an earlier Sunday afternoon when it was docked in Long Beach, Mrs. Morse had briefly been aboard the *Arizona* to deliver a "five lb box" to her sons.]

Nov. 22, 1948
Darling Francis, you would have been 29 years old, dear one. I spend most of my nights in silence and alone, and in prayer. Good night darlings. Mother.

Nov. 22, 1949
Darling son it's been so long since you went away, and mothers never get used to doing without a son's smile. You were

99

always smiling even if things went wrong. I remember when Dady [*sic*] went away, you said don't cry mother, Norman and myself will care for you. How true. Now I will try to carry on for my fighting Hero Family. The same Sun still shines that shined on the same day before all you dear ones left me. God knows best.

December 7, 1954
Thank God for the volunteer work and all work. It is a wonderful thing for me to be able to do Red Cross work after Pearl Harbor, my Pearl Harbor. Others will have their Pearl Harbors, I feel for them very much because I know. God how I do know.

Colorado Heritage, Autumn 1991

Endnotes

1 The Navy still permits immediate family members to serve aboard the same ship upon approval of a formal request and if members sign acknowledgement of the potential perils involved.

2 *Francis Jerome Morse and Norman Roi Morse were awarded posthumous Pearl Harbor Commemorative Medals following the original publication of this article.*

3 Mrs. Morse writes this even though a few months earlier she had confided: " ... long ago I lost my faith in human nature. Please forgive me for this, I have decided to sit by the side lines and let the world go by, and as long as I live my own life so as not to hurt anyone else, I will continue to do so."

R ichard Grove learned how the internal combustion engine's ignition system worked at his father's automobile dealership when he was a boy. "At its heart," Grove wrote later, "was an absolutely brilliant invention: the Tesla coil." Much later, while working as an assistant curator at the Colorado Springs Fine Arts Center's Taylor Museum, he rediscovered his fascination with Nikola Tesla's inventions. Researching local history for an exhibition, he found extensive newspaper coverage of Tesla's bizarre laboratory on East Pikes Peak Avenue. "I was then living in a house on West Pikes Peak," Grove recalled. "The article for *The Colorado Magazine* was irresistible."

Tesla's arrival in Colorado Springs in 1899 generated a buzz among local newspaper reporters. They already knew about his inventions. The Westinghouse Electric Company had made him famous by putting his polyphase system of alternating-current dynamos, motors, and transformers to work at the 1893 World's Columbian Exposition in Chicago. And they had heard about his eccentricities. Now they would have a chance to see the wizard at work.

Grove relied on those reporters, other writers, and Tesla's own limited publications to reconstruct events on Pikes Peak in 1899 and 1900. Shortly after submitting the article, he left Colorado to become the Wichita Art Museum's director. Later he specialized in art education at the U.S. Office of Education in Washington, D.C., the JDR Third Fund in New York City, and the Smithsonian Institution. Before retiring, he served as director of the Henry Gallery at the University of Washington.

The Wizard of East Pikes Peak: Nikola Tesla's Experimental Station

—*Richard Grove*

Everyone agreed that he was an authentic wizard. When he came to Colorado Springs that May afternoon in 1899, a "dark, slim foreigner" with smoldering eyes, eager to begin work on his mysterious laboratory, he found reporters at the door of his apartment at the Alta Vista hotel. Nikola Tesla obliged them with a wizardly statement. "I propose to send a message from Pike's Peak to Paris," he said. "I will investigate electrical disturbances through the air and the earth. There are great laws which I want to discover and principles to command."[1]

Stories of the great inventor had traveled before him. Tesla was a Yugoslavian immigrant, the son of a mother who could, at sixty, "using only her fingers, tie three knots in an eyelash." He arrived in New York in 1884 with four cents in his pocket. Now the cascade of discoveries and inventions which his phenomenal mind produced in unbelievable profusion had made him an international celebrity.

He built and operated a radio-controlled boat. In a public demonstration, he sent electricity through his body so intense that it melted wires held in his hands. Once he accidentally caused a minor earthquake in downtown Manhattan while testing a device "small enough to put in your pocket." He invented a revolutionary electric motor, conceived the complex system which made it possible to harness Niagara Falls and transmit its power to unheard of distances.[2] Today our lives are made easier in a thousand ways by his inventions.

Now the wizard was at the peak of his powers. John Jacob Astor had given him $30,000. Leonard E. Curtis, of the Colorado Springs Electric Company, assured him of the necessary electric power. He could build the laboratory of his dreams; he felt ready to open a new territory of knowledge.

They were astonishing dreams. The grandest of them was a plan to pump tremendous charges of electricity into the earth so that you could plug in anywhere and obtain power. The world would be changed; mankind would enter a new era.

Tesla selected a site outside the city, a hill on East Pike's Peak Avenue "just east of the Deaf and Blind institute," and set a crew of carpenters to work on a strange building of his own design. No one had ever seen anything quite like it. It managed to combine the look of sober practicality with the otherworldly appearance of an alchemist's eyrie.[3]

Colorado Springs buzzed with curiosity. But Tesla was a fanatically secretive worker. He maintained the kind of security we have come to expect from today's atomic energy plants.

One of the ever-present (and ever-frustrated) reporters described it:

> The building is roughly boarded up and is about 50 by 60 feet, with a lean-to on the west, or front, in which are two windows and a big double door. ... The structure is about 18 feet high, with a 12 foot roof, which slopes from near the center toward the four corners, thus enabling the carpenters to construct a fairly large platform or stand on the roof ... the structure was securely braced on all sides except the west ... [4]

Working like a man possessed, Tesla pushed the laboratory to completion in July. Wires on poles connected it to the Colorado Springs Electric Company powerhouse. The roof platform sprouted a four-sided skeleton tower of wood. From it, a collapsible mast some 200 feet in height thrust into the sky, terminating in a shiny metal ball.

Ropes were stretched around the station with big signs on every post warning in black letters, "KEEP OUT—GREAT DANGER." When a *Telegraph* reporter crawled under the rope, a Tesla assistant appeared at his elbow "to kindly warn him that his life was in peril inside the ropes, and that he would be a great deal safer if he would remove himself from the vicinity."[5]

Passers-by in the night saw uncanny bluish flickering lights, for these were the hours when the greatest power was available. The wizard was at work.

Photographs and accounts in local newspapers give us a good idea of the inside of the experimental station. In the center of the great room was a gigantic high frequency transformer, Tesla's "Magnifying transmitter." This was a circular wooden fence wound with wire. Within this stood a smaller coil to which was affixed the tall mast. More than 40,000 feet of wire went into their making. The remaining space was "filled with dynamos, electric wires, switches, generators, motors, and almost every conceivable invention known to electricians. And through this mass of intricate and dangerous mechanism Mr. Tesla walks as fearlessly as if on the streets of the city."[6]

This transformer, or "Tesla coil," was the largest ever built. (On a miniature scale, every car ignition system uses the same principle.) It produced freakishly high voltages, probably as high as 135,000,000 volts. In one of its early tests, the first manmade bolts of lightning spat into the sky from the top of the mast. According to one report, the resulting thunder was heard as far away as Cripple Creek, and the dynamo at the Colorado Springs Electric Company powerhouse smoked and ground to a halt.[7]

Tesla was so excited that he forgot himself to the extent of talking to a reporter. "I have an instrument at my station," he said, "which is capable of killing 30,000 people in an instant." The newspaper man was bug-eyed,

> For if the great electrician finds that it is possible to construct a machine that will hurl such death dealing currents with any degree of accuracy at any great distance, the matter of modern warfare will have been settled ... for no nation will seek a disturbance with another nation that is known to possess such a terrible and certain instrument of death.[8]

Sound familiar?

When the mammoth transformer was in operation, Tesla noted a variety of weird phenomena. Great fountains of flame, sixty-five feet across, writhed and crashed and sizzled through the air, producing a blinding light and an ear-splitting racket and creating a strong draft which rushed up through the opening in the roof. Smaller, unconnected coils placed about the room, or even outside the building, sympathetically produced fiery discharges. A story in the local papers said, "It was found that the dynamos and other electrical apparatus of a Colorado fuel company nearby within 100 yards or so were all put out of business."[9] Tesla said, "The discharge. . . [creates] such a commotion of electricity in the earth that sparks an inch long can be drawn from a water main at a distance of 300 feet from the laboratory."[10] There is no report of a Colorado Springs citizen having been unaccountably electrocuted in his bathtub.

He was asked repeatedly when he was going to make the announced experiment with wireless telegraphy. Because of the publicity given Marconi's accomplishments, radio had captured the popular imagination. But this idea was now crowded out of Tesla's mind by the staggering implications of his latest discoveries. "I don't intend to make such an experiment," he said. [11] He was in the theoretical stratosphere. Small practical applications seemed to him insignificant.

As close-mouthed as ever, Tesla continued to work, following a Spartan regimen which might have numbed an ordinary man. He neither smoked nor drank. Years ago he had ruled out women—too distracting.

> ... His workday is from about 11 o'clock in the morning until the same hour or later at night. ... All his meals but breakfast are served to him at his "shop" and while he eats he is still experimenting. [12]

He emerged once in September to proclaim that he had discovered "a principle entirely new, by which I am enabled to transmit tremendous power to any distance without the aid of wires. ... I am only at the beginning of my work, but I never was more confident of success. I never fail." [13]

Following this assured utterance, he said little else for publication in the local papers. He labored on into the winter months. On January 13, 1900, he boarded the train to New York, stating that he would be back in a few weeks to continue his experiments. [14] But this phase of his work was at an end. Tesla became involved in new projects elsewhere.

He attempted to demonstrate some of his discoveries on a practical level a few years later at a plant on Long Island. He ran out of funds before he could complete it.

Reports persist that Tesla succeeded at Colorado Springs in running small motors and lighting 250-watt bulbs at a distance of twenty-six miles from the station without using wires. He said, "In this new system it matters little—in fact, almost nothing—whether the transmission is effected at a distance of a few miles or of a few thousand miles. ... " [15]

Abandoned, the East Pike's Peak laboratory came to an ignominious end. Unpaid bills for taxes, water, and electricity piled up. The station was torn down and the lumber sold to a man who was building a house in Ivywild. Tesla apparently left the building with a caretaker, one C. J. Duffner. Duffner never received any pay. Five years later, his patience at an end, he sued in the county court for back wages. He won the case and, as

Tesla did not send the money, "several cases of copper wire and electrical apparatus" were sold at a sheriff's sale in 1906. It was a melancholy affair.

> From a business point of view, the sale cannot be chronicled
> as a success, for property said to be worth $4,000 failed to sell
> for enough to cover the judgment of approximately $1,100
> standing against it.[16]

What precisely did he learn at his Pikes Peak laboratory? What were the "great laws" and "principles?" We will never know in any detail. Tesla committed little to paper, preferring to rely on his photographic memory. He seriously planned to live to the age of 125, to use the last quarter of a century for recording his experiments. He died in 1943, an eccentric recluse in a room full of pigeons, at the age of 86.

The Colorado Magazine, October 1958

Endnotes

1 Colorado Springs, *The Evening Telegraph*, May 17, 1899, 1. Hereafter cited as *Telegraph*.

2 See John J. O'Neill, *Prodigal Genius: The Life of Nikola Tesla* (New York, 1944). A good short account of Tesla's life and scientific accomplishment is Kenneth M. Swezey, "Nicola Tesla," *Science*, Vol. CXXVII, No. 3307 (May 16, 1958), 1147.

3 Photographs of the exterior of this building are reproduced in *Nikola Tesla, Experiments with Alternate Currents of High Potential and High Frequency*, new ed. (New York, 1904), 150, 155, 158. Photographs of the interior accompany Nikola Tesla, "The Problem of Increasing Human Energy," *The Century Magazine*, Vol. LX, No. 2 (June, 1900), 175–211.

4 *Telegraph*, June 2, 1899, 5.

5 Ibid., June 28, 1899, 5.

6 Ibid., June 21, 1899, 5.

7 O'Neill, 186–187. Dr. Lee De Forest, inventor of the 3-Electrode Grid Vacuum Tube, said at the time he was interested in the glider flights in the Pikes Peak area, "one of the world's most noted scientists and inventors, Mr. Nikola Tesla, who was suffering from tuberculosis, was living in Colorado Springs for his health. He was experimenting with 'transmission of power without wires,' near the Garden of the Gods, where he built a tower and a small laboratory. ... During those experiments he succeeded in lighting electric lamps by wireless more than a mile away from the power transmitter."—E. N. Pickerell, "Wireless Was Developed in Colorado," *Colorado Magazine* Vol. XXXIV, No. 1 (January 1957), 19–20.—Editor

8 *Telegraph*, Aug. 12, 1899, 2.

9 *Colorado Springs Gazette*, May 30, 1924, 1.

10 Tesla, *Problem*, 190.

11 *Telegraph*, July 29, 1899, 3.

12 Ibid., Aug. 12, 1899, 2.

13 Ibid., Sept. 16, 1899, 5.

14 Ibid., Jan. 13, 1900, 5.

15 Tesla, *Problem*, 209–210.

16 *Telegraph*, March 22, 1906, 3.

M axine Benson will be the first to tell you that gunslingers are hardly her specialty.

A Boulder native, Benson was state historian and editor of *The Colorado Magazine* from 1966 until 1971. Following a year at the Smithsonian Institution, she returned to the Society as library director and advisory editor of publications for the next ten years. She later served as director of publications for the Kansas Historical Society and is now an independent historian.

She wrote her University of Colorado doctoral dissertation on the life of Edwin James, the botanist who accompanied the 1820 Stephen H. Long expedition to Colorado. In 1986, the University of Nebraska Press published Benson's *Martha Maxwell, Rocky Mountain Naturalist* as the first volume in its Women in the West series. Benson is also author of the valuable reference *1001 Colorado Place Names*.

A soft-spoken but authoritative chronicler of Colorado's past, Benson is probably best known as coauthor (with Carl Ubbelohde and Duane A. Smith) of the classic *A Colorado History*. The book's ninth edition—commemorating its fortieth anniversary and featuring the authors' regularly updated chapters—will be published in 2005.

But gunslingers?

In 1965, Benson explains, Harry Kelsey, then state historian and editor of *The Colorado Magazine*, asked her to write a piece on the outlaw Porter Stockton for a special issue focusing on the era of the range cattle industry. At the time, she was deputy state historian and the magazine's assistant editor. Though the topic was and is, she confesses, "a bit outside my primary area of interest," she dove into the research and wrote up the true story of Port Stockton—an unsentimental tale of a ruthless killer (and sometime lawman) who died a violent death while still in his twenties.

Port Stockton, Outlaw

—Maxine Benson

A long with the rancher and the cowboy, the outlaw or gunman was an integral part of the cattleman's frontier. The wide-open cow towns on the raw edges of civilization normally counted a large proportion of cattle rustlers, thieves, and murderers among their residents, men who lived and died by the gun. As law and order was established these gunmen gradually disappeared, leaving behind legends of daring escapades and thrilling escapes.[1]

Although the days of the gunman were soon over, the outlaw has lived on in countless novels, movies, and television serials, and has been romanticized and sentimentalized until it is difficult to speak objectively of him.[2] In reality, however, the life of an outlaw was likely to be brutal and short. Violence was a part of his existence, and few gunslingers lived to recount their exploits to their grandchildren. A typical western desperado was Porter Stockton, an outlaw who roamed the plains of Texas, Kansas, New Mexico, and Colorado and died before his thirtieth birthday.[3]

Like his older brother Ike, who also became a well-known gunman, William Porter Stockton was born in Texas.[4] He was in his late twenties when he died in January 1881; thus the year of his birth was probably between 1852 and 1854.[5] Little is known of the Stockton brothers' early life, but presumably they were active (legally or otherwise) in the cattle business around Fort Worth. It is known that Port married a Texas minister's daughter and that they were the parents of three children.[6]

All that has survived of the first part of Port Stockton's career is a collection of stories, some of which are undoubtedly more fiction than fact. One of the first anecdotes takes place in Kansas. It seems that Port was in Ellsworth in 1873 and witnessed the shooting of Sheriff Chauncey Whitney by Bill Thompson during the course of a fight.[7] After the shooting, so the story goes, Wyatt Earp forced Thompson's brother Ben, who also took part in the affair, to give himself up. George Peshaur, a friend of the Thompsons, then tried to persuade Port to kill Earp. He declined, another cowboy called him a coward, and Port shot the heckler.[8] The next year Ben Thompson, Peshaur, and Stockton were in Wichita, where Earp was deputy marshal. This time, when Peshaur asked him to kill the officer, Port agreed. On the appointed day, however, he was quite drunk, and Earp easily shot the gun from his hand. Disgraced and humiliated, the young desperado soon left town.[9]

Another story dealing with Port Stockton dates from 1873 but places him in the Trinidad-Raton area at the time.[10] In that year a gunman named Chunk Tolbert killed one of Port's friends in a Trinidad brawl and then headed for Raton.[11] According to R. L. "Uncle Dick" Wootton, who had the toll road over Raton Pass, Chunk rode up to his place and had breakfast. Stockton, whom Wootton described as "a great rascal and all round desperado," was already there; but if he saw Chunk, "he must have been afraid to undertake to arrest him," for he soon went away.[12]

That evening Wootton was sitting by the fire when he heard a knock. "The door opened, and a man stepped inside, with a cocked 'six-shooter' in each hand. We were all taken by surprise, and my guests didn't know whether they were to be 'held up' or had a desperado to deal with ... and they looked mighty uncomfortable." Uncle Dick asked Stockton what he wanted, and the outlaw said he was looking for Chunk. Wootton told him that Chunk had left and asked him to put his pistols away, "reminding him that it wasn't a very genteel performance to come into a public house, flourishing a couple of 'guns' and frightening people until their hair stood on end, when there was no occasion for it." Port and the men who were with him went out after the murderer, killed another young man by mistake, and came back without seeking Chunk.[13] He was later done in by Clay Allison, another gunman with a considerable reputation in Colorado and New Mexico, perhaps as a favor to Stockton.[14]

A third anecdote that is told about Port Stockton takes place in Cimarron, New Mexico, in 1876. As Port came out of a bar one day, he was met by a Juan Gonzales, who accused him of being more than friendly to his wife. Irritated by this slur on his character, Port promptly shot and killed Gonzales. Although he pleaded self-defense, he was put in jail by the sheriff. Brother Ike soon heard about this and rode to the rescue. He drew on the sheriff and quickly obtained Port's release.[15]

During the late 1870s the Stocktons made the western part of the Colorado–New Mexico border their headquarters. This country was filled with cattle rustlers, outlaws, and other gunslingers of every description, and the Stockton brothers, Harg and Dyson Eskridge, Frank and George Coe, and Clay Allison were just a few of the desperadoes who congregated there.[16] Violence was the normal way of life, and occasionally the fighting erupted into conflicts on the scale of the famous Lincoln County War.[17] Some idea of the situation in New Mexico can be gleaned from the following letter from Farmington, printed in the *Dolores News*. The correspondent, who signed himself "X.I.X.," wrote: "A dismal gloom hangs over this section of the country. A lawless mob is operating here, driving civil laws and law-abiding citizens from the valley. ... A man's life here is not worth much that does not belong to the mob."[18] Port Stockton took part in the fighting in New Mexico, although it is difficult to determine the extent of his involvement in some of the incidents.[19]

In 1880 Port found himself on the right side of the law for a change, when he was named marshal of Animas City, Colorado.[20] Animas City was a bustling frontier community of several hundred people, located near Durango on the Rio de las Animas "in a very pleasant location."[21] In describing the settlement, a visitor noted that there were "about two hundred persons at present residing in the town, about half of which are miners, gamblers and cowboys."[22] No doubt Port felt right at home in Animas City, and evidently he took his duties seriously.

In the summer of 1880 one Captain Hart came to Animas City carrying a revolver, which would seem eminently sensible under the circumstances. He was not aware, however, that a town ordinance prohibited the carrying of guns. He soon became engaged in a discussion with Marshal Stockton, who ordered him to give up the firearm. According to the *Dolores News*, "some words followed and resulted in Stockton shooting Hart in the cheek, the ball passing out under the nose. Hart was taken care of and is not seriously injured." The paper judiciously concluded: "The facts in regard to the shooting that are in our possession are too meagre to form an opinion as to who is in the wrong."[23] The Animas City *Southwest*, however, had no doubts about the incident. The paper reported:

> Captain Hart, of Montezuma Valley, was shot and wounded
> in the face, last Sunday, while resisting an arrest for violating

an ordinance prohibiting the carrying of firearms. Several
shots were exchanged between the parties. It is to be regretted
that the occurrence happened, but the laws of this town must
be enforced to the letter.[24]

Always quick on the trigger, Port's actions soon caused the *Dolores News*
to comment that he had been "extremely free with his pistol since he had
a little authority,"[25] and in September he was involved in another shooting. On this occasion Stockton went into a barbershop to get shaved, and
according to Charles Naeglin, then a resident of Animas City, the barber
"was afraid of Stockton, who had a bad disposition."[26] While shaving the
marshal the barber inadvertently nicked him. The *Dolores News* reported
that Stockton immediately "pulled his revolver and fired, the ball just graz-
ing the back of the barber's head." Not content with this, "he then took the
pistol and beat the head of the barber in a shameful manner."[27]

This was too much for Animas City, and Mayor Eugene Engley[28]
deputized Naeglin to help arrest Stockton. They found Port and took
him into custody. Then, Naeglin stated, Stockton asked to be allowed to
go home for supper, and "Engley consented and took him over home.
While he was there and Engley was watching the door, Stockton went
out the window and escaped on a horse which he got from Myers and
West." They set out after Port but were unable to catch up with him.[29]

Thus ended Port Stockton's brief career as a lawman. Again he was
an outlaw, and the last months of his life were spent in the pursuits that
had helped make him a notorious western desperado. There are several
different accounts of Port's activities during the last part of 1880 and up
to the time of his death in January 1881. According to Naeglin, after his
escape Stockton fled to the area around Farmington. He stated that
Stockton jumped a homestead claim while the owner was absent, having
gone to Lake City to record the claim. When he returned, "he tried to
get his place back. Stockton shot and killed him, and his wife reported
the killing, and a posse went after Stockton and killed him."[30] It has
been pointed out, however, that a man living in New Mexico would not
have gone to Lake City, Colorado, to record a claim, so it is probable
that Naeglin is mistaken in this instance.[31]

Another version of Stockton's last months was given by Erastus
Thompson in an interview some years later. Thompson, an early resident
of the San Juan area, stated:

There was a good deal of scrapping down on the
Colorado–New Mexico border. ... Once Ben Quick and some
others and I took a bunch of cattle to Durango which
belonged to Pierson Brothers. They wanted us to stay there
and hold the cattle for a couple of days for ten or fifteen dollars
extra apiece. The cattle were to go on to Cascade. There was
nothing whatever wrong about these cattle of Pierson
Brothers, and they had no idea there would be trouble. But
the Farmington outfit got it into their heads the cattle had
been rustled and shot into the bunch that was holding the
cattle. (We had gone back home.) The Eskridges and Ike and
Port Stockton and his wife were among those in the scrap
that followed. Port Stockton was killed, and his widow stayed
right with the fight and had her arm shot off.[32]

As nearly as can be determined, however, Port Stockton was killed
because he got involved in the aftermath of a brawl at Francis M.
Hamblet's ranch near Farmington. Hamblet gave a party on Christmas
Eve but neglected to invite what the Durango *Daily Record* termed three
"ruffians," Dyson Eskridge, Oscar Pruett, and James Garrett.[33] They
tried to crash the party and "conducted themselves in such an indecent
and boisterous manner, using profane and obscene language in the presence
of ladies that they were requested by the host to leave." A young man by
the name of George Brown was watching these events, when "the three
roughs began firing at the house and at the same time retreated as they
fired." Brown was killed and Pruett, evidently shot by his comrades, died
a short time later. The *Record* reported that "the community are greatly
enraged and seventeen of the best citizens are out in pursuit of the
murderers, and a thousand dollars reward is offered for them, dead or
alive. If caught short work will be made of them."[34]

After the Christmas Eve fracas Eskridge and Garrett left the Farmington
area.[35] Apparently the vigilantes decided that the outlaws would go to Port
Stockton's place, and early in January the group rode up to his house.[36] A
few weeks later the *Dolores News* carried the following item:

We omitted to state last week that the lower Animas country
had contributed another killing to its already long list. The
one now referred to is the mobbing of Porter Stockton, well

and unfavorably known throughout southern Colorado and northern New Mexico. A band of 18 unknown men went to his house and were confronted by Stockton and his wife, both armed with Winchester rifles. A bullet tore a splinter from the butt of Mrs. S's gun, which entered her abdomen, killing her. Porter was completely riddled and fell dead.[37]

Whatever the exact circumstances, Porter Stockton's death was generally unlamented. Charles Naeglin was "glad to learn that he had been killed as he had sent word that he would shoot Engley and I on sight, so he didn't get the chance. That was a tough fellow and I was glad he was out of the way."[38] The *Dolores News* wrote that "as he had made threats against the lives of several citizens, it was thought best to give him to the angels, who now minister to his wants."[39] Most of the settlers in southern Colorado would have agreed with the following appraisal of the *Las Vegas Gazette*:

Stockton is a man about twenty-seven years old who came to New Mexico about eight years ago and made for himself an unenviable reputation. His own boast was that he killed eighteen men, but at any rate he has been the means of putting quite a number of men under the sod. He was mixed up in the Lincoln County War and after that was over began depredating in the Indian Nation. For the past year or more Stockton has been stealing cattle in the Lower Arkansas country and it is very gratifying to write the obituary of such a desperado. He died with his boots on.[40]

The Colorado Magazine, Winter 1966

Endnotes

[1] For a concise account of the outlaw's place in the cattle country see Robert E. Riegel and Robert G. Athearn, *America Moves West* (4th ed. rev., New York: Holt, Reinhart and Winston, 1964), 532–33.

[2] Kent Ladd Steckmesser describes the creation of the prototype outlaw-hero, Billy the Kid, in his study, *The Western Hero in History and Legend* (Norman: University of Oklahoma Press, 1965), 57–102.

[3] In various accounts the name is spelled Stogden or Stockdon. F. Stanley, *Ike Stockton* (Denver: World Press, 1959), 1, suggests that the spelling "Stogden" was used by the publisher of the Las Vegas, New Mexico, *Optic* to distinguish the outlaw brothers Ike and Port Stockton from

the prominent Stocktons who owned the Clifton House stage station. The name is given as "Stockdon" in Howard L. Conard, *"Uncle Dick" Wootton, the Pioneer Frontiersman of the Rocky Mountain Region, An Account of the Adventures and Thrilling Experiences of the Most Noted American Hunter, Trapper, Guide, Scout, and Indian Fighter Now Living* (Chicago: W. E. Dibble and Co., 1890), 436–38.

4 Stanley W. Zamonski, "Rougher Than Hell," *1957 Brand Book of the Denver Westerners* (Boulder, Colo.: Johnson Publ. Co., 1958), 300, gives his birthplace as Cleburne, Texas.

5 His age is listed as twenty-seven in the *Las Vegas Gazette* obituary, January 16, 1881, quoted in Stanley, *Ike Stockton*, 103–04. Philip J. Rasch, "Feuding at Farmington," *New Mexico Historical Review* 40 (July 1965), 231, says that Port was born about 1851 or 1852.

6 *Las Vegas Gazette*, January 16, 1881, quoted in Stanley, *Ike Stockton*, 103–04; F. Stanley, *Desperadoes of New Mexico* (Denver: World Press, 1953), 167–68, 175.

7 See Floyd B. Streeter, *Ben Thompson: Man with a Gun* (New York: Frederick Fell, Inc., 1957), 94–98.

8 Stanley, *Desperadoes of New Mexico*, 173–74.

9 Ibid., 175–76. A similar story featuring a young, unnamed Texan who fits the description of Port Stockton is told by Stuart Lake in his *Wyatt Earp, Frontier Marshall* (Boston and New York: Houghton Mifflin Co., 1931), 125–26. One would think from reading the numerous accounts of western gunmen that every outlaw of any importance rode with Billy the Kid, or tried to kill Wyatt Earp or Bat Masterson. While this story is colorful, it is probably more fiction than fact. It is possible that Stockton was in Kansas at the time, but there is some doubt that Earp could have been involved in the incident. According to Nyle Miller and Joseph Snell, who have made a thorough study of Kansas gunmen on both sides of the law, in spite of Earp's statement that he disarmed Ben Thompson after the shooting of Sheriff Whitney, "no contemporary record is known to exist which places Earp in the town at that time." Moreover, although Earp said he arrived in Wichita in May 1874, and was soon hired as deputy marshal, "no evidence of his official police employment could be found in the Wichita city records or in either of the town's newspapers until April, 1875." "Some Notes on Kansas Cowtown Police Officers and Gun Fighters," *Kansas Historical Quarterly* 26 (Autumn 1960), 317. Streeter, *Ben Thompson: Man with a Gun*, 101, also says that Earp did not arrest Thompson.

10 *Trinidad is in southern Colorado and Raton in northern New Mexico; at the time, the towns were important stops along the Santa Fe Trail.*

11 Harry Kelsey, "Clay Allison: Western Gunman," *1957 Brand Book of the Denver Westerners* (Boulder, Colo.: Johnson Publ. Co., 1958), 387.

12 Conard, *"Uncle Dick" Wootton*, 436–37. The book is written in the first person as if Wootton were telling the story.

13 Ibid., 437–48.

14 Kelsey, *1957 Brand Book of the Denver Westerners*, 388. See the *Santa Fe New Mexican*, January 20, 1874, 1, for a contemporary account of the killing.

15 Stanley, *Ike Stockton*, 83–84. Rasch, New Mexico Historical Review 40 (1965), 231, states that he killed Antonio Archbie in Cimarron in 1876.

16 Zamonski, *1957 Brand Book of the Denver Westerners*, 299–300.

17 See Rasch, *New Mexico Historical Review* 40 (1965), 214–31.

18 *Dolores News* (Rico), June 26, 1880, 3.

19 Rasch, *New Mexico Historical Review* 40 (1965), 219; Stanley, *Ike Stockton*, 81, 83.

20 W. P. Stockton is listed as marshal of Animas City in the *State Business Directory of Colorado with Mining and Live Stock Directory Departments, 1881* (Denver: Jackson Printing Co., Publishers, 1881), 137. Zamonski, *1957 Brand Book of the Denver Westerners*, 300, suggests that Port went across the border to Animas City because his band was outnumbered by the Coe outfit.

21 George A. Crofutt, *Crofutt's Grip-Sack Guide of Colorado: A Complete Encyclopedia of the State* (Omaha: Overland Publishing Co., 1881), 72.

22 Letter to the editor from "C.," Hermosa, Colorado, February 8, 1880, in the *Ouray Times*, February 28, 1880, 1. *Crofutt's Grip-Sack Guide of Colorado*, 72, gives the population as 451, while it is listed as

350 in the *Colorado State Business Directory with Colorado Mining Directory and Colorado Live Stock Directory Departments, 1880* (Denver, J. A. Blake, Publisher, 1880), 40.

23 *Dolores News* (Rico), July 10, 1880, 2.

24 *Animas City Southwest*, reprinted in the *La Plata Miner* (Silverton), July 17, 1880, 2. George Coe said that he was told that Hart "got shot in the mouth in a little gambling scrape." *Frontier Fighter: The Autobiography of George W. Coe, Who Fought and Rode with Billy the Kid, as Related to Nan Hillary Harrison* (Boston and New York: Houghton Mifflin Co., 1934), 186. The two contemporary newspaper accounts, however, probably present the more accurate version of the shooting.

25 *Dolores News* (Rico), September 18, 1880, 2.

26 Interview with Charles Naeglin, January 17, 1934, CWA Interviews (La Plata, Huerfano, and Mesa Counties, 1933–34), Pam 362/20, 52, in the library of the Colorado Historical Society. Hereafter referred to as CWA Interviews, CHS.

27 *Dolores News* (Rico), September 18, 1880, 2. Naeglin, CWA Interviews, CHS, calls the barber a Negro; but the Dolores paper, lending a more exotic note to the incident, wrote that while he was "supposed to be a negro and certainly has that appearance, ... in fact he is a Maouri, a race of people in Australia, and is well-educated, intelligent and has travelled all over the world." *Dolores News* (Rico), September 18, 1880, 2.

28 Engley was mayor and also publisher of the *Animas City Southwest*; see the *State Business Directory of Colorado, 1881*, 137–38. Unfortunately, according to the most recent survey of Colorado newspapers, no files of the *Southwest* have survived. Donald E. Oehlerts, *Guide to Colorado Newspapers, 1859–1963* (Denver: Bibliographical Center for Research, Rocky Mountain Region, Inc., 1964), 87.

29 Naeglin, CWA Interviews, CHS. "Meyers and West" are listed as proprietors of a livery stable in Animas City in the *State Business Directory of Colorado, 1881*, 138.

30 Naeglin, CWA Interviews, CHS.

31 Stanley, *Ike Stockton*, 93.

32 Interview with Erastus Thompson, July 31, 1934, CWA Interviews (Otero and Montezuma Counties, 1933–34), Pam 360/109, 535, in the library of the Colorado Historical Society.

33 *Durango Daily Record*, reprinted in the *La Plata Miner* (Silverton), January 8, 1881, 3. Pruett's name is spelled "Puett" by the *Dolores News* in its report of the incident, but the story is similar to that given by the *Record*. The Rico paper, however, couldn't quite believe that Pruett took part in the fight. He was a former resident of Rico, and the *Dolores News* wrote: "During the time Oscar remained in Rico his conduct was that of a quiet, gentlemanly boy, and it is hard to think that he should have acted in the manner above described. ... There may have been circumstances which do not appear on the surface as yet, so we will give the dead boy the benefit of the doubt until the true inwardness is exposed to public gaze." January 8, 1881, 3.

34 *Durango Daily Record*, reprinted in the *La Plata Miner* (Silverton), January 18, 1881, 3. Stanley tells the story in *Ike Stockton*, 100–04, but has Stockton, Garrett, and Eskridge as the three party-crashers, with Pruett and a James Brown listed as guests. However, neither the *Durango Daily Record* nor the *Dolores News* mention Port Stockton in connection with the fight.

35 *Dolores News* (Rico), January 8, 1881, 3.

36 Zamonski, *1957 Brand Book of the Denver Westerners*, 305, says that Alf Graves and Aaron Barker were with the group and distracted Port, while a band directed by Frank Coe killed him. Stanley, *Ike Stockton*, 102–03, has Graves doing the shooting. Coe, *Frontier Fighter*, 187–88, states that Graves got into a "mix-up" with Stockton and a few days later went to Port's house with Frank Coe and others and killed him.

37 *Dolores News* (Rico), January 22, 1881, 3. Mrs. Stockton was not dead, but she was severely wounded. Stanley, *Ike Stockton*, 105.

38 Naeglin, CWA Interviews, CHS.

39 *Dolores News* (Rico), January 22, 1881, 3.

40 *Las Vegas Gazette,* January 16, 1881, quoted in Stanley, *Ike Stockton*, 103–04.

The parallels are intriguing: In a close election contest, the ballot counts of certain counties come under fire, with the result that the ballots themselves must be scrutinized. Republicans and Democrats dispute the election returns with equal tenacity. At one point, the state's Supreme Court must step into the fray and declare a rightful winner. But unlike the presidential election of 2000 and its infamous Florida ballots, the Colorado gubernatorial election of 1904 had the curious outcome of three men taking the office over the course of a twenty-four-hour period. The election was one of the quirkier episodes in Colorado's history—a contest fraught with ballot-box stuffing and accusations of fraud from both sides of the aisle.

Marjorie Hornbein, who earned a master's degree in history from the University of Denver in 1967, focused her thesis on the tangled 1904 election. In this adaptation for *The Colorado Magazine*, she synthesized court documents and news reports to lay out the chain of events that led to one of the most controversial decisions over who controlled Colorado's government. Hornbein's interest in the topic came naturally: Her father, Philip Hornbein—a Zionist leader recognized by the Colorado Bar Association as one of the six greatest lawyers in Colorado history—defended the 1904 election officials early in his career.

In subsequent issues of *The Colorado Magazine* Marjorie Hornbein described Denver's historic struggle for self-government and profiled the visionary union official and politician Josephine Roche. Having served on such civic organizations as the Denver Planning Board, Denver's Community Education Council, the Platte River Development Committee, and the Colorado Bicentennial Commission, Hornbein has also written extensively for the *Western Jewish Historical Quarterly* and *Rocky Mountain Jewish Historical Notes*.

Three Governors in a Day

—Marjorie Hornbein

"Well, we've got to win this election, boys," said Denver Chief of Police Michael Delaney. "You want to do the best you can. We will see that you don't go to jail. You know what to do; do the same as you did before and do all you can. If we don't win this election the chances are we will get ditched. You know what you got before—protection."[1]

These singular instructions were delivered early in November, 1904, at a meeting held in Kopper's Hall. In attendance was a group of several hundred persons of low repute and few scruples—gamblers, saloonkeepers, ex-convicts, and prostitutes. They were the Democratic "repeaters" who were paid to go from precinct to precinct and vote the Democratic ticket at each polling place. Private detective William Green, who later was sentenced to jail for his role in this election, also addressed the gathering and instructed it in the art of repeating. He urged the repeaters to swear in any vote which might be challenged.[2]

These plans for fraudulent voting were only a part of the illegality that marked the Colorado gubernatorial campaign of 1904 in which former Governor Alva Adams, the Democratic candidate, challenged the incumbent, Republican James Peabody.[3] Interest in this contest was so great that it quite overshadowed the presidential campaign between President Theodore Roosevelt and Alton B. Parker. "Never before in the history of Colorado," said Republican attorney John Waldron, "has there been such rancor and bitterness engendered and manifested in any gubernatorial race."[4]

During the same week in which the Democratic group met at Kopper's Hall another political meeting was held—this one in Hastings, the site of the Victor Fuel Company's coal mine in Las Animas County. Here, as in Denver, a captive audience was in attendance; but here Republican county leaders sought to intimidate prospective voters. All

miners, saloonkeepers, and merchants were required to attend and listen
to Delos Chappell, the owner of the Victor Fuel Company. "Old man
Chappell," as he was called by the miners, warned them that "the mine was
working very good at the present time and that if the Democrats should
win we would have to close the mine down. ... If the Republicans should
win and find out that some of the working men voted the Democratic ticket
they would fire him [sic] from employment of the company."5

The Hastings meeting, with Chappell's threat to the miners, indicated
the sad state of the entire Colorado mining industry. During Peabody's
administration the hostility and conflict between the mineowners and
the miners had increased. Continual disputes led to a series of strikes
in the Cripple Creek mines and in all the mills of Colorado City; soon all
the coal and metal mining regions of the state were affected.6

Throughout the struggle, Peabody had worked closely with the
Citizen's Alliance, a group formed in Teller, El Paso, and San Miguel
Counties, whose purpose was to put down any resistance of the miners.
The Alliance was composed of a small conservative circle of Republican
businessmen, soldiers, and other citizens who disliked the immigrant miners
and sought to prevent any improvement in their status. This group,
despite its obvious prejudice and bias, was the one to which the governor
turned for advice before making any decision in regard to labor.7

By September 1904, with the election only two months away,
Republican leaders realized that Peabody's chances for re-election were
declining. Drastic measures had become necessary to insure a Republican
victory in the mining counties, for in that area lay Peabody's only chance
of defeating Adams, who admittedly held strength in Denver.

Therefore, the Republicans engaged in a vigorous campaign which
included widespread coercion and intimidation of the voters, the majority
of whom were the miners. This was not a difficult task, for their employers
were all Republican leaders and members of the Alliance, as well as of the
powerful Mine Owners' Association. (This association controlled the
issuance of "work cards," and without such a card a miner had no chance
of finding employment.) For example, Clarence Fitch, assistant secretary
of the association, told Edgar McDaniels, a miner working in the granite
mine in Cripple Creek, that if the Democrats won "there will be no work
in this camp," and warned him that he would lose his job if he voted for
Adams.8 And Delos Chappell brought a carload of men to the polling
place in Hastings and insisted on registering them. Chappell, though,

denied any intimidation of his men. "I think perhaps I could be construed as advising them," he admitted, however. "I think my remarks were along the line that our interests were mutual in the election."9

Only after election day did the miners tell of their exploitation by the Republicans. McDaniels said: "If the people had been allowed to go to the polls and vote as they seen fit, without any intimidation, coercion of any kind, the Democratic ticket would have been elected by at least a thousand votes." Tony Disneria believed that the miners "would like to vote for Adams awful well, but they were afraid." Emil Pfeiffer said that the Democrats were afraid to work in the campaign or even to go to the polls. 10 The Republicans had done their job well; on election day the miners voted for the man whom they hated and feared. They needed the jobs in the mines, so their ballots were cast for Governor Peabody.

Due to the activity of the powerful Democratic machine, election day in Denver was also marked with corruption and fraudulent voting. The repeaters who had been coached at the meeting in Kopper's Hall moved from precinct to precinct to vote under false names. Frequently they repeated in the same polling place after having disguised themselves. The women wore bathrobes, kimonos, or evening dresses for their different appearances. They were aided by election officials and the police, just as Police Chief Delaney had promised. But the next morning, the police drove them all out of town, for they were no longer of any use, and they might cause trouble. 11

Clearly, both parties had acted in ways that prevented a free election. Both had engaged in fraud in an effort to elect their candidate, for control of the governor was essential to the control of Colorado politics. Nevertheless, when the votes were canvassed and tabulated, they showed that Alva Adams had received 123,092 votes to 113,754 for the incumbent, Governor Peabody. 12 Alva Adams was elected on the face of the returns.

On January 4, 1905, the Colorado legislature met in joint session. Tension was immediately apparent when the State Board of Canvassers presented the election returns. Peabody at once submitted a protest, demanding that all the precincts from Denver be rejected as fraudulent. In response to the governor's demand, Republican leaders presented a resolution to the joint session calling for appointment of a committee of five senators and ten representatives which would investigate the Denver vote. 13 The Democrats and those Republicans unfavorable to Peabody were strongly opposed to any investigation, for if the entire Denver vote were cast out, they feared that Adams might lose his majority. As the Democrats sought recognition to voice opposition to the resolution, noise and turmoil filled the hall. Observers from the press said that a riot was imminent.[14] Both Lieutenant Governor Warren Haggott and the speaker of the house, William Dickson, were at the speaker's desk wielding their gavels. Haggott shouted to the secretary of the senate, and Dickson to the clerk of the house, instructing them to call the roll. They did so simultaneously but their voices could not be heard above the din. Haggott, who had presided at the opening of the session, insisted on the right to continue. He hoped to be able to kill the resolution, while Dickson wanted to occupy the chair to further its adoption as a possible means of seating Peabody. Each one tried to outdo the other in pounding his gavel, but neither could subdue the uproar.[15] "Never has there been such wild disorder in any legislature," *The Denver Post* exclaimed.[16]

The first session of the joint assembly had become a farce. It ended when Haggott, shouting that the assembly was adjourned, left the hall, followed by a group of Democrats and insurgent Republicans.[17] The proceedings had caused a deterioration of the already critical political situation in Colorado. The schism in the Republican party had seriously weakened its effort to seat Peabody.

The Peabody supporters claimed that the dissident Republicans, who had refused to act with the majority of their party, were under the direction of the Colorado & Southern Railroad, which was supporting Adams. Although the mining and utility corporations had worked for Peabody throughout the campaign, and allegedly controlled him,[18] the Colorado & Southern had consistently opposed the governor. This was because of the railroad's fight with the Denver Tramway Company, whose president, William Evans, opposed any expansion of the Colorado & Southern. He feared that if the railroad were successful in building suburban electric roads, such competition would seriously interfere with the profitable interurban runs of the Denver Tramway.[19]

Another group of Republicans was friendly to former United States Senator Edward Wolcott, and hoped to restore him to power in Colorado and eventually return him to the Senate. Wolcott had antagonized many corporate leaders by a speech that he delivered before the Colorado Republican convention on September 29, 1903. There he warned of the growing power of corporations in the state, declaring:

> The moment the corporations of Colorado which depend on municipalities for aid and for franchise assume to dominate the parties of the state and to make political parties an appendage of corporate needs, then comes the death knell of political integrity.[20]

This remark was directed against the Denver Water Company and the Denver Tramway Company, especially its president, William Evans. Hostility had long existed between Wolcott and Evans. It was handed down to Evans by his father, John Evans, and dated back to early political battles between the latter and Wolcott. This animosity also disrupted the Republican party, for Wolcott supporters were not favorable to Governor Peabody, whom they considered to be a tool of Evans. Senator Wolcott, however, did give some support to Peabody during the campaign, but only for the purpose of promoting party harmony. In his last speech, delivered the night before election, the senator gave his candidate a strange tribute:

> No man who knows Governor Adams would believe for a minute that he is affiliated and allied with the Western Federation of Miners. And I do not. But in view of the assurances he has given his party as to the use he would make of the law, or rather the non-use of it, I am led to believe the people of this state would be infinitely worse off with a weak man [Adams], than with a vicious one [Peabody].[21]

After the first stormy session of the legislature, Republican leaders, recognizing the disunity of their party, feared that their hope of seating Peabody could not be realized—at least for the present. Their position was complicated not only by the several antagonistic groups within the Republican party, but just as seriously by a constitutional amendment which had been passed in the November election. It provided for the unification of the Colorado Supreme Court and the Colorado Court of Appeals and for the addition of two new justices to be appointed by the governor.[22]

Until 1904, the Supreme Court was a body of three judges. Its most recent constituents were Chief Justice William Gabbert and Associate Justices John Campbell and Robert Steele. Gabbert and Campbell had consistently supported the Republican position in decisions to which

Steele wrote powerful dissents. Therefore, if a Republican governor did not appoint the new judges, the Republicans might lose their control of the state judiciary. This would be crucial for Republican corporate executives, whose causes were frequently adjudicated by the Supreme Court.[23]

Thus the prized appointments became the basis for a deal between Democratic and Republican leaders. The compromise provided for the seating of Alva Adams, who was actually entitled to the governor's chair as he had been elected on the face of the returns. But the Republicans would agree to withdraw their protest on the Denver vote and to seat Adams only if Peabody were allowed to appoint the Supreme Court justices before he left office. This arrangement was accepted by the Democratic leaders, and Alva Adams was inaugurated as governor on January 10, 1905.

Two days after the inauguration, Peabody filed a notice of contest against Governor Adams with Secretary of State James Cowie. In his petition Peabody alleged that: "Adams was not legally elected and is not now lawfully holding office; that this contestor Peabody did in fact receive a majority of legal votes cast, and the contestee is in truth and fact a usurper.[24] Peabody had apparently disregarded the advice offered by *The Denver Post* in an open letter addressed to him: "Do the best thing you ever did—come out like a man and say 'I was defeated and I don't want the governorship.'" The *Post* also repeated what Democratic leaders had already alleged, namely, that Peabody was controlled by William Evans: "All hinges on Peabody standing by Evans' game. If the governor would say 'No I will not be a catspaw,' and would emphatically repudiate Evans' scheme to count him in, the ground would fall from under the bum Napoleon."[25]

At the same time that the *Post* advised Peabody to quit, the *Denver Republican* published an editorial predicting that "Adams will announce that there shall be no stain on the family shield, and will refuse a tainted office."[26] But as the advice of *The Denver Post* went unheeded, so the prediction of the *Republican* never came to pass. Both newspapers underestimated the tenacity with which each candidate and his supporters sought the governorship, and with it, control of Colorado politics.

On January 18, Lieutenant Governor Jesse McDonald, a Republican who had been elected in the November election, appointed a committee of twenty-seven members to hear testimony on former Governor Peabody's challenge to the legality of Adams' election. W. H. Griffith, a liberal

Republican representative from Teller County, became chairman of the committee, which consisted of twelve Republican representatives, six Republican senators, six Democratic representatives, and three Democratic senators.[27] Each candidate filed a brief in support of his position.

Attorney John Waldron, representing Peabody, claimed:

> The entire city government, and all its officials are tainted
> from core to circumference, with connivance or participation
> in these election frauds. ... There is a low moral tone prevailing
> in this community, and ... unless this body, by its action in
> this case, teaches the lesson that elections must not be stolen
> in the future, you might as well keep away from the polls. ...
> Election frauds have gone on, unpunished by the courts in
> this community, until their commission has become a *quasi*
> legitimate occupation.[28]

In his reply, Adams alleged:

> Divers corporations doing business in the State of Colorado and
> divers mine operators' associations ... entered into a conspiracy
> with each other and with the Republican State Central
> Committee ... to secure the election of the same James H.
> Peabody as Governor of the State of Colorado. ... There was
> sent into the various counties ... by the said corporations ... large
> sums of money, much of which ... was used for the purpose of
> buying votes, padding registration lists, corrupting election
> officials ... to prevent a free, fair, and open election.[29]

After the briefs were filed, the legislative committee prepared to hear testimony. Each side had scores of witnesses and an abundance of evidence to present. Alva Adams secured depositions from more than two thousand citizens who had voiced heated opposition to a decision of the Colorado Supreme Court which in effect had eliminated their votes. The court's decision was made in response to a motion filed by the attorney general which asked it to cast out all the votes from "certain precincts" in Denver on the ground that some of the votes were fraudulent. The court sustained the motion and ordered the election commission to exclude the votes of these "certain precincts" from the abstract of returns.[30]

Of course, the many honest voters who had cast legal ballots were angered to see their votes thrown out simply because others in the precinct were fraudulent. Public feeling about eliminating so many Democratic votes became intense and created antagonism toward the Supreme Court and the Republican party as well. The citizens who testified for Adams felt that they had been deprived of any participation in government, even of their right to vote.[31] Their position was supported by an editorial in *The Denver Post* which observed:

> The people of Colorado of both parties had become so
> accustomed to election fraud that they allowed for false vote
> in estimating the outcome. Many people regarded stuffing
> ballot boxes as nothing worse than getting drunk. Therefore,
> the idea of throwing out entire precincts where there was
> fraud was completely revolutionary.[32]

A strange drama was enacted before the joint committee of twenty-seven legislators whose task was to determine and report to the legislature the legally elected governor. The *Post* exclaimed: "If Mark Twain should drop into Denver on one of those nose-reddening days and spend a few minutes before the legislative committee, what a funny book or play could be written on 'How to Steal a Governor in Colorado.'"[33] Waldron said that he believed that no "history of litigation in the civilized world has ever produced the equal of this contest, in the number of witnesses, in the range the testimony has taken, in the volume and mass of proof to be analyzed."[34] The evidence grew to 180,000 pages, most of which were testimony from the more than 2,000 witnesses.

As an important part of their case, the Democrats sought to place in evidence the election boxes from Huerfano County, where the Republicans had allegedly cast a large number of fraudulent ballots. The Republicans, of course, resisted any investigation of the Huerfano vote, and tried to prevent Adams from getting a subpoena for Juan Montez, election clerk of the county. When Montez was finally handed a summons in his home in Walsenburg, he refused to come to Denver in compliance with the order until he first received traveling expenses. Adams agreed to pay the train fare to Denver, so Montez finally obeyed the summons and appeared before the committee. But he had failed to bring the most important part of the evidence—the ballot box from the Maitland precinct. This precinct, No. 23, was a coal camp run by the Colorado Fuel & Iron Company, and it was here, the Democrats believed, that the Republican vote had been fraudulent.[35]

Montez was arrested for contempt of the subpoena and was sent back to Walsenburg with the sheriff and ordered to get the Maitland box. Shortly after the train left the station, he jumped and fled under the Sixteenth Street viaduct. Police could not locate him until the following day, when he was found on the outskirts of the city. He was ordered to go to Walsenburg immediately and bring back the Maitland box. This time he obeyed the order, but when he did return with the box, it was found to be empty. Not a single ballot, not even a poll book, was inside. Apparently the ballot box had not even been used during the election, and thus the returns from this precinct were not official.[36]

The Democrats charged that the corporation officials of the Colorado Fuel & Iron Company had themselves agreed on the vote and notified the election clerk the number to report. "This is the most flagrantly corrupt incident that has ever happened in Colorado history," the *Rocky Mountain News* charged.[37] However, aside from this startling disclosure before the investigating committee, the Democrats took no action to exclude the votes of Huerfano County from the official returns.[38] While the joint committee was busily engaged hearing evidence in the election contest, the legislature was debating a labor law. This, too, was crucial to the political situation, for labor's struggle against the corporations had been the crux of the gubernatorial campaign. This critical problem involving the rights of the miners and the privileges of the mineowners had been transferred from the mining camps to the legislature, where it still had little chance of being solved.

The assembly did, however, enact a law favorable to labor, but it was a very weak one. It was passed with the support of the conservatives, who feared that the Democrats and the liberal anti-Peabody Republicans might push through a stronger measure. Griffith, the chairman of the joint committee, had the courage to oppose this bill. It provided for an eight-hour workday, as the miners had demanded, but this applied only to "miners." Therefore, Griffith pointed out, all trammers, muckers, and timber men were excluded.[39]

He submitted an amendment which would include all men working in the mines. This proposal was enthusiastically supported by Democrats and the liberal group of Republicans, but the Peabody supporters voiced

Alva Adams   Jesse McDonald   James Peabody

heated objections to its broad coverage. Apparently, they had not yet lost control of the legislature, for the amendment was defeated, and the original bill passed on February 28, 1905.[40]

However, the controversy had caused even more friction in the Republican party, and its leaders feared that Peabody's chances of winning the contest had been weakened. Throughout the contest, the *Denver Republican* published daily editorials admonishing Republican leaders to stand united. One article observed that "the Democrats always stand together, while the Republicans divide and allow differences over minor questions to neutralize their efforts."[41]

But the Republicans did not heed this advice. During the illness of Chairman Griffith, who was obliged to be absent from several committee hearings, more trouble arose among the Republican members of the committee. A few Peabody supporters took advantage of Griffith's absence and attempted to select a subcommittee of three persons to prepare the committee's report for the legislature.[42] A few days later, when Griffith returned to his post, he was furious that such a plan had even been proposed, and his sharp display of anger was noted in all the newspapers.

The *Denver Republican* found such behavior unjustifiable, and said that "Griffith appeared in a most excitable frame of mind and made allegations that could only be due to aberrations."[43] But the *Rocky Mountain News* was critical of the committee, and observed that if the proposed subcommittee had prepared the report, it would actually have been written by John Waldron, the attorney for Peabody.[44] In this controversy, the Peabody group was defeated, and the plan for the subcommittee was rescinded. But its proponents had split the party, and unity now seemed impossible.

While some Republicans, including Griffith, were favorable to Adams, many were opposed to both candidates and felt that neither was entitled to the office of governor. This group started a movement in the legislature to seat Lieutenant Governor McDonald as governor; they asked Peabody to admit defeat and unite with them for the sake of the Republican party, but Peabody refused. He and his supporters still hoped to have enough votes in the legislature to win the contest and unseat Alva Adams. But they had miscalculated their strength, for on March 2, when the committee started preparation of its reports, only fourteen of its twenty-seven members were willing to sign the majority report which stated that James Peabody should be seated as governor.[45]

In addition to the majority report, two others were submitted to the assembly. One was the Griffith report, which was prepared by Griffith and J. B. Thomson of Boulder, also a Republican. It admitted that "gross frauds were committed by the Democrats," but concluded that "it is not clear that there is sufficient evidence to unseat Adams."[46] The group supporting McDonald submitted its report, which was written by Senator Morton Alexander and which set forth an ingenious proposal for the legislature's consideration. Alexander charged that:

> Brazen, shameless and far-reaching frauds were committed [in the election]. ... The complex and confused condition of the frauds thus perpetrated render [sic] it wholly impossible for us to separate the legal ballots from the illegal ones, and equally impossible for us to determine whether contestee or contestor received an honest majority of the legal votes. ... No person was elected governor ... because of said fraud. Therefore, be it Resolved ... that the action of this body in declaring Alva Adams elected Governor of this State be rescinded and revoked and that a vacancy be and is hereby declared to exist.[47]

When Alexander presented this report to the legislature, the entire body was thrown into pandemonium. When the speaker, William Dickson, was finally able to restore decorum, he quickly ruled the report to be out of order. Dickson had been elected speaker due to the efforts of Peabody and William Evans, so he opposed this report, which if adopted, would certainly defeat Peabody. Dickson ruled that the "issue was solely between Peabody, the contestor, and Adams, the contestee, and the decision must be for one of the two contestants."[48]

This denial of the Alexander report seemed to indicate failure for the plan to place McDonald in the governor's chair. But his supporters were not ready to admit defeat, and Senator John Campbell introduced a resolution that appeared to contain a solution. He asked that the legislature submit to the Supreme Court the question of adopting the Alexander report. By this time, the Democrats had little hope of retaining Governor Adams in office. Their only victory could be the defeat of Peabody, so they were willing to submit the query to the court. On the other hand, the Peabody supporters felt confident that the Supreme Court would not admit the Alexander plan, but would affirm the ruling of chairman Dickson. In view of such beliefs by each party, a resolution to submit to the court an interrogatory as to the legality of the report was easily passed. It was entitled *In Re Senate Resolution No. 10*, and in it the assembly asked if it could legally adopt a report of the investigating committee which found it impossible to determine the man elected, due to the impossibility of separating the legal from the illegal ballots. The interrogatory was speedily dispatched to the judicial chambers, and, as the Peabody group had hoped, the Supreme Court ruled that the legislature had no power to declare a vacancy. It must find for one of the two contestants.[49]

Despite the court's ruling, the number of legislators who wanted neither Peabody nor Adams was large enough to circumvent its decision. They worked out a curious and clever scheme whereby Peabody was to be declared "lawfully elected to the office of said Governor ... and entitled to the immediate possession ... of said office."[50] But before he could be sworn in, he would be obliged to sign an agreement that he would execute no business, make no appointments, and submit his resignation in twenty-four hours.[51] When he had complied with this latter requirement, McDonald would be sworn in.

Actually, this plan accomplished the same end that the Alexander report had tried to effect. The court's order was in reality disobeyed, though technically the legislature complied with its instruction. It would find for one of the two contestants, although he was to hold office for only one day. McDonald would be governor, and the Republicans would still control the statehouse.

On March 16, Secretary of State James Cowie received Peabody's signed resignation, although Alva Adams still occupied the governor's chair. In his resignation, the former governor stated: "I initiated the contest before the legislature of Colorado to establish my title to the office of Governor. ... I deemed it my bounden duty to the people of Colorado and to the Republican party ... that I should begin and prosecute such contest to the end that the will of the people, lawfully expressed at the polls, should be carried into effect."[52] The statement continued with an admission of the division within the Republican party, which Peabody felt had caused his defeat. He said:

> To my surprise and regret, I discovered toward the latter stages of the contest, that certain members of the legislature, elected as Republicans, entertained feelings of ill-will and dislike toward me personally; I was of course conscious that an unfortunate schism existed among the members of the Republican party at the time I begun [sic] my contest proceedings, but I was not then aware of the extent to which such schism existed. ... I feel that I have been cruelly aspersed by those who should have stood by me loyally, but it is not meet that I should dwell upon this topic. For the good of my party, for the best interests of the State I love so dear, the step I am about to take seems necessary. ... [53]

In an interview with representatives of the press, the former governor explained his views on the labor disputes which had contributed mightily to his political downfall. He said:

> This contest has not been waged for party purposes, or for a political job. It has been carried on that there might be established in Colorado such conditions as would render life and property safe under the law, and would enable a man to work when, where, and for whom he pleases without fear of intimidation or violence.[54]

After Peabody had submitted his resignation and issued his farewell statement, the legislature met to adopt the committee's report, which, paradoxically, would seat Peabody as governor for one day. The report received only fifty-five votes. Forty-one legislators would not even agree that Peabody should hold office for twenty-four hours, and among these were twelve Republicans.[55]

Shortly after the vote was taken, at 5:00 P.M. on March 16, 1905, James Peabody was given the oath of office by Chief Justice Gabbert, and thus Alva Adams was unseated.[56] Adams, like Peabody, issued a statement to the press. Both men viewed themselves as martyrs for their party and their state. Peabody, according to his own words, had been sacrificed in order that a man would have the right to work "when, where, and for whom he pleased." Adams believed that he had been sacrificed so that the political power of corporations would be curtailed in Colorado. He said:

> The majority of the legislature has bowed to the dictates of corporations. ... Colorado is a province of the fuel company, the smelter trust, the tramway and allied corporations. By command of the corporations a usurper has been placed in the executive chair. ... I am calm and moderate in my statements, but do not deny a feeling of intense resentment at being robbed.[57]

Many Colorado voters, including some legislators, believed with Adams that he had been unjustly thrown out of office. Republican representative James Milton filed a protest before the assembly stating:

> I hereby protest against the action taken here in unseating the legally elected Governor of Colorado, Alva Adams; as I am convinced that the majority knows that James H. Peabody did not make his case, and cite the action of the majority in demanding and getting said Peabody's resignation before they would seat him, as proof that they know he (Peabody) did not receive a majority of the legal votes of this State.[58]

Several other Republicans in the legislature hastened to corroborate Milton's statement. Representative James Garcia declared that he would not vote for Peabody, because he did not make a case. Thomas Dungan commented that "Peabody did not receive a plurality of the votes." Al Metz explained: "I am as good a Republican as any member of the assembly, but

I could not honestly vote for Peabody. Alva Adams was certainly elected." Richard Hoyt, like the above-mentioned representative, felt that Peabody was not the choice of the people.[59]

Former Governor Charles Thomas later wrote an historical essay in which he told of this contest and its strange conclusion. He, too, was critical of the action of the legislature. He thought that:

> This compromise was creditable neither to the assembly nor to Peabody. General sentiment condemned it, but the public had to accept it as an ending to a long and unhappy controversy. The assembly unjustifiably evaded its duty, which was to decide the controversy on its merits.[60]

Regardless of public opinion, the plan to seat McDonald was executed as cleverly as it had been planned. On March 17, at 4:25 P.M., Governor Peabody kept his promise and formally ordered his resignation delivered to Secretary of State Cowie, although it was already in Cowie's possession. Five minutes later, Chief Justice Gabbert appeared in Cowie's office with Jesse McDonald, who was promptly sworn in as governor of Colorado. The Republicans had won the long and bitter contest. Alva Adams, who had been elected on the face of the returns, was defeated. As he prepared to return to private life after his brief term as governor, he received a telegram from Governor Thomas which assured him: "More joy the exiled Marcellus feels than mighty Caesar with the Senate at his heels."[61]

The Colorado Magazine, Summer 1968

Endnotes

[1] Quoted in Colorado, General Assembly, *Journal of the General Assembly of the State of Colorado in Joint Session*, 15th sess., *1905*, XIV, 122. Hereafter referred to as *Joint Session Journal*.

[2] Ibid., 224.

[3] Alva Adams was elected governor for the first time in 1886 and for a second term in 1896. James Peabody had been mayor of Cañon City prior to his election as governor in 1902.

[4] *Joint Session Journal*, XIV, 210.

[5] Deposition of Pasquale Pelino, ibid., III *Contestee*, 2227.

[6] See George G. Suggs, Jr., "Prelude to Industrial Warfare: The Colorado City Strike," *The Colorado Magazine*, XLIV (summer 1967), 241–62.

[7] See George G. Suggs, Jr., "Colorado Conservatives vs. Organized Labor: A

Study of the Peabody Administration" (Unpublished Ph.D. dissertation, University of Colorado, 1964) for a study of this period.

8 Deposition of Edgar McDaniels, *Joint Session Journal*, III *Contestee*, 2080.

9 Deposition of Delos A. Chappell, ibid., V *Contestor*, 449.

10 Deposition of Edgar McDaniels, ibid., III *Contestee*, 2082; deposition of Tony Disneria, ibid., III *Contestee*, 2139; deposition of Emil Pfeiffer, ibid., III *Contestee*, 2026–27.

11 Ibid., XIV, 123.

12 James Cowie (comp.), *State of Colorado: Abstract of Votes Cast at the General Election Held the Eighth Day of November, A.D. 1904, For Presidential Electors, State Legislative and District Officers and the Constitutional Amendments* (Denver: The Smith-Brooks Company, State Printers, 1905), 20.

13 *Denver Post*, January 16, 1905.

14 *Rocky Mountain News* (Denver), January 6, 1905.

15 Ibid.; *Denver Times*, January 6, 1905.

16 January 6, 1905.

17 *Rocky Mountain News* (Denver), January 7, 1905; *Denver Times*, January 6, 1905; *Denver Post*, January 6, 1905.

18 *The People v. Times Publishing Company*, 35 Colo. 287 (1906).

19 *Denver Post*, March 6, 1905.

20 Thomas F. Dawson, *Life and Character of Edward Oliver Wolcott, Late a Senator of the United States from the State of Colorado* (New York: For private circulation, 1911), II, 434.

21 Ibid., 455–56. Senator Wolcott died on March 1, 1905, while the contest was still being debated in the legislature.

22 Colorado, General Assembly, *An Act to Submit to the Qualified Electors of the State of Colorado Amendments to Sections Five (5), Six (6), Seven (7), and Eight (8), of Article Six (VI) of the Constitution of the State of Colorado, Concerning the Supreme Court*, S.B. 9, Session Laws, 14th sess., 1903, 148–51.

23 On December 2, 1904, *The Denver Post* exclaimed: "The corporations insist on having the highest tribunal friendly to their cause, as all their cases are finally adjudicated by that body."

24 *Joint Session Journal*, XIV, 9. See also Colorado, General Assembly, Senate

Journal, 15th sess., 1905, 64–65.

25 December 3, 1904.

26 December 21, 1904.

27 *Denver Republican*, January 18, 1905; *Denver Post*, January 18, 1905.

28 *Joint Session Journal*, XIV, 208–09. See also *Senate Journal*, 65.

29 *Joint Session Journal*, XIV, 39–40.

30 Decision "On Motion to Restrain the Election Commission from Canvassing Returns from Certain Precincts and to Exclude such Returns in Making up the Official Abstract of Votes," *The People* ex rel. *the Attorney General v. Tool* et al., 35 Colo. 243–52 (1905).

31 The testimony of Selene Forrester was typical: Q. "You were surprised, I suppose, when you heard that your ballot was thrown out?" A. "I never was more surprised in my life. ... I would like to get the expert here; I would give him a little tongue lashing. ... I would just as soon have voted Republican as Democratic if he is a good man, but such a man as Peabody is ought to be ground under our feet." Deposition of Selene Forrester, *Joint Session Journal*, VII *Contestee*, 5541–42.

32 December 22, 1904.

33 February 9, 1905.

34 *Joint Session Journal*, XIV, 244.

35 Ibid., III *Contestee*, 1934–47. See also the *Rocky Mountain News* (Denver), February 12, 1905; *Denver Times*, February 15, 1905.

36 *Joint Session Journal*, III *Contestee*, 1934–47.

37 February 16, 1905. Other evidence revealed repeating by the Republicans. Frankie Hayes and Clara Chase, prostitutes from Pueblo, testified that a Republican worker, George Fariss, had told them that they must vote. They could not refuse this request, for Fariss collected their fines regularly, and was able to admit or exclude them from certain areas. Neither was registered, but each admitted having voted twice. Deposition of Frankie Hayes, *Joint Session Journal*, II *Contestee*, 1372–74; deposition of Clara Chase, ibid., 1376–78.

38 Such action was not necessary, for the Democratic party had won the election on the face of the returns.

39 *Senate Journal*, 350. See also the *Denver Times*, February 10, 1905, and the *Rocky Mountain News* (Denver), February 11, 1905.

40 Colorado, General Assembly, An Act to Declare Certain Employments Injurious and Dangerous to Health, Life and Limb; Regulating thee Hours of Employment in Underground Mines and other Underground Workings, in Smelters and Ore Reduction Works, in Stamp Mills, in Chlorination and Cyanide Mills, and Employment About or Attending Blast Furnaces, and Providing a Penalty for the Violation Thereof, H.B. 1, Session Laws, 15th sess., 1905, 284–85.

41 February 24, 1905.

42 *Denver Post*, February 10, 1905.

43 February 21, 1905.

44 February 21, 1905.

45 *Joint Session Journal*, XIV, 178.

46 Ibid., 403; see also the *Denver Times*, March 2, 1905.

47 *Joint Session Journal*, XIV, 407–08.

48 Ibid., 403; see also the *Denver Times*, March 8, 1905.

49 *In Re Senate Resolution No. 10 Concerning Governorship Contest*, 33 Colo. 307–15 (1905). See also *Senate Journal*, 385–89.

50 *Joint Session Journal*, XIV, 423–24.

51 *Rocky Mountain News* (Denver), March 16, 1905.

52 Resignation of James H. Peabody, Executive Record No. 17 (1905), 35, Colorado State Archives.

53 Ibid., 35–36.

54 *Rocky Mountain News* (Denver), March 18, 1905.

55 Senator William McCarthy was excused from voting, thus making the total vote cast ninety-six. *Joint Session Journal*, XIV, 423. See also the *Rocky Mountain News* (Denver), March 17, 1908.

56 *Joint Session Journal*, XIV, 424. See also the *Denver Times*, March 16, 1905; *Denver Post*, March 17, 1905; *Denver Republican*, March 17, 1905; *Rocky Mountain News* (Denver), March 17, 1905.

57 *Rocky Mountain News* (Denver), March 19, 1905.

58 *Joint Session Journal*, XIV, 424.

59 *Denver Times*, March 17, 1905.

60 Charles S. Thomas, "Fifty Years of Political History," *History of Colorado*, ed. James Baker and LeRoy R. Hafen (Denver: Linderman and Co., Inc., 1927), III, 936.

61 *Rocky Mountain News* (Denver), March 18, 1905.

R unning from north to south and splitting Colorado down the middle is a vast, jagged strip of the Rocky Mountains.

Through those mountains meanders the imaginary line known as the Continental Divide. To the east of the divide the waters run toward the Atlantic, and the western side's waters run toward the Pacific, much to the eastern side's chagrin.

The eastern side of the mountains has long since been dubbed the "Front Range," a name that reflects the barrier the range posed to westward-journeying settlers and prospectors. Along that eastern slope now stretches the state's primary urban corridor, and from there the Great Plains sweep away toward Kansas. To the west of the divide is the Western Slope, and what historian Duane A. Smith will tell you is a land unto itself.

Anyone who has tapped into the rich history of the Western Slope knows Smith's books, which include *Mesa Verde National Park: Shadows of the Centuries*, *Rocky Mountain Boom Town: A History of Durango*, and *Condemned by Many, Read by All: Durango's Newspapers, 1880–1992*. Professor of Southwest studies at Fort Lewis College in Durango, Smith is a coauthor of *A Colorado History*, appearing in 2005 in its fortieth anniversary edition. Smith's 2002 book, *Henry M. Teller: Colorado's Grand Old Man*, offers an authoritative study of the Central City senator, and he has written the definitive biography of silver tycoon H. A. W. Tabor with the 1973 volume *Horace Tabor: His Life and the Legend*.

Smith wrote his profile of the Western Slope while coauthoring with Duane Vandenbusche a history of that region, published in 1981 as *A Land Alone: Colorado's Western Slope*. Himself a Western Sloper, Smith pulls both personal insight and historical perspectives into this look at what makes Colorado's western half a hardheaded entity all its own.

A Land unto Itself:
The Western Slope

—Duane A. Smith

The fall of the land toward the Pacific is so distinctive that it
has received its own name. When speaking of the Mississippi
side of the mountains, one uses the term "eastern slope" as a
matter of geographic convenience. Western Slope by contrast
is spelled with capital letters. It is a human as well as a phys-
iographic entity. It is also a mystique. The people of the
Western Slope feel superior to lesser mortals. [1]

Thus wrote David Lavender, a native son, to describe to those "lesser
mortals" what the Western Slope symbolizes. This represented no
easy task for even so talented a writer as Lavender. In many ways the
sweep of the land and its individualistic people defy mere words to
capture them, and they laugh at attempts to paint their "soul," as they
would those who try to capture the wind.

Lavender's argument rests on two basic premises: that there is and
always has been a Western Slope, and that Western Slopers have different characteristics. There may be geographic sections, such as the San
Juan Basin and the plateau country, within the whole of the slope, but
they are only components of a more complex entity, mere man-made
definitions, which do not capture the feeling, the mystique, and the sig-
nificance that surround the Western Slope.

A majestic, sometimes foreboding, land of 14,000-foot mountains,
desolate plateaus, and fertile river valleys, the Western Slope covers
nearly two-fifths of Colorado. Once divided into three huge counties, it
evolved into the twenty counties of today, several of which would give
some eastern states a run for total size. [2] From the time of the first

Anasazi village to the farmers and city dwellers of today, water has directed (perhaps dictated would be more nearly accurate) Western Slope settlement. Where people found water they settled; where they did not, they tried to bring it to them, using canals and diversion. James Grafton Rogers expressed it extremely well when he wrote that "water is the limit of life in the far West. Its quantity fixes the number of men who can live in the plains, plateaus and mountains. It limits the crops they grow, the cities they build. Everything else is plentiful—coal, oil, forests, minerals, space, opportunity. Water alone is scarce."[3] As yet no one has tamed the land. Some have gazed with wonder at the scenery; others have tried to reshape it; but the most successful have learned to adapt to the environment, not transform it. Once this lesson was learned and relearned, settlement proceeded more swiftly and smoothly.

The land is there and always will be there; the same cannot be said for Western Slopers. Setting aside the Mesa Verde people and the Ute, settlement covers only a little over one century, hardly a yawn in the total history of the region. In that time span man has scarred, dug, and tampered with the Western Slope more than his predecessors ever did. How permanent this intrusion will turn out to be cannot be judged. On the other side of the coin—is the impact of the Western Slope on people evident in unique ways? Did the environment produce a Western Sloper? Lavender says it did, and history supports his contention.

The isolation, the vastness of the land, and the simple fact that the area and its people were left so long to their own devices produced an independent nature, which Lavender and others sagely discerned. There

As an example of overanticipation, Gunnison, in 1902, attempted to encompass an "area two miles square."

was a self-reliance, too, as a correspondent from Breckenridge noted in the August 8, 1860, issue of the *Rocky Mountain News*. He observed that the people generally know their own business, attend to it promptly, and "let others alone." Yet, there was an openness, provided the visitor did not infringe upon the right of privacy of others. Well-known Victorian traveler Bayard Taylor, on a Breckenridge visit in the summer of 1866, commented on just that point and said, "I shall always retain a very pleasant recollection of Breckenridge."[4]

Further insight into Western Slopers was furnished by two ministers who knew them in the 1870s and 1880s—George Darley and James Gibbons. Darley, who saw it all, from red-light district crib to church pew, wrote, "nor could a more intelligent, plucky, warm-hearted set of men be found." Gibbons concurred, going on to say that the region attracted "only the energetic and the robust, who have the hardihood to endure the severe cold that prevails in those altitudes [San Juans]."[5]

Western Slopers tend to be optimistic. "Everybody looks forward," wrote Ernest Ingersoll in the early 1880s, referring to mining and the prospects of selling a claim. "Perhaps this delicious uncertainty is a part of the fun." It must have been, because so many prospectors never struck a profitable deal. That characteristic prevailed, whether in miner, farmer, or merchant. Routt County residents agreed with the *Steamboat Springs Pilot* in 1899, when it prophesied that "the dawn of prosperity" was breaking for them.[6] No matter that the editor had said the same thing before and would again. They treasured this faith, this optimism.

That eternal optimism has propelled Western Slopers into trouble more than once. For instance, mining engineer Thomas Rickard, arriving in Gunnison in 1902, was dismayed by what he found. "Gunnison was a boom town, and when the wind goes out of a boom the wreckage is not enlivening." The town attempted to "cover an area two miles square," and Rickard was never sure whether he was inside or outside of the city, riding on a main street or out on the prairie.[7] Few Western Slope communities did not pass through similar manias of overbuilding and overanticipation.

It is fair to ask if these traits are unusual or different from other similar western experiences. The answer must be a qualified "no"; the chemistry of these various ingredients produced a Western Sloper, who by the early twentieth century was different from his, even then, more urbanized eastern slope counterpart. And it is still true, as David Lavender wrote, not that physical differences are apparent when Western Slopers mingle with Denverites on Sixteenth Street in the capital city. They do not stand out, except perhaps when gaping at the traffic, buildings, and crowds and shaking their heads over the noise and the smog. The traits that make the Western Sloper what he is are the frontier heritage and the struggle of life, yesterday and today. These things are not observable in casual conversation.

Historically, the concept of the Western Slope dates almost from the beginning of Colorado, although the term came into general use several decades later. The words used to describe the area explain much about the early perception of this region. Miners referred to it as "the land beyond the snowy range." By the early 1870s Denverites had taken to lumping the whole area as "beyond the Divide," a place that, except perhaps for mining, held little interest for most of them. The mountain barrier, then, set it apart initially. When adventurers penetrated this barrier, they found a land of promise. As early as October 1859 a correspondent to the *Rocky Mountain News* praised the Blue River diggings as beating "California out and out." Twelve years later the Western Slope appeared to Sidney Jocknick to be a Garden of Eden. An old frontiersman told him that "the whole 'Western Slope' was a hunter's paradise, a region fit for the gods." Entranced, Jocknick moved there and stayed.[8] So, slowly, did others.

A land beyond the mountains, a land of potential, the Western Slope was both. Nevertheless, it received more than its share of bad press. Colorado newspaperman and author Ovando Hollister referred to it as a vast mountain wilderness (1867), and the *Denver Rocky Mountain Directory* (1871) described it as very nearly uninhabited land; one, however, known to be replete with valuable minerals. Traveler Samuel Bowles would not even say that, as he tersely dismissed western Colorado as "many a fable of rich mines, of beautiful valleys ... it has few settlers and no especial history." To Bowles the rest of the state was "in every way" more interesting. As the 1870s closed Frank Fossett could still call it an "unknown land," especially to the world at large and even to Colorado.[9]

The Western Slope lagged in development in the 1870s, primarily wilderness territory of questionable potential. The land beyond the snowy mountains came to mean west of the Continental Divide.[10] There was no need for further geographical discussion. As far as its potential, that meant one word—mining. Or did it?

Bowles, for all his negativism, nearly lapsed into ecstasy over Hot Sulphur Springs when he visited there in August 1868. With springs for bathing and rivers for fishing, the "old grew young and the young joyous." Could the fountain of youth offer more? Promoter and Colorado booster William Byers of the *Rocky Mountain News* owned the springs and had big plans for his park. He was one of the earliest eastern slopers to boost the Western Slope. The Reverend Isaac Beardsley and his party rode to the springs from Georgetown in August 1871, no easy feat in itself over the trails of those days. Beardsley returned home "invigorated and strengthened" and "healthier, wiser, and better."[11] The scenery had already lured the tourist, and the "vigorous" climate and "health" springs beckoned the weary and the invalid, of whom nineteenth-century Colorado claimed many. The Western Slope enticed the health-seeker and the tourist, as well as the prospector and the miner. Hard upon their heels came the rancher, the lumberman, the railroader, the merchant, the city promoter, and the farmer.

By the time of statehood, the Western Slope had become a recognized entity in Colorado. Yet, its development trailed as much as a generation behind the eastern slope. The placer deposits of the Blue and Snake Rivers in the Breckenridge area opened barely a step behind those of Central City and Georgetown. In the early 1860s they caught up and were, in truth, widely acclaimed as one of the great mining regions of the territory. Prospectors even penetrated the far distant San Juans in 1860–61.

Then realities began to take their toll. Isolation, Ute resistance, rugged mountains, and shallow gold deposits ended the San Juan flirtation; and isolation, lack of capital, and exhaustion of placer gold deposits slowed Breckenridge to such a degree that it rapidly lost its early prominence. By 1872 United States Mining Commissioner Rossiter Raymond could write that the Western Slope, aside from "partial development" of a few mineral resources, was "today, nearly as wild and unimproved as it was when first entered by white men."[12]

When Raymond was writing, Denver already had connected with the transcontinental railroad, and a web of rails slowly inched out of the capital city. Urbanization, nineteenth-century variety, was taking hold of several eastern slope communities besides Denver, while all that could be found west of the divide were a few forlorn mining camps, not even one that could honestly claim the title of mining "town." A population of five thousand in Denver probably tripled that of the entire Western Slope, although incomplete reports make it impossible to know for sure. Agriculture, ranching, and even limited industrialization on the eastern slope promised that the mining/smelting-based economy would become more balanced. Eastern and foreign investors, when they thought of Colorado, thought of Central City, then Leadville, not Saints John or Silverton.

The Leadville silver millions made the difference for both eastern and western slopes. Silver pouring out of the Little Pittsburg, Chrysolite, and a score of other mines helped build Denver into a state and regional mining, social, business, and political center and encouraged prospecting everywhere in the mountains of Colorado. If there was one Leadville, then surely there were more buried in some unprospected glen. Off went the prospectors, followed by money to buy those claims that would assuredly gush silver.

In the 1880s the Western Slope finally began to mature. The Ute people were removed after the Meeker troubles and the outbreak of 1879, and the railroad came in 1881. Prospectors and miners were searching everywhere, and their persistence finally paid off when Aspen emerged to challenge the predominance of Leadville in the late 1880s. A decade later the San Juans became one of the great mining districts in Colorado. With mining came lumbering, agriculture, urbanization, and tourism. The Western Slope was a wilderness no more. Sparsely populated areas could still be found, in northwestern Colorado and in the southwestern corner, about which a promoter wrote in 1890 that it "has been until recently a *terra incognita* to all save the cowboy and Indian and a few adventurous explorers."[13] The Western Slope never developed evenly.

After their slow start, Western Slopers endeavored to catch up, a familiar refrain that still rings true. An understanding of the slope is dependent upon a thorough grasp of this fact: Western Slopers have long been subjected to a semicolonial, exploited status, dependent upon the eastern slope and beyond for financial support. This subservience has colored their outlook and molded their philosophy and is best expressed in their attitude toward Denver, the symbol of their frustrations.

To strike at something so nebulous as the term "eastern slope" was tantamount to boxing the wind. This was not so with Denver, a physical entity, where resided the financial, political, and social powers that seemed to dictate Western Slope development. Denver became the convenient scapegoat. The city earned a good portion of the rhetorical brickbats thrown its way. Rhetoric proved to be about all that the politically and economically impotent nineteenth-century Western Slope could fire. A few illustrations of attitudes and reactions will suffice. These are, however, only the tip of a mountain of complaints. Editor Caroline Romney accused the "Queen City of the Plains" of trying to "freeze out" and blight Durango in 1881. Why?—because Denver feared new cities that would contend with her for the honor, trade, and rewards of the "metropolitan mart" of the West.[14] Durango, all of nine months old at the time, had high aspirations.

The *Lake City Times* complained that quite a few local people were traveling to Denver to buy goods.[15] This was a real concern, especially when, as the editor pointed out, these same people owed hometown merchants for goods already purchased on credit. Not even the largest town on the Western Slope could compete with the variety, size, or prices of the business community in Denver. Dave Day, the most outspoken Western Slope newspaper editor of his day, carried on a decades-long feud with Denver from Ouray and later Durango. He repeatedly called upon his fellow Western Slopers to rally to the unity banner. Amazed over Denver prices for fruit, he thumped, "we must quit Denver commission pirates" and market elsewhere. When Denver lost a fight to get better roads, he shed no tears.[16] Day took on anyone and everyone, but Denver held its place as a prime villain.

Part of the problem obviously lay with envy and resentment of Denver on the part of the Western Slope communities, as well as a lingering assumption that Denverites cared little about the land to the west. Except for those large mining communities and districts where profit could be made, Denver ignored the area. The persistence of Denver newspapers in 1904 to locate Rifle in Routt County amused a few, seemed trivial to most, and thoroughly infuriated Rifle residents. Back in 1890 the newspaper editor in Meeker wondered, after reading that Denver had hired seven new post office clerks, when his town was going to be noticed. Meeker residents wanted daily mail service, not new clerks.[17]

Part of the image problem of Denver came from the companies headquartered there. The Denver & Rio Grande Railroad, which did so much to open and develop the Western Slope, was not always seen as a generous benefactor by the people and communities dependent upon its service. From its own company-created town of Durango, through Grand Junction and beyond, came complaints that rose and fell with the issues and the times. Nor was the D&RG alone. The *Meeker Herald* in March 1913 attacked the Denver-based Mountain States Telegraph and Telephone Company as an "octopus" that spent a lot of money in Denver papers to thwart the independent lines.[18]

There was always, of necessity, an ambivalence in the relationship between Denver and the Western Slope, something like a love/hate courtship. The *Steamboat Springs Pilot* on November 24, 1897, touched the heart of the matter when it printed that "when Denver prospers the whole state will prosper." Although this truth was not always readily accepted, few arguments could refute it. The Western Slope, chronically underfinanced, needed the money that had to come from Denver. Grand Junction, like all slope communities of any pretension, aspired to become the major urban center. Such aspirations, of course, generated regional jealousy and newspaper feuds. The idealists insisted it could be accomplished alone; the realists knew it would take outside help, meaning Denver. Grand Junction and Mesa Counties were active in trying to attract Denver capital in 1890 for that very reason. To them it would mean more rapid development.[19] Such courtships generally proved rocky and often sired only animosity; even a consummated marriage promised little peace. No money or assistance came without strings and interest rates attached. Thus, when the relationship soured, Denver, as the creditor, received the heartiest share of the scorn.

What was the solution to dominance by Denver and the eastern slope? The hotheads talked of secession. In the 1870s, when the San Juans represented the major region of interest west of the divide, several movements flared in that direction because of real or imagined problems. An 1875 failure to achieve fair legislative representation prompted cries that echoed those of the colonies a hundred years before. Tired of being at the mercy of "cow punchers and Mexican peons," as opposed to King George and the Tories, Hinsdale and La Plata Counties organized to select their own candidates to represent their "vast and growing interests." The impasse was not resolved, and two years later a movement was afoot to organize a new territory, to be called San Juan. The reasoning for this radical step was interesting and was reiterated throughout the next century. Colorado had become too large as a state, and the "great mountains" were almost an insurmountable barrier to intercommunication for a large part of the year. The "great majority of the inhabitants," as well as the greatest wealth, resided in the "north" (Denver and its neighbors), which thereby secured senators and representatives unacquainted with the San Juan region and its needs. No common interests bound the two sections, and it seemed impossible to secure "fair and equal representation" in the administration of state government. Not to mention that the capital was located over there, a vexing travel problem at the very least.[20] The 1870s movement fizzled, opposed even in the San Juans as impractical. The idea did not die, though; as late as the 1960s it came to light in conversation and newspaper print.[21] While the separatists contemplated creating San Juan out of southern Colorado and northern New Mexico, more practical people strove for Western Slope unity.

The first indication of a slope-wide organization came just before and with the hard times of the 1890s. A Western Slope Congress was organized in 1891 to include the counties on the Pacific slope of the state. Meetings were held in Grand Junction, Durango, Ouray, and Aspen before the panic of 1893 and the depression ended the support. The congress published several promotional pamphlets, which included minutes and speeches from the meetings. It organized to further the interests of that section of the state and to call attention to the "great resources" that awaited development.[22] A second pamphlet praised the area in all those well-worn phrases, such as "garden spot," "center of mining,"

Breckenridge in the 1860s *(Photo by W. G. Chamberlain)*

and so forth.[23] Such familiar prose was expected, but the speakers and writers did not stop there.

"The Western Slope is a world of itself," wrote Richard McCloud of Durango. Aspen mayor E. P. Rose generally concurred: "the Western Slope is an empire in itself so far as its resources go." This "empire" was at variance with the rest of Colorado. The "great" Continental Divide naturally split the state; geography, natural resources, and rainfall all differed. "Never has nature supplied with such a lavish hand those things that make a country prosperous and rich as in this section called the Western Slope of Colorado."[24]

Having delimited it and explained why the Western Slope was distinguished from the rest of Colorado, the group turned its discussion to the reasons that required unification. Judge John C. Bell, later to serve in Congress, explained very simply that "united we are powerful, divided we are weak." "Our interests are mutual," he went on, and "we intend" to allow no discrimination against any section "that is west of the range." An editorial, reprinted from the *Grand Junction News* of August 21, 1891, expounded that "it is only through united action that our resources, our natural wealth, and our many opportunities for the profitable investment in capital can be made generally known." It was absolutely necessary, the author concluded, for western Colorado to take "earnest, energetic and united action" to protect and advance her interests. Mayor Rose, soaring in a flight of oratory, called for working "shoulder to shoulder" for the "common weal."[25]

Implicit in all this activity was the feeling that the Western Slope was being short-changed, treated as a second-class citizen by Denver and the eastern slope. Alva Adams, ex-governor and leading Democratic spokesman from Pueblo, had been invited to attend the Western Colorado Congress in 1891 but was unable to do so. Sensing the attitudes, he sent a consoling message that the Western Slope "is the living heart of Colorado—the ebb and flow of your prosperity is reflected at once in our every industry. When you prosper we flourish. When you languish we are depressed."[26] It sounded almost like William J. Bryan's famous "Cross of Gold" speech several years later. Adams's appeal failed to evoke much of a response; the listeners agreed with the viewpoint but mistrusted the motives.

Western Slope sentiments were expressed as clearly as they ever would be at these meetings and they strike sympathetic chords today. In subsequent years other Western Slope organizations have been tried, chambers of commerce, historical societies, pioneers' associations, and various groups to protect water rights. Only briefly have any of them been able to rally the troops; some were intended only to promote the common heritage.

The bitterness and the parochialism toward Denver and the eastern slope have continued through the years. Lucille Loving wrote from the lumber town of McPhee that "if the state of Colorado has money to spend on roads, why don't they spend it on roads that are in daily use, such as the Rico road, instead of million dollar highways for folks to use mostly to enjoy the scenery."[27] In 1927 tourists spent their money largely along the eastern slope, a fact their more numerous legislators did not overlook when appropriating funds. Two years later, 98 percent of the hard surfaced roads of the state were on the eastern slope, a percentage no less lopsided ten years later.[28]

Other statistics compiled for 1937–40 found Western Slope counties ranked in the lower one-half of the sixty-three counties for bank deposits, number of automobiles, and value of manufactured products. Several counties had no bank and most no manufacturing. What these dry facts portrayed was a rural land that lagged well behind the rival eastern slope, further fueling the jealousy. Since World War II the gap has narrowed in some areas and widened in a few. The feeling of second-class citizenship with regard to economic development and state appropriations endures, rightly or wrongly.

More recently the bitterness has focused on water problems; the rift between east and west on this issue runs long and deep. For years Western Slope spokesmen have pointed accusingly at Denver, demanding that it limit demands, conserve its own water, and stop coveting theirs.[29] The dispute strikes at the very heart of the future of Colorado. ...

The Western Slope must never be ignored by those who aspire to comprehend Coloradans and their history. Historically a poor country cousin and upstaged by Denver, the Western Sloper retains more of what is cherished as western than does his urban opposite. Decrying it for its insignificant historical impact, Western Slope critics miss the pivotal point. In his novel *Red Mountain* David Lavender has one of his characters speak to what it took to work and live at Red Mountain, a mining district above Ouray. "What made them go was a sort of urge, a frame of mind. One man that had it would take it up the hill with him and work his guts out, while the fellow next door with the same feeling would use it sitting on his ass scheming out ways to cheat the first one. A third fellow would save a life and the next one would kill just as fast and easy. ... Yes, that's right. That's what built Red Mountain—the frame of mind of the people."[30] That feeling, the proud individualism, the heritage, are what count—David Lavender's "mystique."

Excerpted from "A Land unto Itself: The Western Slope,"
The Colorado Magazine, Spring/Summer 1978

Endnotes

[1] David Lavender, *David Lavender's Colorado* (Garden City, N.Y.: Doubleday & Co., 1976), 86.

[2] Frederic Paxson, *The County Boundaries of Colorado*, University of Colorado Studies 3, no. 4 (Boulder: August 1906), 197–215, traces the county development for the whole state.

[3] James Grafton Rogers, *My Rocky Mountain Valley* (Boulder: Pruett Publishing Co., 1968), 164.

[4] Bayard Taylor, *Colorado: A Summer Trip* (New York: G. P. Putnam and Son, 1867), 112–15.

[5] George M. Darley, *Pioneering in the San Juan: Personal Reminiscences of Work Done in Southwestern Colorado during the "Great San Juan Excitement"* (Chicago: Fleming H. Revell Co., 1899), 18; James J. Gibbons, *In the San Juan: Colorado Sketches* (Chicago: Calumet Book and Engraving Co., 1898), 187.

[6] *Steamboat Springs Pilot*, May 17, 1899; Ernest Ingersoll, *The Crest of the Continent: A Record of a Summer's Ramble in the Rocky Mountains and Beyond* (Chicago: R. R. Donnelley & Sons, 1885), 154.

[7] T. A. Rickard, *Across the San Juan Mountains* (New York: Engineering & Mining Journal, 1903), 92.

[8] Sidney Jocknick, *Early Days on the Western Slope of Colorado and Campfire Chats with Otto Mears, the Pathfinder, from 1870 to 1883, Inclusive* (1913; reprint ed., Glorieta, N.M.: Rio Grande Press, 1968), 32. See also [Charles Harrington], *Summering in Colorado* (Denver: Richards & Co., 1874), 130. *Rocky Mountain News*, October 20, 1859.

[9] Ovando James Hollister, *The Mines of Colorado* (Springfield, Mass.: Samuel Bowles & Co., 1867), 336–37; *Rocky Mountain Directory and Colorado Gazetteer for 1871* (Denver: S. S. Wallihan & Co., 1870), 50; Frank Fossett, *Colorado, Its Gold and Silver Mines, Farms and Stock Ranges; and Health and Pleasure Resorts: Tourist's Guide to the Rocky Mountains*, 2nd ed., rev. and enl. (New York: C. G. Crawford, 1880), 564; Samuel Bowles, *Our New West* (Hartford, Conn.: Hartford Publishing Co., 1869), 85.

[10] Paxton, *The County Boundaries of Colorado*, 199. The Colorado Supreme Court in 1886 settled the definition once and for all in favor of the Continental Divide.

[11] Bowles, *Our New West*, 116–19; Isaac H. Beardsley, *Echoes from Peak and Plain; or, Tales of Life, War, Travel, and Colorado Methodism* (Cincinnati: Curts & Jennings, 1898), 338–40. For Byers's role, see Robert L. Perkin, *The First Hundred Years: An Informal History of Denver and the Rocky Mountain News* (Garden City, N.Y.: Doubleday & Co., 1959).

[12] Rossiter W. Raymond, *Statistics of Mines and Mining in the States and Territories West of the Rocky Mountains; Being the Fifth Annual Report of Rossiter W. Raymond, United States Commissioner of Mining Statistics*, 42nd Cong., 3rd sess., 1872, H. Exec. Doc. 210, 82.

[13] *The Montezuma Valley in Colorado* (Cortez: Colorado Consolidated Land & Water Co., 1890), 2.

[14] *Durango Weekly Record*, June 25, 1881.

[15] *Lake City Times*, October 1, 1896.

[16] *Durango Weekly Democrat*, January 12 and 19, 1912.

[17] *Rio Blanco News*, December 13, 1890;

Routt County Courier, March 20, 1904.

18 *Meeker Herald*, March 15, 1913. See also *Grand Junction Weekly Sentinel*, April 7, 1914. For the Denver & Rio Grande, see Robert G. Athearn, *Rebel of the Rockies: A History of the Denver and Rio Grande Western Railroad* (New Haven: Yale University Press, 1962).

19 *Grand Junction News*, March 22, 1890.

20 *Lake City Silver World*, August 14 and 21, 1875; *Engineering and Mining Journal*, July 21, 1877, 42; *Ouray Times*, October 6, 1877.

21 *Boulder Daily Camera*, March 2, 1969, describes a movement to create the state of Western Colorado. Back in the late 1940s a similar idea was generally ignored. Both suffered a common fate.

22 Western Colorado and Her Resources: Report Made to the Western Colorado Congress in Aspen, December 15, 16, and 17, 1891 (Aspen: Aspen Times, 1892), 2.

23 Western Colorado Congress, Western Colorado (Grand Junction: Grand Junction News, 1893).

24 *Western Colorado*, 86. *Western Colorado and Her Resources*, 4, 5, 7.

25 *Western Colorado and Her Resources*, 4, 7, 9.

26 Ibid., 69.

27 *Dolores News*, June 3, 1927.

28 Colorado, State Board of Immigration, *Year Book of the State of Colorado: 1928–1929* (Denver, 1929), 218; State Planning Commission, *Year Book of the State of Colorado: 1939–1940* (Denver, 1940), 284.

29 See, for example, *Durango Herald-News*, January 7, 1955.

30 David Lavender, *Red Mountain* (Garden City, N.Y.: Doubleday & Co., 1963), 517.

I n 1981 *The Colorado Magazine* gave way to two new publications: the scholarly series of *Essays and Monographs in Colorado History* and the illustrated *Colorado Heritage* magazine. For its inaugural issue, *Colorado Heritage* tackled a western icon—the cowboy. Articles examined a diary of the cattle drover, the cowboy in Hollywood films, the history of cowboy songs, and the legacy of Denver's long-running

Louis L'Amour, circa 1947, in Virginia City, Nevada

National Western Stock Show. Setting the stage for it all was a profile of the cowboy—his history, his legend, and his reality—by novelist Louis L'Amour.

Born in 1908, L'Amour was the son of a large-animal veterinarian in the farming community of Jamestown, North Dakota. A voracious reader of adventure fiction, history, and natural history, he grew up around cowboys and soon joined their ranks, working at ranches and farms in Texas and New Mexico. Work later took him to the mines of the Southwest and the lumber camps of the Pacific Northwest. He enjoyed a brief career as a boxer and sporadically rode the rails with hobos. Through it all, he absorbed a sense of frontier life that he channeled into a prolific career as a writer. Selling more than 270 million copies and translated into more than twenty languages, his novels pull readers into a rich fictional world that has the true West at its core.

The first editor of *Colorado Heritage*, Cathryne Johnson, approached L'Amour knowing his skills at character study and his reputation as a meticulous researcher. In the essay that resulted, the acclaimed novelist looked at the demographics of the cowboy, the chores that went into his day, and the beginnings of cowboy literature, which go back farther than one might think. In conjunction with the magazine's publication and on the occasion of the 101st annual meeting of the Colorado Historical Society in 1980, L'Amour gave an extemporaneous talk and the keynote address at a two-day event honoring the legacy of the western cowboy.

Though he never smoked, lung cancer claimed L'Amour's life in 1988. Late in his career, he served on the Presidential Committee on Space, took part in a Ute-Comanche peace treaty, and sat on the board of the Library of Congress's Center for the Book. In 1983, L'Amour received the Congressional Gold Medal; he was the first writer since the poet Robert Frost to earn the honor, which requires a unanimous vote in both houses of Congress. A year later, he won the Presidential Medal of Freedom, the nation's highest civilian award.

The Cowboy: Reflections of a Western Writer

—Louis L'Amour

Teddy Blue, who was a real cowboy, said that the only two things a cowboy feared were a decent woman and being set afoot.

Fortunately, due to men like Teddy Blue and fifty others we could mention, we do not have to rely on fiction for our picture of the cowboy. We know who he was and what he was like. We have his picture clearly drawn by men who were cowboys or who were there at the time, by women who loved them, married them, and sometimes survived them.

In fiction the cowboy is usually portrayed as an illiterate, and no doubt many were but just as many were not; some had excellent educations, going on to achieve a reputation in other fields. Granville Stuart, Eugene Manlove Rhodes, Charlie Siringo, and many others have told of the cowboy's reading habits.[1]

No other type of man has been the subject of so many written words as the American cowboy. Yet he not only inspired literature and produced literature, he was to a considerable extent a product of his literature. From the very beginning the cowboy was, in the minds of those who wrote about him, a dashing and romantic figure. Moreover, although he would never have admitted it, that was how he saw himself. He knew the realities but believed the illusion. He was, after all, A Man on Horseback.

The Bedouin of the desert, the armored knight, the Cossack—all were figures of romance. The cavalry charge is the essence of poetry, the bayonet charge is not.

A few years ago an eastern writer with a great air of debunking it all commented contemptuously that a cowboy was nothing but a hired man

150

on horseback. Of course. What else? The cowboy knew his job and was happy with it. In most cases he wished for nothing more. He wanted, above all, to be considered a top hand.

Give him a job to do while mounted and he would work from daylight to dark. Ask him to dig a posthole and you had a sour, discontented man. He would dig the posthole but he did not have to like it and he did not.

He had to know horses and cattle, and he needed skill with a rope. His average working day during the early years on the range was fourteen hours, from can-see to can't-see. His night's sleep was usually six hours but when driving a trail herd he could expect to do a stint on night guard, usually about two hours.

His work consisted of rounding up and branding cattle, gathering strays, riding fence, pulling cattle out of bogs, treating cuts or abrasions for screwworms, building and repairing fences, cleaning out water holes, or whatever needed doing.

In the old open-range days he carried a running-iron and branded whatever he found on the range. If an unbranded calf was running with a branded cow he usually applied her brand to the calf. If there was any doubt he branded for the home ranch, whatever it might be. After a few years when fences became common the running-iron disappeared and the stamp-iron was introduced and most of the branding was done during the seasonal roundups.

Over the years the character of the cowboy's work changed considerably. In the earliest days the cattle were Longhorns and they were unlike any cow critter around today. Longhorns were wild animals. Often they hid in thick brush, coming out to feed only at night. They were big, strong, and fierce and would fight anything that walked. As long as a rider was in the saddle he was reasonably safe. Caught afoot, he had two choices—run for his horse and get into the saddle or shoot the steer. Usually he elected to run, as the boss did not look with favor on dead steers, but many a cowhand has blessed the Good Lord and Sam Colt for the pistol he carried.

The saddle stock on most of the ranches consisted of half-broken mustangs. They were small horses, incredibly tough, very agile, and soon developed an instinct for working cattle.

Later, when fences came and ranches became settled operations, horses were bred for the job and the saddle stock became better. It also needed more careful handling. On northern ranges the horses were larger for they were often required to buck snowdrifts and harsher conditions.

Stories of the West are said, by those who do not read them, to be about cowboys and Indians. Actually, that is rarely the case. More often the protagonist is a ranch foreman, a town marshal, a Texas Ranger, an army officer, or a scout for the army. When a cowboy is the protagonist he is usually a drifter, and very rarely is shown at work, doing what has to be done on a ranch.

Usually cowboys were between fifteen and twenty-five years of age, although some were as young as twelve or as old as eighty. By and large they were a hardy breed. Their work was hard, brutal, and demanding. Their food was, in the earlier years, largely beef, beans, and cornbread with molasses for sweetening.

The cowboys were, as a rule, Anglo-Saxon or Irish (as were the bulk of the early pioneers) and they came from every state in the Union and a half dozen European countries.[2] The first cowboys were Texans who learned how to handle cattle from the Mexican *vaqueros* who had begun cultivating the art in the time of Cortez.

Boys from the border states soon added to their number. From Illinois, Iowa, Arkansas, Missouri, and Tennessee, to name a few, boys came to ride north with the trail herds. Boys in those states grew up handling stock, and a point to be remembered is that they grew up hunting meat for the table.

Often those who comment on shooting in the West fail to realize that most boys in the border states grew up shooting. If they did not kill their meat they did not have it to eat, and as ammunition could not be wasted in plinking away at any target that appeared, they took their time and made every shot count. The pioneer boy was usually an excellent shot who wasted no ammunition. Many a girl shot equally well, with Annie Oakley as an example. She began shooting game for her own table and then began hunting for the market.

One professor at a western university has commented that "it was generally agreed that the six-gun was a hard gun to shoot accurately." This is absurd. Among the many men I have known who used such guns, none would agree. There are many dead men who wish it had been true.

The six-gun, for its time, was an exceptionally efficient gun, and in the hands of a man who knew his weapon, his bullet would go exactly where he wished. The Grand Duke Alexis, after seeing the Smith and

Wesson .44 demonstrated by Buffalo Bill Cody, ordered 250,000 of them for the Russian army.

There are literally thousands of cases to demonstrate the effectiveness of the cowboys' marksmanship. There were bad shots then as there are today, but most of the gunfighters served their apprenticeship as buffalo hunters, practicing their marksmanship day after day. Quanah Parker and his Kiowa-Comanche warriors discovered just how well they could shoot at the Battle of Adobe Walls, where twenty-eight buffalo hunters stood off hundreds of his braves.

Cowboys came from everywhere. Teddy Blue, who left an account of his cowboy life in the western classic *We Pointed Them North*,[3] was born in Norwich, England, and was a typical cowboy. Frank Collinson, whose *Life in the Saddle* is another true story of western life, came from Yorkshire, England.[4] Jeff Milton, a cowboy who became a famous western peace officer, was a son of the governor of Florida.[5]

Unfortunately, from the very first the cowboy and the West in general have suffered from the writings of various "authorities" who assume certain things to be true because they are, to their thinking, logical.

The cowboy's attitude toward women, for example, was far different from present attitudes. If we are to understand his times we must know something of his education, family background, and the customs of his time as to what was acceptable conduct and what was not. The cowboy must always be measured by the standards of his time, not ours. Conditions and manners were vastly different.

Moreover, many who presume to write of the western story take altogether too narrow a view of what is "Western" and what is not. The western story is one of the few truly American forms of literature; no other has so captured the world's imagination, and the stories can be found everywhere.

Not only has the western story and film excited readers and viewers everywhere, but western attire has also captured the imagination. Its clean lines and distinctive style have an appeal of their own. Western jeans, boots, belts, and shirts are eagerly sought after, although to the cowboy himself his clothing was simply the most efficient for the man and the work he had to do.

A cowboy's clothing was just what he could afford. In the beginning years he wore any cast-off clothing he happened to have, but the clumsiness of heavy boots or shoes in the stirrup soon brought change.

Many items of his clothing were adapted from those already proven by the Mexican *vaquero*.

The boot with the pointed toe enabled his foot to slip quickly and easily into the stirrup, an important attribute when riding the half-broken or spirited stock on the ranches. The high heel kept the boot from slipping through the stirrup and gave him more to dig in with when roping on foot, as was occasionally the case.

There has been much talk about how unlike the real thing some of the more modern-day costumes are, but you can bet there were few cowhands who would not have worn modern cowboy shirts, boots, and jeans if they had been available.

His first item of expense was his hat, and he wanted the best he could afford. In fact, he often wore both hat and boots that he definitely could not afford. His next major item of expense was his saddle, and here again the cowboy bought the best he could find for the money he could scrape together.

Women were not as scarce on the western frontier as we have been led to believe. Many of the homesteaders had daughters—as did the ranchers themselves. There were always women in the towns, although the cowboy's opportunities for meeting them were few. Dances were not infrequent and there were box suppers from time to time. The red-light districts in most western towns, however, did a brisk business.

Necessarily, the writer dealing with the West will choose its more dramatic moments. Usually, the cowboy of fiction is not too dissimilar from the real thing except that the working cowboy spent most of his time doing just that—working.

Western stories began to be written almost as soon as the West came into being. The mountain man, the cavalry soldier, and the cowboy were exciting material for a writer, and even before this the Indian and the settler had been written about by Chateaubriand and dozens of others.

It has been said that the western story began with Owen Wister's *The Virginian*. This is pure nonsense. Dime novels based on western life had begun appearing about 1860, but Capt. Mayne Reid, an Irish soldier of fortune, had written *The Rifle Rangers* in 1850 and such others as *The Scalp Hunters*, *The War Trail*, and *The Lost Rancho*, to name a few. All this was long before Wister had come West, and some of them were written before he was born.

The flood of dime novels that followed 1860 is a phase of our literature that requires study, not alone as a publishing phenomenon but for its influence on the developing country, for despite the casual way in which the dime novel has sometimes been treated, it had a far-reaching and profound effect.

Following Sir Walter Scott, and borrowing from him, the dime novels did much to influence the behavior of the new generations growing up in the border and western states. Sir Walter Scott, read throughout the East but particularly in the southern states, was a major influence on western behavior. Those who came westward after the collapse of the South at the end of the Civil War brought with them little but their pride, their sense of honor, and something of the code of the cavalier, acquired from Scott.

This same code of behavior was carried along in the dime novels read by many a boy on the farm or in the city before coming West and helped to create some of the ideas as well as situations that developed later.

Far from the wild young ruffian some considered him, the average cowboy came from a Christian, church-going family, and most of his wildness was expressed in charging into town on horseback and firing harmless shots into the air, after which he would head for the nearest saloon and a drink.

The town marshals often were fairly shrewd judges of the character of the men with whom they had to cope. They could quickly distinguish between a healthy young cowhand wanting to blow off some steam and a hard-nosed troublemaker. Marshals also learned to recognize the difference between the would-be gunman and one who was truly dangerous, and acted accordingly.

The boy or man who came West to become the cowboy rode into a land empty but for occasional Indian villages, and while learning much from the land itself, he brought with him a baggage of folklore, song, story, and remembered history, and from this was created a new folklore, a new literary tradition, even new songs.

Along with him he also brought a code, a way of thinking and believing that is still very much alive in America today. Although ignored by many, and dismissed with glib, cynical comments by others, it remains in our subconscious, a strong factor in our social and political thinking.

The cowboy has not ridden off into the sunset, he rides with us, into the future.

Colorado Heritage, 1981, Issue 1

Endnotes

1 *Granville Stuart*, Forty Years on the Frontier as Seen in the Journals and Reminiscences of Granville Stuart, Gold-Miner, Trader, Merchant, Rancher and Politician, *edited by Paul C. Phillips (Cleveland: The Arthur H. Clark Company, 1925). Eugene Manlove Rhodes,* The Rhodes Reader: Stories of Virgins, Villains, and Varmints, *selected by W. H. Hutchinson (Norman: University of Oklahoma Press, 1957). Charles A. Siringo,* A Texas Cow Boy: Or, Fifteen Years on the Hurricane Deck of a Spanish Pony—Taken from Real Life (*Chicago: Rand, McNally & Co., 1886).*

2 *Some historians have estimated that fully a third of western cowboys were African American, but Quintard Taylor, the noted historian of black American history, would agree with L'Amour's assessment. In his* In Search of the Racial Frontier: African Americans in the American West, 1528–1990 *(New York: Norton, 1998), Taylor writes: "If historians have exaggerated the number and influence of western cowboys, they have also erred in their estimates of African Americans in the industry. ... Overall, black cowboys were about 2 percent of the total in the West." He discusses the point further, stating: "Historians' inflated estimates of the number of black cowboys stemmed from a loose interpretation of figures provided by Philip Durham and Everett L. Jones in 1965 [The Negro Cowboys] and Kenneth W. Porter in 1969 ['Negro Labor in the Western Cattle Industry, 1866–1900,' Labor History]." He does go on to say: "While the number of black cowboys was smaller than previously assumed, census data nonetheless show them throughout the region."*

3 *Edward Charles Abbott ("Teddy Blue") and Helena Huntington Smith,* We Pointed Them North: Recollections of a Cowpuncher *(New York: Farrar & Rinehart, 1939). Illustrated with drawings by Ross Santee, and photographs; includes songs with music.*

4 *Frank Collinson,* Life in the Saddle, *edited and arranged by Mary Whatley Clarke; drawings by Harold D. Bugbee (Norman: University of Oklahoma Press, 1963).*

5 *See J. Evetts Haley,* Jeff Milton: A Good Man with a Gun *(Norman: University of Oklahoma Press, 1948); drawings by Harold D. Bugbee.*

I n more than twenty booklets and two book-length histories, Caroline Bancroft carved herself a memorable niche among Colorado historians.

History was in her blood. Her grandfather, the Civil War surgeon Frederick J. Bancroft, cofounded the State Historical and Natural History Society of Colorado, today's Colorado Historical Society. Colorado's Mount Bancroft is named for him. Though as a young woman Caroline Bancroft went east, graduating from Smith College and briefly pursuing a dance career, she was perhaps inevitably drawn back to Colorado.

Through her work as a journalist, she met Colorado's old-timers, and she got them talking. Their tales became her own. In the books and booklets she wrote from the 1940s into the early 1980s, she led readers to the jeep trails, the ghost towns, the lost treasures, and the stories of Colorado's past. She did it in a format that she thought people would read, rather than merely consult. And she was right: Decades after she wrote those booklets, and long after her death in 1985, six of them are still in print and still being read.

In these histories, Bancroft's own voice is always center stage, even when her characters are talking. In her studies of legendary Colorado figures such as Baby Doe Tabor and Margaret "Molly" Brown, she stretches reality to reinvent these women as larger-than-life characters. But in this profile of author Mari Sandoz, we see another side of Caroline Bancroft. Here, we see her affection and admiration for a dear friend and fellow writer, and we see subtle facets of their friendship quietly revealed and fondly remembered.

Mari Sandoz in Colorado

—Caroline Bancroft

"She has long, red hair!" William M. John explained to me delight-
edly in Denver in the summer of 1940.

Bill John was a prominent member of the Colorado Authors' League,
a writer of fiction who had won an O'Henry Memorial Award for short
stories based on his early life in a small town of southern Colorado. He
knew the high plains country well (his father had owned cattle and sheep
ranches), and naturally, with Bill's interests, he would be one of the first to
seek out the newest celebrity on the Denver literary scene—Mari Sandoz.

As a symbol, I have always remembered that statement. The length
of her hair told of her affiliation with the nineteenth century; its color
represented both her warmth of heart and her firebrand political bias.
Both the color and the politics may come as a surprise to people who
knew her in the 1950s. By that time, she was dyeing her hair blonde, and
her anticapitalistic criticisms had faded materially in the light of later
political developments. It was not long after Bill's enthusiastic description
of her that a poet friend brought us together. So began a friendship of
over twenty-five years standing.

At that time, Mari was forty-six years old, having been born on May 10,
1896. Her grueling childhood and early poverty were already known to the
world. Mari's first book, *Old Jules*, which won the *Atlantic Monthly's* $5,000
nonfiction prize in 1935, had told all. Ostensibly, it was a portrait of her Swiss
father, an immigrant to the Niobrara country of northwestern Nebraska.

Sandoz was a rancher, tough pioneer, fine shot, brave outdoorsman,
and a friend to the Indians. But as a husband, he was demanding and
autocratic, going through four wives, and as a father, he was cruel, and,
from my personal point of view, terrifying.[1] Mari's book *Old Jules* was not
only her father's biography but a picture of the whole family and pioneer
life on the regional primitive ranches at the turn of the century.

Apparently Sandoz had some charm, despite his fierce independence (although the first trait never came through in the book to me), and
he was able to command great loyalty and what passed for love from his
children. And of these children, Mari was the oldest. In addition to the
toughest of the ranch work, a large amount of the nursing of her younger
sisters and brothers fell upon her slim shoulders. Yet, despite all of these
harsh duties and grim discouragements, she was able to learn how to read
and write by lamplight, and as her knowledge expanded, she increasingly
yearned for a different life.

Old Jules attempted to suppress these tendencies in his eldest daughter,
but to no effect, for she had inherited his fierceness, his independence,
and his bravery, and what must have been a constitution of barbed-wire
strength. By the time she was in her late teens and for a period of five
years, she taught in a one-room ranch schoolhouse in order to augment
the family finances; while at the same time, she continued sitting up after
she corrected papers, studying by kerosene lamplight to give herself
enough of an education to get into the university at Lincoln.

Of course, Old Jules disapproved. He thought she ought to get married, work hard on a ranch, have children, and live the life dictated by
what (to me) were the standards of the original "male chauvinist pig." Yet
Mari was finally able to slip away to Lincoln, live a hand-to-mouth existence, doing any kind of menial work to keep herself alive, and attend
classes at the University of Nebraska. She could not be accepted as a
qualified student because she had no high school diploma. But that did
not prevent her from attending classes and receiving an education nor
from writing and sending out manuscripts.

Her bent had always been toward the history of the Rocky
Mountain West or of the Plains Indian tribes, whom she had come to
know at the Sandoz ranch. (In fact, later in life she was formally inducted
into the tribe of the Oglala Sioux.)[2] Inevitably, her first manuscripts
were submitted to local journals and publications where their appearance
helped give her confidence. Gradually, she made the big time. Her stories
began to appear in national magazines, even the *Saturday Evening Post*.
Simultaneously, she obtained the position of associate editor of the
Nebraska History Magazine, requiring work with the Nebraska Historical
Society. Now she was on her way.

Mari's first major breakthrough was, however, *Old Jules*, which the
critics deemed a "true American epic" and still do. Two years later her first

novel, *Slogum House*, was published—about which *The New York Times* said: "You may have the feeling it was written on sandpaper with a piece of barbed wire." By 1939 her second novel, *Capital City*, appeared. In this, she attacked the Fascist movement in the United States and gained mixed reviews. Nevertheless, it gave her the courage to break work-a-day ties with her home state and, in 1940, to move to Denver. She wanted to concentrate on research for a biography of Crazy Horse, an Oglala Sioux who was one of the truly great Indian chiefs. She also sought an opportunity to be free in its writing, divorced from all former associations and precepts.

During the two and a half years of Mari's residence in Denver, she lived in an apartment house at 1010 Sherman Street, named the Thomas Carlyle and next door to the Robert Browning and across the street from the Mark Twain, the three forming an appropriate literary cloak for her own poetic and peculiarly American work. Many is the night that we sat

Caroline Bancroft on a 1964 Jeep outing somewhere in the mountains of Colorado

there until three or four in the morning discussing, and discussing some more. Mari and I shared a preoccupation with the nineteenth-century history of the Far West and contemporary politics. But we were also interested in poetry, art, people, horses, wildflowers, architecture, parties, psychic phenomena, and almost anything else that crossed our outer or inner vision. To this day, when I am jeeping in the high country, if someone asks me the name of a wildflower that I have forgotten, I will reply, "Well, I'd know it if Mari Sandoz were here."

That sounds silly. But it is a fact. Even after she left Colorado, Mari would return nearly every summer for a stay of a month or six weeks at the Lazy VV Ranch, four miles north of Nederland in the scenic Colorado Rockies.

This ranch was unique. Although it had working aspects, it was mostly a lavish summertime plaything and was so glamorous that two Hollywood companies used it for short documentary travel films. It was owned by mutual friends of ours, Rose and Lynn Van Vleet of Denver. Here the Van Vleets entertained in the manner in which a Newport millionaire would have entertained on his yacht.

Lynn Van Vleet's business was the Trinidad Bean Company, of which he was president and principal stockholder. But his avocation was breeding thoroughbred Arabian horses, and these were moved each summer from the main brood ranch at Boulder to the Lazy VV for the delight of guests and visitors. Each Sunday a free Arabian horse show was staged, exhibiting Van Vleet's beautiful and unusual stock. Forty-odd years ago, a thoroughbred Arabian was a rarity in the Far West.

Their hospitality was prodigious, and as their houseguests, Mari and I would ride horseback on Arabian mares morning and afternoon along the mountain trails of some 12,000 acres. During these rides, we would talk about everything but particularly the identification of flowers and trees. My mind is much more dreamy and vague than Mari's and not nearly so retentive. But each summer as soon as we would set off, waves of knowledge that I had forgotten in the interim would surge back—in some way associated with Mari's psychic powers.[3]

No doubt others, writing memoirs of Mari, will comment on her generosity, which gave time and encouragement to any struggling writer or artist, her warmth, her fantastic vitality, her versatility, her crusading zeal in many dear causes—particularly for justice and aid to the Indians— her courage, her independence, and her far-encompassing wisdom, well salted with practicality. But she was a person of many facets, and she did not always choose to turn the flashing sides of her jeweled personality in all directions. In spite of her outgoing nature, I never saw her in any relationship, including ours, where some deep reserve did not compel her to withhold a part of herself. To many people, sufficiently sensitive and perceptive to reach beyond the surface, Mari was an enigma.

Her interest in ESP (extrasensory perception) and her denial of all religion were a part of this puzzle. She was fascinated by psychic happenings, particularly the powers of certain mutual acquaintances and of many Indians. Yet, she never permitted herself a full explanation. She was firm in her belief that there was no personal afterlife. Religion, in her view, was mankind's necessary emotional crutch, not worthy of more than a historic or an economic assessment. Yet, she lived a saintly life. She was, however, capable of temper, of impatience or irritation, and, on occasion, of long-dwelling personal resentment. These emotions were usually ephemeral, and only once in the early 1950s did her temper flare in my direction. This was a momentary impulse that sputtered out in twenty-four hours.

During the early 1940s while she lived in Denver, our politics more or less coincided. We were both very pro-Ally. I had been one of the five Colorado incorporators of Defend America by Aiding the Allies and, after Germany invaded Russia in June 1941, went on the board of the Foundation for American-Soviet Friendship. To aid these causes, I was doing considerable speaking and organizing, of which Mari approved and to which she gave donations.

But by 1950, I had become completely disillusioned with the Soviets and was definitely anti-Communist. During one of my nearly annual visits to New York City, Mari and I were having dinner in Greenwich Village, not far from her small walk-up apartment at 23 Barrow Street. She had grown to admire the Communist system more and more and was berating me sharply for my shift. I said very firmly that this was a topic we would have to drop completely from both our present and future conversations. Her temper flared, and our dinner ended on a fairly sour note. (I do not know if Mari was ever a card-carrying member of the Communist party, but there were a number of years when I was suspicious.) The next morning she phoned me at my uncle's apartment where I was staying, issued me a nice invitation, omitting any mention of the night before, and so no rift ever marred our friendship.

With her charm, Mari had made myriad Colorado friends, but she did not choose to keep many through the years. After the Van Vleet ranch was sold in 1951, her visits to Denver were for only a couple or three days in order to complete some piece of research, to appear at an autograph party, or to give a lecture. At these times, so far as I am aware, she notified only a distant cousin who lived in Denver, the Van Vleets, and myself. It was always my custom to take her to her departing plane or train, picking her up usually an hour or so early so that we could sit and leisurely converse at the station or airport before she left.

She had a special affinity for public places. No one who knew Mari well could have failed to note an ambivalence about her setting. She was a lone spirit (and I do not mean lonely). The great sweeping spaces and the elemental grandeur of the high plains country with their bordering Rockies were a complete part of her. She loved their distances and loneliness. I can see her now, standing beside her horse on the ridge of a mountain, while she fought with the winds that wanted to rip a map from her hands. (We also shared a love of maps.) Mari was completely at home.

Yet, when she worked, she often went to a saloon and sat in a booth, while a jukebox blared, drunks fought, and glasses clinked. Here, she would read proof or edit a script. Even when she worked in her own apartment, the radio was a constant accompaniment. With her psychic powers, she could concentrate on her own writing until her subconscious told her something was being said that she wanted to hear. (We did not share this proclivity—mine is strictly a single-path mind, capable of working only in undistracted silence.)

I remember my phone rang close to midnight on November 7, 1942. (She knew that I habitually read or worked until one or two in the morning.) With great excitement, she told me she had just heard on the radio that the Americans had landed in North Africa. (It was already the dawn of November 8 there as we were talking.) Naturally, she was elated and knew that I would be also. She could not wait to let me have the news. But she picked this intelligence out of the air, while she was concentrating on preparing and assembling her notes, some to go with her to New York in December and some to be stored in Denver.

Crazy Horse, her fourth book, had just appeared. In many ways, this 1942 book remained her favorite work. Aside from her long-time affinity with Indians, she had a particular admiration for Crazy Horse and his cleverness in leading Sioux and other warriors during the Battle of the

Little Big Horn in 1876. They succeeded in surrounding the white soldiers under General George A. Custer and in annihilating them. To understand all of their maneuvers, Mari had walked over every hillock of the battlefield, visualizing where each detachment had been stationed or advanced. Before that detailed study, she had interviewed personally dozens of Indians and whites whose lives had in any way touched that of Crazy Horse, thus adding to the meticulous research she had already done in the War Department and at the Bureau of Indian Affairs.

There was a great deal of anguish about the book's publication. She had already signed a contract with Alfred A. Knopf of New York, and Paul Hoffman was acting as her personal editor. He was the same editor who had formerly been with Little, Brown, and Company of Boston and had been instrumental in seeing that she had won the *Atlantic Monthly* $5,000 prize. They were good friends.

But when the manuscript of *Crazy Horse* arrived from Denver, neither Alfred nor Blanche Knopf were enthusiastic about its completion. They sent Paul Hoffman out to Denver to negotiate with Mari. Their orders directed Mari to shorten the manuscript materially, to soften the Indian bias, and to rewrite the picture of Crazy Horse's tragic and treacherous death, stabbed by a white man in 1877 at an Indian agency.[4]

Mari was incensed and flatly refused. She held Paul responsible for not defending her position more stoutly to the publishing house. In a temper, she ended their close friendship.

Meanwhile, *Crazy Horse* appeared in time for the Christmas trade and received very negative reviews. The critics were not prepared to understand a book written entirely from the Indians' viewpoint nor to grasp the mass of details that Mari had assembled. Clifton Fadiman ended his review (probably in an effort to mitigate its generally negative tone) by saying, "Unquestionably, her book, the product of studious labor, will rank among the important records of the history of the American Indian." Fadiman had no idea how prophetic he was. Forty years later, *Crazy Horse* is rated as a masterpiece and, by many, as Mari's finest book.

Mari held her head high and settled into the life of the Village from the base of her little apartment. She made her living by writing articles and short stories, with occasional private teaching. In 1945 the Van Vleets asked her to spend the entire summer, all expenses paid, at the Lazy VV, and there she began work on her novel *The Tom Walker*. Mostly, she reveled in the horseback rides, in the life of the ranch, and in the beauty of the Colorado mountains.

In the winter of 1946, back in New York, a bit of serendipity occurred that had a helpful influence on Mari's emotional and professional life. Having originally met Paul Hoffman in Denver through Mari, our friendship had grown despite the split between the two of them. Paul had been hurt by Mari's action, but he had never lost his affection for her nor his admiration for her talent. Making my usual visit to New York to stay with my uncle, Paul asked me to dinner, and I suggested he come to the apartment first for cocktails. Naturally, he asked about Mari.

On the spur of the moment, I said: "Why don't we ask her to join us for dinner?"

"She won't come," Paul answered.

I went to the phone, caught Mari in, and explained the circumstances.

"All right," she answered, "if you don't mind coming to the Village. I'll meet you in an hour at our little restaurant."

Paul could hardly believe my report, but we finished our drinks and headed for the Village, where we spent an evening that was an unmitigated success. Paul had left Knopf and gone with J. P. Lippincott of Philadelphia, which Mari knew through her sales to the *Saturday Evening Post*, one of Lippincott's holdings. The two old friends had lots to talk about. Not only was their friendship recemented, but through Paul's influence, Westminster Press, another Lippincott holding, published Mari's charming young adult books, *Winter Thunder*, and one of my pets, *The Horse Catcher*.

The Colorado years and associations made an emotional impact on Mari that influenced her life more deeply than can be outlined here. I am happy to say that in the conflicts and strains of those years (many of them confidential), I was not involved other than as a listener. My copy of *Crazy Horse* has an autograph that reads with typical Mari-generosity: "For Caroline Bancroft because she listened to much of this in progress, but—chiefly because she will someday write a better book than this herself. Affectionately, Mari Sandoz."

This flattery was part of Mari's technique. She had an enormous maternal instinct, which she used in full measure on all of her protégés, alternating praise with a spur. In my case, she was determined that I would write well, and if she had anything to do with it, my efforts would prove her correct. (At the time of our meeting, I had been a writer for newspapers and magazines, a literary columnist, and a book critic, but I could not claim any very lasting achievements.) She never gave up with her exhortations and demands.

Nor did she give up the demands on herself. Work was her real passion. In the intervening years, her industry had produced a series of successes: *Cheyenne Autumn*, *The Buffalo Hunters*, *The Cattlemen*, and *Love Song to the Plains* in the nonfiction field; two novels, *Miss Morissa* and *Son of the Gamblin' Man*; and three collections of short pieces, *Hostiles and Friendlies*, *These Were the Sioux*, and *Sandhill Sundays*. *Cheyenne Autumn* had also sold to the movies for a handsome price.

These years also brought many long-delayed honors. In 1950 the University of Nebraska awarded her an honorary degree of Doctor of Literature. In 1954 the Nebraska governor created an annual Mari Sandoz Day, while the state's Native Sons and Daughters gave her an Award for Distinguished Achievement. From 1947 through 1956 she was in charge of Advanced Novel Writing during the summer sessions at the University of Wisconsin. Four of her books were selected in 1955 for the list of "One Hundred Best Books on the West" by the Chicago Corral of Westerners. In 1961 the National Cowboy Hall of Fame gave her a Western Heritage Award and in 1965 the Mari Sandoz Hall was erected at the University of Nebraska.

But now Mari was trapped by a severe illness.

My last meeting with her was in June 1965 in her high-rise apartment at 422 Hudson Street in the Village. She was leading a very secluded life because she knew she had bone cancer, and during our visit, we spent some time evaluating the possibility of the bone cancer abating. Optimistically, she added that there were case histories of persons who had been able to live a moderately normal life for ten years after the first virulent attack. Mari was hoping for a similar surcease because she had eight more books in progress, most of them under contract.

I had known about six of these scripts for years. Two of them were new developments, and we discussed these at some length. There was one big omission—a script that I had read some ten years before, set in Colorado, and never published. It was based on Mari's desire to picture L. W. Van Vleet (always familiarly known as "The Boss") and his relationship to a favorite of the four thoroughbred Arab stallions, stabled each summer at the Lazy VV Ranch.

Colorado was once again a cross-pulling factor in Mari's life. Her friendship with The Boss was as complicated and as contradictory as was each of their natures. He was a short, Napoleonic sort of man who wielded power with egotism, tyranny, and even sadism. As a financial tycoon, he was not interested in the usual social pursuits of the Establishment. He backed away from Denver society and sought out celebrities who had color or brains. He was enormously original and dynamic, and he was in a position to implement most of his ideas and conceits.

Between Mari and The Boss there was a great friendship. He thoroughly enjoyed having her as a houseguest, both at the ranch and at the Van Vleet residence in Denver, and he was sometimes exaggeratedly possessive about her. It was not, however, because he financed many of her trips to Colorado and was exacting his due; it was based on some submerged emotional pull between them, perhaps a compensation unrealized by either. My private opinion, at the time, was that Mari felt a similarity between The Boss and Old Jules and gloried in the fact that here was a man as ruthless and domineering as her father but who delighted in her knowledge and creative powers. Old Jules had rejected her because of her mind and talent, but The Boss embraced them. This was a compensation for Mari's hurt that was tied and knotted out of rawhide leather.

The Boss was a good friend despite his idiosyncrasies—generous, thoughtful, and considerate, when he had a mind to it. If he was belligerent, scornful, and demeaning, which he could be (especially under the influence of alcohol), I would fight back. I would match each rudeness of his with equal rudeness, despite being his houseguest. But not Mari. She would be soft and feminine. Yet, the next day during one of our horseback rides, she would be extremely critical of his behavior and penetratingly analytical of his predilection for causing scenes. But never to his face.

That was what was wrong with the script titled "Foal of Heaven." It was almost the only thing I ever read of hers that was not basically and totally honest. It was as if she wanted to write a novel for him, not for herself. As with all of her work, there were marvelous passages, especially her descriptions of the Arabians and the Colorado scenery, but the really vital and interesting picture of the character, a portrait such as she had done once in Old Jules, was just not there.

Also, her usual tenacity and determination were not there. She once told me that Old Jules had been submitted to some thirty-odd publishers before it won the $5,000 Atlantic Monthly prize in 1935. It had already been rejected by the same publisher that eventually took it. She normally never gave up, and she was never afraid of rewriting. Almost anything she wrote went through three or four drafts as a natural work procedure, and her major works had passages and chapters that had been through seven and eight versions.

Why, then, did she try this Colorado script in only two or three versions with only two or three publishers? I do not know. By the time we were talking of her work in 1965, The Boss had been gone long enough for her to have gained detachment, both about him and about the script. But she no longer had the emotional impulse. It struck me as odd. I never knew her to give up on any other script.

All of the other scripts that were in the hopper imbued her with optimism and offered aspects for shoptalk. She had completed a partially successful version for a book about Custer and hoped to finish it soon, despite her illness.[5] During our long conversation that afternoon, I found it hard to think of her as ill. I still sensed the old enthusiasm, the driving ambition, and the fond memories of Colorado.

But sadly, time was all too short. She died March 10, 1966.

"Two Women Writers: Caroline Bancroft Recalls Her Days with Mari Sandoz," *Colorado Heritage*, 1982, Issue 1

Endnotes

[1] Bancroft had a similar view of her own father, George, who was known for cruelty and alcoholism.

[2] As former Colorado Historical Society chief historian David F. Halaas points out, tribes do not induct non-Indians into their ranks, although many non-Indians continue to assume they do.

[3] Bancroft was an avowed believer in psychic powers and also in ghosts, which she was convinced haunted Denver's Capitol Hill and the mining town of Central City.

[4] It remains unclear as to who actually killed Crazy Horse. While it appears that a Lakota, Little Big Man, may have held Crazy Horse's arms while a soldier bayoneted him, some historians—and Lakotas—dispute this version of the events.

[5] The book was published posthumously as The Battle of the Little Bighorn (Philadelphia and New York: J. B. Lippincott Company, 1966).

A t the time of this article's publication in 1982, Omer Call Stewart was a distinguished professor emeritus of anthropology at the University of Colorado at Boulder and a recognized authority on Native American cultures. After receiving his Ph.D. in 1939, he devoted much of his professional career to furthering the understanding of Ute customs, including practice of the peyote religion. His 1987 book, *Peyote Religion: A History*, and this earlier essay from *Colorado Heritage* remain key sources in the debate that still rages over the Native American Church and its use of peyote—the spineless, hallucinogenic cactus around which one of the church's most sacred ceremonies revolves.

A staunch supporter of the rights of Utes and other tribes, Stewart testified in the 1962 trial in California in which (two years later) that state officially recognized Native Americans' religious freedom, thereby legalizing ceremonial use of the cactus. Stewart later testified in a similar trial—with a similar outcome—in Colorado, the first state with an antipeyote law on the books. In the 1967 trial, Denver artist Mana Pardeahtan, an Apache and a member of the Native American Church, defended his right to possess and use peyote. The judge ruled in his favor, deeming the prohibition of peyote to be unconstitutional and thus reversing a fifty-year ban on its use. The artist, meanwhile, shared his hope that the case would not popularize the cactus among "beatniks and such."

Today, federal law allows Native Americans to ingest the mescaline-bearing peyote cactus in religious ceremonies, but the Controlled Substances Act forbids its use to anyone else, beatnik or otherwise. In the ongoing argument over whether peyote should be forbidden altogether—or whether its use should be extended beyond the reservation—Omer Stewart remains an oft-cited champion of the sacred rights of the Native American.

Peyotism in Colorado

—Omer C. Stewart

While still a graduate student in anthropology at the University of California at Berkeley in January 1938, I was invited to be a participant-observer in an all-night peyote meeting, held near Towaoc on the Ute Mountain Ute reservation in southwestern Colorado. This was my third experience with the Ute peyote religion in a few months, experiences that were to have a profound effect on the course of my career. Since that time my continuing research on the Ute and on the peyote religion has uncovered a great deal of information about this little-understood Native American religion. Over the years I have recorded the similarities in the ceremonies and rituals of the peyote religion in more than twenty-seven tribes from Oklahoma to Canada and from Wisconsin to California. Especially have I fought to protect the religious freedom of those who practice the peyote religion as formalized in the Native American Church.

Those early experiences in 1937–38 made me acutely aware of the vast public misunderstanding over peyote and its use. This prompted me to do a radio broadcast later in 1938 for a University of California radio program over NBC in San Francisco. I then wrote an article about the ceremony in Colorado and Utah, which was published in a local newspaper. These were my initial efforts at applying my discipline of anthropology to further general public education. In the meantime I continued with my scholarly research, writing my Ph.D. dissertation on Washo–Northern Paiute peyotism in 1939.

Following my discharge from the army in 1945, I returned to academic work with an appointment to the University of Colorado in Boulder. As a professor there, I worked to inform the general public as well as my students and fellow anthropologists about peyote and the peyote religion. Late in 1946 I began lecturing, and it seems like I lectured on the peyote religion in at least twenty towns, demonstrating the ritual objects—drum, fan, staff, and rattle—and singing several peyote songs in the American Indian style that I had learned. The questions and discussions that followed my demonstrations revealed that the old prejudices against the word "peyote" remained. I became well aware that a single lecture would probably change none of these long-held opinions.

Throughout my professional career as an anthropologist, I have published a number of works on the subject of the peyote religion. In 1948 the first volume in the University of Colorado Studies Series in Anthropology was my "Ute Peyotism: A Study of a Cultural Complex," completed in 1938, but its publication was delayed by World War II. Over the years I have published extensively in the *American Anthropologist, Southwestern Lore*, the *Delphian Quarterly*, and other scholarly journals. ... [1]

Although my research has uncovered many documented facts on the early use of peyote, much of what I have learned comes from oral tradition. While it is most inexact at fixing dates and is also limited in accuracy, I have received information from old Southern Ute informants that supplements the early written documents and also serves as a corrective to some of the written reports.

Peyotism has been practiced by the two southwestern Colorado Ute tribes—the Southern Ute and the Ute Mountain Ute—since the turn of the century. Yet peyote and its use are not native to Colorado. The peyote cactus grows in a limited area near Laredo in Texas and in Mexico from the Rio Grande to the region of San Luis Potosí. While it can be documented that peyote was widely used in ceremonies in Mexico in the sixteenth century, the development of the rituals associated with its use in the United States occurred near Laredo, Texas, and came from the Lipan Apache. They invented new Apache-style ritual songs and music and may have added some ritual elements to the Carrizo Indian peyote ceremony they learned. The peyote ceremonies contain Christian features and qualities. Since the religion indigenous to the Ute contained none of these concepts or ritual elements, the peyote religion spread to them as a cultural complex.

The documents establish that both the Lipan and the Mescalero Apache knew about peyote and Christianity by 1770—nearly a century before the earliest documented evidence of peyotism in the United States. The transmission of the peyote ceremonies was direct from Laredo by known Lipan Apache, who were named as the first teachers of peyotism to the Kiowa and the Comanche on their reservation in Oklahoma in the late 1870s and early 1880s.

Buckskin Charlie, a Southern Ute chief, was one of the first to become acquainted with the use of peyote. Oral tradition states that he was introduced to the peyote ceremony while visiting the Cheyenne and Arapaho Indian agency in Oklahoma in 1896.[2] The Kiowa and Comanche then introduced the peyote ceremony to their neighbors, the Arapaho and Cheyenne.

The accounts differ as to when the Ute first learned the peyote ceremony; all of them document its introduction by the Cheyenne and Arapaho into southern Colorado. Over the years the Southern Ute have been questioned on the early history of peyotism. In 1948 Tony Buck, Buckskin Charlie's son, stated that in 1900 an Arapaho came to Ignacio two or three times and stayed for extended periods, bringing peyote and teaching the ritual. Tony also said that he had attended ceremonies for forty-eight years and that his father was an early leader. In 1949 it was again stated that peyotism began among the

A Peyote Ceremony

The meeting place is a tipi with its entrance to the east. A crescent-shaped altar and fire are prepared according to custom. A drum, feather fan, eagle humerus whistle, gourd rattle, Bull Durham tobacco, and sagebrush complete the necessary ritual equipment. The chief or leader usually supplies the peyote for the meeting. Members bathe before the meeting, and about nightfall they gather in small groups outside the tipi—first the chief, then the chief-drummer, the cedarman, next the men, then the women and children with the fire-chief last—all making their way into the tipi.

The leader places the "chief peyote" upon some sagebrush leaves on the top of the altar and prays. Everyone is invited to speak of their ills and struggles, so that prayers may be voiced in their behalf. The Bull Durham tobacco is passed and cigarettes are made and lit from the glowing fire-stick. Each person blows the first four puffs of smoke toward the "chief peyote" on the altar and prays. The cigarette butts are then placed at the base of the altar.

Next sprigs of sagebrush are passed and the leaves are rubbed between the hands, sniffed, rubbed over the limbs, and beaten four times against the chest to purify the body. A sack of peyote follows the sage, and each adult takes four buttons. Since the peyote is extremely bitter and nauseous, coughing and spitting often succeed the arduous swallowing. Everyone sits as still as possible until all have finished eating the medicine, because the partaking of the divine plant during meetings is a sacred procedure and supposed to be accompanied by silent prayer.

Southern Ute in the Ignacio area and spread to the Ute Mountain Ute at Towaoc, reiterating that the first leader was Buckskin Charlie, who had been visited by Cheyenne Indians who taught him its use.

In 1948 Isaac Cloud was recognized as the leader of the peyote religion among the Southern Ute. In an interview he stated that he commenced directing services in 1915, having learned the ritual from Buckskin Charlie and his wife, Emma Buck. Emma had obtained a supply of peyote from Sam Lone Bear, the notorious Sioux peyote supplier and missionary who had settled among the Uncompahgre Ute at Dragon, Utah, in early 1914.

During these early years of peyote use, the Ute must have been very secretive or the officials of the Bureau of Indian Affairs (BIA) were very nonobservant. In 1916 and again in 1919, the Bureau of Indian Affairs agents of both the Southern Ute and the Ute Mountain Ute denied its existence on these reservations.[3]

After the eating, the chief holds the staff and fan, shakes the rattle, and sings the Opening Song, accompanied by the chief-drummer's rapid drum beats. Only four songs have to be sung at fixed times: the Opening Song, the Midnight Water Call, the Morning Water Call, and the Closing Song. During the remainder of the ritual each man sings any song he wishes when it is his turn to lead, holding the staff and fan in one hand and shaking the rattle with the other. Women neither hold the staff to lead the singing nor beat the drum.

With midnight and the Midnight Water Call, the fire-chief replenishes the fire, the Midnight Song is sung, and prayers are offered through four puffs of smoke. All drink water. Singing then continues with renewed vigor, each using their own equipment. Personal supplies of peyote may be consumed after midnight, and prayers continue to be offered.

A special morning ritual duplicates some features of the Midnight Water Call; the fire is refueled and the central altar area cleaned. The chief then sings the Morning Water Call, and following the four blasts on the whistle, a woman, usually the chief's wife, brings in the water and kneels. After ceremonial duties, the water is again spilled on the ground, a breakfast follows, and the Closing Song is sung, followed by more lengthy prayers and blessings. All equipment is dismantled and put away, and then the fire-chief leads the exit, followed by the chief. Once the ritual is over, the women leave to prepare the noon feast and the men to rest, relating their spiritual experiences and visions.

—Excerpted and edited from Stewart, "Ute Peyotism," 1948.

It is indeed surprising, then, that in 1917 the Colorado state legislature would pass the Crowley Bill, prohibiting the use of peyote in the state. This law, of course, did not affect peyote use on the reservation, where the Ute were subject only to federal laws, but did prohibit its transfer through the United States mails and use outside reservation boundaries. Colorado became the first state to pass an antipeyote law. The year before, federal legislation in the form of the Gandy Bill had failed to pass the United States Congress. The campaign against peyote in Colorado was led by women's organizations, such as the Parent Teacher Associations and the Women's Christian Temperance Union. The precipitating force for the final passage of the Crowley Bill, however, was Gertrude Bonnin, a Yankton Sioux who had worked for fourteen years as a social worker among the Ute of Utah. While in Utah, she became an opponent of the Sioux peyote proselytizer, Sam Lone Bear, who appears to have been a peyote supplier also to the Southern Ute. Bonnin lobbied to

Omer C. Stewart and members of the Ute Mountain Ute tribe following a peyote service at Towaoc, Colorado, in January 1938. Front row, left to right: John Cuthair, Herbert Stecker, Alfred Lang. Rear row, left to right: Stewart, Charlie Lang, Edward Eytoo (or Tom Root Jr.), Louis Wing.
(Courtesy of the Omer C. Stewart Collection, 2nd Accession 58—Ute Photos, Archives, University of Colorado at Boulder Libraries)

have the Gandy Bill passed in Washington, D.C., in 1916, and following its defeat, transferred her efforts to Colorado, where she met with success.

The passage of the law did not, however, prevent the practice of the peyote religion among the Ute. In fact, in a 1926 letter to the BIA, Mrs. C. W. Wiegel, who was chairman of the committee on Indian welfare of the Colorado Federation of Women's Clubs in Denver, stated that "it has been reported to me that during the past winter the practice of using Piota [sic] medicine and the form of worship that goes with it has been introduced to the Ute Indian Reservation at Ignacio and is spreading rapidly among them. The better class of Indians are filled with consternation and are appealing for help to stamp it out before it ruins all the young people."[4] In answering the accusations to the BIA, E. E. McKean, the superintendent at Ignacio, defended peyotism, stating that "it is very clear that her information is indefinite and exaggerated. It is true that there has been a small amount of peyote coming at different times to a few of the Indians on this reservation. I would also add that these Indians are among the better class, both from the point of industry and abiding by the law. ... There is small grounds for alarm of its spreading among these Indians."[5]

Many years later, while testifying in 1953, Isaac Cloud used the period of 1919 to 1928 when E. E. McKean was in charge of the BIA in Ignacio, as a time marker. Isaac said that about that time Sam Lone Bear brought peyote and ran meetings three times in Ignacio, but he knew that Sam had been convicted and had spent time in prison. Isaac also named men from Oklahoma who came to Ignacio for meetings: Sam Buffalo, Claude Hill, George Hill, Albert Hofman, Brown Flocko, and John Peak Heart. In addition to being the first important and continuous peyote proselytizer to the Ute Mountain Ute, John Peak Heart had attended the well-known Indian school at Carlisle in 1886–87 and was a peyote leader among the Cheyenne. Although Sam Lone Bear had visited the Ute at Ignacio and at Towaoc about 1915 or 1916, it was Heart who, repeatedly each summer, brought peyote to the Ute Mountain Ute and remained with them for weeks to teach them how to conduct the peyote ritual.

The first local peyote leader at Towaoc appears to have been James Mills, a twenty-seven-year-old Ute Mountain Ute. He had impressed Heart sufficiently to be invited to return to Oklahoma with him and to be an apprentice in peyotism. Beginning in 1918, Mills was Heart's assistant in Colorado each summer and remained as the resident peyote leader between his visits, which continued until the early 1950s.[6]

While peyote ceremonies continued to be held, subsequently formalized in the incorporation in various states as the Native American Church, such rituals, dependent upon the use of peyote, were illegal in Colorado and in several other states. In 1962 the antipeyote law was challenged in California, and although my testimony was stricken from the record, it was restored by the California Supreme Court in 1964 and was used when that court ruled that the state had an obligation to protect the religious freedom of the Native American. The 1917 law in Colorado was then challenged in 1967, following the arrest of Mana Pardeahtan for possession of peyote. I also testified in this case. Citing the precedent of the California case along with the other evidence and documents provided, the Colorado court declared the 1917 law unconstitutional.[7]

Bringing the First Amendment fight to an end, this 1967 ruling greatly influenced the Colorado state legislature to amend its narcotic law in 1969 to permit the use of peyote in the religious services of the Native American Church. After fifty years, the right of a people to practice their religion in freedom had been upheld. The struggle to educate and to inform people about cultural practices that are different from their own, however, continues.

"Friend to the Ute: Omer C. Stewart Crusades for Indian Religious Freedom,"
Colorado Heritage, 1982, Issue 1

Endnotes

[1] *Stewart's authoritative* Peyote Religion: A History, *was published five years after this essay (Norman: University of Oklahoma Press, 1987).*

[2] Woodson, Darlington, Oklahoma, to Day, Ignacio, Colorado, 13 July 1896, Federal Records Center, Denver.

[3] West to Larson, 2 November 1916, from Ignacio; also denied by Symons to Larson, 14 November 1916, from Towaoc; McKean to BIA, 14 April 1919; Johnson to BIA, 15 April 1919 (Federal Records Center, Denver).

[4] In 1926 Sioux antipeyotist Gertrude Bonnin was a national lecturer for the National Federation of Women's Clubs and may be suspected of having been the "better class of Indian" who spurred

Mrs. Wiegel to action. Wiegel to Burke, 19 May 1926, Federal Records Center, Denver.

[5] McKean to BIA, 9 June 1926, Federal Records Center, Denver.

[6] David F. Aberle and Omer C. Stewart, *Navaho and Ute Peyotism: A Chronological and Distributional Study*, University of Colorado Studies, Series in Anthropology, No. 6, 1957.

[7] In the County Court in and for the City and County of Denver and State of Colorado, Criminal Action No. 9454, *The People v. Mana Pardeahtan*, finding of 27 June 1967, Judge William Conley. Reported, with photo of Judge Conley and attorneys Deikman and Cook, *Rocky Mountain News*, 28 June 1967.

Rarely seen without a tweed jacket and his trademark schoolboy's backpack, popular University of Colorado at Denver history professor Tom "Dr. Colorado" Noel waltzes into classrooms, offices, and conference rooms with a broad grin and a hearty handshake. He greets everyone by first name, even those he has only met once or twice before. He likes libations and lots of friends to share them with. So why did Colorado's king of conviviality take up the story of antagonistic "Big Bill" Haywood, "the most hated and feared figure in America"?

Noel knows a good story when he sees one. The author or coauthor of more than two dozen books, he is never without a batch of index cards to write down interesting bits of Colorado history picked up from reading or casual conversation. Those notes embellish his historic preservation and western history lectures, his weekly *Rocky Mountain News* column, and the countless tours he leads through Colorado's historic places for the Colorado Historical Society.

On his most popular tour, Noel takes participants into Denver's oldest saloons, where he serves up a concoction of social, cultural, and industrial history. His stories borrow from his 1982 book, *The City and the Saloon: Denver, 1858–1916*, a project that sparked his interest in labor history and introduced him to William Haywood.

Taverns, Noel wrote, sometimes served as impromptu union halls. Workers gathered there to socialize, drink, and discuss miserable, unfair working conditions. Knowing this, labor organizers such as Haywood used bars as recruitment centers and strike headquarters.

Using bar tours to teach labor history to public audiences typifies Noel's ability to relate academic subjects to everyday life. That style carries through to his writing as well, as this short biography demonstrates.

William D. Haywood:
"The Most Hated and Feared Figure in America"

—Thomas J. Noel

Big Bill Haywood was born in sixtynine in a boardinghouse in Salt Lake City.

He was raised in Utah, got his schooling in Ophir, a mining camp with shooting scrapes, faro Saturday nights, whiskey spilled on pokertables piled with new silver dollars.

When he was eleven his mother bound him out to a farmer, he ran away because the farmer lashed him with a whip. That was his first strike.

He lost an eye whittling a slingshot out of scruboak. ...

When he was fifteen he went out to the mines in Humboldt County,

Nevada,

his outfit was overalls, a jumper, a blue shirt, mining-boots, two pair of blankets, a set of chessmen, boxinggloves and a big lunch of plum pudding his mother fixed for him. ...

At Silver City, Idaho, he joined the W.F.M., there he held his first union office. ...

From then on he was an organizer, a speaker, an exhorter, the wants of all the miners were his wants; he fought Coeur D'Alenes, Telluride, Cripple Creek,

joined the Socialist Party, wrote and spoke through Idaho, Utah, Nevada, Montana, Colorado to miners striking for an eighthour day, better living, a share of the wealth they hacked out of the hills.

—John Dos Passos

"I don't know of any Socialists or Communists in the Colorado labor movement today," Harold V. Knight reflected in 1984, "but there are some Republicans." Knight, the first director of the Colorado American Civil Liberties Union, a longtime columnist for the *Colorado Labor Advocate*, and author of *Working in Colorado*, adds that "with a few exceptions, the unions are declining in numbers and in clout." In recent years, successful union busting of the air traffic controllers, the Adolph Coors Company, Continental Airlines, Frontier Airlines, and the Monfort Packing Company has swelled the ranks of non-union firms. This decline of the labor movement has come at a time when unions are, as Knight puts it, "more conservative than ever before."

Labor has not always been so tame. Once Colorado workers were championed by a man who delighted in stepping before a crowd and bellowing, "I'm a two-gun man from the West!" After a dramatic pause, he would draw a crimson Socialist party membership card from one pocket and a red IWW card from another. He was William Dudley Haywood, the first and last major Colorado labor leader to glory in socialism, in communism, and in the class struggle.

William D. Haywood was probably Colorado's most notorious character in the early twentieth century. President Theodore Roosevelt condemned Haywood and his sidekicks as "undesirable citizens" who belonged behind bars. *The New York Times* called Haywood "the most hated and feared figure in America." And Haywood looked the part. He was a big, burly bulldog, standing six feet tall and weighing over 220 pounds. The loss of his right eye in a childhood slingshot accident gave him a sinister look, as did his characteristic scowl. Friend and foe alike learned to call him Big Bill.

Within the labor movement this feisty cyclops lurched to the left wing of every organization he joined. He helped steer the Western Federation of Miners (WFM) out of the conservative American Federation of Labor and into the Socialist Party of America. Then Haywood left the WFM to help found the more radical Industrial Workers of the World (IWW or Wobblies) in 1905. He was too radical even for the Socialist party, which expelled him from its national executive committee in 1912. Other Socialist leaders denounced Haywood as a champion of the Red faction advocating violent overthrow of the capitalist system.

Haywood was America's leading radical with the exception of his friend Eugene V. Debs, the head of the American Railway Union and a quadrennial Socialist candidate for president of the United States. Haywood was a comrade of Emma Goldman, Mary ("Mother") Jones, Mabel Dodge Luhan, and John Reed; they cherished and cultivated Big Bill as the grass-roots radical of the Rockies.

Born in Salt Lake City in 1869, Haywood experienced a childhood that helps to explain his extremism. In his autobiography he recalled the burial of his father, a miner felled by pneumonia when Bill was three. That, Haywood boasted, was the last time he went to church. Like many others on the labor-short western frontier, this youngster became a wage earner early. Haywood began working at the age of nine and graduated to underground work in the mines at sixteen. He spent his adolescence following mining booms throughout Utah, Nevada, and Idaho. In between mining jobs, Haywood worked for farmers, ranchers, and shopkeepers.

After his marriage, this itinerant worker tried homesteading. Sharing the fate of the majority of homesteaders, Haywood sank hard work into his place but was never able to prove up and take full possession. After the federal government ordered him off his Nevada spread, Haywood wrote that "it seemed as if a black curtain had been pulled down on the future; there was no ray of hope. ... There was nothing left; no compensation for the work I had put into the homestead, for the house I had built, the fences I had run, the trees I had set out."

To make matters worse, the Haywoods lost their land in 1893, the year of the depression and the collapse of silver mining. Feeling "more depressed than I had ever been in my life," Haywood considered joining Coxey's Army, which he later celebrated as "one of the greatest unemployed demonstrations that ever took place in the United States."

Big Bill began to sour on the American dream. He was not alone. Thousands of others had rushed into the Rocky Mountain West filled with visions of gold, silver, and property ownership. After 1893 many of these fortune seekers found themselves landless and jobless with backaches and lung problems, begging to toil ten to fourteen hours a day for twenty-five cents an hour. The mining frontier had evolved into a depression-cursed corporate world of huge underground ore factories and hot, smoky smelters.

In 1896 Haywood found work in Silver City, Idaho. He discovered how dangerous underground work was when he saw a falling slab of rock crush his workmate's face against a drill. Haywood helped pick up the body and take it to the waiting family. Shortly afterwards, Haywood almost lost his right arm when it was pinned between a mine car and an ore chute 3,000 feet underground. Neither his dead companion's family nor the unemployed Haywood was compensated in any way. Miners, as Haywood discovered firsthand, assumed horrible risks and bore the full consequences. Broken equipment was repaired—broken men were simply replaced.

Big Bill was ready to listen when Edward Boyce, president of the WFM, came to Silver City to preach the union gospel. The union, formed in 1893 in a Butte, Montana, jail cell by Boyce and other imprisoned strikers, had grown rapidly, particularly after its successful 1894 strike in Cripple Creek, Colorado. There the WFM achieved its greatest victory, getting mineowners to recognize the union and to pay a three-dollar minimum wage for a maximum workday of eight hours.

Haywood became a zealous WFM convert. He boasted of never missing a meeting and soon became the WFM's star recruiter. Long before the "closed shop" was legal, Big Bill made it the law in the mines by routinely telling miners to join the WFM or "hit the trail." Everywhere he went Haywood talked, argued, and fought for his union. Down in the mines, up in the saloons, in the union halls, and on the picket lines—his toughness became legendary.

Bill Haywood awaits trial for the murder of Idaho's ex-governor, 1907. The jury found him not guilty.

181

Both Boyce and Charles Moyer, who succeeded him as WFM president, were impressed with the one-eyed giant. He was a good, if unorthodox, administrator who stored notes, membership forms, and receipts in his hatband. Haywood was particularly hard-nosed about collecting union dues and keeping financial records straight. He helped the WFM avoid the fraud, theft, and mismanagement that plagued some of the other unions.

After occupying every office in the Silver City local, Haywood was selected as the union's national secretary-treasurer. When the WFM moved its national headquarters from Butte to Denver in 1900, Big Bill came to the Mile High City where he would direct the WFM's bitterest, bloodiest, and last major campaign.

With his wife and two small daughters, Haywood settled into a house at 1250 Evans (now Cherokee) Street. From there he took the streetcar to his office, room 625 of the Mining Exchange Building at Fifteenth and Arapahoe Streets (demolished in the 1960s to build the Brooks Towers Apartments).

Haywood also worked on the WFM's monthly *Miners' Magazine*, which declared in its first issue in January 1900:

> We will at all times and under all conditions espouse the
> cause of the producing masses, regardless of religion, nation-
> ality or race, with the object of arousing them from the
> lethargy into which they have sunk and which makes them
> willing to live in squalor, while their masters revel in the
> wealth stolen from labor.

Haywood stuck to this conviction to the end of his life.

Although the support of Colorado Governor Davis H. Waite had made possible the WFM's achievement of a three-dollar, eight-hour day in the Cripple Creek mines in 1894, subsequent strikes helped to convince Haywood that labor could not depend on the conventional political process. After the WFM struck Leadville mines in 1896, the mineowners came up with a new tactic. They persuaded Governor Albert W. McIntire (who succeeded Waite in 1895) to send in the Colorado National Guard to protect their mines and their strike-breakers. The National Guard, however, did nothing to prevent the harassment of Eugene Debs, who had come to Leadville to rally the strikers.

Haywood was much impressed with Debs and followed him into the Socialist camp in 1897. Shortly afterwards Haywood helped persuade the WFM to join the Socialist coalition.

Three years after the Leadville strike was snuffed out, Governor Frank Steunenberg used the same tactics to crush a WFM strike in northern Idaho. Steunenberg, a Populist, had been elected governor in 1896 with WFM support. Once in office, however, his sympathies shifted from labor to management.

Haywood's skepticism about working within the existing political system was deepened by the obfuscation of Colorado authorities on the eight-hour day law. Colorado Governor Charles S. Thomas and the legislature approved an eight-hour maximum workday law for miners, smelterworkers, and certain other occupational groups in 1899. In 1902, however, the Colorado Supreme Court declared the law unconstitutional even though the United States Supreme Court had upheld Utah's 1895 eight-hour law.

In November 1903 Colorado voters would approve a constitutional amendment for an eight-hour day by a margin of 72,980 to 26,266. The Colorado legislature, however, would frustrate the electorate by enacting a watered-down, loophole-ridden version that enabled mine and smelter owners to continue using ten- and twelve-hour workdays. This allowed

In 1903, the Colorado National Guard sent hundreds of men to Cripple Creek to crush the hopes of Haywood and the Western Federation of Miners for an eight-hour day for all Colorado mine and smelter workers.

management to use two instead of three shifts per day. The eight-hour workday was a simple issue that management and its allies in state government turned into a complex and difficult-to-enforce measure.

In June 1903 representatives of Denver Smeltermen's Union No. 93 proposed a strike to Haywood and other members of the WFM executive board. Representatives of the Globeville local reported that 70 percent of Denver's smelterworkers still toiled twelve hours a day while the remaining 30 percent worked ten-hour days. Starting pay for the twelve-hour day was $2.50. Ten-hour-a-day workers received $2.00 at the Globe smelter and $1.75 a day at the Grant smelter.

Haywood, who had successfully spearheaded unionization of the smelterworkers beginning in 1902, went to a mass meeting of smelterworkers at the Globeville town hall on July 3, 1903. After a unanimous declaration at midnight, the WFM began its strike on July 4. "There were no rest days, no Sundays, no holidays" for smelterworkers, according to Haywood, because "the fires that melted the ores, like the fires of hell, must never cool." Workers walked out of the huge Grant smelter, allowing the fires to cool and causing the metal and slag to congeal and freeze the furnaces. The American Smelting and Refining Company never reopened the Grant smelter but did rekindle the neighboring Argo and Globe smelters.

"Now that we had to fight for the eight hour day," Haywood wrote later in his autobiography, "it would involve one strike after another, some of which would become very bitter." This was precisely what happened. WFM miners, even those receiving good wages, joined a statewide sympathy strike in support of the striking smelterworkers in Denver and Colorado City (an industrial area of Colorado Springs where Cripple Creek gold ores were processed).

Between July 1903 and July 1904, Colorado experienced its bitterest, most widespread labor war. Several dozen men lost their lives during the conflict, making it Colorado's second-deadliest labor war. Only the 1914 coal miners' struggle, where over a hundred lives were lost in the violence that culminated with the Ludlow Massacre, was more violent.

As WFM President Charles Moyer spent most of his time jailed on charges that were later dropped, Secretary-Treasurer Haywood spearheaded the strike. Soon the struggle shifted from the eight-hour day to the survival of the WFM. Mineowners hired guards to protect their mines and defend strikebreakers. Mineowners also persuaded Governor

James H. Peabody to declare martial law and to send the Colorado National Guard into Cripple Creek, Telluride, and other hot spots.

Governor Peabody, a Republican businessman from Cañon City, showed little sympathy for the striking miners. In his July 30, 1903, statement to the people of Colorado, the governor blasted "the socialistic, anarchistic objects and methods of the Federation" under "the evil influences of a criminal leadership." Haywood responded in kind and also brandished his favorite weapon—humor. *Miners' Magazine* carried one apparently bogus letter to "His Excellency, the Governor of Colorado" from Czar Nicholas II of Russia. Therein the czar commiserated with the governor, confiding that "I have had the same insubordination to deal with in the convict mines of Siberia."

When violence and murder flared, Governor Peabody and the mine owners attributed it to the WFM. With the notable exception of Thomas M. Patterson's *Rocky Mountain News* and David Day's *Durango Democrat*, many newspapers in Colorado blamed the "Western Federation of Murderers."

Even the Catholic bishop of Denver, Nicholas C. Matz, told his flock in the *Denver Catholic Register* on June 20, 1903, to "choose between the Western Federation and your church." Haywood thereupon denounced the bishop as an "ecclesiastical parasite" and a "brazen and palpable liar" and offered to donate $1,000 to the Immaculate Conception Cathedral building fund if the bishop would "submit an honest itemized statement of his stewardship."

The bishop, however, had other financial resources. These included J. P. Morgan, the New York money mogul, to whom the bishop wrote an assurance that "our timely stand in behalf of order and in defense of capitalism has had considerable to do with our successful opposition to strikes and the stamping out of lawlessness in our labor troubles."

With the church, the state, public opinion, and the mine and smelter owners united against them, the WFM began looking for a way out of the strike. On December 5, 1903, the executive board passed a resolution that "the Western Federation of Miners has, at all times, been ready and willing to go more than halfway in meeting the mine operators of the state, and to use every honorable effort to bring to a close this conflict, that has left scars upon the welfare and prosperity of every citizen of the state."

Management's response came from Adjutant General Sherman Bell, whom Peabody sent to Cripple Creek with the Colorado National

Guard. Upon his arrival in the gold region, Bell announced that he was there "to do up this damned anarchistic federation." General Bell and his guardsmen, in collusion with private guards hired by the mine owners, proceeded to force pro-union Teller County officials to resign, to arrest strikers and imprison or deport them, to destroy WFM union halls and stores, and to ransack the office of the district's pro-union newspaper, the *Victor Record*.

By August of 1904 most Colorado mines, mills, and smelters were back in operation using non-union labor. WFM members were blacklisted and refused jobs unless they repented. By December 1904 all eight of the Cripple Creek district WFM locals had been exterminated and statewide the forty-two strong WFM locals of 1902 had been reduced to thirty feeble locals. By June of 1905 Haywood recommended that assessment of the locals be dropped, and the WFM discontinued paying benefits to sick and injured union members. Although the strike was broken and the WFM would never fully recover, it never officially called off the 1903–04 strike for an eight-hour day.

Haywood and the WFM continued their hopeless struggle in an effort to attract national attention to what was happening in Colorado. This tactic did work. Two 1904 articles in *McClure's Magazine*, editorials in *The New York Times*, and other coverage focused national attention on the Colorado labor war. A rash of books and pamphlets published from 1904 to 1906 also appeared to credit and discredit the various parties to the strike. One of the most thoughtful and reliable evaluations came from Henry M. Teller, Colorado's senior statesman. Teller, who served in the United States Senate from statehood in 1876 to 1909, except for a stint as secretary of the interior under President Chester A. Arthur, was widely respected in most quarters. Without naming Governor Peabody or any of the other principals, Teller concluded:

> The acts of the military authorities, not less than their utter-
> ances, show conclusively that they do not recognize the fact
> that their true and only function is to protect the rights of
> both parties. ... On the contrary, they act upon the theory
> that they are employed to disrupt the unions, and, indeed,
> they have openly declared that to be their purpose. The gross
> injustice of such a position is evident to all the world, and has
> brought our state into undeserved disrepute.

In this statement, published in the *Rocky Mountain News* on July 24, 1904, Senator Teller listed some of the consequences of Colorado's efforts to crush the WFM:

1.) The State has incurred a great debt which will bear heavily upon the people in the immediate future. But what is of greater importance to us than the loss of money and payment of extra taxes is the disgrace inflicted upon our state by the course of the military government.

2.) The press of the United States is almost a unit in condemning the methods employed by the military.

Both Teller and Senator Thomas M. Patterson had petitioned President Theodore Roosevelt to investigate the situation in Colorado. Roosevelt, who had recommended his former fellow Rough Rider Sherman Bell for the adjutant generalship of the Colorado National Guard, saw no need for federal intervention.

Haywood continued to draw attention to the tactics used by the state of Colorado until a knock came on the door of his Denver home shortly before midnight on February 17, 1906. A deputy sheriff without a warrant arrested him. At the county jail, Haywood discovered that WFM President Charles Moyer and George Pettibone, a blacklisted WFM miner, had also been jailed. Early that morning the three were taken to the Oxford Hotel and then whisked onto a train in the early morning darkness.

This was perhaps the most bizarre of Haywood's encounters with the "law and order" element. Pinkerton Detective Agency reports reveal that James McParland, manager of the western division of the Pinkerton Detective Agency in Denver, had carefully planned the arrests in cooperation with Governor Jesse F. McDonald of Colorado and Governor Frank R. Gooding of Idaho.

Pinkerton detectives had been shadowing Haywood, Moyer, and Pettibone for weeks. "We may have considerable trouble in extraditing them," McParland wrote to Governor Gooding on February 2, 1906. In an earlier letter to Gooding dated January 30, 1906, McParland promised to "keep close shadow" on Haywood because he "has said on several occasions [that friends] would get him off on a boat to some foreign country."

In the coded correspondence between McParland and the two governors, Haywood was known as "Viper," Moyer as "Copperhead," and Pettibone as "Rattler," while McParland called himself "Owl," Governor Peabody "Elk," and Governor McDonald "Antelope." "Justice" was the code name for Pinkerton's National Detective Agency. All went according to the Pinkerton plan. The three labor leaders were arrested separately and each was "placed in a hack and taken to 40th Street where the special train that you [i.e., the governors] arrange should be stationed to pull out when all three prisoners are placed on board. ... No stops should be made until after it has passed the Colorado line."

On the train, Haywood recognized Bulkeley Wells, manager of the Smuggler-Union Mine in Telluride, who had been put in charge of the Colorado National Guard in San Miguel County's campaign against the WFM. "Later Bulkeley Wells came into the car with a bottle of whisky and asked us to have a drink," Haywood recalled in his autobiography. "We did, handling the glass rather awkwardly on account of the handcuffs." From Wells, Hayward learned that they were on a special train headed for the Idaho State Penitentiary in Boise to be charged with the murder of Frank Steunenberg, Idaho's ex-governor.

Harry Orchard had set the bomb that killed Steunenberg at his home and after repeated sessions with Pinkerton agent McParland, Orchard had produced a confession. It declared that Haywood, Moyer, Pettibone, and the "inner circle" of the WFM had commissioned him to kill the governor, who had helped to crush the WFM strike in the Coeur d'Alene region. Haywood countered that Orchard, an unstable criminal whose real name was Albert Horseley, had been hired by the mine owners to infiltrate and discredit the WFM.

Clarence Darrow, the celebrated Chicago defense attorney, agreed to represent Haywood, Moyer, and Pettibone. Haywood's trial came first, after he had spent thirteen months in the Idaho penitentiary. *The New York Times* of April 21, 1907, called this trial "the most important event that occurred in Western America in recent years." Writers Jack London and Maxim Gorky came to Haywood's defense, as did 50,000 protesters in Boston and 20,000 in New York City. In Colorado, Haywood was the Socialist candidate for governor and, although imprisoned in Idaho, received 16,015 votes in the 1906 election.

After a jury of Idaho farmers found Haywood not guilty, he walked out of prison as a hero and headed back to Denver. Although local authorities had turned off the electric WELCOME sign on the arch at Union Station, hundreds of supporters greeted the exonerated labor leader. Haywood moved to 3304 Franklin Street in Denver where he lived until 1917 according to the Denver City Directory.

Haywood, now an international star of militant unionism, spent a good deal of time in Chicago. Eugene Debs, Mother Jones, and other founders wanted "one big union" for all workers, including racial minorities, women, and unskilled and migrant workers shunned by other unions. Haywood declined the presidency of the IWW but later became secretary-treasurer. He helped direct the successful 1912 Lawrence Woolen Mills strike in Massachusetts, the unsuccessful 1913 Patterson silkworkers strike in New Jersey, and many other IWW battles.

When World War I erupted, some IWW members condemned it as a capitalist's war in which the working class would do the fighting and dying to enrich war profiteers. For these views, Haywood and over a hundred other Wobblies were arrested. Judge Kenesaw Mountain Landis (later famous as the commissioner of professional baseball) gave Haywood the maximum penalty allowed under the Espionage Act of 1917—a $10,000 fine and twenty years' imprisonment. Haywood appealed to the United States Supreme Court, but his attorneys were not optimistic that the lower court's decision would be overturned.

Big Bill was in the IWW cellblock of the Cook County Jail when news arrived that the October 1917 Bolshevik Revolution had succeeded. He and about 100 other incarcerated Wobblies broke into cheers and sang from the IWW's *Little Red Songbook*. After years of frustration, hopeless struggle, and talk about a socialist revolution, it had actually happened in Russia. There the Bolshevik party had seemed as small and as inconsequential as the IWW in America.

When Haywood finally got out of jail after a $30,000 bond was posted, he fled the United States. Sailing out of New York harbor on March 31, 1921, the long-persecuted labor leader saluted "the old hag with her uplifted torch," telling her: "Good-by, you've had your back turned on me too long. I am now going to the land of freedom." Vladimir Ilyich Lenin welcomed Haywood to the Soviet Union with open arms. Haywood was given a suite in the Lux Hotel in Moscow and put in charge of a mining project in the Donets region. He was wined and dined and brought out on occasion to tell Soviets and foreigners about the evils of American capitalism.

Haywood died in Moscow on May 12, 1928, after a stroke. At his request, his ashes were divided. Half were sent to the Waldheim Cemetery in Chicago to rest with the radicals executed after the Haymarket Riot. The other half were placed in an urn wrapped in red ribbons and flowers. A large crowd gathered for the sunset ceremony. The ashes were laid to rest in Red Square under the walls of the Kremlin near Lenin's embalmed body.

Big Bill Haywood makes for a dramatic study in international radicalism. But what did he do for Rocky Mountain miners? This difficult question might lead to speculation that although Haywood ultimately failed to radicalize the labor movement, he did shove management into a reactionary stance. Some mine owners voluntarily improved working conditions to preempt unions and preclude the rise of another Haywood. However, improved wages, hours, and working conditions came primarily because of federal legislation passed during the New Deal, not because of union pressure. To this day Colorado unions rely heavily upon federal laws and enforcement mechanisms in their struggles with management. Employers, the general public, many state and local officials, and even some workers see little need and feel little sympathy for unions. This sentiment is probably due to a popular consensus that unions have served, if not over-served, their purpose. It can hardly be called a reaction to giants like Haywood, who fought once-radical problems with radical solutions.

After the 1903–04 strike, the WFM limped along for another decade with greatly reduced membership, expectations, and achievements. The IWW, characterized as the "I Won't Works" and the "I Want Whiskeys," never gained a significant following in Colorado. In 1916 the WFM reorganized as the International Union of Mine, Mill and Smelter Workers (IUMMSW).

A tradition of radicalism continued to haunt the IUMMSW, as did retaliation from mine owners. In Silverton on August 30, 1939, for example, the management of the Shenandoah-Dives Mine, then the biggest gold and silver producer in the San Juans, inspired a mob of 200 to charge into the union hall and break up a strike meeting. A. S. Embree, a former IWW organizer then working for the IUMMSW, and the secretary of the Silverton local were forced into an automobile and deported. The mob took possession of the miners' union hall and its hospital in the name of a company union.

A year later, at a National Labor Relations Board (NLRB) hearing in Durango, San Juan County commissioners admitted that they had paid goons to escort the two union men out of town. The NLRB ordered the Shenandoah-Dives company union to pay back the union dues it had collected and to return the union hall and the union hospital to the IUMMSW. Owners of the Shenandoah-Dives were ordered to reinstate with back pay seventy-eight blacklisted miners of Silverton IUMMSW Local No. 26. Today the old WFM-built union hall is an American Legion post and the WFM hospital has become the headquarters for the Standard Metals Company, which operates the non-union Sunnyside Mine.

Like its predecessor, the IUMMSW made its headquarters in Denver. But it never became as important to Rocky Mountain hard-rock mining as the WFM had been. The new union suffered from low membership, financial difficulties, and a Red reputation. During the Red Scare of 1919 and the McCarthy era of the 1950s, the IUMMSW was colored pink by some. All of these problems made it easier for the United Steelworkers of America—with their patriotic acronym USA and middle-of-the-road reputation—to begin recruiting mine and smelter-workers in the 1950s and 1960s. In 1967, the IUMMSW gave up the ghost and merged with the United Steelworkers of America. Three years later workers at the Climax Molybdenum Mine—then the largest underground mine in North America—voted to affiliate with the Oil, Chemical and Atomic Workers International Union (OCAW), which had backed away earlier from merging with the IUMMSW because it was "tainted red." OCAW still represented Climax workers in 1983 when AMAX (legal name of the merged American Metals and Climax Molybdenum companies) closed Climax to concentrate their efforts on their non-union Henderson Mine.

Not only the miners' unions but the entire Colorado labor movement has been losing ground in recent decades. Between 1960 and 1980, union membership slipped from 23.3 percent to 13.8 percent of the nonagricultural work force in Colorado. In the eighty years since Big Bill Haywood led a radical young union into battle, the Colorado labor movement has never recovered its militancy.

Colorado Heritage, 1984, Issue 2

I n 1987 the Colorado Historical Society published a special issue of *Essays and Monographs in Colorado History* consisting of papers presented at the Santa Fe Trail Symposium held the previous year. Meeting astride the trail's mountain branch in Trinidad, historians, preservationists, poets, and museum specialists explored the 700-mile trade route's history and impact.

David Lavender, a Colorado native and author of more than three dozen books on the American West (including novels), presented a paper that reexamined one of his favorite topics: Bent's Fort. By the time of the symposium, his 1954 book, simply titled *Bent's Fort*, had become a classic. Lavender's engaging narrative style, rigorous scholarship, and treatment of Charles and William Bent as men caught up in an epic adventure enthralled serious students and casual readers alike. His style transformed big concepts—such as American expansion and cultural conflict—into demystified personal experiences that readers could relate to and learn from.

Lavender returned to this style in his symposium paper. Once again, he wrestled a lofty theme to the ground by focusing on the people that were shaped, and in this case, destroyed, by its forces.

Bent's Fort and Manifest Destiny

—David Lavender

In one thousand and seventy-eight days between the formal annexation of Texas on March 1, 1845, and the signing, on February 2, 1848, of the Treaty of Guadalupe Hidalgo, ending the war with Mexico, the United States added nearly 1.2 million square miles to its national domain. The vast sprawl of Texas, the American Southwest, the Oregon country south of the forty-ninth parallel—all were gobbled up during this single, extraordinary surge of expansionism. So, too, were many lives and landmarks. The Alamo, Chapultepec, Bent's Fort, the Bent brothers—destiny used them and destroyed them, just as it came very close to destroying the federal union it so radically enlarged.

Destiny. Manifest Destiny. Just what *are* we talking about? If we can sort out the strands and reach a definition, then perhaps we can see how the Bent tragedy fits into and illuminates, in its small way, some of the characteristics that marked the headlong growth of our nation.

Although the words *manifest* and *destiny* were not paired politically until 1845, the energies they came to represent were as old as the Pilgrims. "Go West, young men—and women—and find a better world": that faith ignited and sustained one of the greatest mass migrations in history. It brought the United States into being and sent Lewis and Clark to the Pacific on a trip whose impact has never left the American imagination. That faith also led Silas Bent, the father of the four fort-building Bent brothers, to move from Massachusetts to Ohio and then to Missouri, where he became principal deputy surveyor in charge of recently founded Louisiana Territory. Other human atoms in the continuing migration were the St. Vrains, one-time nobles in France. Ruined by the Revolution there, they too eventually reached Missouri. [1]

The magnet kept tugging at some of the next generation of Bents and St. Vrains. After a variety of separate, sometimes dangerous, and seldom

Bent's Fort, drawn by Lt. James Abert, 1845

profitable adventures in the Rocky Mountains and what is now the Southwest, Charles and William Bent—Charles nine years the elder—and Ceran St. Vrain came together as partners in the Santa Fe trade. An outgrowth of that commercial union, of course, was the adobe fort on the Mountain Branch of the Santa Fe Trail.

The building of the post was occasioned by a significant shift in the pattern of the fur trade. Initially the quest had been for beaver. Initially, too, Indians had been the chief hunters, and the pelts they harvested were bartered from them at conveniently located trading houses. As the fur frontier reached the upper Missouri, the Rockies, and the mountainous parts of the Southwest, however, whites turned out to be more proficient trappers than the horse Indians were. Most fixed posts lost their reason for being. Fur brigades roamed far and wide. The trappers in the north came together at annual summer rendezvous to turn in their catches, squander their pay, and gather supplies for the following winter.[2]

Farther south, the rendezvous did not take hold, partly because the Mexican government would not have allowed so blatant an intrusion by foreign fur companies. Trappers there worked in smaller parties. They sold their pelts and bought their supplies from merchants who maintained small, odorous general department stores in Taos, somewhat removed from the scrutiny of the officials in Santa Fe. The merchants also sold goods to local inhabitants, and if unsold items accumulated, they were carted off as far, sometimes, as Chihuahua, Durango, or even California—goals, also, of storekeepers in Santa Fe. It was in Taos that the original firm of Bent & St. Vrain took shape in 1829.[3]

By the early 1830s, overhunting had reduced the availability of beaver throughout the West. Scarcity, however, did not raise prices, for beaver hats were losing their popularity. Concurrently, more and more easterners were using buffalo robes as winter lap robes in their sleighs and as throw rugs in front of their fireplaces. As a result, the price of buffalo hides, along with that of the choice edible parts of the huge beasts, began edging up. Quick to note this, the principal fur companies adapted their procedures to take advantage of the change.

In a sense, this was a step backward. Indians again became the principal hunters—preparing buffalo robes was a grubby work whites gladly left to red women they called squaws—and bartering for the pelts reinstituted fixed trading posts. Considerations of safety were also involved. The Plains Indians might not trap beaver, but they had made a life ritual out of hunting buffalo and would have fiercely resisted attempts by whites to muscle in commercially on their principal natural resource.

Though the halcyon days of trapping were over by the early 1830s, the industry was by no means dead. Accordingly the firm of Bent & St. Vrain—soon to become Bent, St. Vrain & Company with the addition of brothers Robert and George Bent and Marcellin St. Vrain—wanted to locate its new post where it could be reached both by the mountain men who roamed the southern Rockies and the Cheyenne, Arapaho, Ute, Kiowa, and Comanche, who crisscrossed the southern High Plains. The new fort, they told each other, should also be close to the company stores at Taos, yet not on Mexican soil, where it would be subject to arbitrary taxation and interference by New Mexico's unpredictable governors. The last-named consideration necessitated a location north of the Arkansas River, which in those days served as part of the boundary between the United States and Mexico.

The task of locating and building the post fell to William Bent. Just how calculated his early experiments were cannot be said. Probably trial and error as well as pressure from competitor John Gantt, who built an adobe post near the site of present-day Pueblo, guided him as much as logic did. In any event he did construct, in 1833 or so, a wooden stockade close to the junction of Fountain Creek and the Arkansas River, near Gantt's establishment. It seems likely, too, that Bent had another stockade at the Big Timbers, an extensive grove of stately cottonwoods down river toward today's Lamar, Colorado. Neither location suited demands as they were perceived at the time, and in the end he settled on a riverbank site roughly nine miles above Purgatory Creek and close to the place where the Mountain Branch of the Santa Fe Trail swerved southwest up Timpas Creek toward Raton Pass.[4]

The adobe castle that resulted was powerful for the era. Walls fourteen feet high, with eighteen-foot bastions at opposite corners, formed a rectangle 130 feet wide by 180 feet long. There was a wedge-shaped corral along one side, wagon sheds and a wagon yard to the rear. Living and work rooms surrounded an inner plaza. Their roofs could be used for promenades, and the outer walls, which rose about four feet higher than the roofs, could be used as parapets in case of attack. Eventually a billiard room and bar and a few dwelling rooms would be added to form a partial second story. In the center of the plaza, as prominent as a statue or an identifying fountain, was a wooden press for compacting buffalo hides into bales that could be readily loaded into freight wagons.[5] Adventures in commerce were definitely and always a primary motive behind the western urge—or to put it another way, of imperialism on the home front.

The fort was probably built in 1834, though Sam Arnold has argued cogently that it did not come into full use until 1835.[6] By that time, nearby competition had been stifled, and soon (probably 1837) the firm had located a branch store, eventually named Fort St. Vrain, on the South Platte River, within reach of the Oregon Trail.

Significantly for our discussion, the 1830s was also the decade when the first missionaries, precursors of settlement, faced westward along the trail that led past Fort Laramie (built in 1834) and over South Pass into the Oregon country. During that same decade the Choctaws, Creeks, Chickasaws, Cherokees, and Seminoles were pressured into ceding their lands to the United States and moving along the notorious Trail of Tears into Indian country (present Oklahoma), out of the way of southern cotton planters. It was the decade when rebellious Texans won independence from Mexico. President Andrew Jackson, looking westward toward what he called, in the best public relations fashion, "new areas of freedom," sent William Slacum off by ship to spy on Oregon and California. The latter province he offered to buy, along with Texas, from Mexico.[7] Though Mexico turned him down, destiny was clearly gathering headway.

Unfortunately for Jacksonian Democrats, the Panic of 1837 interrupted the march. Whigs took over the government in 1840, installing William Henry Harrison as president. To small avail. A month after the nomination, Harrison died of pneumonia, and John Tyler, who was really a Democrat in Whig clothing (he had left the Democratic party because he could not stomach Jackson), stepped into the White House.

Because Tyler was neither fish nor fowl, the Whigs declined to nominate him in 1844 and instead substituted, as their presidential candidate, Henry Clay. The Democrats responded with James Knox Polk, who boldly chose to campaign on an expansionist platform of reannexing Texas and reoccupying Oregon. The naked imperialism just barely worked. Polk's margin in a popular vote of roughly 2.6 million was a thin 37,000—less than one tenth of 1 percent of the total! A scant shift of a few thousand votes in New York, which commanded a large block of electoral votes, and in Michigan would have defeated him. Because of New York, however, the electoral college vote looked respectable—170 to 105.[8] Of greater importance, several war-hawk Democrats were sent to Congress. Reading the results as a mandate for expansion, the hybrid Tyler renewed efforts he had made earlier in his presidency to annex Texas. This time he succeeded by means of a joint congressional resolution. In spite of Mexico's strenuous objections, he signed the act on March 1, 1845, three days before Polk's inauguration.

Though Charles Bent seldom, if ever, voted in an American election— no polling places were near the scene of his activities—his sympathies were with the Whigs. After learning from Manuel Alvarez, the United States consul in Santa Fe, of Polk's election, he replied glumly that he wished the choice had been Clay. The Democratic victory, he wrote, was likely to stir up trouble between the United States and Mexico.[9]

He was familiar with the frontiers of both countries. When he was not on the trail to and from Missouri, supervising the progress of the company's wagonloads of pelts and merchandise, he lived in Taos. About 1835 he married a local beauty, Ignacia Jamarillo, but never took out Mexican citizenship. He was the self-appointed protector of Americans in northern New Mexico. He helped gain "drawback" rights for himself and his fellow merchants—a law that enabled a trader who had paid U.S. custom duties on the goods and afterwards paid additional Mexican duties on the same goods to obtain a refund. He protested discriminatory tariffs against American traders. On at least four occasions he railed at the Mexican authorities for not bringing the murderers of American citizens to justice, and he officiously did what the police neglected doing: he gathered up the victims' personal possessions for return to the nearest kin.[10] Though only five feet seven inches tall, he could be a mountain of belligerence. On being threatened with a suit by a Mexican national, he snorted contemptuously, "I had rather have the satisfaction of whiping [sic] a man that has wronged me than to have him punished ten times by the law."[11]

His bête noir was Padre Antonio José Martínez, parish priest of Taos and a leading member of the rich "big family" of northern New Mexico. Martínez has had a bad press in the United States, mostly because Willa Cather chose to make him the gross, treacherous, lustful antithesis of her hero, Jean LaTour (actually Archbishop Lamy) in her New Mexico novel *Death Comes for the Archbishop.* Charles Bent disliked Martínez fully as much as Cather did. In a letter to the consul, Alvarez, he accused Martinez of worshiping Bacchus more than any other god, of vanity, physical cowardice, and flagrant dishonesty—but not of sexual immorality, Cather's favorite denigration.[12]

Whatever the priest's personal foibles, he was a patriot and sought to improve the lot of his fellow citizens. He opened the first school in the area. His aim was to prepare likely young men for the priesthood, for there was a dire shortage of trained ecclesiastics in New Mexico—and, indeed, several of his students did become priests. In order to provide his pupils with books and catechisms, he bought the only printing press in New Mexico and turned out with his own hands the material he needed. He also used the press for a short while to print New Mexico's first newspaper, *El Crepúsculo de la Libertad* (The Dawn of Liberty).[13]

More to the point, Martínez wrote and, on November 28, 1843, printed a ten-page pamphlet analyzing the ills of the department. He mailed copies to President Santa Anna and to New Mexico's most influential inhabitants. In the pamphlet, he leveled an accusing finger at American hide traders, by whom he clearly meant Bent, St. Vrain & Company. Those unscrupulous men, he charged, debauched the Indians with alcohol and thus persuaded them to kill so many buffalo cows that they were depriving themselves of their future livelihood. To obtain booty for whiskey, he went on, the Indians also preyed on the helpless ranchers of New Mexico.[14]

The accusation seemed substantiated early in 1846 when heavily armed Utes made off with several thousand head of livestock belonging to the "big family." The priest blamed Bent traders for arming the Indians, a charge Charles Bent vehemently denied. Shortly thereafter Bent found an additional cause for fury. An unruly Taos mob beat up his brother

George and a companion, Francis Blair, of the influential Blair family of Missouri. During the fracas, the town justice, Martínez's brother Pasqual, looked on approvingly.[15]

The real sticklers, however, were the enormous land grants Governor Armijo began passing out in the early 1840s. He had two justifications. First, New Mexico's population was growing and demands for land could be met if energetic grantees undertook to colonize the vacant areas in the northern part of the territory. Second, the colonies, if established, would create a buffer against land-hungry Americans and, even more, against the rambunctious inhabitants of Texas, then an independent republic suspected of casting covetous eyes on New Mexico.

Because Charles Bent was not a citizen of Mexico, he could not legally obtain a land grant anywhere in that nation. Ceran St. Vrain and other former aliens could, however, for they had taken out citizenship papers. So could their prosperous Mexican acquaintances. Eight of these people applied for and were granted tentative title to more than seven million acres. Charles Bent was quietly given a sixth interest in two of the holdings.[16]

Discovering the illegality, Martínez reacted vigorously. He was not necessarily being altruistic. His relatives had also applied for a pair of huge grants in the north, and if all went through, real competition for suitable colonists would develop. So he fought hard against the grants in which Charles Bent was involved, but to no avail. Governor Armijo had also been quietly given a sixth interest in the same two massive properties, and after delays for the sake of appearances, the title was confirmed.[17]

Such is a sparse outline of Charles Bent's relations with the territory in which he had chosen to make his home. But how does this fit in with the broader picture of Manifest Destiny? By defining the term, perhaps we can tell.

The wedding of the words *manifest* and *destiny* did not occur until 1845. The matchmaker was John O'Sullivan, prolific writer and editor of several partisan journals. He first introduced the term to the public in the July-August issue of the *Democratic Review*.[18] Why, he demanded rhetorically, did many Whigs and a few recalcitrant Democrats still complain about the annexation of Texas? Couldn't they see that other nations—he meant Britain and France—were meddling there in the hope of checking "the fulfillment of our manifest destiny to overspread the continent allotted by Providence for the free development of our yearly multiplying millions?"

Never one to let a good phrase lapse, O'Sullivan returned to the two words in the *New York Morning News* of December 27, 1845. The quarrel with Britain over title to Oregon was growing tense. Impatient with the legalistics of the diplomats, the journalist cried out, "Away, away with all these cobweb tissues of rights of discovery, exploration, settlement, continuity, etc. ... Our claim to Oregon ... is by the right of our manifest destiny to possess the whole of the continent which Providence has given us for the development of the great experiment of liberty and federated self-government."

This time the phrase caught on. Within a week Manifest Destiny was being hailed in Congress as "a new right in the law of nations." The power of suggestive language: American expansion was now seen as God-ordained and irresistible, hence blameless.[19]

Now to consider what all this actually meant. First, those lofty words about "the great experiment of liberty and federated self-government": They were not to be taken too literally, as Professor Thomas R. Hietala of Dartmouth College argues in chapter five, "Continentalism and the Color line," in his book *Manifest Design*, published in 1985. White pioneers were the ones who were going to overspread the continent for the development of the great experiment. If nonwhite Mexicans or Indians or amalgamations of the two were too stubborn or too numerous to be absorbed, that was their hard luck. Away, away with them. They were not worthy of the gifts of liberty and self-government.[20]

Slandering your enemy is an old ploy, of course. Listen to Senator Edward Hannegan of Indiana. The Mexicans, he declared, were "utterly unfit for the blessings of liberty. ... [T]hey cannot comprehend the distinction between regulated freedom, and that unbridled licentiousness which consults only the evil passions of the human heart."[21] Now listen to Charles Bent. "They are not fit to be free. ... [E]very speses of vise in this country is a recomendation to public office. ... The Mexican caracter is made up of stupidity, Obstanacy, Ignorance duplicity and vanity." (This strange screed, written as war approached, is still preserved among the Bent-Alvarez papers in the Read Collection at the Museum of New Mexico.[22] As far as I know it was never given public airing; Alvarez may have acted as a restraining force. Nevertheless, the document fits squarely with the racist traditions of Manifest Destiny.)

Let us turn back now to journalist O'Sullivan's initial definition of Manifest Destiny as "the free development of our yearly teeming millions." The awkward phrase "yearly teeming millions" apparently refers to a startling revelation made by the census of 1840. America's population was doubling every twenty-three years. It is part of Professor Hietala's thesis that anxious Democratic leaders, worrying over how to care for this relentless growth, deliberately designed the program that O'Sullivan labeled, in a flash of linguistic genius, Manifest Destiny.[23]

One part of their solution was the development of commercial outlets for both agricultural and manufactured products. The Orient was seen as the best potential market—after all, the far side of the Pacific had been a merchant's dream ever since 1785, the year that marked the return of the ship *Empress of China* to New York via Cape Horn with a hold full of Far Eastern exotics. In 1845 Representative Caleb Cushing, member of a Massachusetts shipping family that already was trading in Hawaii and Oregon, managed to talk the reluctant Chinese rulers into a formal trading treaty.[24] Simultaneously Asa Whitney, a merchant who had long dealt with the Chinese, was advocating a transcontinental railroad that would eliminate the long, taxing journey around Cape Horn.

There were problems, to be sure. The nascent plans could not be truly successful unless America acquired ports on the Pacific. Puget Sound was one possibility; San Francisco Bay was another. The English, until eliminated by a surprising treaty completed early in 1846, were a barrier to the first. Mexico held the second. It was a loose hold, however, and could probably be broken by a combined land and naval assault. Though several hundred miles of the land route lay in Mexican territory, a fifth column of American traders, Bent, St. Vrain & Company included, was already firmly established at the trail's head. If war developed, the company and its adobe post on the Arkansas would inevitably play a role. In short, commercial Manifest Destiny was ready to march, via Bent's Fort.

Another worry awakened by the census of 1840 was the growth of industrial urbanization. True, cities produced goods for trade, but in the minds of many observers, they also brought about poverty, overcrowding, evil, and a tragic loss of self-reliance. The best safety valve for these ills, expansionists argued, was the maintenance of a strong agrarian society, as recommended years before by Thomas Jefferson. Skeptical Whigs pointed out that large tracts of undeveloped land were still available inside the country, so why stir up trouble by adventuring outside? Pointing to the census, Democrats retorted that the population explosion would soon devour those internal tracts. Meanwhile reports were coming in about bountiful fields not just in Texas but in Oregon and California as well.[25]

Less was said about New Mexico, yet it offered, as did Texas and California, a wondrous wedge, the land grant. A noisy, longtime booster of the West, William Gilpin, destined to be the first territorial governor of Colorado, later bragged that he had mentioned the opportunity to certain Santa Fe traders while traveling with Frémont's expedition of 1843–44. Soon New Mexico would fall into American hands, he predicted.[26] Was it not wise to prepare?

Other tales say Frémont himself made the suggestion. Perhaps so, though the Bents and Ceran St. Vrain had long been familiar with Spanish land grants in Missouri; St. Vrain's family had even owned one for a time. So their own knowledge could have prompted them to act with dispatch when land grants became available through Governor Armijo. Speculating on a growing nation's hunger for land—that, too, was a part of America's westering urge. By the early 1840s this rampant speculative urge had reached New Mexico.

Finally, of course, there were the inescapable factors of geography. Bent's Fort and Raton Pass lay athwart the southern route to California. That self-evident truth had led Stephen Watts Kearny and his dragoons to the Arkansas post after they had scouted the Oregon Trail as far as South Pass in 1845. What questions Kearny asked during his consultations with the Bents and St. Vrain were not recorded, but a guess that they involved matters of military logistics and New Mexican attitudes probably would not be wide of the mark.[27]

A few weeks after Kearny had departed, Lieutenant John Charles Frémont rode in with sixty heavily armed men. They were on their way to California, just to keep an eye on things. With Frémont was Lieutenant J. W. Abert, under orders to return to Missouri by way of the Texas Panhandle, making maps as he went. He also completed detailed drawings of Bent's Fort, presumably because the army might want information about the frontier bastion. The Bents, of course, were fully aware of what Abert was doing.[28]

The next summer Charles Bent and Ceran St. Vrain again conferred with Kearny, this time at Fort Leavenworth in the northeastern part of present-day Kansas. By then, disputes with Mexico over the southern boundary of Texas had brought about Polk's formal declaration of war. As part of a military strategy already laid down, Colonel Kearny, soon to be elevated to a general's rank, was struggling to put together an army capable of invading the Mexican northwest, currently our Southwest.

William Bent

The tentacles of that army quickly embraced Bent, St. Vrain & Company. Seventeen hundred uniformed men and their supply columns, plus a heterogeneous mob of traders and their teamsters, came together in a chaotic rendezvous at the fort. There final plans for the invasion were completed. Because Polk cherished a hope that the troops could reach California before winter, Kearny wanted a peaceful conquest of New Mexico. To that end he issued proclamations promising to respect Mexican lives and property and bring a halt to the Indian raids that harassed the province. Emissaries were sent ahead to subvert Armijo if possible, and when the army began its advance, William Bent led the party of scouts that reconnoitered the way.[29]

Whether Armijo was bribed or whether he hoped to retain, after the war, his secret share in two of the land grants he had issued, or whether he simply lost his nerve, cannot be stated with firmness. In any event, he fled and the conquest was as peaceful, during its initial stages, as Polk and Kearny had desired.

Following the president's instruction, the general established a civil government with Charles Bent at its head. The lieutenant governor, Donaciano Vigil, was a relative of Charles's wife. Vigil also served as registrar of lands and would handle grant matters, even though he was a principal claimant, along with Ceran St. Vrain, to the four-million-acre Las Animas grant just south of the Arkansas River. Charles Beaubien, one of the territorial judges appointed by Kearny, claimed, together with Guadalupe Miranda, 1.7 million acres south of the Las Animas grant. Charles Bent and Manuel Armijo each held a sixth interest in those two grants. And the rest of Kearny's appointments were either friends or business associates of Bent's. Ironically, this list of officials and a new code of laws for running the government were printed on the press that belonged to Padre Antonio José Martínez.

Irony plagued the rest of the narrative. Territorial expansion, which Polk's anxious Democrats hoped would bind the Union together, actually exacerbated the differences over slavery and almost destroyed the federation. Charles Bent was killed during an uprising in Taos. Confirmation of the grant titles he so earnestly tried to protect created, during subsequent years, spectacular frauds and no little violence.

Epidemics of cholera introduced by the onrushing whites caused havoc among the Indians. That and their sense of what was following in the footsteps of the army led to outbreaks of war. William Gilpin, who led some of the punitive campaigns against the tribes, used Bent's Fort as one of his bases. The Indian trade declined. Seeing a more prosperous future in New Mexico, Ceran St. Vrain dissolved his partnership with William Bent.

In 1849 Bent's Fort was set afire and partly destroyed, whether by Indians or Bent himself cannot be said with assurance.[30] In any case, Bent moved downstream and built a new, smaller fort. There he became an Indian agent, handing out government doles to the once-proud people among whom he had found his first two wives. In time he sold this new fort to the army and moved to a stockade at the mouth of the Purgatory River. There he watched Chivington's troops march toward the Indian encampment at Sand Creek, where three of his mixed-blood children were staying with their mother's friends and relatives. A world split in that fashion could end only in dismay—and it did, in the horrors at Sand Creek and its aftermath, all of which bring to mind a slightly revised version of the old proverb: "Be careful what destiny you seek, because you are likely to get it."

Essays and Monographs in Colorado History, No. 6, 1987

Endnotes

1 For the ancestry of the Bents and St. Vrain, see David Lavender, *Bent's Fort* (Garden City, N.Y.: Doubleday & Co., 1954), 18–23, 49–52, 376–78. Short sketches in LeRoy Hafen's ten-volume *The Mountain Men and the Fur Trade of the Far West* (Glendale, Calif.: The Arthur H. Clark Company, 1965–71) include Harold Dunham, "Charles Bent," 2:27–48, and "Ceran St. Vrain," 5:197–316. See also Samuel P. Arnold, "William Bent," 6:61–84.

2 The Rocky Mountain fur trade is well covered in Dale Morgan, *Jedediah Smith and the Opening of the West* (Indianapolis and New York: Bobbs-Merrill, 1953); Bernard DeVoto, *Across the Wide Missouri* (Boston: Houghton Mifflin, 1947); and Don Barry, *A Majority of Scoundrels* (New York: Harper & Brothers, 1961).

3 For the Southwest fur trade, see David J. Weber, *The Taos Trappers: The Fur Trade in the Far Southwest, 1540–1846* (Norman: University of Oklahoma Press, 1959) and Robert Glass Cleland, *This Reckless Breed of Men: The Trappers and Fur Traders of the Southwest* (New York: Knopf, 1950).

4 George Hyde gives an Indian version, its dates demonstrably wrong, of how the fort was located, in *A Life of George Bent, Written from His Letters*, ed. Savoie Lottinville (Norman: University of Oklahoma Press, 1968), 42–43, 59–60. See also Janet Lecompte, "Gantt's Fort and Bent's Picket Post," *The Colorado Magazine* 41 (Spring 1964) and Samuel P. Arnold, "William Bent," as in note 1 above.

5 J. W. Abert's detailed sketch of the fort appears in Hyde, *Life of George Bent*, 102ff.

6 *Arnold, "William Bent." The National Park Service uses an 1833 date of construction in published brochures, while Lavender offered a case for 1832 in* Bent's Fort, *414, n. 12.*

7 John W. Caughey, *California: A Remarkable State's Life History* (Englewood Cliffs, N.J.: Prentice Hall, 1970), 156–57.

8 Thomas A. Bailey, *The American Pageant*, 2 vols. (Lexington, Mass.: D.C. Heath & Co., 1971), 1:306.

9 Bent to Alvarez, January 24, 1845. Most of Bent's letters to Manuel Alvarez were published in the *New Mexico Historical Review* (hereafter *NMHR*) sporadically from 1954 to 1957. The originals (which I used when preparing *Bent's Fort*) are in the Read Collection, Museum of New Mexico, Santa Fe.

10 Dunham, "Charles Bent." Also Bent to Alvarez, April 23, 1843, in Harold Dunham, "Sidelights on Santa Fe Traders, 1839–1846." *Denver Westerners Brand Book*, vol. 6 (Denver: University of Denver Press, 1950), 276–77. *Bent to Alvarez*, December 1, 1840; March 2, 1846; April 26, 1846, in NMHR, 1954 et seq.

11 Bent to Alvarez, February 19, 1841, *NMHR* 29 (October 1954): 315.

12 Bent to Alvarez, January 30, 1841, ibid., 313–15.

13 For starters in the literature defending Martínez, see Pedro Sánchez, *Memories of Antonio José Martínez*, ed. Guadalupe Baca-Vaughn (Santa Fe: Rydal Press, 1978); C. V. Romero, "Apologia of Presbyter Antonio J. [José] Martínez," *NMHR* 3 (October 1928): 325–46, E. K. Francis, "Padre Martínez: A New Mexican Myth," *NMHR* 31 (October 1956): 265–89; Ralph Vigil, "Willa Cather and Historical Reality," *NMHR* 50 (April 1975): 123–34.

14 William Keleher, *Turmoil in New Mexico, 1846–1868* (Santa Fe: Rydal Press, 1952), 66–70.

15 Bent to Alvarez, May 3, May 10, June 1, 1846, *NMHR* 31 (April 1956): 160ff.

16 Harold Dunham, "New Mexico land Grants," *NMHR* 30 (January 1955): 1–22, and "Coloradans and the Maxwell Grant," *The Colorado Magazine* 32 (April 1955): 131–45.

17 Protesting the grants: Dunham, "New Mexico Land Grants," Myra E. Jenkins, "Taos Pueblo and Its Neighbors," *NMHR* 41 (April 1966): 107; Louis Warner, *Archbishop Lamy* (Santa Fe, 1936), 78–79; *Bent to Alvarez*, March 2, 1846, April 19, 1846.

18 *In* Mistress of Manifest Destiny: A Biography of Jane McManus Storm Cazneau, 1807–1878 (Austin: Texas State Historical Association, 2001), Linda Hudson asserts that political writer Jane

McManus Storm Cazneau wrote the "Annexation" article in the United States Magazine and Democratic Review *and should be given credit for using the term "manifest destiny" for the first time in print.*

19 Julius Pratt, "The Origin of Manifest Destiny," *American Historical Review* 32 (July 1927): 795–98.

20 Thomas R. Hietala, *Manifest Design: Anxious Aggrandizement in Late Jacksonian America* (Ithaca, N.Y.: Cornell University Press, 1985), 152–60.

21 Ibid., 156–57.

22 Bent-Alvarez papers, date uncertain but probably in 1845.

23 Hietala, *Manifest Design*, passim. Note especially 110–11.

24 Ibid., 62, 198–201.

25 Ibid., Chapter 4, passim.

26 Dunham, "New Mexican Land Grants with Special Reference to the Title Papers of the Maxwell Grant," *NMHR* 30 (January 1955): 3–4.

27 Dwight L. Clarke, *Stephen Watts Kearny, Soldier of the West* (Norman: University of Oklahoma Press, 1961), 85–100.

28 J. W. Abert, *Western America in 1846–47*, ed. John Galvin (San Francisco, 1966).

29 Clarke. *Stephen Watts Kearny*, 116–62. Other accounts of the war on the New Mexican front are too numerous to be listed here.

30 Lavender, *Bent's Fort*. 315–16, 413–14.

J ames Pickering's story of Agnes Vaille's death on Longs Peak on January 12, 1925, reads like the script for a blockbuster film. It has all the right elements: An athletic and daring woman and a young Swiss mountaineer face an impossible alpine challenge during a deadly winter storm. But this is no silver-screen drama.

Tragic true stories often suffer from a lack of reliable primary sources and an excess of sensational hearsay. Not this one. Pickering supplemented official reports, secondhand accounts, and newspaper articles with the so-called "Hewes manuscript," a journal entry containing a record of the tragedy as told by Walter Kiener—the Swiss mountaineer himself—to his friend Charles Hewes. Hewes wanted to publish the account in 1932, but Kiener, perhaps still scarred by Vaille's death, refused. "I believe," he wrote, "that the time has not yet come to publish that story." Then he advised Hewes to keep the manuscript as "an integral part of your Journal."

Hewes did not do so. Eventually his journal found its way to the Estes Park Museum, minus Kiener's narrative. The missing excerpt, Pickering discovered, had been circulating among members of the Colorado Mountain Club for some time. The story of how he learned of its existence, included within this article, adds a serendipitous twist to an already exciting tale.

James Pickering is an English professor at the University of Houston where he has served as dean, provost, and president. In addition to his articles for *Colorado Heritage* he has written or edited some fifteen books on Colorado history, including *"This Blue Hollow": Estes Park, The Early Years 1859–1915*, which received the Colorado Endowment for the Humanities Publication Prize in 1999 and was a finalist for the Colorado Book Award in 2000. Its sequel, *America's Switzerland: Estes Park and Rocky Mountain National Park—The Growth Years*, will be published in 2005.

Tragedy on Longs Peak: Walter Kiener's Own Story

—James H. Pickering

L ike all great mountains, Longs Peak has known its share of tragedies. Since Major John Wesley Powell and his party made the first known ascent on August 23, 1868, thousands have followed. Over the years, a number of men and women have died in the undertaking, through care-lessness for the most part, but under circumstances ranging from the prosaic to the highly dramatic. None of these was more dramatic, however, than the tragedy of Agnes Wolcott Vaille (1890–1925), the daughter of one of Denver's pioneer families, a graduate of Smith College, and a woman well known in Colorado climbing circles, who lost her life on January 12, 1925, following the first successful wintertime ascent of the 1,630-foot East Face. Her companion on that occasion was a young Swiss mountaineer named Walter Kiener (1900–1959), whom Agnes Vaille had come to know through the activities of the Colorado Mountain Club.

Born in Bern, Switzerland, the son of a sausagemaker, Kiener had been forced to leave school at fifteen to enter the family business. His spare time, however, was spent climbing in the Alps; it was not surprising, therefore, that when Kiener quarreled with his father and came to America, he should find his way to Colorado. Arriving in Denver some-time in 1923, Kiener went to work as a butcher and almost immediately became involved with the Colorado Mountain Club.

Walter Kiener, six feet tall and two hundred and twenty-five pounds, was a veritable giant of a man who prided himself on his strength and endurance as a mountaineer. At twenty-five he was at the very height of his physical prowess. Though he managed to survive the ordeal on Longs Peak, Kiener nonetheless brought away with him scars, psychological as well as physical, that would irreparably alter his life. Moreover, as is so often the case, tragedy was compounded by tragedy, when Herbert Sortland, a young man of twenty-two or twenty-three, one of the members of the rescue party sent out from Longs Peak Inn to find Vaille and Kiener, lost his way in the storm. Despite a prolonged search of the area, a search which included his two brothers who came down from the family farm in North Dakota to help, Sortland's body was not recovered until some six weeks later, on February 25, 1925, when it was found within several hundred yards of his caretaker's cabin at the inn.

Given Agnes Vaille's prominence (at the time of her death she was serving as secretary of the Denver Chamber of Commerce), her ill-fated climb with Walter Kiener and its tragic aftermath received front page coverage in the Denver press. The official version of the incident was authored by Roger Toll (1883–1936), superintendent of Rocky Mountain National Park and Agnes Vaille's cousin. Toll, who was headquartered for the winter in Denver's Post Office Building, had arrived at Timberline Cabin below the Boulder Field at 4:30 A.M. on Tuesday, January 13, within hours of Kiener's return with the original rescue party. His account of what happened, based on the firsthand accounts of the surviving participants, including Walter Kiener, was included in his regular monthly report to the National Park Service in Washington. This version was then edited, expanded to include the details of the various rescue operations, and made available to the Colorado press under the title "Official Report."

Agnes Wolcott Vaille

209

Though Walter Kiener talked willingly enough with Toll and with local reporters before being taken off to a Denver hospital, there is no evidence that he himself ever committed his own version of events to writing. In its aftermath, in which one or more joints of each finger, except for the right index finger, and all the toes on one foot and several on the other had to be amputated because of frostbite, the naturally private Kiener preferred to keep the memories of that night to himself. On one occasion, however, Kiener did tell his story. Fortunately, Charlie Hewes was a good listener and, just as importantly, an accomplished writer.

Charles Edwin Hewes (1870–1947), who had come to Estes Park in 1907 and stayed on to build and operate Hewes-Kirkwood Inn (now Rocky Ridge

Walter Kiener
(National Park Service photograph, courtesy of James Pickering)

Music Center) near the Longs Peak trailhead, can only be described as a character. Hewes aspired to be a poet and a novelist, and for more than thirty years, from 1913 to 1944, he kept a daily journal of his life in the Tahosa Valley. No event, large or small, went unrecorded, whether it was the activities of his famous neighbor (and nemesis) Enos Mills, the amount of snow that fell during a given day, or what he saw during a morning's walk through the woods. This journal, neatly typed on 1,116 manuscript pages, together with the first volume of an equally remarkable autobiography, was discovered in an Estes Park bank vault following his death. On the evening of December 29, 1931, in front of the large stone fireplace at Hewes-Kirkwood, Walter Kiener gave Charles Hewes a detailed account of what took place that night six years earlier on Longs Peak. That account, hitherto unknown, and for many years unaccountably lost, is published for the first time below.

Prior to the Agnes Vaille tragedy, Hewes and Walter Kiener had never met. Hewes would recall in his journal entry of January 13, 1925, that his dog Jim had been awakened the previous Saturday night by the sounds of Kiener and Vaille skiing towards Timberline Cabin on the Longs Peak trail a half mile to the north. In that same entry Hewes also recorded a lengthy and detailed account of what two of the three surviving members of the original rescue party (Jac Christen and Oscar Brown) had told him earlier that morning. Four days later, on January 17, Hewes got some additional parts of the story from Hugh Brown, Oscar's father and the caretaker of the nearby Columbine Lodge. Hugh had been with the party that had reached Timberline Cabin and then accompanied Kiener back to where Agnes Vaille had been left. Three fourths of a mile up the trail Hugh Brown had turned back, and Hewes noted that "his face was a fearful sight, [with] thick ointment spread over his frozen features."

Hewes's friendship with Walter Kiener developed during the several summers beginning in 1925 when Kiener was hired by Rocky Mountain National Park as a seasonal employee to staff the fire lookout on top of Twin Sisters Mountain across the Tahosa Valley from Hewes-Kirkwood. It had taken Kiener four months in a Denver hospital to recuperate from his ordeal. Though his bills were paid by Agnes Vaille's father, Kiener's injuries were such that he could no longer practice his trade as a butcher. Roger Toll's offer to tend the seven-foot-square lookout on top of the Twins, which had just been taken over from the U.S. Forest Service, thus came as an act of great and timely generosity. It also brought Kiener and the affable Hewes into periodic contact with one another, and the relationship they established continued after Kiener left Colorado to enroll at the University of Nebraska to study biology. In time Kiener chose the alpine vegetation on Longs Peak as his academic specialty and during his visits to the area, Hewes-Kirkwood became his base of operations. Though Hewes himself apparently never raised the story of Agnes Vaille with Kiener, it was perhaps only a matter of time before that topic should arise.

That occasion was the 1931 Christmas season. On the evening of December 21, Kiener, on holiday from the university, unexpectedly arrived by car at Hewes-Kirkwood to spend Christmas with Hewes. A week later, on December 29, Hewes made the following entry in his journal:

> The Wallace party left us today just as a hard blow started off the Range. This evening was a most notable one for us. As I was reading the papers Walter Kiener suddenly spoke up and said, "Charlie, did I ever tell you the story of Agnes and my ascent of the East Face in 1925?" Stating that he had never done so and expressing my keen interest in the same he gave us the following narration of what will probably be the most dramatic event ever staged on Longs Peak. I do not know what prompted him to do this. As I look back at [it], it seems as tho he was almost inspired by an unknown prompter; yet with the gale surging heavily and cold outside, and we four so comfortable inside in front of the great fire, with the three dogs lying so ... comfortable in their different corners, it surely made an ideal setting for a great story; and in spite [of] the many notable and interesting scenes that have been staged within the old cabin, surely the one this evening was not the least of them; and I am inclined to think, that the tale I have recorded below, will, in time, become the classic of the Longs Peak region, involving as it does, the mysterious agencies of Fate and Providence working in the lives of some extraordinary human characters. Thus follows Walter Kiener's own story, told in the presence of Julia [Julia Morrissey, Hewes's housekeeper], Gordon Heddin [a young man from Ohio, who did odd jobs around Hewes-Kirkwood], and myself.

No story of mountain adventure and tragedy could possibly have had a more enticing or dramatic introduction. Yet when one turns to the next manuscript page of Hewes's journal, Walter Kiener's story simply is not there.

Hewes did record Kiener's story that evening. But when Hewes subsequently retyped his journal and produced the draft which now survives in the Estes Park Area Historical Museum, he deliberately, and for reasons I will touch on briefly below, chose not to include Kiener's story, though he did include its exciting prologue. That portion of the original Hewes journal, thirteen and a half typed pages in all, was placed for safekeeping in an old filing cabinet that somehow found its way a decade ago to a used furniture store in Boulder. "When we took out the drawer to clean it," the current owners recall, "we discovered some old papers that belonged to the family that previously owned the filing cabinet. Behind the drawer, crumpled and old, was the Hewes manuscript. We contacted the previous owners of the file cabinet, but they had no knowledge of it."

At the top of the first page of the manuscript is a single-spaced typewritten notation: "Dec. 1931. Extract from the journal of Charles Edwin Hewes under the date of December 9 [sic], 1931. Being a personal relation

The timberline cabin, where Agnes Vaille and Walter Kiener began
their climb and to which Kiener returned for help.

213

of Walter Kiener of the facts and circumstances of the ascent of the East Face of Longs Peak in Jan. 1925 by Agnus [*sic*] Vaille and himself." What follows is "Walter Kiener's own story." As editor I have taken the liberty of silently correcting Hewes's few errors of spelling and punctuation. I have also made minor emendations of the text where sense and readability clearly seemed to demand it.

Kiener's Story

Our inclination to climb the East Face of Longs Peak came when Mr. and Mrs. Herman Buhl and ourselves had just ascended Mt. Evans early in the fall of 1924; and while resting on the summit of that peak, we looked off north and beholding the grand appearance of Longs, we resolved to climb its East Face in the near future. With the reputation that Agnes enjoyed in the Colo. Mt. Club as the equal of any member, man or woman, for daring endurance, and other qualifications of an able mountain climber, and my own experience in both Switzerland and America, we felt that we could make a successful winter climb, as the previous ascents had been made in late summer or early fall when the face of the mountain was about as dry and free from ice and snow as it ever gets.

One Sat. evening in the following Oct. we made the first attempt. Motoring to and camping on the Longs Peak campground in Rocky Mt. National Park, above Hewes-Kirkwood Inn, we took the trail to Chasm Lake and proceeded on up the glacier to the foot of Alexander's Chimney [named for James Alexander, the Princeton professor who made the first successful ascent of the East Face on September 7, 1922]. The going was good despite the snow which covered the glacier. My examination of the Mt. in that vicinity convinced me that we should advance up the glacier to its junction with Broadway, then proceed along that ledge until we found an opening above it which looked promising as leading to the summit. Agnes, however, got so interested in the chimney that I gave way to her desire to explore it. Upon entering we were soon involved in difficulties—the interior was lined with ice and for nearly every foot we climbed, steps had to be cut in the ice. Finally, in order to get around and up over a mass of rock which blocks the upper end, we had to cut niches in a vertical wall of ice, and tho succeeding at last in gaining the top of the wall, I dropped my ice axe which made further progress impossible. Calling to Agnes, I told her the situation and that we must return. Having a very precarious footing on the steeply inclined wall, I succeeded in finally lodging my partner in a place where she could hold on; then, for the second time in my life—the first time, a tight place in Switzerland—I loosened the rope from my body, so that in case I slipped and fell she would not be dragged down. On account of the long time we had been employed in cutting steps in the ice, darkness had come on, and I soon realized that I was in a difficult situation. Soon, however, my body was wriggling over the edge of the wall, with fingers clinging to the slight indentations in the rocks and with my feet finally finding the niches previously cut in the ice I made my way down to safety and we returned to camp.

The next trip was made in the following Nov. We had taken a couple of Agnes' friends, two young ladies, with us up on the first trip, who remained at the camp while we were on the mountain; and we were accompanied by Carl Blaurock, a fellow Mountain Club member, on the second trip. Although the weather was fine and the going good, such serious errors were made in choosing the route involving a long and protracted retreat to cover the true course, that night was upon us almost before we realized it; and after a laborious descent in the darkness, in which the rope was resorted to until we reached the glacier, we again gave up the task and returned to Denver.

The following Dec. Agnes and I motored to the campground again and ascended to the foot of the East Face through a heavy blizzard; but admonished by one of the strictest rules of mountain climbing to attempt no difficult ascents in adverse weather—and there being no prospect of any abatement of the storm, we turned back for the third time.

At this juncture a sort of disagreeable, unhealthy situation developed in our East Face efforts. Agnes became the object of considerable adverse criticism on the part of those who tried to dissuade her from any further attempts to climb the East Face. Members of her family, fellow mountain Club members, friends and others contributed to this—and with the highest motives, the belief that the climb was too dangerous, until they became a unit in asserting that it was impossible to ascend the East Face of Longs Peak in winter. In opposition to this was Agnes and myself, both of us believing that it could be accomplished. Thus a regrettable but definite challenge arose in the matter which we proposed to meet; although, moving in almost wholly different strata of society from hers, I was not subjected to this criticism as she was, and I too endeavored to dissuade her from going again, stating that when the talk quieted down

215

we could slip up to the peak and make the ascent almost before anyone knew we were going. To these remarks, however, she was not favorable; and although not feeling happy over the situation, I accepted her invitation and the following January again found us on the mountain.

Upon this fourth, and last, and successful attempt so far as attaining the summit was concerned, we encountered new difficulties, for there had been a heavy wind and snow in the region since our last visit, drifting the roads and forcing us to park our car several miles north of our former campground, about a mile below Bald Pate Inn; and from that point we skied to the timberline cabin on the old Longs Peak Trail, arriving there well after midnight, Sunday morning January 11. Our companion on this trip was Elinor Eppich. There was a strong wind blowing and we spent the balance of the night dozing in our heavy clothes around the old stove there. When daylight came the prospects for the ascent were not favorable for there was a heavy gale blowing and lifting the snow considerably. After eating breakfast, and joking and visiting awhile, Elinor gave a sudden exclamation and told us to look out of the window at the peak, for as if by magic the wind had ceased and the appearance of the mountain was so magnificent that every drop of blood in my body anticipated its conquest, with the girls equally enthusiastic. The storm over and the sky clear, we said goodbye to Elinor who returned down the trail to Longs Peak Inn where she was to wait until we came back.

Although we made a late start I felt that we could attain our object if we could maintain a reasonably rapid speed. Reaching the glacier we climbed to Broadway and traversed that ledge to its junction with the Notch Couloir, the galley which descends from under the great notch of the peak on the east side. The day remained calm and beautiful but the couloir was filled with snow and ice and we spent about four hours in cutting our steps up its steep incline. Then another two hours was occupied in getting from the top of the couloir north on the face of the mountain to a point that had been selected from which we could finish the climb up through the little notch to the summit. It was four o'clock in the afternoon and darkness had set in, and although I felt strong and fit for the remainder of the ascent I was greatly perturbed and grieved to note that my companion's strength was about spent. For some time I had noticed that she was far from being in the wonderful form and endurance that she was noted for, and for the past two hrs. She had been almost helpless; and often as we paused she complained and apologized for being such a burden on my hands. Although I had long since abandoned all hopes of rapid ascent, I tried not to betray it, and encouraged her all I could; but it was soon evident that she was helpless to proceed, and for close to twelve hours I had to cut the steps alone, handle the rope, and pull, lift and assist her, until we finally reached the summit about four A.M. This last twelve hours of the climb was made in complete darkness, and the way exceedingly tantalizing, for the face of the mountain at this point is a series of projections, like great steps; and at this time of year being covered by a blanket of snow and ice, one step would be on the sheer rock face just under a thin covering of ice, and at the next we would sink to our waists in snow—thus every step we advanced became an effort won only by dogged labor. We lost our two lanterns on this slope, and here I took the only thermometer reading of the trip—14 degrees below zero. We found it fairly quiet on the summit and Agnes suggested that we register as proof we had made the ascent, but anxious to get off the mountain on account of her exhausted condition and fearing a now gusty wind would bring in something stronger, I said jokingly, "What's the use? Of course it would be proof we reached the summit, but by which side and that's the point. Let's go on." By this time the summit began to be enveloped in clouds; we lost our way, we wandered off toward the northwest, when a fortunate opening in the clouds occurred just at day break and I got our location exactly, seeing Mount Lady Washington to the east, the Boulder Field below me, and our route down the north face. My joy and exultation in this observation were suddenly dispensed, however, when the light of dawn revealed the features of my brave companion; for they were those of one who was doomed—that most appalling lines of suffering, anguish, pain, haggard and deep drawn, had developed in the countenance of that heroic woman; her eyes were fearfully bloodshot and she talked in tones that seemed supernatural. I did my best to conceal my own intense agitation and despair; but even as far advanced as she must have been into the spirit, kept still on earth by her dauntless will and courage, she read my glance, and then there was born a friendship in the presence of death that must have risen to God as a thing immortal. The apologies she sought to make for being in such a condition were heart breaking, but I passed them over by asking as gently as I could, if she felt that she could go on; and nodding in the affirmative though she seemed on the verge of actual dissolution, we started down the north face near Chasm View for the Boulder Field below. Reaching the point where a large rock jams the long lateral crack where the cable is now, I tried to get her to go around instead of over it, but probably too far gone to heed the suggestion she went over the top of it, and slipped, as I feared she would, she fell and skidded a long ways down over the smooth, snowy slope, and lay there until I could descend. It was broad daylight now with the wind steadily rising from the west, and as the sun rose over the distant plains we discussed the situation. She was so weak that she could not hold onto me, and I was so far gone that my knees shook and I fairly tottered; and all the time she was insisting, in that supernatural voice that smote and terrified me, that a half hour's sleep would restore her. Assisting her—to some rocks that seemed to offer protection from the wind, I put her knapsack under her head as a pillow, placed her ice axe in her hand, for she seemed to cling to it as a treasured thing; and then with all the speed at my command I started across the Boulder Field for help. It was not long before I was brought up quick by two or three terrible falls made between the great boulders which were covered with the treacherous snows; and as I lay recovering in one place, I wept at my miserable weakness and helplessness; and debated whether to return and die with her, or push on for blankets, restoratives, and aid to bring her off the Boulder Field; and as the latter plan offered the only fighting chance for life there was, and hoping that she still had enough endurance left to last until I could return with the cherished aid, I went on. This was about 11 o'clock Monday morning, the twelfth. By 1 P.M. I managed to reach the timberline cabin and found to my great surprise and joy that a rescue party had been organized by Miss Eppich, who had become alarmed at our long absence and the rising gale, and which consisted of Hugh Brown, his son Oscar, and Herbert Sortland, the caretaker at the Longs Peak Inn, and Jacob Christen, all of whom had been putting up ice at the inn. I told them the situation, we took the blankets and restoratives they brought and the elder Brown, Sortland, Christen, and myself started for the rescue. By this time the wind had risen to a terrible gale and it was intensely cold. On account of being so poorly dressed, Brown had to give up and return within a short distance; then Sortland called out that he could not stand it, and he left us; but as I remember, the timberline cabin was still in view, and both Christen and I thought he could make it, never dreaming that it was the last time that anyone would see him alive.

When Christen and I reached Agnes she was dead and frozen, but during my absence she had partially risen, turned over and was lying face downward still clutching her ice axe. The gale was raging in unabated fury, driving the cold against our bodies without cessation or mercy—there was nothing to do but return, for we could not carry the body; later, when it was recovered, it took eight men in calm weather to carry it. We would do well if we got back alive ourselves. How many times I fell on this last journey I could not tell. It was one long, horrible nightmare of slip, plunge, groan, prostration, painful recovery among the jagged boulders, and again staggering on with the aid of the brave Christen. There was no visibility—all was one vast welter of blinding snow; but the way was downward and that was our cue. My knees were battered to pieces it seemed to me and I could feel the blood trickle down them, and stiffen, and freeze. My feet had long since ceased to have any feeling. They were just stumps that I tried to balance myself on against the wind like a pair of stilts; and my hands were gone with the fingers frozen and rattling like icicles whenever my gloves fell off. The wind never let up, but roared and beat upon us like a furious monster that is determined to kill and devour his prey. About half way back my eyes began to freeze and I could not see, and Christen had to lead me by hand. When I fell he would help me up. Sometimes he would get ahead, and then when I fell I hoped he would never come back it seemed so restful as I lay upon the snow and rocks; then when he did come back yelling, and shaking me, I was glad when I got up again. I had no real sleep since the previous night—had worked under heavy nervous strain and exposure for the past 36 hours, and it was now late Monday afternoon—I was a wreck. For the last mile or so Christen had to lead me by the hand for I was blind and almost helpless. Finally reaching Timberline Cabin about 7:30 P.M. and sitting near the fire that had been built on the stove, it looked only like a dim candle seen far off. The National Park Rangers arrived at the cabin three hours later. The next morning Mr. Toll, the superintendent, came. He was a cousin of Agnes and his official report tells the balance of the story—how I was badly frozen and taken to a Denver hospital; the disappearance of Herbert Sortland, whose remains were found near Longs Peak Inn six weeks later; and the recovery of Agnes' body by the rangers a couple of days later when the storm was over. (Here ends Kiener's personal narrative as told by him to Charles E. Hewes, the evening of December 29, 1931, in Hewes['s] cabin near Longs Peak.)

Why then, did Hewes deliberately choose to exclude Kiener's story when he retyped his journal? Why (and for whom) did he make the "extract" reproduced above? And how did that document find its way to the filing cabinet in Boulder? Answers to these questions do not come easily, if at all. It seems likely, however, that Hewes's decision not to include Kiener's story in the draft of his journal intended for posterity had to do with his sensitivity to the controversy that had arisen following Agnes Vaille's death about where responsibility lay—responsibility not only for Agnes's death but for the death of the unfortunate Sortland as well.

Virtually everyone agreed that the attempt to ascend the East Face under prevailing conditions was foolhardy and reckless. The Colorado Mountain Club, of which both were members, was quick to issue a disclaimer. *The Denver Post*, quoting an unidentified source, assured its readers that the event had not been an official club undertaking: "Club rules require, on an official climb, that at least four persons must participate. In case of an accident to one member, one person can be left to stand guard while the other two seek help." By implication, of course, this was precisely what had been so wrong about the Vaille-Kiener expedition.

But who was at fault? Was it Agnes Vaille, headstrong and determined, a woman who had served in Europe as a nurse in World War I and who, in many particulars, seemed to personify the "new" American woman of the 1920s? She, of course, was Kiener's senior by some ten years, and far more knowledgeable than the Swiss about the peaks and perils of Colorado's mountains. Or did the fault belong to Walter Kiener, the experienced Swiss mountaineer, a man whom Agnes Vaille had apparently chosen precisely for his expertise?

To the extent that her contemporaries were willing to cast blame at all, they tended to be critical of Agnes Vaille. The reasons were easy enough to come by. Agnes Vaille at thirty-five had a reputation for determination and toughness, and it was this reputation—the ability to compete with men on their own terms—that had earned her the position of secretary of the Denver Chamber of Commerce the year before. As a writer for the *Rocky Mountain News* noted in reporting her death ("Agnes Vaille Dies in Blizzard on Longs Peak") on January 13, 1925,

> Miss Vaille believed that a woman could do anything that a man could do and never for a moment hesitated to undertake tasks that would have made many a man quail. ... [She was] often paid the tribute by business men with whom she came in contact that she had "the brains of a man." She gloried in competing with men and attaining those things which men said were impossible.

Agnes Vaille was an accomplished mountaineer. Over the years she had scaled all but sixteen peaks in the United States above 14,000 feet, and her previous attempts to make a winter assault on Longs Peak were widely known. "Each failure," observed the *Estes Park Trail* in a story of January 16, 1925, "made her more determined to accomplish the feat. Her determination led her to seek out Mr. Kiener as her companion on this trip, because of his endurance and experience. Friends sought in vain to dissuade her from her plans." The editor of *Trail and Timberline*, in a post-script "note" to Roger Toll's "Official Report" which appeared in the February 1925 issue, was even more critical:

> Agnes's desire to ascend the East Face of Longs Peak this winter had become an obsession. Arguments and entreaties of relatives and friends did not move her. Kiener's work was almost super-human. No man could have done more. ... Agnes's relatives do not attach the slightest blame to Kiener for the sad out-come. They feel he did everything that a man could do. No criticism of his work or his decisions has been made by any-one with even a rudimentary knowledge of conditions or the slightest acquaintance with the peak or the route followed. ... In justice to a brave man who performed the almost impossible, whose course of action is above criticism and who nearly paid with his life, this statement is made.

Other contemporary authorities also tended to be critical of Agnes Vaille, though usually in muted and oblique terms. Carl Blaurock, for example, is one of Colorado's most highly seasoned mountaineers and had climbed with Agnes Vaille before. As he recalled in his book *A Climber's Climber*, he had been a member of the aborted second attempt in November and made no secret of the fact that he had tried to dissuade Agnes and had been rebuffed. "Agnes, you're not going to try that East Face," Blaurock recalled having told her prior to that trip.

> "Don't do it Agnes! You know how uncertain the weather can be in late fall. I think it's foolish. I wouldn't do it if I were you." But she persisted, so then I called Kiener and tried to talk him out of it. He was a smart aleck. "Oh, we can do it," he said. "We'll be all right." So I called Agnes back and said,

221

"Would you object if I went with you. I think the three of us
would have a better chance of making it."
"I would sure be glad if you would," she said.

Having failed, Blaurock counseled them to wait until spring: "I tried
to talk them into waiting, but no, they wouldn't."

One of the key participants in the event, however, had a much different view of where the blame should be placed. Elinor Eppich, the
secretary of the Colorado Mountain Club and a longtime friend of Agnes
Vaille, had accompanied Vaille and Kiener as far as Timberline Cabin
that Saturday night, and it was her concern when the two did not return
at the prearranged time that caused the rescue party to be dispatched to
search for them. Her unpublished account, dated November 20, 1963,
some four years after Kiener's death, is blunt and to the point:

> Because the subject seems still to come up periodically I think I
> should write down what I know of Agnes Vaille's winter climb
> of the East face of Longs Peak in 1925. I believe my recollection
> is accurate, and I know it is for those details which disturbed
> me so much in the official report because things hadn't hap-
> pened that way. At this point it occurs to me to wonder that
> Roger Toll did not talk to me before sending the report, but I
> suppose his concern—his business as Superintendent of the
> Park was with the rescue operation—which he certainly knew
> better than I—rather than with what preceded it.

As far as Elinor Eppich was concerned, the blame lay exclusively with
Kiener. "This lack of maturity," she wrote, "must be the reason for those
actions of his, those judgments, and the development of the trip, which
have made me so resent the judgment of the world on Agnes. I can now
view it with a little more charity. Walter Kiener was a big man, and slow."
Agnes Vaille, Eppich admitted, was "persistent and indefatigable in following her objectives. She had that drive that all the particularly successful people I know have." Based on her recollections of what took place at
Timberline Cabin during the hours prior to their departure, Eppich was
convinced that it was Walter Kiener, not Agnes Vaille, who forced the
issue. "The next morning [Sunday, January 11] the sun was shining," she
recalled,

but it was very cold and the wind was cruel. I asked Agnes something about their going and she said, "I don't think we'll go." I went outside for a few minutes, and when I came back here were Walter Kiener and Agnes, all ready to take off. I believe it was at this time that Walter Kiener made the attempt to persuade me to go with them, although I did not have proper climbing shoes with me nor other necessary equipment—which he knew because I told him. It must certainly have been at this time. It is these few minutes, and because I know from these two incidents that the final decision to make the climb on that day was not Agnes's, and that the judgment of Walter Kiener was not necessarily infallible or even good (*nobody* goes on a climb like that in ski shoes, without crampons or ice axe or even proper gloves). [It is because of this] that I have resented so, and so fought against, the general assumption of the world, of practically everyone who had heard the story, that it was all Agnes's stubbornness and poor judgment that were responsible for the whole tragedy. That simply is not so. Afterwards, when Walter Kiener came to me and told me that his friends thought that he should sue Agnes's family for damages on account of this trip, I said to him, "Wasn't this just as much your trip as hers? Didn't you want to go, too?" And he agreed that it was so.

The extent that Kiener himself secretly shared Eppich's view, or came to it as the years went by, can only be inferred. What we do know is that he talked very little in later years about the Vaille tragedy and that he never committed his version to writing. If Eppich is correct, however, about Kiener's role, the aftermath in which he lost most of his fingers and toes to frostbite would have been a source of tremendous guilt and anger, notwithstanding his ability to overcome the handicap. What we do know is that Walter Kiener lived out the remainder of his life alone. Following the completion of his B.A. at Nebraska in 1930, Kiener embarked at once on graduate work. He earned an M.A. in 1931 and a Ph.D. in biology in 1940, with a thesis on the alpine vegetation on Longs Peak. That same year, Kiener became an ecologist for the university's Conservation and Survey Division, and in 1943 he founded the Nebraska Game Commission's Fisheries Research Department. Then in 1955, suddenly and without warning,

Walter Kiener, at the very height of his career, announced his retirement. As a writer for the *Lincoln Sunday Journal* reported in a 1961 story, "He turned completely to his lichen collection, shut himself in his home-converted laboratory, and devoted all his attention to the plants." Kiener died of cancer in August of 1959, leaving his collection of some 25,000 specimens to the University of Nebraska. Twelve people attended his funeral.

The mystery surrounding the Hewes manuscript most likely will never be unraveled completely. But let the last word belong to Charles Edwin Hewes. Speaking of the Walter Kiener that he came to know, the Walter Kiener who for a series of some five summers lived alone on top of the Twin Sisters as fire lookout, Hewes wrote:

> In a way his new situation seemed to intensify the tragedy in his life, for from this station on the Twins, Longs Peak, and its East and North faces, the scene of his sorrows, were constantly under his gaze. Looking often at the point where Agnes perished, he must have constantly pictured the circumstances of that last fearful journey in her company. But apparently they were at peace with each other. They were not lovers— but they were, *friends*. Often he was forced to repress the thought of what might have been if she had survived.

Colorado Heritage, 1990, Issue 1

The year 1993 marked the 100th anniversary of women's suffrage in Colorado. For the occasion, the Colorado Historical Society published an edition of *Colorado Heritage* devoted to the state's legacy as the nation's first to grant women the vote by public referendum. Authors examined the many ways in which women participated in the suffrage crusade.

One of those authors was Stephen J. Leonard, chair of the history program at Metropolitan State College in Denver. A frequent contributor to *Heritage*, Leonard has chronicled such topics as life in Denver during World War II, the city's tramway strike of 1920, and Denver's modernizing postwar mayor, Quigg Newton. His 1977 article on the Irish, Germans, and English in Denver for *The Colorado Magazine* won the Society's Hafen Award as did his 1989 article in *Essays and Monographs in Colorado History* about the 1918 flu epidemic. In 2003 he coauthored the Society monograph *Honest John Shafroth: A Colorado Reformer*.

Leonard has recently written *Lynching in Colorado, 1859–1919*, an insightful look at law and order, justice and injustice as evidenced in more than 175 lynchings throughout the state. He is the author of the award-winning *Trials and Triumphs: A Colorado Portrait of the Great Depression*. He is also coauthor of several other titles, including *Thomas Hornsby Ferril and the American West* and *The Art of Charles Partridge Adams*, both published by Fulcrum Publishing; *Colorado: A History of the Centennial State*; and with Tom Noel, *Denver: Mining Camp to Metropolis*.

With a good ear for a telling quote, here Leonard offers a concise look at how the women of Colorado convinced the state's men to grant them the right to vote.

"Bristling for Their Rights": Colorado's Women and the Mandate of 1893

—Stephen J. Leonard

As "Dane," an anonymous correspondent for a Wisconsin newspaper, traveled through southeastern Wyoming in the summer of 1871, he found little to his liking. He characterized the landscape, which he deemed unsuitable for farming, as "an immense bed of small gravel." The political landscape troubled him as well: "Wyoming, if great in nothing, has at last achieved notoriety by being the first to admit women into the political kingdom. Here it was that we first beheld that political monstrosity [—] a female voter."

Wyoming's territorial legislature gave women the right to vote in 1869, putting that sparsely settled future state far ahead of the rest of the country in granting suffrage unfettered by gender. Governor Edward McCook, hoping that his Colorado Territory would quickly follow Wyoming, asked lawmakers in 1870 to sanction equal voting privileges for men and women. Approval by the territorial legislature, coupled with congressional concurrence, could have made McCook's proposal law, since a territory could broaden the voting franchise without an election among the people. Colorado's legislators, however, refused to follow Wyoming's lead. Instead, most of them heeded George A. Hinsdale, president of the territorial council. He declared that allowing a woman to vote would "destroy the symmetry of her character."

Suffragists did not give up. In 1871, two of the movement's national leaders, Susan B. Anthony and Elizabeth Cady Stanton, journeyed west to win converts. Dane warned that "Colorado appears to be the vineyard wherein the female suffragists are laboring assiduously, probably expecting to reap the harvest of another territory victimized into committing itself to their cause." In Greeley, Dane heard Stanton indulge "in the customary pathos when speaking of the galling serfdom of women and how they are tyrannized over by the monster, man."

Not all men were "monsters"; a few of them interpreted rules broadly and allowed women to vote. In the early 1870s some Colorado women voted in areas where there were sympathetic registrars, and in Greeley, says historian Beverly Beeton, a candidate for postmaster "begged women to go to the polls and vote for him." Such practices, however, were of dubious legality. Rather, to guarantee their rights women needed the official sanction which leaders of the Women's Suffrage Association hoped to obtain in 1876 from drafters of Colorado's state constitution. Two legislators, Agipeta Vigil, representing Huerfano and Las Animas Counties, and Henry Bromwell of Denver, favored writing equal suffrage into the constitution, but their colleagues disagreed. By a vote of 24 to 8, they approved a constitution limiting women to voting in school district elections and upon issues affecting schools. The question of a full vote for women was left for males to decide during an election in 1877.

Susan B. Anthony again came to Colorado, as did Lucy Stone. Again they failed to persuade most men. Dismissed by Presbyterian minister Thomas Bliss as "bawling, ranting women, bristling for their rights" and by Roman Catholic Bishop Joseph Projectus Machebeuf as "battalions of old maids disappointed in love," women found that frontier Colorado held fast to the past. Agipeta Vigil aside, most Hispanics in southern Colorado opposed votes for women. In northern and central sections, males bred in the United States or Europe also generally followed tradition. Only Boulder County approved equal suffrage in the 1877 balloting, which failed by a count of 14,053 to 6,612.

The Colorado Equal Suffrage Association, which angered some women by electing a man as its president, replaced the moribund Colorado Women's Suffrage Association in early 1881—the same year that a measure providing suffrage in the state's municipal elections met defeat. Twice rejected, the state's women temporarily put the suffrage issue aside and concentrated their energies elsewhere.

The Woman's Christian Temperance Union (WCTU) established its Denver chapter in 1880, attacked liquor interests, demanded laws protecting women and children, and campaigned against vices ranging from prostitution to promiscuous expectoration. Mary Shields, the organization's president from 1880 to 1887, put equal suffrage high on her agenda because votes would give power to temperance advocates. Although the WCTU failed to give suffrage full support, it nonetheless organized women and convinced many of their need for political clout.

Other groups focused the power of women. The Young Women's Christian Association (YWCA) opened a Denver clubhouse in 1887. In addition to providing recreational and social activities, it campaigned against child labor and gave food and shelter to homeless visitors. Many upper- and middle-class women joined literary and musical societies such as the Denver Fortnightly Club (1881), the Tuesday Musical Club (1891), and the Clio Club and Sphinx Club (both 1892). Additionally there were neighborhood organizations such as the North Side Woman's Club, philanthropic societies, political and reform associations, and task-oriented groups such as the Denver Free Kindergarten Association (1890). Such organizations statewide gave women a powerful network which proved invaluable in their 1890s drive for suffrage.

Outside such organizational mainstreams, publisher Caroline Nichols Churchill also encouraged women to demand their rights. Churchill began the monthly women-oriented *Colorado Antelope* in 1879. Three years later she shifted to a weekly schedule and renamed her

Minnie J. Reynolds, a *Rocky Mountain News* writer, helped win the support of 75 percent of the state's newspapers during the 1893 campaign. She is shown here in her later years at the national suffrage headquarters.

Denver-based paper *Queen Bee*. For more than a decade the *Bee* buzzed loudly, damning the logic of those opposing equal suffrage. "All women," Churchill declared, "are victims, more or less; all suffer in one way or another from a preponderance of masculine influence." Why did men subjugate women? "Young men," wrote Churchill, "fear her emancipation will be the death blow to their pet vices and darling sins." She had no doubt that if "the paternal [instinct] were half as strong as the maternal, the numbers of beggarly children and dead mothers would be vastly lessened." At times her vision was broad: "Society will never construct a government worthy of the respect [of its citizens] ... until women form a part of its councils." At other times she waxed sarcastic, suggesting that an anti–equal suffrage editor in Silverton was going bald because his brain could not furnish "sufficient vitality or nerve ... to sustain the growth of hair."

In December 1887 Churchill gained a journalistic ally when Albina Washburn began publishing a woman's column in Denver's *Labor Enquirer*. Washburn, who had been pushing women's rights through her membership in the Grange, believed that city women and farm women should join workers to defeat the "mob of rich men—rich only in stolen wealth—crying for our blood." And she told her readers: "It is right and just that women would command equal pay for equal work with men." Noting that women only received half a loaf in being permitted to vote in school elections, she predicted that one day they would "intend to have the other half ... and perhaps other loaves and a few of the fishes." In 1892 Washburn hastened the day of the full loaf by helping convince the People's party, whose members were known as Populists, to take a pro-suffrage stance.

Support from the Populists proved important to the suffragist cause, but even more vital was the work of the Colorado Equal Suffrage Association (later renamed the Non-Partisan Equal Suffrage Association) formed by six women in 1890. With headquarters in Denver, the association attracted many of the city's most able women—writers Ellis Meredith, Minnie J. Reynolds, and Patience Stapleton; teacher Martha Pease; physician Mary B. Bates; and club leader Elizabeth P. Ensley, an African American. Society leaders lent their names, and Baby Doe Tabor donated office space in her husband's Denver opera house for the suffrage effort.

Sensing in 1893 that a third suffrage campaign might succeed, local women again sought help from national suffrage leaders. Several discouraged the idea. "Have you converted all those Mexicans?" Susan B.

Anthony skeptically asked, because few southern Colorado Hispanics had supported the previous suffrage effort. "Why did you introduce a bill now?" queried Lucy Stone, the movement's grandmother. "I have talked with no one who feels there is the slightest hope of success in Colorado," wrote Carrie Chapman Catt.

"Are you sure you have talked with anyone who understands the situation here?" replied Denver newspaperwoman Ellis Meredith. Women in southern Colorado, she asserted, were threatening to run their anti-suffrage state senator out of the county; Populist Governor Davis Waite endorsed suffrage as did Republican ex-Governor John Routt. Thirty-three newspapers which were surveyed approved suffrage; only eleven opposed. Thomas Patterson, publisher of the widely circulated *Rocky Mountain News*, was not partial to equal suffrage, but kept his paper neutral. Writer Meredith, whose father was managing editor of the *News*, conceded that "we may fail, but there is a very strong chance our enemies may let it go by default."

Solidifying the alliances formed by Meredith and her co-workers were even larger forces in the women's favor. The 1890 census revealed that Colorado's male voters outnumbered the potential female electorate. More than 80 percent of the state's females over age nineteen were married or widowed; fewer than 20 percent were classified as single. Given this stable, domestic contingent which, if enfranchised, would constitute less than 40 percent of the electorate, men were not risking political suicide by endorsing equal suffrage. Indeed, American-born males fearing the loss of their economic and political power to naturalized citizens may have thought that abandoning one tradition might help preserve others. By enfranchising women, natives gained more ballots than did the foreign-born.

Comforting though such statistics may have been to Meredith and friends, their hopes were tempered by financial realities. "We might just as well talk of raising mountains as money," Meredith told Carrie Chapman Catt. Lucy Stone sent $300, a welcome addition to a war chest that contained only $25 at the campaign's outset. Anthony gave free advice. She specifically warned against linking suffrage to temperance, insisting that advocates "push nothing but suffrage pure and simple." Fearful that the Colorado effort would fail, Anthony stayed away, but Catt agreed to lecture. "I have a voice like a fog horn and can be heard in out-of-door meetings" she assured organizers. She was also ready for the pious: "I have a Sunday school speech—'the Bible and Woman Suffrage'—which will not offend the most orthodox and has done some good among conservatives."

National leaders suggested that Coloradans import Mary Lease, the fiery hell-raiser from Kansas, to snare the Populists. Meredith, knowing that local Populists endorsed the women anyway, rejected Lease as "too ultra," preferring instead the help of Emma DeVoe, whom Catt recommended. To the voices of out-of-staters were added the journalistic talents of *Rocky Mountain News* society columnist Minnie J. Reynolds and novelist Patience Stapleton. Grand Junction's Dr. Elizabeth Strasser, Colorado Springs' Dr. Anna Chamberlain, and Dr. Jessie Harwell of Salida joined teachers such as Denver's Martha A. Pease, president of the

Elizabeth Ensley, treasurer of the Colorado Equal
Suffrage Association in 1893, campaigned for suffrage
in Denver's African American community.

Equal Suffrage Association, to convince men that women were intellectually capable. By electing Ione T. Hanna to a Denver-area school board in May 1893, women dampened the anti-suffrage argument that females did not *want* to vote.

The suffragists' decision to push for a referendum in 1893, a year in which a light vote was forecast, may have helped their cause. Anthony's absence and the widespread involvement of local women may have forced men to recognize that Colorado's women wanted the vote, and that they were not being manipulated by outsiders. There were other factors suggesting that the upcoming vote might favor the women: By publishing an anti-suffrage pamphlet inadvertently containing a brewery advertisement, the opposition revealed the source of some of its support. Meredith delighted in that misstep: "We got out nearly 150,000 pamphlets," she exclaimed, "but not one was so valuable as theirs." Additionally, the chaos spawned by the 1893 silver collapse and resultant depression in Colorado served the women well, as men voiced dissatisfaction with existing conditions by broadening the voting franchise.

By November 1893, at the crescendo of the campaign, no fewer than sixty suffrage chapters and 10,000 Colorado women were working for "equal rights and justice for all." In Cañon City, Emma G. Curtis convinced coal miners to support suffrage. Lillian Hartman-Johnson of Durango took charge in southwestern Colorado, her task made difficult by the opposition of David Day, then editor of the *Durango Democrat*. Men also joined the crusade, one of the most effective being Denver attorney Jared Warner Mills, who drafted the bill authorizing the 1893 suffrage referendum. Toward the campaign's end, even Susan B. Anthony appeared mildly optimistic. She briefly considered traveling to Colorado, but opted not to. If the measure passed, she told Meredith, "Colorado will be the first state that has so many noble and just men."

On election day, November 7, 1893, Colorado's men approved women's suffrage by a vote of 35,698 to 29,461. For the first time in the United States, males were asked the question of a full vote for women, and responded "yes." Although she failed to take a significant part in the crusade, Susan B. Anthony nonetheless exulted: "Well—I can't yet believe it is true—it is too good to be true! Oh—how glad I am, that at last we have knocked down our first state by the popular vote."

Epilogue

Equal suffrage did not guarantee women equal economic and social rights, nor did it reward the Populists with the support they expected in return. Defeated for re-election in 1894, Populist Governor Davis Waite turned against the women, whom he considered ingrates. Susan B. Anthony remained upset at Colorado's women, who had managed to win the vote without her. She did not bother to send congratulations to Ellis Meredith until two weeks after the election. During an 1894 Women's Suffrage Association meeting in Washington, D.C., Meredith was scheduled to be the initial speaker but Anthony called on six others first. With only a few minutes to review the Colorado victory, Meredith exceeded her allocated time and was ordered to stop. The slight so angered the audience that Anthony was forced to allow Meredith more time. Anthony yielded to the audience: "You shall have your sweet will."

Until California sanctioned equal suffrage in 1911, thereby enfranchising women in San Francisco and Los Angeles, Denver remained the largest United States city in which women could vote equally with men. Some remained opposed to the woman's vote in Colorado: When state Senator John Hecker suggested in 1911 that Colorado rescind women's voting rights, he was confronted by four women legislators who suggested taking the vote away from men. Hecker hastily claimed that he was just kidding.

With ratification of the Nineteenth Amendment to the U.S. Constitution in 1920, women nationwide gained suffrage rights equal to those of men. Even before 1920, many states had extended suffrage to women. Among them, Colorado occupied an honored position.

Colorado Heritage, Spring 1993

I n 1989, Patricia Nelson Limerick wrote a one-page statement titled, "What on Earth Is the New Western History?" She distributed it to colleagues attending a Santa Fe symposium that kicked off the traveling *Trails Through Time* exhibition. Limerick had intended to provide focus for discussion about recent trends in western historical interpretation. Instead, she heralded a new school of thought and created a national controversy.

That controversy has all but died. The paradigm, as they say, has shifted. The New Western History is no longer new; it is mainstream. Few, if any, contemporary historians cling to Frederick Jackson Turner's concept that the advancing western frontier—"the meeting point between savagery and civilization"—shaped and defined America's development. Though quick to credit the work of other historians, Limerick's 1987 book, *The Legacy of Conquest*, had something to do with the change. "The reality of conquest," she wrote, "dissolved into stereotypes of noble savages and noble pioneers struggling quaintly in the wilderness. These adventures seemed to have no bearing on the complex realities of twentieth-century America."

Limerick juxtaposed those stereotypes and realities in an essay included in the catalog for *The Real West*, a cooperative and ambitious exhibition staged by the Colorado Historical Society, Denver Public Library, and Denver Art Museum in 1996. Her thoughts reflected the project's goal: to use western symbols—such as the tipi, the Rocky Mountains, the cowboy hat—to examine how the West was shaped by diverse peoples struggling for survival and dominance. Limerick, using her trademark conversational tone, offered insights into the imagined and real West. But she did not provide a final, authoritative definition. Instead, she offered a more flexible viewpoint: "Everybody has a story to tell and each story has its own claim to legitimacy."

Limerick continues to explore the complexities of western history as professor of history and environmental studies at the University of Colorado at Boulder. She backs up her belief in making knowledge of the past relevant to the present by speaking to a range of community groups and writing for local and national newspapers. Currently, she chairs the board of the Center of the American West.

The Real West

—Patricia Nelson Limerick

Begin with this intellectually and visually stimulating exercise. Look at Vroman's photograph *Red Mountain Reflection, Ouray*. Then decide if the mountainous scene you are looking at is right-side-up. Here is a warning: This will feel like an easy question.

Now look at the same photograph, inverted this time. Is the scene upside-down? Is it right-side-up? Does something seem to be going wrong with your judgment? Photographs, we have been trained to think, are images very directly drawn from reality. Light bounces off a landscape and transports its message to film. Painting is, of course, a different matter: Light bounces off a landscape, transports its message to the artists' minds, and the

Adam Clark Vroman, *Red Mountain Reflection, Ouray, Colorado*, c. 1890.
(Courtesy of the Denver Art Museum Collection:
Gift of the Strauss Collection, 1981.177)

235

artists then do what they damn well please with that information. But photographs are supposed to be very close mimicry of reality. Even though we know the photographer plays a role in choosing an angle of vision and a frame to limit the view, we should be able to trust photographs, in some minimal way, to anchor and orient us to the real world out there.

And thus one can work oneself into something of a frenzy with this photograph, turning it one way and then the other, trying to figure out which arrangement will comply with the rules of gravity. Surely two of the most basic measures of a person's grasp on reality are these: a) the ability to tell up from down and b) the ability to distinguish a three-dimensional, weighty, solid landscape from its image reflected in water. This photograph gracefully and pleasantly steals both of those capacities from the viewer. Up and down, landscape and reflection, become indistinguishable and interchangeable, and the sensation produced is not entirely pleasure. While burdensome and restricting of free movement, gravity can also be something of a comfort.

In the late twentieth century, the search to distinguish "the Real West" from "the Fake West" has come to resemble the quest to tell up from down in the image of Red Mountain. Here, in a nutshell, is the problem: For nearly two centuries, a great deal of creative, literary, artistic, and commercial energy has gone into the production and distribution of an imagined West. The content of the imagined West is deeply, endlessly familiar: cowboys, open range, adventure, good guys, bad guys, gunplay, noble pioneers, encircled wagon trains, brides bringing civilization to rough towns, savage Indians needing to be taught a lesson. As tenuous as its tie to history may be, the imagined West has, in turn, come to shape the behavior of human beings—their direct, consequential, physical behavior—in a million ways. Thus, the Real West and the Fake West end up tied together, virtually Siamese twins sharing the same circulatory system. The intellectual surgery required to separate them would be an almost guaranteed failure. And yet, from time to time, irritation—over the way the myths of the West keep us from facing up to and reckoning with the gritty problems of the West—can produce a compelling desire to yank the western myth apart from the western reality.

Good luck.

Take cowboy clothes. There is every piece of evidence to indicate that what we know as the archetypal clothes of the nineteenth-century cowboy actually emerged from the business of country-western music in the twentieth century. Cowboys did not have the time or money or working conditions that would have permitted them to sport beautiful white hats with snappy and curled brims, or shirts patterned with sequins and embroidery. In the late twentieth century, many westerners—urbanites as well as ranchers—adopt "western wear," with a clear belief that they are dressing like cowboys, and not like country western performers. And the application of cowboy clothes to the outside of the body is only one dimension of this trend. Often enough, the cowboy hat on the outside of the head will shape events and patterns inside the head. The employee of a multinational corporation will put on his Stetson and see himself as tough outsider, riding the corporate range, as well as voting in elections, in an independent, self-reliant, John Wayne–based manner. Science may never figure out the exact process at work here, but the values and images associated with a cowboy hat apparently can be absorbed through the scalp. Thus, whether in matters of self-perception or in matters of perception of the land and its limits, the West is a region where vision has a way of going blurry, with wishes and hopes frequently overruling the prosaic reports delivered by the eye and the optic nerve.

And yet, in theory and partly in practice, the American West is the part of the nation where the view is the clearest. A climate of aridity makes for many days of sunshine, and high altitude and cloudlessness combine to create a particularly intense kind of sunlight. Aridity, moreover, sets up the conditions for sparse vegetation, so the land itself is starkly revealed. Many nineteenth-century travelers to the West turned to the metaphor of nakedness, describing western landforms as unclothed and uncovered. From their earliest encounters, geologists embraced the opportunities presented by the sheer visibility of the western earth.

The West seemed to reveal basic truths about physical nature, truths well disguised and concealed elsewhere in North America. In the same spirit, the West got credit for revealing the truth about human nature. A person's real character, many overland travelers observed, came to the surface under the pressures of the trail. In a mobile, pioneer society, reputation and established status could carry comparatively little power. With so little in the way of prior familiarity, judgments of one's neighbors had to rest on what they actually did and said, rather than on appearances. Western society brought out true human character, just as the western sunlight brought out the true character of the earth.

Or so the theory went. In fact, a mobile society also proved to be perfect turf for con men, for people selling stock in nonexistent mines, for boosters promising easy opportunity, for people manipulating and milking expectation and hope in expert ways. The history of western scams and schemes is an extensive one, and there is little evidence to support the proposition that westerners had or have a particularly developed knack for distinguishing the real from the fake in human nature.

In the same way, nature proved to have a few tricks to play of its own. Fool's gold sparkled as real gold ought to sparkle, but perversely does not. Land that seemed to be securely reclassified as real estate developed alarming mobility, whether through earthquakes, landslides, avalanches, or wind erosion. The clarity of the air led travelers from the eastern United States to mis-estimate distances; a range of mountains would seem to be right ahead, just a few miles away, when it actually meant a journey of several days. The landscape seemed to be open for reading, and yet nearly every explorer's journal records moments of deep, sometimes terrifying, perplexity, when the western landscape seemed transformed into labyrinth. Lt. Amiel Weeks Whipple spoke for many of his fellow nineteenth-century explorers when he recorded a dark moment in December of 1853, during his southwestern expedition. "Where we are to go now," Lt. Whipple said, "is a great question that sits like a night-mare upon my breast."[1] We may try, in sentimental hindsight, to work up a fit of envy for the exhilaration that the explorers of the West must have felt, but the fearful consequences of choosing the wrong route in unknown territory reduced the fun considerably for the participants themselves.

Many of these moments of disorientation came from the rough encounter between simple eastern expectations and a complicated western reality. In one of the most familiar incidents of this kind, Thomas Jefferson told Meriwether Lewis and William Clark to travel to the headwaters of the Missouri River and find a short portage to the headwaters of the Columbia River. But, as Lewis and Clark approached the mountains and the river kept forking, how were they to choose the right direction? Which fork was the real Missouri, and which was an imposter likely to lead them off-track? In their long and dangerous journey over the Rockies and across the Continental Divide, Jefferson's idea of a short and easy connection between the waters of the East and the waters of the West set the precedent for a long-range pattern, by which Americans would ask the West for something simple, and the West would give them something complicated.

The request for the simple and the receipt of the complicated remain a common pattern in western life today. In various episodes of recent cultural history, the American public has asked for a simple view of the West; scholars and museums have given them something complicated; and the public—or at least its most audible spokespeople—has responded with threat and anger. In 1991, in the most publicized of these incidents, while American nationalism flared up in the Gulf War, the Smithsonian's Museum of American Art opened an exhibit called *The West as America*. The exhibit featured lovely paintings of the American West, juxtaposed with wall commentary that interpreted these images as justification for and evasions of the often unhappy and ugly reality of the conquest of the West. The guest book, placed at the end of the exhibit to record visitor reactions, reached record levels of emotional heat from the first page. While many viewers wrote favorably about the exhibit, many others were apoplectic, enraged by what they saw as an attack and smear on the nation's proud past. Two western senators threw themselves into the fray, threatening to cut the Smithsonian's budget for this lapse in patriotism.

Newspaper reporters, writing about the *West as America* fight, drew a picture of scholars who claimed to have identified the reality of the West, and who claimed as well that those outraged by the exhibit chose to live in the comfort and simplicity of myth and falsehood. But the late-twentieth-century conflict between the preferences of scholars and the preferences of the public is quite a different matter from the comparatively simple opposition between reality and myth.

Far from claiming to have uncovered the real and true history of the West, scholars are up to something a great deal more annoying. Academics writing about the West, like academics writing about virtually everything else these days, are questioning the very ideas of reality and truth. Rather than opposing a true story to a fake story, they are, instead, saying that everybody has a story, and each story has its own claim to legitimacy. Human beings, by definition, are story-makers and story-tellers. Historical stories may well reveal a great deal about events and occurrences, but they reveal as much about their tellers as they do about the events and occurrences. Rather than scholars imperiously telling the public what is true and what is untrue, scholars are instead declaring that each and every story about the West is a complicated swirl of truth and

untruth, of events of the body and events of the mind, of interior experience and social exchange. Reality, contemporary scholars never tire of
telling us, is a social and cultural construction—a proposition which is
profoundly unsatisfying as a foundation for living one's life.

In fact, as one of the more prosaic-minded inhabitants of that exotic
environment known as the "university," I am quite willing to say that a
full embrace of the idea that reality is constructed would be dangerous
and destructive. A full embrace is, fortunately, impossible. Imagine a day
in which you experienced every moment with full awareness of the arbitrary, even whimsical, assumptions you were making and acting on. You
awake in the morning, and you immediately have to wonder why you
have awakened in the morning. Other species are nocturnal; some people thoroughly adapt to working the night shift; Benjamin Franklin's
adages about "early to bed and early to rise" aside, there is nothing in
human programming that says it has to be this way.

You struggle past the relative meanings of morning and go to take a
shower, but you are immediately overwhelmed with a recognition of
how strange a development contemporary society's preoccupation with
cleanliness is. From the weekly custom of "the Saturday night bath" a few
decades ago, we have now gotten wild with enthusiasm for the frequent
use of soaps, bathing gels, shampoo, and deodorant. Out of the shower,
you try to get dressed, but you are knocked off your feet by an awareness
of the inexplicable arbitrariness of our definitions of the appropriate in
dress. Why on earth must men tie nooses around their necks in order to
convey a condition of professional reliability and steadiness? Why must
women sheathe their legs in a transparent, stretchy material composed of
petrochemicals, even when that material is oppressive and clingy in summer, and almost useless in resisting cold in winter?

If you made it through the performance of all these baffling rituals,
then the cultural construction of breakfast would bring the day to a halt.
Here we have the survival of one persistent set of understandings, by
which breakfast means eggs, buttered toast, bacon, or ham. Thanks to
recent changes in the cultural construction of medicine, that definition
of breakfast is now under siege (though by no means defeated, as any
restaurant menu shows), with an alternative meaning of breakfast, as
juice, fruit, and a bread or cereal product, capturing many minds. And
this still leaves unaddressed the whole strange and mysterious social construction of a morning beverage. The ritual brewing of coffee carries

such a powerful freight of associations in American society that a distant observer (say, one from a different planet) might think that there was a religious content to this carefully observed morning ceremony.

Drinking coffee in the morning, moreover, is often accompanied by the reading of a newspaper, an astonishing social artifact in itself—paper and print arranged in odd categories and degrees of urgency. The front page quotes some not entirely sincere remarks made by people who would sincerely like to be our rulers and who are engaging in a very peculiar act of social theater known as a campaign. The inside front page gives us detailed knowledge of the sayings and doings, the romances and quarrels, the marriages and divorces, of people designated as "celebrities," people we have not met but whose lives we nonetheless consider legitimate turf for snooping. Sometimes the newspaper tells us that we are being poisoned by the coffee we are sipping; sometimes the newspaper raises our spirits by telling us that its previous story was misleading, and our loyalty to this ceremonial beverage will not, in fact, kill us off.

So there one would be, if one tried to live every moment with an awareness of the arbitrary construction of what we know as reality, nearly dead of self-consciousness before one had gotten up from breakfast. Every moment would be one of open-ended choice: "Do I embrace this clearly arbitrary construction of reality, or do I reject it? Or do I just call in sick, go back to bed, and hope that sanity will return if I get more rest?"

Fortunately, nobody—even the scholars most ardent about pursuing this line of analysis—can live this way. Postmodernist male academics rise in the morning and tie the required nooses around their necks without a moment's thought; breakfast gets eaten and the newspaper gets read before anyone gets around to thinking, "What in heaven's name do we mean by *breakfast* and *newspaper*?"

So is scholarly self-consciousness of this sort a useless waste of time, the sort of thing intellectuals do with their idle hours when they have no more important function to perform? On the contrary. In measured doses, the model of reality as a construction could make us better people, certainly better citizens, and maybe better westerners. Persuading readers of this proposition may take a little more time, but it is central to the project of *The Real West*.

Take the challenge posed by this exhibit and catalogue, the challenge to viewers to ask themselves what adds up to "reality" in our understanding of the West. Exercising a mind on this proposition, treating the question

Albert Bierstadt, *Estes Park, Colorado,* 1877.
(Courtesy of the Denver Public Library, Western History Collection)

like a sort of weight-training machine for the intellect, makes for a better and stronger mind.

Take the question of reality as it applies to photographs and paintings. For many viewers (and I am myself in this group), a photograph immediately looks "more real" than a painting. There is, first, the fact that painters put themselves and their imagination into every line and shape, while the photographers just click the button that opens the lens to admit the light. The photographs, moreover, are usually black and white, which causes them to give the impression that they are straightforward, direct, and truthful. To put this very informally, photographs look much less gussied up and therefore more believable.

So viewers asked to be self-conscious about their own ways of measuring "realness" can end up having to make this peculiar admission: Black-and-white photographs look "more real" to us than do brightly colored paintings, even though only those poor souls afflicted with color-blindness actually see a world without color. Thus, in this curious definition of comparative reality, we betray and discount our own primary visual experience. By another, seemingly more sensible standard of judgment, the sheer presence of color in a painting should make its content instantly "more real" than the image presented by any black-and-white photograph.

This attribution of reality clearly presents us with an occasion for reconsideration. We must face up to the powerful role played by the

Vance Kirkland, *Fantasy Landscape*, 1948.
*(Courtesy of the Denver Art Museum Collection: Gift of
Vance H. and Anne O. Kirkland, 1982.431)*

photographers' choices of framework, boundaries, point of view, and subject matter. In many ways, the photographers' images end up as contrived and shaped by artifice as the painters' images. Equally, one's initial impressions of the difference between nineteenth-century paintings and twentieth-century paintings can mislead, though in an opposite direction. Compare, for instance, Bierstadt's *Estes Park, Colorado* with Vance Kirkland's *Fantasy Landscape*. Initially, Kirkland's painting seems obviously more stylized, more shaped by artistic convention, more a matter of the artist taking a great deal of liberty with the representation of the mountains themselves. But this initial attribution of greater realism to the nineteenth-century paintings almost instantly reveals itself to be a testimony to the greater familiarity and wider popularization of the works by Bierstadt and Moran. Their paintings look more familiar, and thus more real, because we have been looking at their paintings much longer and much more frequently. In fact, the nineteenth-century painters were as stylized and mannered in their representations as are the twentieth-century painters; it just happens that the nineteenth-century style and manner make a better, more comfortable fit with the habits of our minds, in part because these paintings shaped those habits.

And yet, as we start to settle into the familiarity of the nineteenth-century paintings, a faith in the realness of their representations instantly encounters a doubt: Can these paintings be believable when they are so pretty? Here, then, is the signal to the good standing and power of cynicism in our times: If something looks too beautiful and attractive, we are likely to think it is fake. And yet the American West is well-supplied with places and people that seem to be, genuinely and powerfully, beautiful and attractive.

In western landscape photography, the appropriate subject was, for many years, natural beauty. Men like Ansel Adams and Eliot Porter took photographs of a gorgeous and stunning West, of pristine and appealing landscapes often threatened by human schemes and plans of development. In the last fifteen or twenty years, a reaction against the "Beauty School" approach has inspired landscape photographers to refuse to search out properly beautiful scenes. Highways, dams, suburbs, and tourist traps have become perfectly legitimate subject matter. Rather than struggling to edit out evidence of human presence, contemporary landscape photographers highlight cars and jet trails, buildings and litter. And yet, paradoxically, a number of these photographs of ugly things are quite arresting in their own aesthetic beauty.

One's first inclination might be to say that the more that it addresses unattractive, or at least unconventionally appealing, sights, the more realistic photography has grown. If an image is stern and even ugly, then, it will strike many viewers as more real than an image that is pleasant and pretty. In this frame of judgment, one lets the artifacts of industry claim the category "real." Thus, William Henry Jackson's *Arkansas Valley Smelter* looks hard-edged and realistic. Tough-minded American capitalism is in

William Henry Jackson, *Arkansas Valley Smelter*

244

John Gast, *American Progress*, 1872

charge. The nice pictures of lovely landscapes may be soothing and spirit-lifting, but here, in this smelter, the rubber meets the road and things get down-to-earth, practical, and unsentimental.

Well, maybe. In the maddening way of late-twentieth-century academics, one has to say that it depends on one's point of view. As the writer Edward Abbey used to put it, what we call practical people are the ones who get emotional about money. It was and is just as possible to make a heavy investment of sentiment in the Arkansas Valley smelter as it was to make such an investment in any of the more conventionally appealing, officially more natural landscapes. In our time, we may lament the injury done to the atmosphere by industrial emissions, but for many Americans in the late nineteenth century, a smoke-filled sky was a sign of prosperity and possibility. From that point of view, one could look at the smoke belching from a smelter's chimney and see, not an environmental mess, but a sign of economic success.

This wavering definitional boundary between mess and success is, surely, the center of irritation in the late twentieth century's reinterpretation of the western American past. In *American Progress*, John Gast personified westward expansion as a huge white lady drifting through the skies, in a white gown held in place more by destiny than by any of the material

John Charles Frémont
(Courtesy of the Denver Public Library, Western History Collection)

arrangements available to mortals. Peculiar as it is, this image has been widely reproduced and commented on in the late twentieth century. One suspects that it is a very rare viewer, these days, who responds to Gast's painting with conviction and agreement. The image of a large, aerial white lady in a precarious dress is unlikely to confirm the viewer in a belief in progress, and it is certainly unlikely to strike the viewer as realistic.

Like the lady in Gast's painting, the concept of progress is itself having a hard time earning the public's loyalty. Even those who have taken up the cause of defensive patriotism do so in terms of nostalgia, laying plans to return to and recreate a departed era of American prosperity, confidence, and consensus. Few can convincingly speak up on behalf of the faith that was much more widespread in the nineteenth century: the faith that life really is getting better and better, that progress is no abstraction, but a force at work in everyday life.

Optimism and confidence, in the nineteenth-century West, came in many forms. Look, for instance, at the demonstration of optimism and confidence in both the image and reality of John C. Frémont. Here was a man charging into the future, ready for any challenge ahead. The engraving shows a spirited horse, but an even more spirited rider in charge of the horse and of destiny. Frémont would explore the West, assessing the landforms and the plants and animals, taking notes, and making celestial observations. Out of this exploration would come a firm grasp on the reality of the West and a prosperous and well-rewarded personal career.

After two successful expeditions, the confidence and optimism did more unraveling than rewarding. In the next years, Frémont underwent a court-martial; he failed financially in the management of an estate in central California; he led an expedition into the San Juan Mountains in midwinter, and some of the men who survived did so by eating those who died. In his last years, Frémont published Volume One of his memoirs (never followed by Volume Two because Volume One sold so poorly) and devoted himself to pleading for a government pension, an experience quite different from charging into the future on a spirited horse.

For some individuals involved in the nineteenth-century West, confidence and optimism had pretty well unraveled in their own lifetime. Others would put up a much harder fight against the unraveling. John Chivington, the Methodist minister who led the troops in the Sand Creek Massacre in 1864, never gave up the project of asserting the righteousness of his actions. "I stand by Sand Creek," Chivington said, even though a chorus of white Americans had joined Cheyenne and Arapaho people in lamenting and condemning the attack. Americans questioned the justifications and apologies for Sand Creek, from the day before it happened, through Senate and Army hearings and investigations, down to our times. Chivington and many of his men worked hard to stay in the framework of thought by which the American conquest of the West was so thoroughly justified that the spilling of Indian blood was a small price for progress. Over time, the number of white Americans of a different persuasion has grown, into a sizable population much more inclined to wince over than to cheer the violence that made American occupation possible.

Interpretations of the West, for some observers of American culture, are the markers of change in national self-appraisal. In the movie *Dances with Wolves*, the Sioux became the good guys and the whites became the bad guys, and the reversal of values seemed, to some, to be complete. Now, when the Sioux caught up to the Army and attacked as the troops crossed the river, the audience response was no longer the familiar, "Oh no, the Army has failed to move fast enough, and now the Indians have attacked; what a mess!" The response was, instead, "Oh thank heavens, the Indians have arrived just in time to attack the wicked Army!" It was hard to make the case that *Dances with Wolves* presented a more realistic picture of western history, but it was considerably easier to claim that the audience's receptive response was an indication that something big was shifting in the self-image of white Americans.

For some, this shift represents a very sad state of affairs. When we cheer for the Indians, these critics would say, we show that we have lost our nerve, lost our will, lost our pride, lost our convictions, lost our bearings, lost our sense of direction. We are sniffling over the injuries of the past, and neglecting the needs of the present, the need for forthright and confident assertion of national interests. Realism, to this point of view, means the necessity to be hardheaded, to recognize that progress necessarily means that someone pays a few prices, to take a stand for traditional American faith in enterprise and profit-seeking, to reject this alternative world of relative and shifting values.

And yet an exhibit like this poses a persuasive and telling set of challenges to those still trying to make the case for certainty and unwavering conviction. We look at an apparently realistic photograph of a mountain and a lake, and we cannot tell right-side-up from upside-down. When we are asked to figure out how, exactly, we are able to distinguish and recognize reality, we discover in ourselves a peculiar and even semi-mystical set of standards that govern our judgments.

Accepting an element of uncertainty and self-doubt in one's judgments has one glorious effect: It cuts into smugness the way detergents cut into grease. Once we have questioned the reliability and steadiness of our own understandings of reality, we have less reason to think of those who see the world differently as fools laboring under misguided and dismissible definitions of reality. Thus, my earlier claim: A reckoning with the question of how we define the "real" part of the phrase, "the Real West," could make us better citizens and better westerners. It could make us aware of how much unexamined sentiment shapes our appraisals of the western past and the western present. And that could, in turn, induce tolerance.

Nineteenth-century painters of the West, one learns from this exhibit, were enthusiasts for mist. There they stood, painting the region most characterized by abundant sunlight, the region where landforms were most starkly revealed. While they sometimes embraced and celebrated the joys and power of an unimpeded view, the painters frequently cloaked their landscapes with fog, clouds, haze, and mist. Consider Harvey Young's *The Heart of the Rockies*. Except for one promontory of land, the heart of the Rockies, as conceptualized and portrayed by Young, consists of fog. There is not much that conveys certainty in this image, not much that confidently proclaims the human ability to explore, decipher, and master nature. There is, on the contrary, an acceptance of mystery, and an admission that the closer one gets to the heart of the West, the less one will be able to know for sure, and the more one may be asked to feel and to imagine.

In 1874, in the heart of the Rockies, two explorers climbed to the top of a peak. Taking advantage of the powerful view, they began to sketch the landscape and to put their surveying equipment to work. "We scarcely got started to work," one of them reported, "when we both began to feel a peculiar tickling sensation along the roots of our hair, just at the edge of our hats. ... At first this sensation was only perceptible and not at all troublesome; still its strength surprised us." Finally recognizing that they were in the midst of an electric storm, they continued to work,

Harvey Otis Young, *The Heart of the Rockies*, 1899.
(Courtesy of the Pikes Peak Library District)

even as "the rapid increase in the electric tension marked also an increased velocity in recording angles and making sketches." When they took off their hats, their hair stood on end, and not purely because the view was so invigorating. "We were electrified," the explorers remembered, "and our notes were taken and recorded with lightning speed, in keeping with the terrible tension of the storm-cloud's electricity."[2] The raised hair of these explorers was certainly proof that actual experience in the West can be as peculiar, and seemingly unreal, as any event imagined, exaggerated, and doctored up in western fiction. There is nothing particularly restful in this encounter with the Real West, but the tension itself gives the edge to the story. Taking a trip to a peak to look at a view is one thing, and a fairly prosaic and forgettable thing at that. But having one's hair stand on end, finding oneself "electrified," adds up to a far more memorable and striking experience. In a considerably less life-threatening way, examining one's own appraisal of the reality of the West can electrify and energize the mind. The "terrible tension" of the electric storm has its analogue in the often-wearing tension built into our conflicts over the interpretation of the western past. Let us hope this collection and this exhibit can both reckon with the tension, and relieve it. If the challenges the exhibit poses to our working assumptions can erode some of the smugness and inflexibility with which many of us today put forward our

Adventures of the Bumming Botanists, Nell Stephenson Album

judgments and dismiss opposing judgments, then its opening could prove to be its own important moment in the cultural and intellectual history of the American West.

As an image to keep in mind for this spirit of flexibility, one turns to the photograph *Adventures of the Bumming Botanists* from 1906. Here stands a very appealing group of women and men who give every sign of enjoying their investigation into the Real West. They seem able, as well, to tell up from down, and to distinguish a landscape from its reflection in water. It does not seem to trouble them that there are no plants in sight, a situation which might be disheartening for a group of people who have called themselves "botanists." But these are people who are evidently willing to shift their attention from plants to rocks, if that is what nature chooses to present for their contemplation. They may have asked for one thing from the West, and the West may have given them something else entirely, but that disparity seems to be a source of more cheer than distress. In their visible good humor, curiosity, adaptability, and good will, these attractive human beings are part of the Real West. Quietly electrified by what they are experiencing in the West, they provide us with our moorings.

The Real West, published by the Civic Center Cultural Complex, 1996. Original publication made possible through a grant from the State Historical Fund.

Endnotes

[1] Whipple, reprinted in Mary McDougall Gordon, ed., *Through Indian Country to California: John P. Sherburne's Diary of the Whipple Expedition, 1853–1854* (Stanford: Stanford University Press, 1988), 152.

[2] Franklin Rhoda, "Report on the Topography of the San Juan Country," in F. V. Hayden, *Bulletin of the United States Geological and Geographical Survey of the Territories, 1874 and 1875*, Vol. 1 (Washington: Government Printing Office, 1875), 170–71.

I n his book *In Search of the Racial Frontier: African Americans in the American West, 1528–1990*, Quintard Taylor examines what he calls "a striking ambiguity about race" that surfaces repeatedly throughout the western historical narrative. Nowhere is that uncertainty more evident than in the saga of the Buffalo Soldiers.

After the Civil War, the U.S. Congress formed several regular army regiments composed of African American troops serving under white officers. From 1866 to 1917, some 25,000 men served in the Ninth and Tenth Cavalries and the Twenty-fourth and Twenty-fifth Infantries. The Buffalo Soldiers were stationed throughout the West, including Forts Garland, Lyon, and Lewis in southern Colorado.

"Comrades of Color," published in *Colorado Heritage* magazine in 1996 and reprinted two years later as a chapter in Taylor's *In Search of the Racial Frontier*, delves into the color-coded challenges that the Buffalo Soldiers faced. During the Indian wars, they fought "red men" in order to protect the liberties of white settlers or traders that in turn denied black citizens those same liberties. Meanwhile, they defended native peoples from white men, and in at least one instance, from other Indian tribes. The soldiers took pride in these varied and often ironic duties and hoped that their service would someday be remembered and respected.

This article represents a small fraction of Taylor's contribution to the historiography of African Americans in the West. Currently teaching at the University of Washington, he has written or coauthored several books and more than fifty articles, book chapters, and introductions on African American history.

Comrades of Color: Buffalo Soldiers in the West, 1866–1917

—Quintard Taylor

No group in black western history has been more revered or more reviled than the Buffalo Soldiers, the approximately 25,000 men who served in the U.S. Army's Ninth and Tenth Cavalries and Twenty-fourth and Twenty-fifth Infantries between 1866 and 1917. These troops were, along with cowboys, the first African American western historical figures to capture public attention in the 1960s when the saga of the western regiments was embraced by a nation eager to accept black heroes.

Yet long before the rest of the nation recognized the Buffalo Soldiers, nineteenth- and twentieth-century African Americans derived considerable pride from those soldiers' role as the "sable arm" of the U.S. government. Some of the Buffalo Soldiers consciously embraced that role. "We made the West," boasted Tenth Cavalry Private Henry McCombs; "[we] defeated the hostile tribes of Indians; and made the country safe to live in." William Leckie, the first biographer of the cavalry regiments, reiterated that view when he wrote in 1967 that "the thriving cities and towns, the fertile fields, and the natural beauty [of the West] are monuments enough for any buffalo soldier."

But by the 1970s historians such as Jack Forbes began to probe the moral dilemma posed by the Buffalo Soldiers' actions. Were the soldiers not, Forbes asked, instruments in the subjugation of native peoples for a society that went on to "erect thriving white cities, grow fertile white fields and leave no real monuments" to the memory of soldiers who were brave but denigrated in their lifetimes?

If the legacy of the Buffalo Soldier is enveloped in controversy, the origin of these men certainly is beyond dispute. The Civil War permanently established African Americans in the nation's military. The Fifty-fourth

Massachusetts Infantry Regiment, organized on the day the Emancipation Proclamation took effect, January 1, 1863, was the first officially recognized African American military unit. As early as 1861, however, Union General James Lane incorporated black men into his Kansas defense forces. By the end of the Civil War 180,000 African Americans had worn the uniform of the United States Army and had proven their courage from Fort Wagner on the Atlantic Ocean to Honey Springs in the Indian Territory.

After the Civil War, the army was quickly reduced from 1.5 million troops to its prewar total of 16,000. The prospect of possible intervention in Mexico and of intensified warfare with Native Americans as the postwar nation turned westward prompted Congress in 1866 to increase the army's authorized strength to 54,000. Budget constraints, recruiting difficulties, and desertion, however, kept the size of the army in the West at approximately 25,000 men in ten cavalry regiments and twenty-five infantry regiments. Black soldiers led by white officers were to comprise the Ninth and Tenth Cavalries and Twenty-fourth and Twenty-fifth Infantries, discussed in this essay.

Since most of the assignments of the post–Civil War army were related to frontier defense, the black units, like the other regiments, were organized in the East and then quickly stationed in western military

Buffalo Soldiers spent much of their time in the field conducting campaigns or practice marches. This group from the Tenth Cavalry is serving as an escort for General Wesley Merritt near St. Mary's, Montana, 1894.
(Courtesy of the Montana Historical Society)

outposts. Unlike white regiments, however, which expected to be rotated between the frontier and more populated areas, all four black units remained in the West from 1869 until the Spanish-American War beginning in 1898. The War Department kept black regiments along the western frontiers because it was feared that their presence in eastern states, and particularly in the South, would prompt racial violence. "However senseless and unreasonable it may be regarded," wrote General C. C. Auger, commander of the Department of the South in 1879, "a strong prejudice exists at [sic] the South against colored troops."

Troop assignment in Texas, the only state which experienced both Reconstruction-era violence and frontier warfare, illustrated the role of race in determining assignments. By the end of 1865, federal military power in Texas grew to 32,000 troops including the XXV Corps consisting of 20,000 African American veterans of the fighting in Virginia. The XXV Corps had participated in the siege at Petersburg, and some of its units were the first to enter Richmond in 1865. These Buffalo Soldiers, sent to the Rio Grande Valley ostensibly to "seal off the Mexican border from refugees and bandits," were in fact part of a United States show of force against Emperor Maximilian and the French troops who occupied Mexico. Some discharged black troops, in fact, crossed the Rio Grande to join Benito Juarez's forces.

Nonetheless, the presence of Buffalo Soldiers in Texas epitomized the hated "occupation" of the state by the Union Army, generating an animosity with the European American civilian population which would last for decades. The *Bellville Countryman* newspaper in Texas, for example, concluded that "the idea of a gallant and highminded people being ordered and pushed around by an inferior, ignorant race is shocking to the senses." Opinion evolved into attack in 1866 when two privates from the Eightieth United States Colored Infantry who had ventured into Jefferson, Texas, for a drink of water were shot by deputy town marshal Jack Phillips as they passed him. After emptying a double-barreled shotgun point-blank into the soldiers, Phillips drew his revolver and calmly shot each of the dying soldiers in the head. Phillips was not arrested by military authorities because, as General Phil Sheridan, military commander of Union forces in the Southwest, concluded: "The trial of a white man for the murder of a freedman in Texas would be a farce." Although African American soldiers comprised nearly half of the federal garrison in Texas during Reconstruction, the racial prejudices of white Texans forced the Buffalo Soldiers by 1869 to be assigned to the West Texas frontier rather than heavily populated areas of the state where anti-black violence was common.

Two African American cavalry regiments were organized in 1866 under white officers who had impressive credentials. Colonel Benjamin Grierson, famous for his 600-mile, sixteen-day Union cavalry raid through Mississippi in April 1863, was selected commanding officer of the Tenth Cavalry. After George A. Custer refused the rank of lieutenant colonel with the Ninth, Colonel Edward Hatch, a highly decorated Civil War general, was chosen to head the regiment. The first commanding officer of the Twenty-fourth Infantry was Lieutenant Colonel William R. Shafter who would achieve fame in the Spanish-American War. The Twenty-fifth Infantry was led by Colonel George L. Andrews.

A number of junior officers who would rise to prominence served at various times with Buffalo Soldiers. Lieutenant John L. Bullis of the Twenty-fourth Infantry, who led Seminole freedmen scouts during the various Indian campaigns of the 1870s, became a general. John Joseph Pershing, who by 1917 commanded the American Expeditionary Force in World War I France, and Army Surgeon Walter Reed were at times assigned to black units. Pershing's strong regard for the Tenth Cavalry, which began with his 1896 assignment to the regiment in Fort Assinniboine, Montana, was atypical of the officer corps of the era, but not unusual among those commanding black soldiers. Pershing wrote of his surprise at the number of complaints leveled at black troops by his fellow officers and concluded that he "would make the same appeal to them as to any other body of men. Most men, of whatever race, creed, or color, want to do the proper thing and they respect the man above them whose motive is the same." Pershing's respect for his troops did not endear him to his fellow officers. He received the racist nickname "Nigger Jack" (later softened to "Black Jack") when he was briefly assigned to West Point in 1897. The few African American officers faced much more than a racist nickname. All three nineteenth-century black graduates of West Point, Lieutenants Henry O. Flipper (1877), John Hanks Alexander (1887), and Charles Young (1889), served in western outposts with the four black regiments as did the black chaplains Allen Allensworth, Henry Plummer, George Prioleau, Theophilus Gould Steward, and William Anderson. Each of them faced ostracism from his colleagues. White officers at Fort Duchesne, Utah, and Fort Robinson, Nebraska, complained, for example, that they were discriminated against by the army because it assigned the only two black line officers, Alexander and Young, to their Ninth Cavalry. The War Department responded that the assignments were attributable to existing vacancies.

The reaction of the black officers to discrimination varied as much as did their social and regional backgrounds. During the 1886 Senate debate over his nomination for a commission, Allen Allensworth made it clear to Georgia Senator Joseph E. Brown that "my Southern training has taught me enough to know how to appreciate ... those who are my superiors. I am prepared to guard against allowing myself to give offense." Captain Henry Plummer, in contrast, plunged himself deeply into black nationalist activities culminating in an 1894 proposal to the War Department to lead an expedition of a hundred black soldiers into Central Africa to introduce American civilization and Christianity and to colonize part of the African continent for the U.S. before the European nations had completed their division of the continent. Charles Young devoted so much of his energies to pleasing his superiors with his work performance, even as they regularly upbraided him for "tactical errors," that he rarely concerned himself with his social isolation.

The records of two officers reflect African American success and failure in the officer corps. Chaplain Allensworth expanded the educational role of the army, establishing an innovative program at Fort Bayard, New Mexico Territory, where enlisted men became teachers of other soldiers. His booklet describing the program, *Outline of Course of Study, and the Rules Governing Post Schools of Ft. Bayard, N.M.*, was widely adopted in army posts. Allensworth retired in 1907 as a colonel, then the highest rank achieved by any black officer. In contrast, Henry O. Flipper, the first black graduate of West Point, was court-martialed in 1882 at Fort Davis, Texas, for alleged irregularities in his account as a commissary officer. After leaving the army, Flipper worked for the next thirty-seven years as a mining engineer in New Mexico and Mexico, becoming the first black American to gain prominence in the profession. In 1913 Flipper was employed as a consultant for New Mexico Senator Albert B. Fall's Sierra Mining Company, where from El Paso he dispatched reports on the Mexican Revolution to Washington, D.C.

The first enlisted men in the cavalry and infantry regiments were primarily eighteen- and nineteen-year-olds, too young to have seen service in the Civil War. They represented a cross-section of black America. William Christy and George Gray were ex-farmers from Pennsylvania and Kentucky, respectively. Washington Wyatt was a former Virginia slave. Nineteen-year-old Emanuel Stance, scarcely five feet tall, was a native of East Carroll Parish, Louisiana, who joined the Ninth Cavalry when the regiment was two months old. Stance enlisted in F Troop in 1866 and four years later became the first post–Civil War African American soldier to win a Congressional Medal of Honor.

Black soldiers' motives for joining the army varied as widely as their backgrounds. Former slave Reuben Waller recalled that he joined the Tenth Cavalry in 1867 to fight in "the Indian war that was then raging in Kansas and Colorado." Sergeant Samuel Harris wanted to see the West and further believed that his military service would help him get a good government job.

The possibility of education sparked the interest of two soldiers in the army. "I felt I wasn't learning enough," recalled Mazique Sanco, "so I joined." George Conrad, Jr., recalled how he did not learn to read and write until he joined the army in 1883. "I got tired of looking mules in the face from sunrise to sunset," recalled Private Charles Creek. "[I] thought there must be a better livin' in this world." Private George Bentley, the illegitimate son of an African American woman and a European American man, joined the army to escape an overbearing mother and brother. Others signing up were cooks, waiters, painters, bakers, and teamsters who eagerly enlisted for five years at thirteen dollars a month.

Caleb Benson's saga as a career Buffalo Soldier suggests the geographical and chronological scope of service for African American men in the post–Civil War army. Benson joined the army in Columbia, South Carolina, on February 2, 1875, and remained in the service for the next thirty-three years. Able to sign only an "X" on his enlistment papers, Benson served with both the Ninth and Tenth Cavalries, re-enlisting for the final time in January 1907. During his three decades in the army, Benson served in Texas, New Mexico, Colorado, Nebraska, Montana, Arizona, and California. His overseas service included Cuba (1899–1902) and the Philippines (1907–08). After his mandatory retirement at the Presidio in San Francisco, Benson moved to Crawford, Nebraska, and in 1908 married Percilla Smith, a Virginia native who had migrated to Nebraska from Philadelphia. Shortly after their marriage the Bensons homesteaded land near Crawford but in 1925 moved to New York City's

Harlem, and then returned to Nebraska in 1934. Caleb Benson died in Crawford on November 19, 1937.

African American soldiers faced hazardous duty almost immediately upon their arrival at assigned posts in west Texas and central Kansas of 1867. By that summer, the all-black Thirty-eighth Infantry Regiment, which had already fought in a number of Western engagements with Indian warriors, assisted the Seventh Cavalry in the defense of Fort Wallace, Kansas, against a Cheyenne attack led by Chief Roman Nose. Elizabeth Custer, the wife of Colonel George Custer, recalled that battle and the strange sight of a mule-drawn wagon full of black infantrymen firing at the Cheyenne while it raced to the skirmish line. When they reached their destination, the soldiers jumped out of the wagon and began firing again. "No one had ordered them to leave their picket station," she remembered, but "they were determined that no soldiering should be carried on in which their valor was not proved."

The newly organized Tenth Cavalry arrived in Kansas during that 1867 war which involved numerous campaigns against the Central and Southern Plains Indians—the Comanches, Kiowas, Southern Cheyennes, and Arapahos. Their first assignment was to guard settlers and construction camps of the Kansas Pacific Railroad. On August 1, one of the camps was attacked by Cheyenne Indians, who killed seven construction workers. A thirty-four-man troop followed the trail of the raiders into an ambush. Forced to dismount, they fought off eighty warriors in a six-hour battle, killing six Cheyennes. However, the ambush cost the life of Sergeant William Christy, the first of hundreds of black soldiers to die in various military engagements during the next five decades.

Between August 21 and 24, 1867, some 800 Kiowa and Cheyenne led by Roman Nose and Satanta trapped a company of Tenth Cavalry and a regiment of Eighteenth Kansas Volunteer Cavalry in a ravine near the Nebraska border. The 164 troopers were subject to taunts which indicated the Plains Indians recognized distinctions between black and white soldiers: "Come out of that hole, you white sons of bitches; we don't want to fight the niggers; we want to fight you white sons of bitches." Yet in the ensuing battle blacks and whites fought with equal intensity and the Indians showed no particular mercy toward the African American soldiers.

The foregoing examples illustrate that the African American soldiers' primary mission of Indian "pacification" meant almost three decades of conflict with native peoples in what would be termed "Indian wars."

These wars were in fact a continuation of the longest guerrilla resistance in American history. Bands of warriors, numbering no more than a hundred and often far fewer, attacked vulnerable targets: isolated ranches, stagecoach relay stations, railroad or telegraph construction sites, and on occasion, small military camps. And like guerrilla struggles elsewhere, they found sanctuary by crossing international borders, or taking refuge within the civilian population they were pledged to defend. For native peoples these wars of resistance were necessary, inevitable struggles to defend what remained of their lands and way of life. Achieving victory over far more numerous settlers or the military was impossible. Yet, when faced with what they considered an unacceptable alternative, "pacification," they chose resistance.

Black soldiers protected the region's inhabitants, usually white settlers. On occasion, however, they guarded Native Americans in Indian Territory from other Indians (Chickasaw, Cherokee, and Creek farmers suffered as much from Comanche or Kiowa raids as did white farmers in neighboring states), or protected Indian people from the depredations of white men as occurred in 1879 when Tenth Cavalry troops defended Kiowa women and children from Texas Rangers who had invaded their village intent upon killing and scalping its occupants. Protection of the inhabitants meant repeatedly removing David L. Payne and the hundreds of white settlers called "boomers" whom he illegally led into Indian Territory between 1879 and his death in 1884. In 1887 units of the Ninth protected Ute Indians from Colorado militiamen determined to enter their reservation in pursuit of tribal leader Colorow.

Protection of settlers required the pursuit of elusive Indian horsemen much more familiar with the countryside. Following a series of startling raids by Kiowas and Comanches in the summer of 1869 that extended as far east as Fort Worth and San Antonio, units of the Ninth Cavalry were ordered to intercept all non-reservation Indians. In 1869, ninety-five troopers of the Ninth left Fort McKavett, Texas, on a grueling forty-two-day, 600-mile pursuit of a band of Comanches which had attacked ranches near San Saba. Six years later Colonel William Shafter led a combined force of 220 officers and men from the Tenth Cavalry and Twenty-fourth and Twenty-fifth Infantries on a six-month sweep of the Llano Estacado to destroy Comanchero, Apache, and Comanche camps. The expedition, which covered more than 2,500 miles, crisscrossing the remote high plains in Texas and New Mexico, pursued Indians but it also mapped the country, noting water and fuel supplies, resources, flora, and fauna. Between July 1879 and March 1880, Company C of the Ninth Cavalry chased a small band of Mescalero Apaches over 2,000 miles through West Texas and eastern New Mexico.

An example of dangers inherent in such missions occurred in May 1880 during the campaign against the Apache band led by Victorio. When warned of an impending attack by Victorio on the small settlement of Tularosa, New Mexico, Sergeant George Jordan led twenty-four Buffalo Soldiers of the Ninth Cavalry on an all-night ride to the settlement. Upon arriving, the soldiers transformed a corral and an old fort into a defensive stockade and gathered the frightened settlers into it. Soldiers and citizens fought off repeated attacks by the Apaches who then made an unsuccessful attempt to capture the town's horses and cattle. Anticipating their plan, Jordan sent ten troopers to assist two soldiers and a herder who were earlier assigned to protect the livestock. Sergeant Jordan's decisive leadership and bravery earned him the Congressional Medal of Honor.

A decade later, Ninth Cavalry Buffalo Soldiers endured the bitter cold of a South Dakota winter as they supported the last major military operation against native people, the Ghost Dance Campaign of 1890–91. Prompted by fears that the messianic Ghost Dance religion was attracting a large following on the Sioux Indian reservations at Pine Ridge and Rosebud, the War Department in November 1890 placed 1,400 soldiers on the two reservations. Included were units of the Ninth Cavalry who were stationed at Fort Robinson, Nebraska, and thus were closest to the Pine Ridge reservation. A tense peace ensued for the next month until it was broken on December 29 when 350 Sioux men, women, and children awoke at their camp on Wounded Knee Creek to find themselves surrounded by 500 Seventh Cavalry troopers. Colonel James Forsyth ordered his soldiers to disarm the Sioux. In a confrontation between an Indian and a soldier, a rifle discharged prompting both sides to begin firing. When it ended, more than 250 Sioux (including women and children) and twenty-five soldiers were dead at Wounded Knee.

In the ensuing campaign the Seventh and Ninth cavalries pursued frightened Sioux survivors who fled Wounded Knee. Hampered by internal conflicts, separated from supplies, encircled by a slowly contracting ring of soldiers, and facing the prospect of fighting in the middle of winter, the Sioux were ill prepared for a sustained campaign against the army. By

January 15, some two weeks after the Battle of Wounded Knee, the Sioux leader, Kicking Bear, surrendered to General Nelson A. Miles. As the other army units quickly evacuated the Pine Ridge Reservation, four companies of black Ninth Cavalry were left to guard the Sioux. The men endured a bitterly cold winter with only canvas tents and were not relieved until March. The Sioux, of course, faced even greater privation. Private W. H. Prather, who only months earlier had viewed the Sioux as adversaries in battle, now asked why both Indians and blacks seemed abandoned to a harsh Dakota winter with record snowfalls and temperatures as low as minus 30. "The Ninth, the willing Ninth," he lamented, "[who] were the first to come, will be the last to leave." Prather expressed his bewilderment at why "we poor devils, and the Sioux, are left to freeze."

Buffalo Soldiers' responsibilities for civil law enforcement in the vicinity of their posts required them to pursue outlaws of any race or nationality. An 1870 report by Colonel Benjamin Grierson at Fort Sill, Indian Territory, suggested the dimensions of black soldiers' activities as a frontier

Company G of the Ninth Cavalry served at Fort Garland,
Colorado, from 1876 until 1879.

police force. In the preceding year, soldiers under Grierson's command had tracked and returned more than 250 stolen animals, turned over twenty alleged thieves to civil authorities, and killed several suspects who resisted arrest or tried to escape. A terse 1881 report on the activities of the Tenth Cavalry at Fort Davis, Texas, summarized one example of such duty: "Sgt. Winfield Scott and Pvt. Augustus Dover wounded in the line of duty while attempting to arrest desperado on military reservation— desperado W. A. Alexander was killed resisting arrest."

Police duty occasionally necessitated intervening in civilian disputes. Black troops were embroiled in 1878's Lincoln County War in New Mexico Territory, known primarily because it initiated the career of the notorious gunfighter William Bonny (Billy the Kid). Here, however, the injudicious intervention of Colonel N. A. M. Dudley, the commander at Fort Stanton, near Lincoln, resulted in the black and white troops supporting the Murphy-Dolan group, one of two equally violent factions of businessmen-ranchers. The Murphy-Dolan faction, headed by Lawrence G. Murphy and James J. Dolan, and the McSween-Tunstall group, led by Alexander A. McSween and John H. Tunstall, both recruited dozens of cowboy gunmen while appealing for federal assistance to crush their opponents. In April 1878, for example, Colonel Dudley assigned Ninth Cavalry Buffalo Soldiers to Lincoln to assist County Sheriff John Copeland (a Murphy-Dolan supporter) in making arrests.

By mid-July, tensions between the feuding Murphy and McSween forces led to a showdown. Using an attack on black cavalryman Private Berry Robinson as a pretext, Colonel Dudley on July 19 led a column of eleven black cavalrymen and twenty-four white infantrymen into Lincoln and demanded that Justice of the Peace John B. Wilson issue warrants for the arrest of McSween, William Bonny, and other so-called "regulators." Emboldened by Dudley's action, members of the Murphy faction demanded the surrender of McSween and the regulators who had gathered at McSween's home. When the McSweens refused, the house was burned. In the ensuing five-day battle involving more than a hundred combatants, McSween and three supporters were killed while Bonny and five other cowboys escaped. Although his soldiers did not fire a shot during the fighting, Colonel Dudley's intervention and his opposition to McSween allowed the Murphy partisans to gain temporary control over Lincoln County.

Twelve years after the Lincoln County conflict, Ninth Cavalry troopers again found themselves enmeshed in a civilian dispute between powerful cattlemen and ranch owners in Johnson County, Wyoming Territory. In 1890 small ranchers in Wyoming protested the territory's 1884 law which allowed the major cattle ranches to claim all unbranded cattle. Unable to get the law amended in a legislature dominated by powerful cattlemen, the small ranchers resorted to claiming unbranded cattle, prompting the Wyoming Stockgrowers Association, which represented the large ranchers, to label their opponents "rustlers." In 1892 they hired twenty-five gunmen to drive the small ranchers out of northern Wyoming. Local law enforcement officials, however, supported by the Sixth Cavalry, arrested both the cattlemen and their hired guns for the death of two alleged rustlers near Casper. Angered that the troops and civilians had thwarted its plans, the stockgrowers association telegraphed Wyoming U.S. Senator Joseph M. Carey on June 1, 1892, with specific demands: "We want cool level-headed men whose sympathy is with us. ... Send six companies of Ninth Cavalry from [Fort] Robinson to [Fort McKinney]. The colored troop will have no sympathy for Texan thieves, and these are the troops we want."

The Wyoming Stockgrowers Association relied on both old animosities and a new role that black troops would assume in industrial disputes. The old animosity stemmed from the longstanding tensions between white Texans and black soldiers. The new role arose from the belief that widespread racial discrimination of working-class whites against African Americans ensured that black soldiers would harbor little sympathy for small ranchers in their struggle against Wyoming's cattlemen. Subsequent events seemed to bear out that assumption.

Two weeks after Senator Carey received the Stockgrowers' telegram, 314 Ninth Cavalry troops were transferred from Fort Robinson to Johnson County, Wyoming. On June 13, the troops established Camp Bettens near the town of Suggs, Wyoming, and almost immediately encountered hostility from local residents. Black troopers, of course, were long accustomed to verbal insults and rebuffs from townspeople, but when Private Abraham Champ and Private Emile Smith were chased out of Suggs by townspeople on June 16, most troopers realized that their new assignment posed more than "normal" hazards. On the night of June 17, twenty black soldiers vowing to avenge the attack on their fellow troopers disobeyed orders and, as it was later reported, "penetrated the

264

centre of [Suggs], fired one volley in the air, and then commenced firing through the streets and at some of the houses." The gunfire exchange with townspeople left Private Willis Johnson dead. Two companies of the Ninth arrived in town to disarm and arrest their fellow soldiers.

Immediately after the Suggs incident, John M. Schofield, commanding general of the Army, ordered the men responsible for the attack on Suggs turned over to civilian authorities for trial, and prohibited the remaining troops from contact with civilians until they returned to Fort Robinson. Yet Ninth Cavalry Colonel James Biddle's fear for the safety of the troopers at the hands of local authorities prompted the Army to try the soldiers at Fort Robinson where they were given minor punishments. Unlike Lincoln County of the 1870s—where the Buffalo Soldiers' presence was calculated to reduce tension between warring factions—the introduction of these troops into the Johnson County War by the Wyoming Stockgrowers Association was a cynical ploy calculated to exacerbate racial tension. It was tragic but not surprising that such tension in Suggs resulted in the violent death of an African American soldier.

As in Lincoln and Suggs, civilian animosity toward African American soldiers often posed dangers comparable to their confrontations with Native Americans. Unlike in the South where essentially unarmed blacks could not retaliate against racial violence, the troopers seemed ready and eager to extract revenge for every perceived injustice. The 1867 lynching by vigilantes of three African American infantrymen at Fort Hays, Kansas, generated retaliatory violence by black soldiers which culminated on May 3 with a thirty-minute gun battle in the center of town. In 1885, following the lynching of a black soldier near Sturgis, Dakota Territory, some twenty soldiers of the Twenty-fifth Infantry returned to town and got even by firing on two saloons and killing a civilian.

Such impetuous acts, regardless of the prompting circumstances, intensified civilian-soldier animosity. The *Sturgis Weekly Record* recognized that the black troops harbored resentment over the lynching of a fellow soldier. Nonetheless it argued that the trooper's lynching did not justify the actions of the soldiers who returned to shoot up the town. "Here are soldiers whom we help support [and who] are placed at the post for our supposed protection. ... They take the guns that we bought, march calmly out of the post and mob our town. ... What difference can there be between that and an Indian raid?" The *Black Hills Daily Times* of Deadwood added: "Never has any people been visited by a more horrible

265

murder. Men who think of life so lightly are fit subjects for a cannibal island, and only such a place. ... "

On other occasions hostility toward the Buffalo Soldiers stemmed not from any particular act against civilians but from the perception that black troops were incapable of performing their duties. The editor of the *Las Cruces Thirty-Four* in New Mexico Territory expressed the frustration of many westerners at the army's inability to capture or defeat Indian raiders when he wrote in 1879:

> The experiences ... which the people of Southern New
> Mexico have passed during the past two months are sufficient
> to convince any sane man that the portion of the United
> States Army known as the Ninth Cavalry is totally unfit to
> fight Indians. Let the Ninth be disbanded [so that its members]
> might contribute to the nation's wealth as pickers of cotton
> and hoers of corn or to its amusement as a travelling minstrel
> troupe. As soldiers on the western frontier they are worse
> than useless—they are a fraud and a nuisance.

Hostility toward black soldiers was the most entrenched and enduring in Reconstruction-era Texas. Animosities toward all U.S. military personnel—who represented the victorious Union Army and the hated Republican administrations in Washington and Austin—only increased when the federal troops were African American. Often the hostility was manifested in the refusal of local civilian juries to convict outlaws captured by black soldiers or civilians accused of murdering Buffalo Soldiers. In 1870, John Jackson, a civilian near Fort McKavett, murdered Private Boston Henry, and then in his ensuing flight Jackson killed Corporal Albert Marshall and Private Charles Murray who were part of a unit which was sent to capture him. When Jackson was finally apprehended and brought to trial, a jury set him free.

Five years later, two Buffalo Soldiers were killed when a five-man patrol was ambushed by vaqueros near Rio Grande City, Texas. A grand jury subsequently indicted nine men for the murders but only one was brought to trial and he was quickly acquitted. In 1878, cowboys and buffalo hunters in a San Angelo, Texas, saloon humiliated a black sergeant by removing his stripes from his uniform. Angry troops from nearby Fort Concho stormed the saloon in retaliation and in the subsequent gunfight killed one of the hunters. Nine soldiers were indicted for murder and one, William Mace, was sentenced to death. But when sheepherder Tom McCarthy killed unarmed Tenth Cavalry Private William Watkins in a San Angelo saloon in 1881, McCarthy was indicted for murder, transferred to Austin for trial, and acquitted.

No citizen-soldier clashes occurred in the West between 1885 and 1899. Nonetheless, segregation and racial violence, particularly in the South, increased the national chasm between soldiers and civilians. A correspondent from the *Boston Evening Transcript* captured that divergence when he wrote of black soldiers from four regiments assembling in Tampa, Florida, at the beginning of the Spanish-American War for their new assignments in Cuba. Said the paper: "The Negro soldiers who come here from the West are under the impression that they are as good as white soldiers ... they think that the willingness to die on an equality with white men gives them a claim to live on something like an equality with them." Such views were now publicly expressed by the black enlisted men and officers. When the *Salt Lake City Tribune* urged the War Department to station the Twenty-fifth Infantry someplace other than nearby Fort Douglas, Private Ernest A. Thomas wrote to the paper declaring, "We object to being classed as lawless barbarians. We were men before we were soldiers, we are men now, and will continue to be men after we are through soldiering." Lieutenant Charles Young, speaking before a Stanford University audience in 1903, repudiated the views of Booker T. Washington, suggesting that submission in the face of growing racial oppression would gain nothing. Instead, he suggested, black Americans should be allowed to use their abilities without interference from society. "All the Negro asks is a white man's chance," concluded Young, "Will you give it?" The answer would soon come with the Brownsville Raid and its aftermath.

Most of the soldier-civilian clashes occurred within a context of white-black racial violence characteristic of the 1890–1920 period. Yet conflicts at Brownsville and other Texas border towns reflected tensions between black servicemen and predominantly Latino citizens and the larger triangular (Hispanic, white, black) race relations of Texas. The origins of these black-brown tensions can be traced to the immediate post–Civil War era when south Texas Anglos and Latinos supported the Confederacy and faced a mostly black Union army occupying force along the lower Rio Grande.

Like most Rio Grande border towns, Brownsville had a white minority and a Hispano majority, which in that community of 7,000 comprised 80 percent of the population. As the center of the lower Rio Grande Valley range cattle industry, Brownsville was, according to historian Ann Lane, "filled with rough, rootless, violent men, living in a community as much frontier and western as it was racist and southern." Only ten black families resided in the town. White Brownsvillians maintained a rigid segregation against their Latino neighbors, and both groups opposed the presence of the Twenty-fifth Infantry. One local white resident wrote Texas Senator Charles A. Culberson warning that if blacks misbehaved, the whites would retaliate.

Incidents in July 1906, soon after the first three companies of the Twenty-fifth arrived, suggested the future. In the most serious case, an infantryman attacked Mrs. Lon Evans, and when she screamed the assailant fled. The *Brownsville Daily Herald* recounted the event in lurid detail under the headline, "Negro Soldier Invaded Private Premises Last Night and Attempted to Seize a White Lady." Mayor Frederick J. Combe persuaded post commander Major Charles Penrose to confine all soldiers to the fort to preclude racial violence stemming from the assault. Nonetheless on August 13, 1906, approximately fifteen unidentified men gathered in an alley across from Fort Brown and began firing into buildings along the alley and then ran into a street. Before they stopped ten minutes later, bartender Frank Natus was dead. Wounded were police Lieutenant M. Ygnacio Dominguez and editor Paulino S. Preciado of the Spanish-language newspaper *El Porvenir*.

The Brownsville Raid quickly polarized public opinion locally and nationally. A citizens committee appointed by Mayor Combe concluded after a two-day investigation that black soldiers were responsible for the raid and telegraphed President Theodore Roosevelt on August 15, asking him to replace the Twenty-fifth Infantry with white troops. President Roosevelt sent Major Augustus P. Blocksom, assistant to the inspector general, to Brownsville to ascertain responsibility. Within two days of his arrival Blocksom concluded that although the raid was provoked by civilian mistreatment of soldiers because of their race, African American troops were responsible. He also recommended the removal of all of the black soldiers from the lower Rio Grande Valley as soon as possible. The president complied and the War Department transferred the infantry to Fort Reno, Oklahoma. Texas Rangers, however, acting on behalf of local civil authorities, arbitrarily selected eleven soldiers and one civilian as the most likely responsible parties, in effect holding them as judicial hostages until they or other troopers were specifically implicated by fellow soldiers. When no other soldiers stepped forward to acknowledge responsibility for the raid, Texas authorities reluctantly released the prisoners. President Roosevelt, however, discharged 167 men, arguing that his action would teach blacks that they should not "band together to shelter their own criminals."

Roosevelt's action generated a maelstrom of protest from the African American press; from interracial organizations such as the Constitution League, which sent investigators to Texas; and from some major northern newspapers. The *New York World*, for example, called the president's action "executive lynch law" and *The New York Times* decried: "Not a particle of evidence is given ... proving the guilt of a single enlisted man." African Americans felt particularly betrayed by Roosevelt. Many of them remembered his high praise of the Tenth Cavalry during his campaign for governor of New York. "I don't think any rough rider," Roosevelt declared, recalling the role of black troops in his charge up San Juan Hill in 1898, "will ever forget the tie that binds us to the Ninth and Tenth Cavalry." Most African Americans considered that tie to have been severed by the president's decision to discharge the 167 soldiers.

Eleven years later it was the black Twenty-fourth Infantry's turn to confront Texas animosity, although in this instance the price for the soldiers, for the city of Houston, and for American race relations was much higher. In July 1917, 654 enlisted men and eight officers of the Third Battalion, Twenty-fourth Infantry, arrived in Houston, a city of 130,000 (including 30,000 African Americans), to assume guard duty around Camp Logan, a military training facility then under construction. The Twenty-fourth knew well the experience of the Buffalo Soldiers of the Twenty-fifth Infantry at Brownsville. The troopers were also quite aware of the ongoing conflict between the Twenty-fifth and white citizens in San Antonio in 1911 and 1916 over public accommodations. Soldiers of the Twenty-fourth's First Battalion fought with local police and Texas Rangers in Del Rio where a Ranger killed a soldier in self-defense and the Army court-martialed two others for inciting the brawl. The men also were aware of the state's long history of lynching (Texas ranked third in the nation in that statistic) including the brutal Waco "horror" of May 1916 wherein Jesse Washington was tortured and then burned alive before 15,000 spectators. Only two months before the black soldiers arrived in Houston, a mob of 200 whites hanged a black man in nearby Galveston.

Most of the soldiers of the Twenty-fourth, realizing the well-entrenched pattern of segregation and racial subordination in Houston, obeyed the law. Conversely, many local white Houstonians, eager to maintain lucrative federal contracts, followed the pronouncement of the chamber of commerce that "in a spirit of patriotism, the colored soldiers would be treated right." Nonetheless some black soldiers tested the city's Jim Crow policies, sitting in the front seats on public trolleys or removing "colored only" signs which they kept as "souvenirs." The greatest tension, however, was between the soldiers and the Houston police. Some white citizens regarded police brutality against African Americans conducive to effective law enforcement. As one white Houstonian said immediately after the riot, "Our policemen have to beat the niggers when they are insolent."

On August 18, two policemen chased, beat, and then arrested two black soldiers when the soldiers protested the officers' brutal handling of a black youth. Later that day two other soldiers were assaulted by police for objecting to being called "nigger," while the following day a Harris County deputy sheriff pistol-whipped a soldier for resisting arrest when the officer found him in the white-only section of a streetcar. These incidents were a prelude to the Houston Riot on the night of August 23, 1917, the worst interracial violence in the city's history. Earlier that day in 102-degree heat, two mounted Houston police officers, Rufus Daniels and Lee Sparks, arrested Private Alonzo Edwards for interfering in the arrest of a black woman. When later in the afternoon Corporal Charles Baltimore, the provost guard, tried to obtain information from the police officers about Edwards' arrest, policeman Sparks struck the soldier with his pistol and then fired at the corporal as he fled. Sparks and Daniels caught Corporal Baltimore in an unoccupied house and beat and jailed him. News of the attacks, embellished by the false rumor that Baltimore had been killed, reached the Twenty-fourth Infantry camp just outside the city. Several Buffalo Soldiers vowed to avenge Edwards and Baltimore and to "burn down the town" even as the officers and some noncommissioned officers tried unsuccessfully to calm the men with promises of an official investigation.

As Major Kneeland S. Snow pleaded with one group of soldiers to remain calm and loyal, Private Frank Johnson slipped to the rear of the assembled body and yelled, "Get your guns, boys! Here comes the mob!" The frightened men grabbed arms and ammunition and began fifteen minutes of confused, indiscriminate firing. The military officers unsuccessfully attempted to regain control over the company but the mutiny leaders, shouting "Stick by your own race" and "To hell with going to France, get to work right here," gained the allegiance of most of the men. The mutiny leader, Sergeant Vida Henry, commanded his followers to "fall in" for the march on Houston. "Get plenty of ammunition and save one for yourself," he advised, "because there will be no Third Battalion. ... We are in it now ... [and] have to go." Most of Company I, joined by men from other companies, about 100 soldiers in all, marched out of the camp at 9:00 P.M., headed for Houston.

Intent on exacting their vengeance upon the Houston police officers who attacked their comrades, the Buffalo Soldiers bolted through the heavily black San Felipe district where they confronted policemen Sparks and Daniels. Daniels and three other lawmen were killed while Sparks escaped. The soldiers then disagreed on their next course of action. Sergeant Henry called on them to attack the police station. Most refused and began to make their way back to Camp Logan. Members of one group, however, took refuge in homes of black Houstonians where they were captured the following day by policemen and other black troopers. The death toll in the one-night orgy of violence was twenty dead—fifteen of them whites (including five policemen), one Mexican American, and four black soldiers including the insurrection leader Henry. The Houston Mutiny and Riot became the nation's second deadliest racial confrontation of 1917, exceeded only by the East St. Louis Race Riot on July 2, in which thirty-nine people died.

(Courtesy of the National Archives)

271

Once military investigators persuaded eight participants to testify against the others, the first sixty-five of the 118 soldiers arrested were brought to trial in three separate courts-martial in San Antonio and El Paso between November 1917 and the following March. The combined trials became the largest court-martial since the Mexican War. On November 30, thirteen soldiers were sentenced to death and were executed at dawn on December 11. Among them was Corporal Charles Baltimore. Forty-one others were given life in prison. The army later tried the remaining fifty-three in December and February, sentencing sixteen to hang and twelve to serve life terms. Seven soldiers were acquitted while the remainder received prison sentences ranging from two to fifteen years. President Woodrow Wilson commuted the sentences of ten soldiers to life imprisonment after receiving an NAACP petition with 12,000 signatures requesting executive clemency for the condemned soldiers.

The consequences of the Houston Riot extended far beyond Texas and 1917. The incident provoked renewed calls for the complete elimination of African Americans from military service. While the soldiers' supporters in Congress blocked outright dissolution of the units, the War Department limited the four regular black regiments to menial labor, thus excluding the majority of black soldiers from World War I combat. The decision, viewed as a temporary response to the misconduct of some black soldiers, ultimately removed the four highly decorated Buffalo Soldier regiments from combat roles until World War II.

The Texas mutiny reflected and inspired a growing militancy among African Americans. While many African Americans disagreed with the impulsive, destructive actions of the black soldiers, black citizens nonetheless lauded the troopers' refusal to succumb to second-class citizenship. Eventually black Americans would transform the soldiers' impetuous defiance of segregation laws and customs into a larger, more controlled civil rights movement. Historian Garna Christian writes that the "New Negro" of the post–World War I period—assertive, decisive, and proud—was the younger cousin of the black fighting man of earlier decades.

Both nineteenth- and twentieth-century African Americans were understandably proud of the Buffalo Soldiers. Many of those black troopers, in turn, accepted their special role in the as-yet small pantheon of African American heroes. "[Black soldiers] are possessed of the notion," wrote Chaplain George M. Mullins of the Twenty-fifth Infantry in 1877, "that the colored people of the whole country are more or less affected by their conduct in the Army." The *Langston Daily Herald* (Oklahoma) called them "a brave and courageous company of men of whom the race may well feel proud." Years later, historian Rayford Logan remarked that African Americans "had little, at the turn of the century to help sustain our faith in ourselves except the pride that we took in the Ninth and Tenth Cavalry, the Twenty-Fourth and Twenty-Fifth Infantry. ... They were our Ralph Bunche, Marian Anderson, Joe Louis and Jackie Robinson." Yet, considering the racism these soldiers stoically faced, the horrible living and working conditions they experienced, and the violence they inflicted on others and themselves, this small group of black men paid a dear price in their bid to earn the respect of the nation.

The tragic irony of the late-nineteenth-century black soldiers in the West escaped most contemporary observers. In an era when the vast majority of African Americans in the South were without the protection of local, state, or federal officials in the face of unprecedented terror, black soldiers in the West were the indispensable arm of the United States government arrayed against Native Americans, striking white workers, eager land claimants, outlaws, and others who by varied circumstance found themselves challenging that power. Thus historian Logan's understandable pride must be tempered by W. E. B. DuBois's poignant eulogy for the first thirteen soldiers executed following the Houston Mutiny: "Thirteen young, strong men; soldiers who have fought for a country which never was wholly theirs; men born to suffer ridicule, injustice and, at last, death itself."

Black men in the Army of the United States confronted the dilemma faced by virtually every African American who donned the uniform of the U.S. armed services. They risked "ridicule, injustice ... and death itself" to defend a nation which denied them the rights they were asked to preserve for others. Yet African American soldiers, and thousands of other blacks who never wore the uniform of the United States military, believed such service, however flawed, implied a social contract with the nation that must eventually be honored with equal justice and equal rights.

Excerpted from "Comrades of Color: Buffalo Soldiers in the West, 1866–1917,"
Colorado Heritage, Spring 1996

F or the second volume of its *Colorado History* journal, the Colorado Historical Society published *La Gente: Hispano History and Life in Colorado*. Edited by Dr. Vincent C. de Baca of Denver's Metropolitan State College, this 1998 volume brought together the voices of thirteen authors whose writings capture, as de Baca writes, "the full expression and diversity" of the state's Hispano peoples. The book culminated a several-year effort that also resulted in the opening of *La Gente*, one of the core exhibitions of the Colorado History Museum in Denver.

Both the exhibit and the book explore the rich 150-year history, and the centuries-old legacy, of Colorado's Hispano population. The experiences of Colorado's Mexican Americans encompass personal journeys, political movements, and—as José Aguayo demonstrates—backbreaking labor and agricultural know-how.

Aguayo graduated from the University of Denver with a master of arts degree in cultural anthropology. His research has focused on Mexican culture and history from the post-conquest period through the Revolution of 1910–20. At the time of *La Gente's* publication, Aguayo was executive director of the Museo de las Américas in Denver. Founded in 1991, the museum is one of a scant few in the region that showcases the artistic traditions of all Latin American cultures. Today Aguayo serves on the Museo's board of trustees.

In *"Los Betabeleros,"* Aguayo draws on the accounts of his own family and a wealth of other sources to weave a portrait of the lives of beet-workers in the fields of Colorado's northern plains.

Los Betabeleros
(The Beetworkers)

—José Aguayo

"The safest investment on earth *is* earth." "One-way colonist fares for homeseekers." Advertisements like these, following the completion of rail connections to eastern markets, spurred the settlement of the Colorado plains in the late 1880s and early 1900s. Settlers came to farm the arid prairie—until then described as useless and uninhabitable.

The channeling of winter snow melt from the state's major rivers and tributaries added the missing element, allowing a dramatic increase in tillable acreage. Irrigation permitted farmers to experiment with crops other than grains watered only with natural rainfall. The sugar beet was one such crop, planted on land bordering the South Platte River, which slices the state diagonally from south of Denver northeast to the Nebraska border. The cultivation of sugar beets eventually dominated farming in this South Platte Valley, growing at a rate that exceeded the pool of local labor available to tend the crop.

The Great Western Sugar Company contracted with farmers to grow a specified number of acres of sugar beets within designated factory districts. The company taught the farmers the latest techniques developed out of research conducted at its Longmont Experimental Station, established in 1910. Great Western fostered the development of better planting, cultivating, and harvesting equipment, even buying new equipment and lending it to the growers. University-trained Great Western fieldmen assisted farmers in the selection of suitable land for growing sugar beets and supervised the planting, fertilization, tending, and harvesting of the crop, the control of pests and diseases, and the transport of the crop to the factory for processing. The fieldman also oversaw relations between the grower and the laborers, who were

275

recruited annually to do the seasonal handwork required to produce maximum tonnage from each acre.

Farm families and local labor tended the beet crop for only the first few years of production, when planted acreage was small. An article in the Great Western publication *Through the Leaves* proclaimed: "The youngster, when employed in bunches, enjoys the work, which is not really hard, and it gives them self-confidence." But other assessments of beet work described it as backbreaking, tedious labor that not many would choose to do voluntarily. Labor-saving innovations in machinery and "scientific" agricultural techniques came too slow to help the beleaguered farmer. It became necessary to import field hands from neighboring areas.

From the beginning, Great Western adopted the unprecedented policy of nurturing its product from field to market. The company brought in German Russian families from Nebraska, who had experience working in that state's beet-producing areas. Japanese "solos"—single males—were also recruited starting in 1903. The company transported the laborers to beet-growing districts and arranged contracts with the farmers. German Russian laborers were preferred because they arrived in family groups that eventually settled permanently, eliminating the need to provide annual transportation from the Midwest to the Colorado beet fields. By 1909, sufficient numbers of German Russians lived in the South Platte Valley to satisfy labor requirements. But permanent residency created another problem: Within ten years, the German Russian laborers were becoming tenant farmers and landowners themselves. Some of the earlier settlers resented the laborers' climb up the economic ladder. An excerpt from a Lafayette farmer's 1918 article in *Through the Leaves* titled "Does Beet Labor Respond to Good Treatment?" is typical of popular sentiment toward immigrants trying to better their lives: "You simply can't treat them as you would treat people you have around the place, for if you tried that, it wouldn't be thirty days until you would be living in the shack and the Russian would be riding in your 'fliver.'"

By about 1916, German Russians had left the fields of northern Colorado as laborers. The Japanese "solos," now married, also became permanent residents and farmers. Great Western ranged farther afield in its efforts to find reliable workers willing to do the seasonal drudgery necessary to bring in the required sugar beet tonnage to keep its chain of Platte Valley factories operating.

Great Western employed agents whose sole duty was the recruitment of field laborers. The company advertised in local newspapers, even calling door-to-door in southern Colorado, New Mexico, and Texas. Hispanos who had settled the region as of 1598 were experiencing economic difficulties, forcing them to seek employment away from their ancestral villages.

Magdalena Arellano recalls an agent's visit to her home in Antonito, Colorado, in 1922. She was fifteen at the time and employed by a wealthy family to care for their children at five dollars a week. "I was lucky," she says. "I was working, but the other members of my family could not find employment. When the agent for '*la compañía azucarera*,' the sugar company, came, my mother, uncle, aunt, and I left Antonito for Fort Collins. The sugar company paid our rail fare and put us up overnight at the Linden Hotel when we arrived in Fort Collins. The next morning we were contracted out to a farmer, living in a shack '*en el rancho*' while we worked in the beets."

Between 1912 and 1916, Spanish Americans satisfied the need for beet laborers. The start of World War I and the continued growth of the agricultural industry caused another surge in the demand for unskilled laborers. Mexican *peones*, driven by the violence of revolution (1910–20), population pressures, and general economic chaos scrambled north seeking rumored prosperity. Crossing the border was a simple matter in those days. The war and changes in immigration laws had stemmed the flood of immigrants from eastern and southern Europe. Agriculturists in the western states actively lobbied Congress to exempt Mexicans from restrictive immigration quotas, arguing that they would not become permanent residents. Instead, they would return to Mexico every year after the harvests. Before 1900, immigration from Mexico was negligible, averaging less than seven hundred a year. The numbers quickly escalated. Between 1900 and 1930, more than a million Mexicans came to the United States to work, mostly in Texas cotton fields and California vegetable and citrus industries. Forty-five thousand came to Colorado in search of rumored high wages in the tending of sugar beets. Initially, many of the migrants did return to their homeland, buying small parcels of land in Mexico or living during the off-season on their earnings in the United States. Upon returning to Mexico, they also described the opportunity for a better life north of the border. Some returned to Colorado, often bringing relatives or friends with them. Each new wave of migrant laborers was larger than the last and, as it receded back into Mexico, left increasing numbers of permanent residents in its wake.

The survivors of the Ortega family were some of the many who fled the terrible conflict between revolutionary and federal armies in Mexico. Seven-year-old Jovita remembers the family gathering only the possessions they could carry and jumping over corpses in the streets of Chihuahua as they hurried to the train station:

> My father, José Ortega, a soldier in Pancho Villa's Army of
> the North, died in 1912 during the siege of Chihuahua.
> Before he died, he told my mother that if she didn't survive
> the Revolution, I was to live with my *tía*, aunt, Severa Varela,
> and my two sisters should be sent to live with their *madrina*,
> their godmother. My mother died of diphtheria during the
> second battle for Chihuahua in 1915, so my grandmother and
> all of her family came to the United States, crossing the
> bridge at El Paso, Texas.
>
> When we arrived at the Chihuahua train station, there
> was already a huge mob of refugees pushing and shoving fran-
> tically to board the train. The coaches were full and we
> couldn't find space. Desperate with fear, we boarded a freight
> train. I remember vividly the crowded cattle car, the floor
> matted with straw, and the wind blowing from side to side
> through the slatted wall as we sped to the border.

Jovita Ortega did not come directly to the Colorado beet fields. Her family lived in Texas for twelve years. In El Paso, they settled at 301 Spruce Street, only steps away from the Mexican border. They lived reasonably well with income from *abuelo* (grandfather) Matias Gonzales's junk selling and *abuela* (grandmother) Albina's enterprises. Every day, after school, Jovita's abuela sent her to sell eggs around the neighborhood.

Jovita loved school despite her aunt's constant maneuvering to keep her at home. Tía Severa inevitably pleaded illness, so Jovita had to do all of the housework. ... Tía Severa took Jovita out of school for good at age eleven. Cooking, housecleaning, washing, and ironing became her daily routine:

> In May of 1927, after my grandmother died, we came to the
> beet fields of Ovid, Colorado. We had many boys in the family,

278

so we could earn much money. My tío [uncle] would light the stove for me at 3 A.M. and I would wake up to make a hearty breakfast for everyone working at thinning and topping the beets. After breakfast, at about 4 A.M., I would also go out to the fields to work, but not before making a large stack of tortillas and putting beans to cook. I would return at noon to help my tía prepare the noon meal. While the boys rested in the shade, I would wash dishes and then return to the fields with them until it got dark. After dinner, I ironed clothes, finally going to bed at 11 P.M. Oh, those were tough times, so many boys in the family, so many clothes to wash and iron.

Most of the early Mexican immigrants who came north seeking to better their economic condition came from the agrarian states of Guanajuato, Jalisco, San Luis Potosí, Michoacan, and Aguascalientes. Though Great Western preferred to contract families because of their stability, an increasing number of the Mexican immigrants were single males between the ages of eighteen and thirty. Marciano Aguayo fit the typical profile exactly.

Aguayo left an abusive father and the grinding poverty of their tiny *rancho* in *La Barranca de las Cabras* (Goat Canyon), Aguascalientes, at age fifteen. Geronimo Aguayo was accustomed to leaving young Marciano to protect the distant *milpas*, cornfields, from birds and rodents for days at a time. Marciano, desperate at times, was forced to roast the immature corn and squash to satisfy his gnawing hunger. Their rancho, isolated in a spectacularly scenic canyon, barely produced enough food to sustain the Aguayo family. The scarcity of food, perhaps, compelled grandmother Maria Hernandez to lasso the towering *peñascos*, escarpments, and climb up to savor the delicious *tunas*, cactus fruit, growing high above the canyon. There too were honeycombs she wrested from the protesting bees.

One by one, the Aguayo family left *La Barranca de las Cabras* for the capital city of Aguascalientes, where there was more opportunity. Following his older brother Ciriaco to Aguascalientes, Marciano first worked as a blacksmith in the railroad roundhouse. He was too young to be hired officially, but Ciriaco convinced the foreman that Marciano was a hard worker. The foreman gave him a job but told him, "On payday, when the superintendent comes around, I want you to hide behind the locomotives."

Though railway workers were noncombatants, they played an important role in the revolution. They had to keep the trains that transported troops from city to city rolling. Pancho Villa often used more than a dozen trains to carry his troops into battle. At the roundhouse Aguayo learned to operate monstrous steam-powered hammers to shape replacement parts for the steam locomotives. This experience may account for his lifelong fascination with the railroad.

In Aguascalientes, near the end of the war, railroad workers including Aguayo petitioned victorious general Alvaro Obregon to make good the paper money issued to them by Villa's administration in northern Mexico. Obregon contemptuously replied, "When this arm that I lost to Villa's artillery grows back, I will make good that money." Aguayo's foreman was confident that President Carranza would eventually pay their back wages and urged him to stay, but Aguayo left Mexico for good about 1919. Penniless when he arrived at the border, he could only look hungrily at the bread in bakery windows. He spent a cold and hungry night before crossing the border the next morning.

Prosperity was not there for the taking in El Paso, although conditions were certainly better than what Aguayo had abandoned. The average daily wage in Mexico had been about eighty centavos (.80 pesos). Farm laborers in the United States earned five times that at $2.02 per day (4.04 pesos at the current exchange rate of two pesos to the dollar). Anxious to again join his brother Ciriaco, who had preceded him to the United States, Marciano went north to Tyler, Texas, where he worked for a few months on the railroad extra gang at $1.25 per day. Moving on, he lingered awhile in Blackwell, Oklahoma, cutting four and a half cords of firewood daily at twenty-five cents a cord. He eventually teamed up with Ciriaco again in Pueblo, Colorado. Together they "worked the beets" near Sugar City on the Arkansas River. Compatriots returning to Mexico lavishly described the opportunity for high wages in the South Platte Valley, so, like hobos, they rode the truss rods of freight cars, jumping off near Merino, Colorado, in the spring of 1921.

Not all of the beet laborers were recruited by the sugar company. Some, like the Aguayos, approached the growers directly and negotiated their own contracts.

Tending sugar beets is a cyclical task requiring several "passes" over the same acreage. In *My Childhood on the Prairie*, Clara Hilderman Erlich describes the phases of sugar beet growing in 1904. The seed is planted in spring using a horse-drawn, four-row beet drill. It is planted generously to ensure a good stand. The seed germinates by the time school is out in early June. When the plant develops four leaves it is time for thinning—*el desaihe* to Mexican laborers. The field is "blocked" by cutting out plants in the rows with a hoe so that clusters or blocks of plants are evenly spaced about eight to twelve inches apart. Next, thinning of blocks by hand or again with the hoe removes all but one plant from each cluster. As the plants mature, two passes are made to remove weeds and any double plants missed in the thinning—*la limpia*. The field is then furrowed to prepare it for irrigation and machine cultivated to keep the dirt around the furrows loose. In late September, a special plow is set to cut deep down, severing the taproot and loosening the dirt so that the beet can be pulled out with one hand and the leaves or top cut with a long knife held in the other—*el tapéo*. Topped beets are piled and then loaded into wagons, transporting one-and-a-half to two tons at a time directly to the sugar factory or to beet dumps located near the railroad for transport by rail car. The leaves are left in the field as nutritious feed for cattle.

In later years Marciano Aguayo often paid farmers to allow him to turn his small herds of cattle into the harvested beet fields to fatten on the beet tops. In poor health just before his death in 1979, Aguayo lamented the fact that he could no longer tend the cattle and pigs that he always managed to have around for extra income. "Since I was a small child, I have tended animals," he wrote in a letter to his son. "Now they are taking that joy away from me."

To maximize production and efficiency, Great Western compared the tending of sugar beet acreage among the various ethnic groups of laborers, passing on their findings to the contracted growers. According to the studies, a German Russian family could efficiently tend twelve acres of beets from thinning to topping. Japanese and Mexican "solos" could tend seven acres.

Using various incentives, Great Western attempted to increase the quality and quantity of field work. The company advised growers to "hold back" some of the wages from thinning and cleaning the fields in the spring to ensure that the contract laborer would remain to do the topping in the fall. Laborers accused growers of excessive "hold back," or of neglecting to pay at harvest time the earnings held in escrow, and the practice was outlawed in 1930. Another incentive was bonuses to laborers for tonnage harvested above the district's average. This incentive also discouraged excessive or sloppy thinning of the beet crop in the spring—a practice attributed to laborers wanting to lighten their workload when the beets were pulled in the fall.

The company conducted its operations like athletic competitions: The factory processing season from October to March was called a "campaign," and factories vied to win the "pennant" for highest production. Marciano Aguayo held many certificates of merit issued by Great Western as incentives to help maximize the beet crop and to identify, for the growers, laborers who were reliable and efficient. Aguayo's certificates, dated 1925 to 1931, indicate that he was an exceptional beet laborer, tending from nineteen to twenty-six acres per season with a quality-of-work grade of "A."

Everyone wanted to be Aguayo's partner. The family of Jovita Ortega, Aguayo's future wife, urged relatives to work with him because *"es muy trabajador"*—he is a hard worker. Aguayo was proud of his reputation and, in later years, told his children how hard he worked to earn it:

> I was accustomed to waking up at 3 A.M. every morning. I walked to the fields, arriving by first light when one was just able to see the individual beet plants. I would walk in the furrow between rows, thinning and hoeing two at a time. I continued this pace until well past dark, lighting my way with a carbide lamp mounted on a miner's cap. I was home by 10 P.M. every night to catch a few short hours of sleep before repeating the routine all over again.

Beetworkers' wages varied considerably from year to year and from one district to another. Magdalena Arellano remembers being paid eighteen dollars per acre in the Fort Collins factory district in 1923. Marciano Aguayo's receipts in the Ovid factory district show a breakdown of wages for 1929 of seven dollars per acre for thinning, two dollars per acre for hoeing, and nine dollars per acre for topping, with an additional bonus at harvest of $.775 per acre for exceptional production. Aguayo's earnings for the 1929 sugar beet season totaled just $482. Before he married, similar amounts had to last through the winter, for he had made the decision early on to make the United States his home. With his seasonal earnings he could purchase a hundred pounds each of beans, potatoes, and flour and a bit of lard, sugar, and coffee. In later years, Aguayo demonstrated the skill at making tortillas he developed as a bachelor. Even Jovita, an award-winning tortilla maker herself, acknowledged that his perfectly round, thin, and fluffy tortillas were better than those made by most women!

After beet harvest, Aguayo augmented his winter survival fund and earned a little "fun money" by picking corn in the hills rising south of the Platte River at Sedgwick. Aguayo and two or three companions would pile into his 1926 Model T Ford and drive to Denver. "We stayed in the best hotel—the Shirley Savoy," he would later tell his children. He would point to a studio photograph of two young *Mexicanos* in cowboy garb and say, "I bought this fine hat, a John B. Stetson, at the Daniels & Fisher store." Then, laughing, he would continue, "After one of these trips, a friend and I were determined to return to Mexico. We started out, catching a southbound Rio Grande freight train. But outside of Denver we were robbed at gunpoint. The robber took my friend's new shoes, leaving as replacement the smelliest pair of boots imaginable. After this incident, I decided that I would stay in the United States."

Spanish Americans and Mexicans alike measured their early years in Colorado by the names of farmers for whom they worked: "Those were the years that I worked for *la Señora* Frink," or "*Cuando viviamos en el rancho del* Toyne." They were not any more welcome as permanent residents than the German Russians who preceded them. To the white farmers they were all immigrant Mexicans—no matter that some of their ancestors

Pulling sugar beets near Greeley.
(Photo by Llewellyn A. Moorhouse, Courtesy of the Denver Public Library, Western History Collection)

had settled the Southwest more than four hundred years earlier. As they put down roots in Fort Collins, Greeley, Longmont, Brighton, Eaton, Loveland, and other beet-growing towns in northern Colorado, they also began to leave the fields and farm-labor shacks to settle in previously all-white communities. They learned the language, laws, and customs of their adopted land.

When they purchased homes, they were usually shunted to the fringes of the community, it seems, to live among "their own kind." These neighborhoods, and the clusters of houses subsidized by Great Western on land near its factories, became the Mexican *colonias* of Colorado.

Initially, immigrant laborers lived in housing provided by the farmers with whom they contracted. The housing was nearly always substandard and inadequate for sheltering large extended families. Jovita Ortega, newly married to Marciano Aguayo in 1929, recalls crowding into a one-room labor shack with another couple and Marciano's brother Ciriaco. The sparse furnishings included an iron bedstead and a wood-burning stove. A later home was somewhat better—two rooms made of brick—but Jovita had to place their two infant daughters in a washtub balanced on two chairs to keep them safe from rats as big as house cats.

In *Through the Leaves*, the sugar company, recognizing the critical role played by Mexican labor in its operations, implored growers to provide better housing: "Do not expect a high class of labor if you have a poor place for them to live."

One benefit of working on a farm was the patch of land provided by the farmer on which to grow vegetables that could be canned to last through the winter. The Aguayos kept a large garden, eventually taking up half a town block, throughout their lives. When their children came to Sedgwick on summer visits in later years, bags of fresh cucumbers, tomatoes, chiles, and melons went home with them to Greeley and Denver. Marciano and Jovita's garden produce were perennial first-place winners at Sedgwick's annual harvest festival. The Aguayos were justly proud of the relatively bountiful life that the garden represented. Marciano delighted in taking the newest grandchildren to see and taste the powerful *chorro* (stream) of water pumped from his thirty-foot-deep, hand-dug well.

Great Western created a program for beet laborers to build their own houses of adobe. Laborers were issued building materials on credit against earnings from the next growing season. Purchase of the land on which they built could be extended over a four-year period. The company newsletter even carried information about construction technology, including how to make adobe—recommending it for its insulating qualities and economy and noting its familiarity to the Mexican and Spanish American beet labor force.

Colonias sprang up in Greeley, Kersey, Loveland, Hudson, Brush, Fort Morgan, Brighton, Fort Collins, and Ovid. Some were no more than a cluster of two or three houses. Most were viewed by the white population as an appropriate means of keeping the Mexicans together. Even Spanish American families, who managed to edge into the fringes of the white communities, sometimes looked down at their compatriots living in the *colonias*.

Magdalena Arellano bought a house on Howe Street in Fort Collins for five hundred dollars. She arranged for the loan and made several payments from her earnings as a domestic before her husband was even aware that they were becoming homeowners. Marciano Aguayo traded his Model T for some land and a one-room, tar-paper shack on the outskirts of Sedgwick. A few years later, he used a team of draft horses to drag a two-room clapboard building from Main Street to attach to the shack. This was the Aguayo family home until the 1970s, when Marciano and Jovita moved into the more genteel center of the small community.

Mexican laborers faced many obstacles in their adopted land. Marciano Aguayo's personal files are filled with letters he wrote to the Mexican Consulate in Denver requesting investigations of dishonest practices by company fieldmen. Some accused the fieldmen of favoring growers by shortchanging unsuspecting laborers when measuring the beet acreage they tended. Other growers allegedly refused to pay wages held back from the laborers' spring earnings. Local merchants were suspected of overcharging laborers for goods and services and conspiring with growers to deduct these exorbitant store charges before paychecks were distributed to them. Because most Mexican laborers did not speak English and did not understand the laws of the United States, it was easy to defraud them. They relied on compatriots like Aguayo, who learned to speak English and gained a working knowledge of the local economic and legal systems to communicate their concerns to the appropriate authorities. Aguayo also served as intermediary for Mexican laborers being repatriated during the 1930s and helped locate the families of single laborers who died in northern Colorado, far from their homes in Mexico.

As further defense against prejudice and exploitation, Mexican immigrants in northern Colorado formed mutual aid societies like the *Comisión Honorífica*. Spanish Americans, especially in southern Colorado, formed *Sociedad Protección Mutua de Trabajadores Unidos* chapters for similar purposes. The primary function of these organizations was to build solidarity within the Mexican and Spanish American communities, to educate their members about the laws and institutions of the United States, to welcome new arrivals to the communities, and to plead cases of injustice before the appropriate authorities. *Comisiones Honoríficas* also organized festivals and social gatherings designed to build pride in their heritage, to reinforce loyalty to their homeland, and as a means to meet and visit. The Aguayo brothers led organizers of festivals on two important Mexican national holidays, *Cinco de Mayo* (Fifth of May) and *Diez y Seis de Septiembre* (Sixteenth of September).

Patriotic red, white, and green posters printed in Denver announced the festivals held in Sedgwick and Ovid throughout the 1920s. Candidates for festival queen rode on elaborately decorated farm trucks with both the Mexican and American flags flying. Programs for celebrations in Fort Collins and Sedgwick listed musical presentations, poetry recitals, and waltz, polka, and two-step dances. Red, white, and green and red, white, and blue strings of bulbs lighted the rented halls above Jankovsky's Store for the events in Sedgwick. These were memorable celebrations, where people of Spanish and Mexican descent could express pride in their heritage while acknowledging loyalty to the United States. More than a few marriages, including Jovita Ortega's to Marciano Aguayo, resulted from introductions at these festivals.

The Aguayos and Arellanos were among those who found ways to establish themselves permanently within the white communities. In 1941, after years of applying, Marciano Aguayo was finally able to land a job with the Union Pacific Railroad section gang in Sedgwick. In characteristic fashion, he worked hard maintaining the railroad right-of-way from Ovid to Crook. He was already forty-three, but this stocky, muscular man could hoist an eighty-pound railroad cross-tie onto each shoulder and run to place them in position. He never missed a day of work in thirty-two years with Union Pacific, no matter if he was ill or how severe the weather. Aguayo's children remember running to meet his sheepskin-overcoated figure as he walked home on cold and snowy winter days, his eyelids nearly frozen shut.

Working somewhat regular hours for the railroad left Aguayo time in the evening to entertain his children with stories of his childhood in Mexico. He was a talented raconteur, and his accounts of village *brujas* (witches), buried treasure, and the Mexican Revolution created vivid images. ... Though he and Jovita proudly became citizens of the United States in the 1950s, he always maintained and instilled in his children a fierce loyalty to Mexico and their *Mestizo*—Indian and Spanish—heritage.

Also in the 1950s, when a workforce reduction caused him to transfer to the Crook, Colorado, section of the Union Pacific, Aguayo faced unusual hardship in order to maintain his family. Always obsessed with punctuality, Aguayo rose at 4 A.M. (as he had when he worked in the beet fields) to ride "el loco," the local Union Pacific freight train, the seven miles to Crook. Arriving before anyone was stirring in the small community, he would curl up in the cement water troughs at the abandoned stockyard to catch a bit more sleep before reporting for work at 7:30. El loco took him back to Sedgwick well after dark. Grateful for the relatively steady employment, he never complained. One day in the 1970s, Aguayo suffered a heart attack while returning to Sedgwick on the section gang motorcar. The foreman merely braked the motorcar long enough for him to dismount. Aguayo rested awhile beside the track before walking to the Sedgwick Lumber Company to ask for help.

All beet laborers, Spanish American or Mexican, suffered the prejudice, intolerance, and discrimination seemingly always directed toward the most recently arrived ethnic group. The Mexicans, perhaps, suffered more because they looked different and spoke a different language as well. In northern Colorado during the 1920s, it was not uncommon to see signs posted in public places stating "No dogs or Mexicans allowed" and "We cater to the white trade only." Filigonio Arellano often said, "During wartime and when they need votes, white people call me an American; if I need a loan, I am Spanish; and if I am applying for a job they call me Mexican." Arellano's ancestors, of course, became citizens at the end of the Mexican War in 1848, when nearly half the Mexican Republic, including what would later be the states of Texas, New Mexico, Arizona, Nevada, California, and parts of Colorado and Utah, was ceded to the United States.

The children of beet laborers were unwelcome in northern Colorado schools. School boards characterized Mexicans as unsanitary and proposed separate schools or classrooms to protect white students from this misperceived health hazard. No extra effort was made to ensure that immigrant children attended school in compliance with the law. According to some white educators, Mexicans lacked ambition and possessed limited intellect. School administrators in Larimer and Weld Counties made it easy for families to keep their children out of school for the spring beet thinning and fall harvest seasons. They made it extremely difficult for Mexican children to feel that they belonged in school, let alone to compete or excel.

None of this deterred Jovita Aguayo. She brought to Colorado her love of learning, developed in the schools in El Paso, Texas. Some of the older children born to her and Marciano Aguayo worked in the fields, but they did so only when school was out. While Marciano worked on the railroad, Jovita and some of the older children picked potatoes to earn extra money for school clothes. None of her children would be deprived of an education: There were few illnesses and no event important enough to keep anyone out of school. The Aguayo children nearly always brought home perfect attendance certificates. All learned from these outstanding and hardworking parents the value of education, graduating at the top of their high school classes and earning one Ph.D. and five master of arts degrees among them. Still, the Aguayos are not unique. Many Mexicans and Spanish Americans of the war years generation overcame the obstacles placed in their path and succeeded in various professional careers.

Today, the descendants of Colorado's Spanish American and Mexican beetworkers are fully assimilated. The sugar beet industry in Colorado is just a shadow of what it once was. What little land is planted in sugar beets is tended completely by machinery. The sugar factories that vitalized the communities along the South Platte River stand empty except for those in Loveland, Greeley, and Fort Morgan. Still, Colorado's Hispanics and Chicanos appreciate the hardships and obstacles overcome by their parents and grandparents so that they could capture a share of the American Dream. And many are thankful for the rich legacy of social and moral values carried down to them by their indigenous and Spanish forebears.

Excerpted from "Los Betabeleros (*The Beetworkers*)," *La Gente:*
Hispano History and Life in Colorado, 1998

G rowing up in a small community on Colorado's expansive eastern plains of the 1930s and 1940s was unlike growing up in the big city or even in a mountain town. The city had movie shows and trolley cars and alleys to prowl (slingshot in hip pocket); a mountain kid could fish and (courage permitting) explore deep old mineshafts and hike to where snow was still on the ground in July.

On the plains, however, a young person had fewer opportunities and had to rely on his or her imagination for amusements, which sometimes translated into mischief.

Sharon Springs, Kansas, and Hugo, Colorado, were both that kind of town, and Keith A. Cook was that kind of kid. As for Hugo, today's observer might suspect that the most exciting thing there was when the Union Pacific train rumbled through, eastbound to Kansas City or westbound to Denver. The town may not have had trolley cars or amusement parks, but it had the Plains Café and Doc Daniel's Rexall pharmacy and Hap Wooldridge's hardware store and the Hugo National Bank—all places to hang around—and occasionally Hugo offered a good duck-hunting adventure.

Former *Colorado Heritage* editor Clark Secrest published Cook's reminiscences in the spring of 1998 after lengthier versions first appeared in the *Eastern Colorado Plainsman* of Hugo. The following are just a sampling of those reminiscences.

Keith Cook was a homebuilder in Denver for many years and now lives in Missouri. Occasionally he returns to his hometowns on the Colorado and Kansas plains.

A Whiskey Train and a Doughnut Day: Coming of Age on the Eastern Colorado Plains

—*Keith A. Cook*

A writer once said of hometowns that when you are young, you want to get away and when you are old, you want to go back. I had two hometowns: Sharon Springs, Kansas (1928–39); and—106 miles west of there—Hugo, Colorado (1939–46). I didn't want to leave Sharon Springs, but we moved to Colorado to be near my elderly grandparents. There were no nursing homes in those days; a family took care of its own. It was the right thing to do. No nursing homes; no Medicare; no Medicaid.

I was ten months old when the stock market crashed in 1929, the start of the Great Depression, followed by Drought and then the Dust Bowl. I called them the three Big Ds. There were suicides related to one or all of the Big Ds. Men *did* abandon their families when they could not find work. Families *did* disappear overnight, never heard from again. Women *did* have nervous breakdowns due to the wind, the constant never-ending wind. Do you know what it's like to be in wind that never, ever, stops?

Young boys did a man's work and our generation learned the value of a penny—disregard a dollar. People were hungry yet proud, and one cannot eat pride. Banks went broke; ours did in Sharon Springs. We had one dollar and forty-seven cents to last two weeks.

North of Sharon Springs we had rabbits by the millions, and grasshoppers that would eat paint off the house. I was in high school at Hugo when the World War II troop trains came through on the Union Pacific every day. Some of our own Lincoln County boys went to war; only a few of them returned to our county to reside, and a few of them came back in caskets. Our high school played a football game at Limon, and the entire team suited up in Hugo and we rode in the back of a stock truck to the game. Hugo had small-town places like Doc Daniel's drugstore and Hap Wooldridge's garage and store; I worked at both of them.

My dad was a conductor on the Union Pacific that ran through Hugo from Kansas to Denver. He worked for the U.P. fifty-one years. He told me there were thirty-five trains a day in his early days! He received his last and final telegram in Hugo probably not fifty yards from where he first started calling crews in 1912.

There were many adventures in growing up in a small town on those endless eastern Colorado Plains in the 1930s and '40s. I have written down some of them.

Depression, Drought, and Dust

Never before in the history of modern times had mankind been subjected to these three phenomena at once, especially to the extent that they struck at eastern Colorado and west Kansas. Let me start with the Depression. How did the Depression affect us, trying to survive?

My dad was out of a job. Our local bank in Sharon Springs went broke. There was *no* money. Even the schoolteachers were paid by warrants pledging that if there were ever money again, they would get some. The principal real property taxes that were being collected in eastern Colorado and western Kansas were from the Union Pacific. The few banks still open refused to loan. When my uncle moved to Cheyenne County in Colorado there were thirty-three families on his mail route; this was in 1922. When he sold out in 1965 there were three. Where did these people go? I don't know. I remember children in my first grade class in Sharon Springs who were in school on Friday and gone on Monday; the year was 1934. They simply disappeared. There were no food stamps and a lot of people went on relief. That meant they could get food staples free but many were too proud. In Sharon Springs, when our hometown physician Doc Nelson passed away, his daughter found over $100,000 in accounts receivable in his large rolltop desk.

A drought just means that the rains never come. When there is a drought there is no grass for cattle, so there are no cattle shipped in or out. When there is a drought there is no wheat and thus no work on the winter wheat run. Then a variety of things occurred: Millions of rabbits and zillions of grasshoppers, and the Union Pacific freight had to halt because the driver wheels were sliding. Land in Wallace County, Kansas, could be had for a dollar an acre, cash.

Dust. My uncle in Cheyenne County replanted his feed crop three times one year. One time a group of us youngsters was east of Sharon Springs swimming in the Smoky Hill River, and we saw this huge cloud of dust in the west. The air was very still and seemed charged with electricity. We ran for the car; we were just four miles from town. We never made it; the static electricity grounded out the car and it wouldn't start. We covered our faces with our wet swimsuits. Dad and a neighbor man finally found us. Another time it was so dark they let school out; Dad and I tried to drive just three blocks and we got lost. The children were issued surgical masks, and where the nose was, was black with dust. Mother stuck kitchen knives in the edges of the windows to cinch them tight because they howled so loud. She put wet sheets over the doors. The streetlights went on at 2 P.M., and one was afraid to push the button on the light switch because a spark would shoot out three inches. Dust blew in the attics of many houses, and the weight of the dirt caused ceilings to fall in. Even the birds were afraid to fly.

Folks, that's what a dust storm was, and once you have been in one, you'll never forget it.

Junor's 180

The Teel boys lived across the street from us when I was a lad in Sharon Springs. They were Junor and Gene, son of Pop Teel, who was the town plumber, fire chief, and hardware clerk. We were ages ten, eleven, and twelve.

Pop Teel decided to build us boys a swing, and it was a doozie. He dug two holes about two feet deep, set two twelve-foot four-by-fours in concrete, and put a half-inch diameter of pipe across with hooks to hold the rope for the swing. He threaded the pipe ends and installed caps so the pipe couldn't slip out of the four-by-fours. Safety first. Those days, you didn't go out and buy a plastic swing set at Wal-Mart.

Someone had taken the swing and given it a big flip and it wound around the pipe once. We swung it back over the pipe and that gave us a good idea. Put one of us in that swing and do a 360; go all the way around. Wouldn't that be a thrill! It would be a first—never done before!

We selected Junor as he had the most weight. We put him in the swing seat; Junor would pump his legs and Gene and I would push him every time he came back. But no luck, we just couldn't get him high enough.

Gene came up with the idea of getting the six-foot folding stepladder and Gene could get on the top with one foot on the ladder shelf where you put the paint can; I would get on the step below, and we would push the swing from that elevation.

We really got Junor to going; got him right up near the apex when the kitchen window flew up and Mom Teel hollered, "What are you boys doing?!" At that very moment, Junor hit the 180 and plummeted straight down about twenty feet but he stayed in the saddle. You could hear his jaw pop for a block.

Mom Teel hurtled out the back door; "You've killed my first-born!" Gene and I were laughing hard as we could and rolling around in the dirt. Junor's freckles were kind of pale and he and Mom Teel wobbled into the house. He was okay.

When the three of us got together, it always spelled trouble, but that's what you did those days in a little town. Kids today probably wouldn't think of it and anyway you could never do a 360 on a Wal-Mart swing because it isn't made that way.

Now in 1998, Junor Teel is dead; Gene found him in his apartment out in Bremerton, Washington. I hope he's swinging on a star because he deserves it.

The Freight Train "Computer"

When I was a small boy, I should think about age four, we lived in a rental house next to the West Hotel in Sharon Springs. I could sit on the front porch and watch Dad "make up" a Union Pacific train. Some people think a freight train is assembled by the engineer backing up to a bunch of railroad cars and then taking off for Denver. It was not that easy.

In 1932 or 1933, Dad was conductor on the largest freight train, 120 cars, ever to leave Sharon Springs for Denver. There were three locomotives; this was called a triple-header. Since the U.P. was a land-grant railroad, it was under a ninety-nine-year obligation to transport the mail. This was done on passenger trains carrying Railway Express cars, and these trains had priority over standard freight trains.

This priority was the real problem for Dad. He had to consider when the passenger/mail train was due, and by that time have all freight trains on sidings so the passenger/mail could pass. The difficulty was that he had no siding that would hold 120 freight cars. I can still see Dad gracefully catching a freight car going past at twenty miles an hour, and then looking at his watch, checking the mile markers on the Western Union poles, and calculating distances to the upcoming sidings. The 7-percent grade into Firstview, Colorado, between Cheyenne Wells and Kit Carson, was a widow-maker. Dad told me how the head brakeman had to assist the fireman in continuously shoveling coal into the firebox to keep up the steam to get up that hill. Sometimes they would cut the train in half and make two trips over the hill; this was called "doubling the hill."

They split Dad's 120-car train into *thirds* and each locomotive pulled a third of the train west over toward Kit Carson. *Tripling* the hill! There was a side track at Arena, so he left part of the freight train there, and then other parts of it were switched and "set out" onto various small-town sidings. The passenger/mail got past safely.

When they pulled Dad's freight train into Hugo there were 128 cars—eight more than when the train left Sharon Springs. These were empties they picked up along the way.

And they did it all without computers, just by looking at their Hamilton railroad pocket watches which they kept tucked into the bibs of their overalls, and knowing how many cars each siding would hold, and knowing how close the approaching mail train was. Yes, there was professionalism in railroading and Dad was a pro, working almost sixteen hours a day when they were juggling cars onto sidings.

And not getting any time-and-a-half, either.

Ladies Aid Doughnut Day

I got my first bicycle in about 1937. It had balloon tires; all the other kids' bikes had narrow and hard tires. Balloon tires rode easy, but with the sand burrs and a weed called "road tacks" all around Sharon Springs, I mostly was in the tire repair business. I did run errands for some of the elderly, get their mail, groceries. They usually paid me a dime, and I made enough to go to the Strand Theater picture show and buy a sack of popcorn on Friday night.

Along came the first Saturday in October, when the Sharon Springs Methodist Ladies Aid Society had its annual doughnut sale. Mother volunteered me to deliver the doughnuts. The telephone was in the parsonage next door. A lady took the orders, a little Sunday school girl ran the orders over to the women in the kitchen, and I delivered. On doughnut day, the church ladies arrived in their starched dresses and aprons, hair all done up, some even in their Sunday hats. The farm women brought about ten gallons of lard, built a fire in a coal range as big as a piano, and began putting the doughnut dough in the bubbling lard. The temperature in that kitchen was about ninety. They made plain cake doughnuts and sugar-coated; someone asked me if I wanted the doughnut holes and I happily accepted.

I was watching the lady blot the hot, greasy doughnuts on inky newspaper pages and then put them in sacks—munching all the dough-nut holes as I watched—and she put *thirteen* doughnuts into each sack! Now anybody knows that there are *twelve* in a dozen. I started out on my deliveries—I could get about ten sacks into my bike basket—and I took one doughnut out of each sack, munching as I rode along. A dozen should be a dozen.

Things were pretty slacked off by 4 P.M.; believe me, those Methodist ladies didn't look quite as starched and done-up at 4 as they had at 10! I took a sack of doughnuts home to Mother. She remarked that I looked kind of pale, and then up came all the doughnut holes and all the thirteenth doughnuts.

Mother wanted to know how many greasy doughnuts I had eaten; it must have been thirty or forty.

Incidentally, she said that thirteen is a "baker's dozen." I didn't know that. I was just the delivery boy.

I think I liked the cake doughnuts better than the sugar-coated.

Duck Hunters Are Different

The men in our family have always liked to hunt ducks, even as far back as my great-grandfather when he shot a hole in the bottom of the boat and swam to shore. He was eighty at the time.

When my Grandpa Cook lost his homestead—960 acres down on Rush Creek (the address was Swift, Colorado, east of Karval)—to the Federal Land Bank in the early '30s, he bought the Standard station and cottage courts there in Hugo. My how he hated that filling station! Disliked living in a metropolis such as Hugo, and said all he did at the gas station was sell air and water. However, he did trade a tank of gas for a .410-gauge shotgun and it became my duck-hunting gun at age seven. The shop and physics teacher in Hugo, Glen Garrabrant, and I would go duck hunting together.

When L. H. Fields sold his fine ranch to Bob Jolly, every autumn there appeared an advertisement in the *Eastern Colorado Plainsman*:

NO HUNTING OR TRESPASSING
ON THE JOLLY RANCHES!!

Every other fencepost on the east side had a "no hunting" sign as well.

Problem was, duck hunters develop a reading problem, even if they are teachers or students. Plus, my dad and I had received prior permission to duck hunt from Mr. Fields before he sold the ranch to Bob Jolly, so I assumed there was a codicil in the deed that we could hunt. Once hunting permission is granted, it is into perpetuity; possibly one might consider it as eminent domain.

Garrabrant and I were out there long before sunrise; eased the '38 Plymouth door open; ducks out on the pond, quacking. We must have gotten at least nine. I had just laid my gun down and was reaching for the first duck when a rifle bullet hit the frozen ground about ten feet away and ricocheted toward the rising sun.

That is an uncomfortable sound. There is no other sound quite like it. It gets a duck hunter's attention.

I stood up and there was Bob Jolly on horseback with his .30-30. Didn't holler much, just "Leave the ducks and get off the place!" This was no time to discuss codicils, perpetuities, eminent domains, or possessions of the kill.

We stepped lively to the Plymouth; Garrabrant ripped his trousers jumping the fence; he hurried back to Hugo to change his pants for school. When that .30-30 slug hit, I thought I might need to change my pants, too.

The worst part of duck hunting is cleaning the ducks. I was delighted that Bob Jolly had to clean ours, and I always have hoped they tasted good to him.

A Young Entrepreneur

It was along in the autumn of 1941, when I came home from school and noticed a car with Denver license plates in front of our house. Used to be, you could look at a Colorado license plate and know immediately where somebody was from. If the license started with "1," it was automatically Denver; "2" was Pueblo, "3" was Colorado Springs. It was done according to population. Our small Lincoln County was "33." I walked in the house and Mother was happy as could be. Without any consultation, no discussion, I was Hugo's new newspaperboy for the *Rocky Mountain News.* I got the job because Bud Sterling was studying for the West Point examinations and didn't have time to deliver the paper. It must have worked because Bud became a general.

The papers came in a bundle on the Greyhound bus. The driver dropped them off in the nearest mudhole he could find at Farrell Hines's Texaco station. The *News* charged me 3.5 cents and I sold them for 5 cents. If it hadn't been for the Plains Cafe I would have made money. Instead, I stopped in the Plains each morning for a short stack and coffee, and that cost me twenty-five cents a day.

I just was not making money equaling the effort. But right after Pearl Harbor, business picked up because troop trains began coming into Hugo, three or four a day. I would ride down the side of the train on my bicycle, paper bag on the handlebars, soldier recruits hanging out the windows, and I'd peddle my papers.

Still, I wasn't earning enough. Then I hit on the money-maker. It was booze. I became the youngest bootlegger along the Union Pacific.

When Prohibition was removed in 1933, W. A. (Doc) Daniel at the Hugo drugstore received a liquor license and he bought a hundred barrels of raw and unaged whiskey, to remain at the distillery for six years. Those six years were up in 1940. The whiskey salesman came back and said it was now time to bottle it, and what should we name it. They settled on "Doc's Private Stock." When the pints and fifths began arriving, I had the job of stamping Doc's liquor license number on every label. The whiskey was stored in a basement room with a large padlock.

There was a man in Hugo who hung around the pool hall and who would purchase liquor for the high school boys. I had him buy me just two pints at a dollar seventy-five each plus fifty cents each for his trouble. So that totals two dollars and twenty-five cents each. I hid the two pints down amongst the newspapers but enough of the top showed so that the soldier boys could see the booze caps from the train. I peddled my papers and the booze in about five minutes for five dollars a pint!

But it got better. Once I had a pint left, and pedaled up to the cook car while the locomotive was taking on water. The cook looked down and saw the pint. "I'll give you two big slabs of corned beef and a crate of cabbage for that pint." The reason they had to get rid of the food was they had to clean the cook car before they got to Denver; then he would dead-head back to Kansas City and come west again.

My friend Butch Robbins, who ran the Hugo Locker Plant, stored the food and he put an ad in the next *Plainsman* for corned beef and cabbage, no ration stamps required; forty-nine cents a pound for the meat and a dime a head for the cabbage. I could make more on trading booze for food than with the straight sales program.

That train with the cook came through Hugo about every four days. The next time I traded for four hams. I made a profit, Butch made a profit, and the *Plainsman* made an advertising profit. This was business at its finest.

Hugo had a men's bridge club, and one day during a game at our house Dad remarked to one of our fine upstanding bankers that I could hardly pay my bill to the *Rocky Mountain News*. The banker bid two clubs and responded to Dad: "Keith is sure doing better on that paper route than Bud Sterling did. He's got about six hundred dollars in a savings account."

I never could lie to Dad. He told me I could get Doc Daniel in a lot of trouble and to stop my bootlegging. He kind of smiled, though. My little nest egg at the First National went for the remodeling of our living room, but my folks didn't know about an extra couple hundred I had stashed in a fruit jar in the basement crawl space. I used that for school clothes and had some left over.

I always thought bankers had a fiduciary obligation to their depositors. I learned a couple of important lessons from my entrepreneurship. Never put all your money in one place and beware of bankers. I haven't trusted one since that bridge game.

The Old Jail

When my Grandpa Cook was the Hugo town marshal, they lived in a house adjacent to the jail. Grandma cooked for the prisoners and was paid by the town. The Union Pacific paid Grandpa or the town a set sum for his taking hobos off the freight trains. "Hobos" or "tramps" were transient vagabonds; today the more polite term is "homeless." Grandpa rode a saddle horse on his rounds, and his dog Queen would sit up on the rear of the saddle with her paws on Grandpa's shoulders. As Grandpa rode alongside a freight and Queen sniffed a hobo, all Grandpa had to do was tell them to come on out or he'd sic the dog on them. They came along peacefully.

During World War II, the Hugo Boy Scouts had paper-collecting drives, and the papers were all stored in the old jail, which looked like a castle. The first time I was in the jail, female nudity and poetry seemed to be the themes on the walls. Odd how jailbirds out on the Plains had either artistic or poetic leanings. Troop 52 learned a lot about art and poetry while stacking newspapers into that old jailhouse.

The Whiskey Train

I was a senior in Hugo High School in the autumn of '45 and worked mornings at Doc Daniel's drugstore. I got off at 11 and then went to school. Our small town of Hugo was fortunate to have a fine weekly newspaper, the *Eastern Colorado Plainsman*, edited by Ember Sterling and Jerry Missemer. They were very proficient at their journalistic trade, making sure that every subscriber got his or her name in the paper at least once a month. That's the wise way to run a small-town newspaper.

The *Plainsman* often encountered a news item that it felt was sufficiently important to not save until the next weekly edition, and in those cases it posted the news item in the front window of the newspaper office. Frequently there would also be this posted announcement: "$5 reward for the finder of Jerry's dentures. Lost someplace in Hugo Saturday night." Jerry would go on a liquid diet on Saturday nights, following a week of journalism.

I was on my way to school one morning when Jerry came flying out of the *Plainsman* office with his camera. He hollered at me, "Hey Cook, you want to go up to Bovina and see the Rock Island train wreck? Sounds like a bad one!"

How often does a kid get to see a good train wreck? Jerry drove a 1941 Buick and as far as he was concerned it had just one speed, and that was fast. We flew north to Genoa, then east on 24 to the wreck site. No fires, no injuries, just tipped-over railroad freight cars. We had hardly reached the first overturned freight car when Jerry's nose went right up; he had the scent, he looked like a golden retriever. Right there was an overturned freight car full of Cutty Sark, good Scotch whiskey.

Jerry tossed his camera in the front seat of the Buick. "Come on, Cook, we'll get loaded up before Merlin Koerner (the sheriff) or the railroad inspectors get here!" One must remember that very little whiskey was distilled during the war; grain was going to feed the world. Now Jerry had struck the mother lode, the El Dorado of all drinking men, alcohol heaven.

Well he jumped right up in that freight car like a man in his prime—a milestone he had passed several decades ago. He commenced to hand me those cases of Cutty Sark. I filled the trunk, the back seat, and put a case on the front seat floor. I was becoming concerned if I was going to get a ride back to Hugo.

Jerry jumped down and we started the ride back to Hugo, and then we met the sheriff headed the other way. I thought Merlin would surely know Jerry was up to something because he was driving slow like he had a carload of eggs, and the Buick was down on the axles due to all that weight. Merlin waved and we waved.

When we got to the school corner I told Jerry to stop, but he said, "Nope. You have to help me unload, then I'll take you to school and tell Superintendent Peck you were helping me on a story, and you will have a legitimate excuse that way."

We carefully backed that Buick into his garage, unloaded the Scotch, and closed the garage door. He took me to school. I never saw Jerry open that garage door again while I was still in Hugo. His garage was situated so that the sheriff could look right into it from the courthouse.

The next week when the *Plainsman* came off the press, I looked for a large article about the Rock Island wreck. I knew there would be no photos, but I thought the story might even mention my name. There was the story back on page 3, one column wide, not more than two inches in length.

Then there was an ad: "$5 reward for the return of Jerry's dentures." The people who later found them said they smelled distinctly of Scotch whiskey. Couldn't be. Everybody knew there hadn't been any Scotch whiskey in Lincoln County since 1941.

Excerpted from "A Whiskey Train and a Doughnut Day: Coming of Age on the Eastern Colorado Plains," *Colorado Heritage*, Spring 1998

I n June 1984, Clark Secrest was working as a writer for *The Denver Post*. He held various writing and editorial positions in his twenty-four years at the paper; at the time, he was covering television and radio.

Late in the evening, when he was home sick with the flu, he got a call from the night city editor. The news was as bad as it gets: Secrest's old friend, the talk-radio host Alan Berg, had just been shot to death in his Denver driveway. Secrest had known the outspoken Berg for twelve years—in fact, he had been a guest, as he often was, on Berg's program just two weeks before. Secrest's editor gave him five minutes to write a column about his late friend and colleague for the next morning's paper.

"I'm a fast writer, but I'm not that fast," Secrest says. "I got the call at about 10:00. Working at my kitchen table on an early Radio Shack laptop, I had them a column by 10:09." It ran on page one of the *Post* the next day.

"There was a time when Alan Berg, by his own admission, was a hateful, unhappy person," Secrest's column began. "But he defeated that misery, just as he defeated his business and professional failures, his alcoholism, memories of his bad marriages, and a life that he occasionally found unkind."

Fifteen years later, in 1999, Secrest was working at the Colorado Historical Society as editor of *Colorado Heritage* magazine, a post he held for eleven years. Again he found himself writing about his friend Alan Berg, this time for an issue of the magazine devoted to 1980s Colorado. But now, rather than recalling his own friendship with the controversial radio personality, he detailed the events leading up to Berg's murder by anti-Semitic extremists.

Alan Berg, as seen by *Denver Post* artist Bonnie Timmons

The Last Back Fence in Town: The Assassination of Alan Berg

—Clark Secrest

At 9:45 on Monday night, June 18, 1984, a black Volkswagen Beetle enters Adams Street just south of Denver's East Colfax Avenue, proceeds the half-block to the townhouses at 1445 Adams, and swings in to park in front of the garages.[1]

The driver switches off the engine, drags from his filterless Pall Mall, retrieves a 7-Eleven bag from the seat beside him, and opens the Volkswagen door.

PopPopPopPopPop.

Gunfire sprays the Volkswagen, the driver's upper torso, and the garage doors. With thirty-four bullet wounds, the man falls backward onto the driveway, cigarette still afire. Thus ends the life of Alan Berg, lawyer turned radio phone-in-show host, slain because he was Jewish and talked about it, and because of his open disdain for fringe extremist groups such as the Ku Klux Klan and neo-Nazis.

One might not anticipate the Berg killing to become the huge and ongoing international news story that it will. But that indeed will be the course that this case will take, because of its racial, political, and who-dunit ingredients. In fact, the Berg murder eventually will involve the Federal Bureau of Investigation, the Internal Revenue Service, the Secret Service, and law enforcement agencies in sixty cities and eighteen states. It becomes the biggest domestic terrorism case in FBI history.

Alan Berg was born in Chicago in 1934, the son of a Jewish dentist and a clothing shop operator. As a youngster, Alan enjoyed bright red hair and a temper to match. His hobbies were golf, stamp collecting, photography, and doing magic tricks. At age seventeen he went off to college at the University of Colorado in Boulder where he was happy to be away from his father, whom Alan viewed as a hypocritical anti-Semite. Always slender and rather unusual looking, Alan Berg was known around campus for his dandified appearance—custom-made suits, fancy shoes, and nicer shirts than most of his fellow students had, or cared to have. And he talked! Alan Berg would not shut up.

After two years at Boulder, Berg transferred to the University of Denver; then the University of Miami in Florida, De Paul University in Chicago, Northwestern University, and then back to De Paul, finally graduating from its law school. In 1958 he married Judy Halpern of Denver and the couple settled in Chicago where he would practice law. He was an able and successful criminal defense lawyer—although his clients more often than not were of sleazy nature—and his affable glibness in front of juries served him well.[2]

Berg began experiencing epileptic-like grand mal seizures, certainly surviving them all but often experiencing depression. Then he discovered martinis, which calmed him and soothed the anxieties he could not otherwise get rid of. He abandoned his law practice, and he and Judy moved back to Denver where he entered St. Joseph Hospital to dry out. Always the clotheshorse and particularly fond of fashionable shoes ("I was a helluva shoe salesman"), the Fontius store hired him, and then fired him. So he opened his own clothing shop, the Shirt Broker, in Seventeenth Street's Albany Hotel. In the haberdashery business, it was the interacting with people that he liked most. He could spontaneously talk about anything with anybody.

Larry Gross, a friend, had a talk show on tiny little KGMC radio in Englewood. Because Berg was such a good talker, Gross invited him behind the microphone as a new adventure. Words. Alan Berg loved words, and they poured forth. KGMC was so anemic and unimportant next to behemoths such as KOA that it took a while, but the curmudgeonly and opinionated Berg began to catch on, and he began to work the radio station in scheduled shifts.

In his first days at KGMC, Berg's words were gentle, but as he became more accustomed to the radio business, they were less tamed, more emboldened, more obstreperous, more controversial. This was not Alan Berg's true puppy-dog personality; the abrasiveness was merely show-biz schtick, and it was quite often very humorous. People started tuning in just to see what Berg would do next.

By 1975, Alan and Judy Berg had split; she returned to Chicago and he was running through a series of paramours. Brain surgery by now had eliminated his seizures, and his hair was allowed to grow long to cover the scars; a scraggly beard was nurtured too, and his fuzzy countenance from now on would be one of his trademarks.

The lack of seizures and his welcome sobriety, one might think, would have calmed the bombastic Berg, but by now he understood the broadcast business and knew that the more rude and argumentative he became, the higher his rating would go, and he was correct.

In 1977 Berg joined KHOW, a more powerful station than was KGMC, and his cantankerous ways reached new heights—insulting listeners, shouting putdowns, waving an index finger toward the ceiling, strewing Pall Mall butts about the control room, and then hanging up on callers. There, two years later, a poll adjudged him to be the most disliked radio host in town—and the most popular. Just the formula for ratings successes!

At one point, local Ku Klux Klan leader Fred Wilkins walked into a radio studio, shook a finger at Berg and exclaimed that Berg was "going to die." Questioned by the police, Wilkins explained that the statement had been a scare tactic and not a threat, and the episode soon was forgotten.

Berg's popularity, the controversies he generated, and the comment he was generating around Denver did not escape management at KOA, then the most influential of all Colorado radio outlets, but where raw rudeness had not theretofore been particularly tolerated. On February 23, 1981, KOA hired Berg to fill a prime afternoon time period. The deal was that he could say anything he pleased, but now Berg was happier with his place in life and his accomplishments than he had been at KHOW, and he began to change. He was provocative, certainly, but his discordant mannerisms were disappearing and his humor was developing.

Throughout his broadcast career, Alan Berg talked about what his biographer Stephen Singular describes as Berg's "Jewishness." On one occasion, an interviewer asked why Berg kept beating up on himself. He pondered that one for a moment.

"I must be punished."

What for?

After a long exhale of a filterless Pall Mall: "I secretly want to be a Christian and don't recognize it."

Berg often characterized talk radio as the final vestige of old-fashioned conversation over a back fence. At KOA, all parts of Alan Berg deepened, including his knowledge of Judaism, and it was a topic often opened for discussion with callers. Often, he would lambaste anti-Semites, the Ku Klux Klan, neo-Nazis, and other right wingers.

Berg's program of June 15, 1983, jumped from topic to topic, from the Holocaust to Christianity to Israel. One of the callers—although Berg could not know it—was a man named David Lane of suburban Aurora, a KKK sympathizer and white supremacist who regarded himself as an old-fashioned patriot. Lane and friends with his same political persuasions—they called themselves the Order—often listened to Berg's radio programs, or if they were out of radio range they made themselves aware of Berg's philosophies, particularly his ethnic beliefs.

In early June of the next year, Order members Robert Jay Mathews, Randy Duey, Bruce Pierce, Gary Yarbrough, Denver Parmenter, and Richard Scutari met in Boise, Idaho, to discuss assassinations. Four possibilities were discussed: television producer Norman Lear, civil rights attorney Morris Dees, desegregationist federal district judge William Wayne Justice, and Alan Berg.

Shortly thereafter, Mathews and Scutari headed toward Wyoming and Colorado from the Pacific Northwest. By this time they knew many of Alan Berg's habits: They knew what he looked like, the kind of automobiles he drove, when he left for work and returned home, the Adams Street address, and where he ate his meals, which almost always was at restaurants. Moving down southeastward from another Aryan Nations location were Bruce Pierce and David Lane, Lane having missed the assassination planning session. They checked into a Denver motel, and on the evening of June 18, 1984, they were positioned around 1445 Adams Street: Mathews and Scutari flanked either side of the apartment unit; Lane was in the getaway car; and Bruce Pierce held the .45-calibre MAC-10 machine pistol, equipped with a silencer.

As the brethren lay in wait, Berg and Judy—she was in from Chicago to visit her parents—dined at the Jefferson 440 restaurant on the near west side of suburban Denver. They discussed the topic of his next day's radio show: gun control. Leaving the 440 together in the Volkswagen, they stopped at the 7-Eleven for dog food for Berg's beloved Airedale, Fred. Berg dropped off Judy at her car and proceeded to his apartment home, 1445 Adams Street, entering the driveway and opening the car door.

PopPopPopPopPop.

Pierce later bragged that Berg "went down as if the carpet had been pulled out from under him."

306

The next morning, the Order members split up and leave Denver: Pierce going west, Lane east, and Mathews and Scutari north. Four months later, three FBI agents—part of an intense task force of perhaps two hundred who are working on the Berg case—drive their Forest Service truck past the "No Trespassing" signs at Gary Yarbrough's property near Sandpoint, Idaho, enter the house and find a three-foot-high portrait of Adolf Hitler, neo-Nazi literature, code names of Order members, and a small arsenal of weapons including the MAC-10. Yarbrough has fled but news of the federal raid quickly reaches Bob Mathews.

The Order is surprised that the killing of Alan Berg has stirred up this much news interest. The story receives prominent display in the news media worldwide, and the nature of the hit-and-run slaying of a media personality for what could be racial reasons is just enough to pique the interest of federal authorities. And once federal authorities are tossed a challenge such as this, they can be more than tenacious.

As autumn passes and winter begins, the Order agrees to split up into separate cells, each with its own function to further the cause. They cannot know that in some instances, they are shadowed by the FBI. And they cannot know that they are being infiltrated by an informer for the FBI.

As the other neo-Nazis are pursued, Yarbrough is arrested, but in Portland, Oregon, FBI agents shoot it out with Mathews, who makes good his escape. Hiding out in a safe house, Mathews issues a document, quoted here in part:

DECLARATION OF WAR
November 25, 1984

It is now a dark and dismal time in the history of our race. By the millions, those not of our blood violate our borders and mock our claim to sovereignty. Yet our people react only with lethargy. How pitiful the white working class has become. Where is the brave Aryan yeoman so quick to smite the tyrant's hand? Rise, rise from your graves white brothers! Rise and join us. We go to avenge your deaths. By ones and twos, by scores and by legions we will drive the enemy into the sea. Through our blood and God's will, the land promised to our fathers of old will become the land of our children to be.

307

As year's end approaches, it is becoming evident to some of the Aryan yeomen that the FBI is onto them. One by one, they are hunted down, surrounded, and arrested. In the first week of December, FBI agents commandeer a home just a few yards from a Washington seaside house where Bob Mathews is hiding out. After repeatedly pleading that he surrender, a helicopter drops illumination flares upon the roof. The house catches fire, and as hundreds of rounds of stored ammunition explode within, Mathews, in his dying gestures, blasts away with gunfire that only strikes the burning walls and the ceilings caving in on him.

PopPopPopPopPop.

By March 1985, nine months after the assassination, fifteen of the twenty-five hard-core Aryan Brothers have been caught, but three of the four Berg murderers are still on the loose: Richard Scutari, David Lane, and triggerman Bruce Pierce. Then one by one, they too begin to fall: The FBI tracks Pierce to Rossville, Georgia, where state and federal agents plus local police surround and arrest him as he attempts to pick up a letter. A federal prosecutor exclaims: "There is great joy in Fedville today."

David Lane has been rambling around the country since the Berg murder, dropping by Denver every so often. By March he is residing in a shack with no electricity and no plumbing, near Charity, Virginia. There, he is writing an Aryan Nations operations manual, titled *Bruders Schweigen*. ("Our Race is Our Nation. We are realists, recognizing that ... we are outnumbered a hundred to one ... by a coalition of blacks, browns, yellows, liberals, communists, queers, race-mixing religious zealots, race-traitors, preachers, teachers and judges. All of these are under the total control or influence of organized jewry. ... ")

On March 29 he is arrested by six FBI agents outside a supermarket in Winston-Salem, North Carolina. Still surprised at the seemingly never-ending hubbub that the Berg murder has provoked, Lane will remark that Berg has been a far more difficult enemy from the grave than when he was alive.

The last of the four Berg suspects, Richard Scutari, is arrested in March 1986 in San Antonio, Texas, where he had been working in an auto body shop.

The federal government charges the Aryan brothers under the 1970 Racketeer Influenced and Corrupt Organizations (RICO) statute, an umbrella device which covers crimes such as robbery, arson, murder, wire fraud, and loan sharking.

Count number 14 of twenty-one counts concerns the murder of Alan Berg; the Order members had been involved in other crimes such as counterfeiting, weapons activities, and armored car stickups to finance their activities.

After trials of almost four months, all of those whose cases were pursued are convicted: Pierce receives a one-hundred-year sentence; Scutari sixty years; and Lane, forty years.[3]

Later, Lane and Pierce will be handed additional sentences for violations of Berg's civil rights, stacking up Pierce's sentences to 252 years and Lane's to 190. None is ever charged in Colorado for murder; Denver District Attorney Norm Early says the city could not afford to stage such trials and points out that the perpetrators are already in jail on the federal charges.

Early falls under intense criticism from Coloradans who believe that the Berg murderers should suffer an eye for an eye ...

Colorado Heritage, Winter 1999

Endnotes

[1] As with the other pieces in the Twentieth-Century Colorado series of Colorado Heritage, Secrest's profile of Alan Berg is written largely in present tense—a device that Secrest, as the magazine's editor, urged as a way to lend immediacy to the stories in the series.

[2] When Berg passed the Illinois bar exam at age twenty-two, he was the youngest person ever to do so. His clients later included comedian Lenny Bruce, whom he defended on an obscenity charge.

[3] In 2003 Scutari, serving his sixty-year sentence in the U.S. Penitentiary in Florence, Colorado, was denied an appeal for parole. The judge who denied his appeal was the same who had convicted him in 1987—Richard Matsch, who more recently presided over the trials of Oklahoma City bombers Timothy McVeigh and Terry Nichols.

*D*enver Post senior columnist Dick Kreck likes beer. In addition to the city column where for almost twenty years he kept readers up to date on people and events of note, Kreck has written weekly profiles of equally notable microbrews and their makers. A journalist who began at the *San Francisco Examiner* and the *Los Angeles Times*, Kreck has been a *Denver Post* reporter, editor, and columnist since 1968. Always with a touch of humor and a breezy style, Kreck's microbrew write-ups capture each beer's unique character and the traditions that go into its crafting.

Kreck also loves history, especially Denver history. His 2000 book, *Denver in Flames: Forging a New Mile High City*, chronicles some of the most catastrophic fires of the city's past. Kreck shows how Denver's fires— beginning with the "Great Fire" of 1863 that leveled much of the fledgling frontier town's business district—have shaped and reshaped the look of the city over the past 140 years. In his 2003 book, *Murder at the Brown Palace: A True Story of Seduction and Betrayal*, he details a 1911 high-society barroom shooting and the well-attended trials that followed it.

So when the time came to publish an issue of *Colorado Heritage* devoted to 1990s Colorado, Kreck was the logical choice to look at Colorado's recent brewpub craze and the debt that this new tradition owes to the saloons of the state's beery past.

"The Napa Valley of Beer": Colorado's Brewpub Phenomenon

—Richard A. Kreck

Little wonder that Denver of the 1990s is a brewpub capital of America. After all, Colorado's constitution was drawn up and signed in a bar.

Alcohol was available almost as soon as settlers arrived at the twin outposts of Denver City and Auraria. In 1859, Richens "Uncle Dick" Wootton opened the fledgling towns' first permanent saloon in a two-story log cabin, serving "Taos Lightning," a particularly potent form of cheap whiskey.

While hard liquor, much of it bad, was often the refreshment of choice, beer, cheaper and made locally, fast became available. Within two years of the first settlers, a half-dozen breweries, the most notable being Zang and Milwaukee, were turning out beer for thirsty miners and multiple waves of settlers. Twenty years after that, thirty-two breweries were operating in Denver.

By 1890, Denver had 81 churches, 46 schools, and 319 saloons. Many of these drinking emporiums were crowded into a few blocks of Larimer, Market, and Blake Streets, which, with some irony, would become the center of the city's renaissance of bars and restaurants a hundred years later.

Alcohol at the century's turn could be regarded as a health aid, and beer was no exception. Historian Thomas Noel notes in *The City and the Saloon* an 1870 newspaper advertisement announcing, "Invalids seeking health and strength are recommended by all physicians to drink Denver Ale Brewing Co.'s Ale and Porter," and points out that beer, in fact, may have been a safer refreshment than the town's frequently polluted drinking water.

Denver's saloons quickly became home to immigrants tromping to the gold fields. Barrooms also served as banks, clubhouses, and, sometimes, churches. Germans, and to a lesser extent the Irish and Italians, were the predominant owners of these oases, leading to a rising popularity of lagers, which were the light, effervescent beers the Germans were fond of in their homeland.

The saloon also could serve as a poor man's club, a low-end copy of the fancy barrooms with gilded mirrors, polished brass, carved woodwork, and paintings of reclining nudes where the wealthier men of commerce sipped brandy and smoked cigars. Just as churches had their congregations, the workingmen's saloons had constituencies of "regulars" who kept them in business. Most customers were laboring-class men, though a few women also participated in saloon life. Although these gathering places were rough-hewn, they could be a welcome departure from the hastily constructed mining camps exposed to the disagreeable elements, or from the city's overcrowded boarding houses. "Workers cultivated bonds of friendship and mutuality based on the similarity of their livelihoods, national heritages, and local acquaintanceship networks," observed Madelon Powers in *Faces along the Bar*, a study of workingmen's bars between 1870 and 1920.

Prohibition, beginning in Colorado in 1916 and elsewhere four years later, eliminated legal saloons and breweries. Coors in Colorado barely survived by producing ceramics and malted milk products instead of beer, and when Prohibition was repealed in 1933 big operations such as Anheuser-Busch, Coors, Miller, Stroh, and Falstaff emerged. Each concentrated on satisfying the American taste for light and fizzy products. The advent of pasteurization and of the metal bottle cap allowed large breweries to ship their products throughout the country.

In the 1990s, the friendly bonding atmospheres which prevailed in Denver's first saloons reemerge in chic new nightspots along the same streets that housed the city's first drinking emporiums.[1] Led by the Wynkoop Brewery in Denver's "LoDo" lower-downtown district, local brewing is enjoying a renaissance and Colorado becomes a focal point of the emerging brewpub and small brewery industry.[2] Permits enabling "microbrewers" to make and sell beer on-site outside of industrially zoned neighborhoods literally took an act of government, but the idea blossomed and by 1990 the brewpub and small brewery phenomena are firmly established in Colorado. But this time, instead of attracting hard-rock prospectors and similar adventurers, these new brewpubs attract consumers who are young, upwardly mobile, and prosperous. In these new barrooms, a certain sense of community prevails, as it did on the same streets a hundred years earlier.

This small-brewing revolution began in the Pacific Northwest, but Colorado and especially Denver catch up quickly. Such enterprises are called "craft brewers," and their products generally can be found no further than their own front doors. John Hickenlooper, the highest-profile of the four partners who open the Wynkoop in the historic former J. S. Brown & Bro. Mercantile warehouse across the street from Denver Union Station, will later recall, "In those days, you could open a brewpub but you couldn't serve wine or spirits. We had to go to the city and get the zoning ordinances rewritten to allow brewing outside the industrial areas and to get permission to serve more than beer."

The Wynkoop founders are four friends—Hickenlooper, a geologist;[3] Russ Schehrer, homebrewer and computer programmer; Jerry Williams, geophysicist; and chef Mark Schiffler. The idea for Colorado's first brewpub comes from a Hickenlooper trip to Berkeley, California. There he observes a brewpub, Triple Rock, where the beer is not fizzy and has more flavor than those turned out by the big breweries. He suspects that such an idea could work in Colorado, although none of the Wynkoop founders has experience in this sort of enterprise. Williams visits the public library and obtains a book on writing business plans.

Fortified with $100,000 from Hickenlooper—the result of a buyout from a failed oil company during the energy crash of the mid-1980s—the foursome receives a $125,000 loan from the city, contingent upon their ability to persuade a bank to loan them additional funds. After being rejected by lenders—including Hickenlooper's own mother—the Women's Bank offers a $50,000 loan, and the group secures $300,000 from additional investors.

After much effort by the foursome, wives, and friends in cleaning, painting, and rehabilitating the 1899 five-story Brown Mercantile building, the Wynkoop opens on October 18, 1988, with the contractor still being owed $40,000. It is one of the few "respectable" places to go in the old lower downtown district. As an opening-night promotion, Colorado's first brewpub (it beats Carver's Bakery and Brewpub in Durango by two months) offers twenty-five-cent beers and the place is mobbed. Thirsty customers, anxious to try the city's first Denver-made beers since the closing of the Tivoli Brewery on April 25, 1969, line up four-deep at the Wynkoop's rectangular, steel-topped bar. Former bartender Dave Schierling remembers, "We ran out of plastic cups. We were taking them out of the trash and running them through the washer." The Wynkoop sold 6,000 cups of twenty-five-cent beer that first night, with Hickenlooper wishing all along he had set the price at fifty cents instead, to help pay down the debt. By 1997, the Wynkoop is the nation's largest brewpub, having served 5,008 barrels of beer over the counter that year. The Wynkoop continues as Denver's flagship pub.

The remarkable success of the Wynkoop inspires numerous competitors, some more interested in making a quick dollar than in making "real" beer abundant with hops and barley and often dark in color and full of flavor. The Wynkoop, which adds a pool room on the second floor, a comedy club in the basement, and three floors of loft residences, is followed in 1991 by the Denver Chophouse & Brewery at Nineteenth and Wynkoop Streets, the Champion Brewing Company in the Larimer Square historic preservation neighborhood, and by the Rock Bottom Brewery at Sixteenth and Curtis Streets.

The Chophouse and Rock Bottom are owned in part by Boulder entrepreneur Frank Day, who eventually will make Rock Bottom a

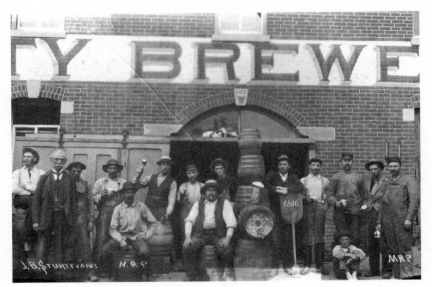

Boulder City Brewery *(Photo by J. B. Sturtevant)*

314

nationwide chain. Day's two establishments are decidedly dissimilar. Increasingly, it is realized that brewpubs must develop distinctive personalities.

In December 1992, Denver's initial four brewpubs are joined by the Breckenridge Brewery in a former automotive garage at Twenty-second and Blake Streets, across the street from what in 1995 becomes the site of the new Coors Field. The ballpark has a profound effect not only on the Breckenridge, but also on all of LoDo's nightspots.

Colorado's beer explosion is everywhere. In 1996, the Boulder-based Association of Brewers, an industry organization, reports there are forty-two brewpubs and microbreweries in Colorado. Just two years later, that figure is seventy-one, more per capita than any other state. By century's end, there are approximately ninety such brewers in Colorado, although a significant failure rate is a concern.

Brewpubs, which produce a three-and-one-half-dollar glass of beer for about thirty-five cents, offer a larger profit margin than breweries, which in addition to production costs must pay for packaging and distribution. Thus the number of breweries opening in the state slows to a near standstill. Industry analysts, however, predict a rise in beer consumption early in the new century as children of baby boomers reach drinking age.

The state's brewers provide more than simply a variety of beers to augment light lagers which pour forth from the nation's three giant breweries. They also pay significant taxes. It is estimated in 1996, for instance, that small breweries will contribute $1 million in excise taxes within three years. The final numbers are even more impressive, however. Denver's Big Three microbrewers—Wynkoop, Chophouse, and Rock Bottom—themselves log an estimated $20 million in sales, resulting in $1.6 million in excise taxes.

Denver hosts the annual Great American Beer Festival, the nation's largest and oldest gathering of brewers. Begun in Boulder in 1981 with forty brewers and 800 attendees, the festival grows until it hosts 400 breweries from throughout the country. In 1999, an estimated 38,000 beer lovers attend the three-day October festival to taste more than 1,700 beers. On any given day in Denver, a thirsty patron can choose from eighty beers not available anywhere else in the country. "I think that's remarkable," says the Wynkoop's Hickenlooper. "Brewpubs are a part of our identity now; they put us on the map. As a friend of mine put it, 'Colorado is the Napa Valley of beer.'"

Denver is the center of all these activities, but the beer revolution covers the state from Durango to Greeley. Communities as small as Castle Rock, Salida, Nederland, Estes Park, and Frisco have at least one pub at this writing. Fort Collins—home of a mammoth Anheuser-Busch beer factory (6.2 *million* barrels in 1998)—also hosts two of the state's largest microbrewers, the New Belgium Brewing Company and the Odell Brewing Company. Founded in 1989, Odell in 1994 moves to an 8,000-square-foot stone-and-steel facility on the east side of Fort Collins, and in 1999 expects to produce 18,000 barrels. Even larger is New Belgium, opening in 1991 in the basement of brewer Jeff Lebesch's home. In its first year, New Belgium turns out 8.5 barrels a week. Propelled by the popularity of its Fat Tire Ale (named after the Colorado mountain bicycle), New Belgium forecasts a 100,000-barrel year for 1999 and expects to reach 125,000 in 2000, placing it among the nation's largest regional breweries.

Boulder, too, is home to two successful breweries, Rockies and Oasis. Rockies was founded in 1979 as the Boulder Brewing Company, which foundered and ultimately died partially because of a bizarre advertising campaign which promoted its "Ugly Beer" containing yeast particles. Rockies makes a comeback with new owners and leadership in 1991. Since its reincarnation, Rockies is headed by Gina Day, and as the 1990s end, approaches production of 25,000 barrels a year.

A late arrival in the brewpub/brewery derby is the Oasis Brewing Company, opening as a brewpub in 1992. It adds a brewing "annex" in 1995, dedicated to producing packaged beers for retail sale. In 1999, Oasis, which also produces Trout Creek beers, wins four medals—a gold and three silvers—at the Great American Beer Festival. Owner George Hanna expects such honors to pave the way for his new brews nationwide. Oasis is the first Colorado microbrewery to produce six-packs, beating Breckenridge and New Belgium to market by a few months. Hanna is among those predicting a big change in the craft-brew industry: more brewpubs, fewer breweries. Observes Hanna: "I can't imagine someone opening a brewery. You'd have to have a lot of money and not care if you lost it."

A trend at the end of the 1990s is tap houses—barrooms which make no beer of their own but offer as many as seventy beers on tap and many more in bottles, and in which food attracts additional revenue.

Notable tap houses operating in year 2000 are Falling Rock, Cherry Cricket, and the Boiler Room in Denver, and the Mountain Tap in Fort Collins.

At dawn of the new millennium, Colorado is the leading producer of beer in the country, with no incidental thanks to the presence of brewing giants Coors in Golden and Anheuser-Busch in Fort Collins. Though it has fewer breweries than California, Colorado has the most breweries per capita of any state.

Denver's brewpubs in 2000 are the Wynkoop (still the biggest), Breckenridge (two sites), Broadway, Bull and Bush, Champion, Denver Chophouse, Dixons, Heavenly Daze, Hops, Mercury Café, Pints Pub, and the Rock Bottom. Seven of those are situated close to each other in lower downtown. In addition, Great Divide runs a brewing-only operation.

As the old century ended, so did the rush to open new beer emporiums. Though the industry grew by 50 percent a year for almost five years, a slowdown beginning in 1997 saw growth at "only" 26 percent. "Most industries would be thrilled with that kind of growth," comments Richard Backus, editor of *The New Brewer* magazine, published in Boulder.

Colorado Heritage, Winter 2000

Epilogue

Since "The Napa Valley of Beer" appeared in 2000, the maturing Colorado brewing industry underwent numerous changes. In 2004, the number of beer makers (breweries, brewpubs, and contract brewers) in the state stands at ninety-five, although the frantic days of the 1990s, when it seemed a new beer outlet opened every day, are long gone.

In 2003, six breweries joined the flock—Fort Collins Brewing, Grand Lake Brewing, Mahogany Ridge Brewing & Grill, Palisade Brewery, and Trinidad Brewing Co.

The industry continues to evolve. Although it still operates a brewery, Oasis Pub, at one time one of the state's most successful brewpubs, ceased operation of the pub in 2003, a victim of the state's anemic economy. Two makers, Odell Brewing and New Belgium Brewing, both based in Fort Collins, moved up from "microbrewers" to "regional brewers" (see endnote 2), meaning that they produce more than 15,000 barrels a year.

In Denver, the Boiler Room and Champion closed, and Dixons and the Mercury Café no longer produce their own beers. Heavenly Daze closed, then reappeared a year later. Seven microbrewers remain in the city—Breckenridge, Bull and Bush, Denver Chophouse, Heavenly Daze, Hops, Pints Pub, and Rock Bottom. Other pubs have supplanted Wynkoop Brewing Co. as the nation's largest brewpub in terms of production but the lower downtown saloon continues to be the spiritual epicenter of the state's microbrewing industry.

Endnotes

1 *As with the other pieces in the Twentieth-Century Colorado series of* Colorado Heritage, *Kreck's article is written largely in present tense—a device the magazine's editor, Clark Secrest, urged as a way to lend immediacy to the stories in the series.*

2 A brewpub is a restaurant/brewery that sells most of its beer on-site. Where allowed by law, brewpubs can offer beer "to go" in jugs, and/or to distribute at off-site accounts. A microbrewery is a brewery producing fewer than 15,000 barrels yearly.

A barrel contains thirty-one gallons. Microbreweries dispense their products to the public through liquor retailers, tap rooms, or brewery restaurant sales. A regional brewery has a capacity of between 15,000 and 2 million barrels annually. A contract brewery is an enterprise that hires an outside company to produce its beer. The contract brewery then markets and distributes the beer.

3 *Denver voters elected John Hickenlooper as their new mayor in 2003.*

At sunrise on November 7, 2003, members of the Cheyenne and Arapaho tribes started a long journey. They planned to run, in shifts and in groups large and small, from the Sand Creek Massacre site near Eads in southeastern Colorado to Denver. The journey would take them from their ancestral homeland to the state capital, reversing the route Col. John M. Chivington's command took 139 years earlier before attacking a peaceful Indian village of some 500 people, mostly women, children, and old men. The runners endured miles of fatigue, pain, and joy to honor the victims and survivors of the massacre, heal a multigenerational trauma, and educate younger members of the tribes and the general public.

When the runners arrived at Riverside Cemetery in Denver three weeks later, they held another sunrise ceremony. This time, they honored two junior Army officers who disobeyed Chivington's order to attack the village and later condemned the slaughter in private letters and public testimony. About two weeks after the massacre, Captain Silas Soule and Lieutenant Joe E. Cramer had written vivid and disturbing letters to Major Edward W. Wynkoop, the commanding officer at Fort Lyon. Scholars assumed that these letters, though mentioned briefly in another source, had been lost.

The historians were—to their delight—wrong. In response to the outrage expressed in federal hearings by Soule, Cramer, and others, the U.S. Congress condemned the attack as a massacre in 1865 and promised reparations to the survivors. The promise was not kept. Then, 136 years later, Congress took up the evidence again.

David Fridtjof Halaas, the Colorado Historical Society's chief historian from 1990 to 2001, facilitated the publication of the letters and spoke to Congress in favor of a bill establishing the Sand Creek Massacre National Historic Site. Now the museum division director for the Senator John Heinz Pittsburgh Regional History Center, Halaas coauthored *Cheyenne Dog Soldiers: A Ledgerbook History of Coups and Combat* and the acclaimed *Halfbreed: The Remarkable True Story of George Bent, Caught Between the Worlds of the Indian and the White Man*.

Gary L. Roberts has studied and written about the events of Sand Creek for forty years and has published widely in the field of western history. He is a retired professor from Abraham Baldwin Agricultural College in Tifton, Georgia.

Written in Blood:
The Soule-Cramer Sand Creek
Massacre Letters

—Gary L. Roberts and David Fridtjof Halaas

At ten o'clock on the evening of April 23, 1865, Provost Marshal Captain Silas S. Soule and his bride of three weeks stepped out of a Denver theater. Suddenly, down the street, they heard gunshots. Leaving his wife behind with friends, Soule pulled his revolver and ran to investigate. As he approached the Lawrence Street Church near F (later Fifteenth) Street, two blue-clad soldiers with pistols drawn jumped from the darkness and opened fire. Although taken by surprise and mortally wounded, Soule squeezed off a shot before falling to the street, dead.

The killing shocked Denver, for Soule—who as provost marshal was responsible for maintaining order among military personnel in town—was well-known and popular. His marriage to Hersa Coberly had received considerable attention in the city's newspapers, and his even-handed enforcement of the law had earned him the respect of soldiers and civilians. Yet, since his arrival in Denver in January, repeated attempts had been made on his life, and the day before his death he told friends he expected to be murdered. Why did assassins target this popular Army officer? The answer lay in his relationship to his military superior, Colonel John M. Chivington, and the Army's recent attack on Black Kettle's Cheyenne village at Sand Creek in southeast Colorado Territory.

On November 29, 1864, three great events of the Civil War were transpiring: General William Tecumseh Sherman was moving through Georgia on his march from Atlanta to the sea; General John M. Schofield was preparing for an assault by Confederate forces under General John B. Hood at Franklin, Tennessee; and General Ulysses S. Grant was holding

320

position in Petersburg, Virginia, in a costly siege that had already taken thousands of lives. On that same morning, half a continent away, Colonel Chivington led U.S. volunteers in an attack on a Cheyenne and Arapaho camp at Big Sandy Creek—Sand Creek to history. By contrast to the great campaigns of the Civil War, the Sand Creek incident seemed little more than a skirmish, its casualties trivial by comparison to the mass slaughter then taking place on eastern battlefields. Yet in a matter of months, the Sand Creek Massacre became the subject of two congressional investigations and a military commission hearing, disgraced Colorado's greatest military hero in the eyes of the nation, and unseated its governor.

This remarkable series of events came about largely through the efforts of a few junior officers in the First Colorado Cavalry who were outraged by the atrocities committed at Sand Creek—the soldiers killed and mutilated over 160 Indian men, women, and children. More than any others, they forced upon the American consciousness an awareness that what occurred on that frigid November day was not a battle—but a massacre.

Historians long have suspected that immediately after Sand Creek, two of these officers, Soule and Lieutenant Joseph A. Cramer, played a critical role in the initiation of the investigation when they wrote letters documenting the atrocities committed there. These letters, long thought

Robert Lindneux's 1936 interpretation of the Sand Creek Massacre features an American flag and a white flag of surrender flying over Chief Black Kettle's lodge.

destroyed or lost forever, suddenly surfaced in the summer of 2000. In them, Soule and Cramer not only provide graphic detail of the massacre but also provide new knowledge regarding the tragedy itself.

Soule and Cramer respectively commanded companies D and K of the First Colorado U.S. Volunteer Cavalry. In 1864, the First was a regiment divided against itself, with its imposing commander, John Chivington, the primary focus of contention. The split originated in a quarrel between Chivington and the regiment's commander, Colonel John P. Slough. Following the First's involvement in the 1862 Battle of Glorieta Pass in New Mexico, the troops had stopped the Confederate advance toward the Colorado gold fields. Slough resigned, believing he had been the object of an assassination attempt during that campaign. Slough went east and received a commission as brigadier general; Chivington took command of the First and of the Colorado Military District. The bad feelings in the First continued as Colonel Samuel F. Tappan, the regiment's second in command, became embroiled in his own dispute with Chivington.

In the summer of 1864 tensions between white settlers and native tribes of the central plains provoked an Indian war that interrupted overland travel and created panic in the Colorado settlements. To put down the uprising, Territorial Governor John Evans secured permission from the War Department in Washington, D.C., to raise a regiment of U.S. volunteers for one hundred days' service. But even as Evans and Chivington promoted enlistments into the new regiment—the Third Colorado—the Cheyennes and Arapahos made a peace overture at Fort Lyon, Colorado, prompting post commander Major Edward W. Wynkoop to lead an expedition to the Smoky Hill River, where he conferred with tribal chiefs and persuaded them to accompany him to Denver to meet with Chivington and Evans. During the September 28, 1864, parley at Camp Weld, Evans, although surprised and clearly irritated by the Indian initiative, directed the chiefs to surrender to military authority if they truly wanted peace. In turn, Chivington told the Indians that if they wanted to submit to the government, they should lay down their arms and give themselves up to the post commander at Fort Lyon.

Wynkoop returned to Fort Lyon convinced that peace was at hand. Soon, several Cheyenne and Arapaho bands responded to Chivington's instructions and moved to the fort. This embarrassed Evans, who openly wondered what to do with the hundred-day volunteers. He had lobbied

Captain Silas S. Soule

hard for troops, arguing that an all-out Indian war threatened not only Denver but all of Colorado. Was he now to tell Washington officials that he had panicked, that the Indian war had all been in his mind? Peace also threatened Chivington's grandiose ambitions; he had hoped an Indian campaign would renew his reputation as a soldier, win him a brigadier's star, and provide a stepping stone for a seat in Congress.

Events now moved quickly. In October, Evans left Denver for Washington. At the same time, military officials of the Upper Arkansas district relieved Wynkoop from command at Fort Lyon—the fort lay within their jurisdiction—and named Major Scott Anthony as his replacement. Against Upper Arkansas district orders but in compliance with Chivington's injunction at Camp Weld, Wynkoop had accepted the surrender of several Arapaho and Cheyenne bands and issued them rations. This thoroughly muddled affairs at Fort Lyon. Wynkoop firmly believed the Indians had surrendered, thus entitling them to government protection. The new commander, Scott Anthony, hardly knew what course to follow but finally ordered all the Indians to move over to Sand

323

Creek forty miles distant and there join Black Kettle's Cheyennes. When he received further orders from his superiors, he said, he would send word to Black Kettle and the other chiefs.

At this juncture, with the Third's one-hundred-day limit fast approaching, Chivington made a desperate decision to move against the surrendered Indians on Sand Creek. Marching his troops under a cloud of great secrecy, Chivington reached Fort Lyon on the morning of November 28 and immediately threw a tight guard around the post. He then announced his intention to attack Black Kettle's peaceful village. Both Captain Soule and Lieutenant Cramer numbered themselves among the pro-Chivington clique, but Chivington's announcement shocked them. Both men had accompanied Wynkoop to the Smoky Hill and had parlayed with the chiefs there. Both had gone to Denver to attend the Camp Weld Conference. Both were at Fort Lyon when the tribes responded to Chivington's invitation to give themselves up. In fact, Soule had innocently informed Chivington that the Indians had come into the fort, thus unwittingly alerting his commander to Black Kettle's where-abouts.[1] And both Soule and Cramer had protested when Wynkoop was removed from command at Lyon.[2]

Now, both vehemently objected to Chivington's order to attack Black Kettle's village, arguing that the government had guaranteed the Indians' safety. Both joined Chivington's expedition with the understanding that only the hostile Cheyenne Dog Soldiers on the Smoky Hill River would be attacked and that peaceful Indians would not be molested.

When Chivington's forces attacked Black Kettle's village at dawn on November 29, both Cramer and Soule refused to fire their weapons and both received severe criticism for their actions. Afterward, both so loudly expressed their disapproval of Chivington's behavior at Sand Creek that Major Anthony voiced concern for their safety.

Captain Soule's letter, just discovered, to Major "Ned" Wynkoop follows:

Ft. Lyon, C.T.
December 14, 1864

Dear Ned:
Two days after you left here the 3d Reg't with a Battalion of
the 1st arrived here, having moved so secretly that we were
not aware of their approach until they had Pickets around the

Post, allowing no one to pass out. They arrested Capt. [William] Bent, and John Vogle, and placed guards around their houses. They then declared their intention to massacre the friendly Indians camped on Sand Creek. Major Anthony gave all information, and eagerly joined in with Chivington & Co, and ordered Lieut. Cramer, with his whole Co to join the command. As soon as I knew of their movement I was indignant as you would have been were you here, and went to [Lt. James D.] Cannon's room, where a number of officers of the 1st and 3d were congregated, and told them that any man who would take part in the murder, knowing the circumstances as we did, was a low lived cowardly son of a bitch. Capt. Y. J. Johnson [commander, Company E Third Colorado Regiment], and Lieut. [George H.] Harding [Hardin, First Colorado Cavalry] went to camp and reported to Chiv, [Maj. Jacob] Downing, and the whole outfit what I had said, and you bet hell was to pay in camp. Chiv and all hands swore they would hang me before they moved camp, but I stuck it out, and all the officers at the Post, except Anthony backed me. I was then ordered with my whole company to [accompany] Major A[nthony].—with 20 days rations. I told him that I would not take part in their intended murder, but if they were going after the Sioux, Kiowa's [sic] or any fighting Indians, I would go as far as any of them. They said that was what they were going for, and I joined them. We arrived at Black Kettles and Left Hand's Camp, at day light. Lieut. [Luther] Wilson with Co's. "C," "E," & "G" [First Colorado Cavalry troops which had come to Fort Lyon with Chivington and were not part of the Lyon battalion] were ordered in advance to cut off their herd. He made a circle to the rear and formed line 200 yds from the village, and opened fire. Poor Old John Smith and [Private David] Louderbeck [Louderback], ran out with white flags, but they paid no attention to them, and they ran back into the tents. Anthony then rushed up with Co's "D" "K" & "G," to within one hundred yards and commenced firing. I refused to fire, and swore that none but a coward would, for by this time hundreds of women and children were coming towards us, and getting on their knees for mercy. Anthony shouted, "Kill the sons of bitches." Smith and Louderbeck came to our command, although I am confident there were 200 shots fired at them, for I heard an officer say that Old Smith and any one who sympathized with Indians, ought to be killed and now was a good time to do it. The Battery then came up in our rear, and opened on them. I took my comp'y across the Creek, and by this time the whole of the 3d and the Batteries were firing into them and you can form some idea of the slaughter. When the Indians found that there was no hope for them they went for the Creek, and buried themselves in the Sand and got under the banks, and some of the bucks got their Bows and a few rifles and defended themselves as well as they could. By this time there was no organization among our troops, they were a perfect mob—every man on his own hook. My Co, was the only one that kept their formation, and we did not fire a shot.

The massacre lasted six or eight hours, and a good many Indians escaped. I tell you Ned it was hard to see little children on their knees, have their brains beat out by men professing to be civilized. One Squaw was wounded, and a fellow took a hatchet to finish her, she held her arms up to defend her, and he cut one arm off, and held the other with one hand, and dashed the hatchet through her brain. One Squaw with her two children, were on their knees, begging for their lives, of a dozen soldiers, within ten feet of them all firing—when one succeeded in hitting the Squaw in the thigh, when she took a knife and cut the throats of both children, and then killed herself. One old Squaw hung herself in the lodges—there was not enough room for her to hang and she held up her knees and choked herself to death. Some tried to escape on the Prairie, but most of them were run down by horsemen. I saw two Indians [take] hold of one anothers hands, chased until they were exhausted, when they kneeled down, and clasped each other around the neck and were both shot together, they were all scalped, and as high as half a dozen taken from one head. They were all horribly mutilated. One woman was cut open, and a child taken out of her, and scalped.

326

White Antelope, War Bonnet, and a number of others had Ears and Privates cut off. Squaws snatches were cut out for trophies. You would think it impossible for white men to butcher and mutilate human beings as they did there, but every word I have told you is the truth, which they do not deny. It was almost impossible to save any of them. Charly Aubobee [Arkansas Valley pioneer and rancher Charles Autobees] saved John Smith and Winsers [Charles Windsor, post sutler] squaw. I saved little Charley Bent. Geo Bent was killed.[3] Jack Smith [Interpreter John Smith's mixed-blood son] was taken prisoner, and murdered the next day in his tent by one of [Lt. Clark] Dunn's Co. "E." I understand the man received a horse for doing the job. They were going to murder Charlie Bent [William Bent's youngest mixed-blood son], but I run him into the Fort. They were going to kill old Uncle John Smith, but Lt. Cannon and the boys of Ft. Lyon, interfered, and saved him. They would have murdered Old Bents family, if Col Tappan had not taken the matter in hand. Cramer went up with twenty (20) men, and they did not like to buck against so many of the 1st.[4] Chivington has gone to Washington to be made General, I suppose, and get authority to raise a nine months Reg't, to hunt Indians.[5] He and Downing will have me cashiered, if possible. If they do I want you to help me. I think they will try the same for Cramer, for he has shot his mouth off a good deal, and did not shoot his pistol off in the massacre. Joe has behaved first rate during the whole affair. Chivington reports five or six hundred killed, but there were not more than two hundred: about 140 women and children and 60 bucks. A good many were out hunting buffalo. Our best Indians were killed. Black Kettle, One Eye, Minnemic [Minimic], and Left Hand.[6] Geo Pierce of Co "F" was killed trying to save John Smith. There was one other of the 1st killed, and nine of the 3d all through their own fault. They would get up to the edge of the bank and look over, to get a shot at an Indian under them, and get an arrow put through them. When the women were killed the Bucks did not seem to try and get away, but fought desperately. Charly Autobee [Autobees] wished me to write all about it to you.

He says he would have given anything if you could have been there.

I suppose Cramer has written to you, all the particulars, so I will write half. Your family is well. Billy Walker, Col. Tappan, Lou Wilson, (who was wounded in the arm) start for Denver in the morning. There is no news I can think of. I expect we will have a hell of a time with Indians this winter. We have (200) men at the Post—Anthony in command. I think he will be dismissed when the facts are known in Washington. Give my regards to any friends you come across, and write as soon as possible.

Yours &c
(signed) S. S. Soule

Lieutenant Cramer wrote his letter to Major Wynkoop five days later:

Ft. Lyon, C.T.
December 19, 1864

Dear Major:
This is the first opportunity I have had of writing you since the great Indian Massacre, and for a start, I will acknowledge I am ashamed to own [acknowledge] I was in it with my Co. Col. Chivington came down here with the gallant third, known as the Chivington Brigade, like a thief in the dark, throwing his Scouts around the Post, with instructions to let no one out, without his orders, not even the Commander of the Post, and for shame our Comd'g. Officer submitted. Col. Chivington expected to find the Indians in camp below the Com[mand]—but the Major Comd'g told him all about where the Indians were, and volunteered to take a Battalion from the Post and join the Expedition.

Well Col. Chiv. got in about 10 A.M. Nov. 28th and, at 8 P.M., we started with all of the 3d, parts of "H" "C" and "E" of the First, in com'd of Lt. Wilson [and] "K" "D" & "G" in com'd of Major Anthony. Marched all night up Sand [Creek], to the big bend in Sanday [sic] about 15 or 20 miles, above where we crossed on our trip to Smoky Hill and came on to Black Kettles village of 103 lodges, containing not over 500 all told,

350 of which were women and children. Three days previous to our going out, Major Anthony gave John Smith, Lowderbuck [sic] of Co. "G" and a Gov't driver [Richard Watson Clark], permission to go out there and trade with them, and they were in the village when the fight came off. John Smith came out holding up his hands, and running towards us, when he was shot at by several, and the word was passed along to shoot him. He then turned back, and went to his tent, and got behind some Robes, and escaped unhurt. Lowderbuck [sic] came out with a white flag, and was served the same as John Smith; the driver the same. Well I got so mad I swore I would not burn powder, and I did not. Capt. Soule the same. It is no use for me to try to tell you how the fight was managed, only I think the Officer in command should be hung, and I know when the truth is known it will cashier him. We lost 40 men wounded, and 10 killed. Not over 250 Indians mostly women and children, and I think not over 200 were killed and not over 75 bucks. With proper management they could all have been killed and not lost over 10 men. After the fight there was a sight I hope I may never see again. Bucks, women and children were scalped, fingers cut off to get the rings on them, and this as much with Officers as men, and one of those officers a Major; and a Lt. Col. Cut off Ears of all he came across—a squaw ripped open and a child taken from her, little children shot, while begging for their lives, women shot while on their knees, and with their arms around soldiers a begging for their lives, and all the indignities shown their bodies that ever was heard of, things that Indians would be ashamed to do. To give you some little idea, Squaws were known to kill their own children, and then themselves, rather than to have them taken prisoners. Most of the Indians yielded 4 or 5 scalps. But enough! for I know you are disgusted already. Black Kettle, White Antelope, War Bonnet, Left Hand, Little Robe, and several other chiefs were killed. Black Kettle said when he saw us coming, that he was glad, for it was Major Wynkoop coming to make peace. Left Hand stood with his hands folded across his breast, until he was shot saying: "Soldiers no hurt me—soldiers my friends."

One Eye was killed: was in the employ of Gov't as spy: came into the Post a few days before, and reported about the Sioux, were going to break out at Learned [Fort Larned, Kansas], which proved true.

After all the pledges made by Major A—to these Indians and then to take the course he did. I think no comments are necessary from me; only I will say he has a face for every man he talks [to]. The action taken by Capt Soule and myself were under protest. Col. C— was going to have Soule hung for saying there were all cowardly Sons of B—-s; if Soule did not take it back, but nary take back with Soule. I told the Col that I thought it murder to jump them friendly Indians. He says in reply: Damn any man or men who are in sympathy with them. Such men as you and Major Wynkoop better leave the U.S. Service, so you can judge what a nice time we had on the trip. I expect Col. C— and Downing will do all in their power to have Soule, [Lt. Chauncey M.] Cossitt and I dismissed. Well, let them work for what they damn please, I ask no favors of them. If you are in Washington, for God's sake, Major, keep Chivington from being a Bri'g. Genl, which he expects. I will send you the Denver Papers with this. Excuse this for I have been in much of a hurry.

Very respectfully,
Your Well-wisher
(signed) Jos. A. Cramer

[the following is a postscript]

Jack Smith was taken prisoner and then murdered. One little child 3 months old was thrown in the feed box of a wagon and brought one days march and there left on the ground to perish. Col. Tappan is after them for all that is out. I am making out a report of all from the beginning to end, to send to Gen'l Slough, in hopes that he will have the thing investigated, and if you should see him, please speak to him about it, for fear that he has forgotten me. I shall write him nothing but what can be proven.

Major I am ashamed of this. I have it gloriously mixed up, but am in hopes I can explain it all to you before long. I would have given my right arm had you been here, when they arrived. Your family are all well.

(signed) Joe A. Cramer

The Soule-Cramer letters—only recently discovered in a family trunk—greatly enhance our understanding of Sand Creek and related events. First, they validate much of the testimony taken during the congressional and Army hearings. They establish the presence of white flags in Black Kettle's village—claimed by many witnesses but strongly denied by Chivington supporters, both past and present. They confirm that the officers in command lost control of their troops and allowed the Third Regiment to disintegrate into a mob. They confirm that rank-and-file soldiers, as well as staff officers—notably Major Hal Sayre and Lieutenant Colonel Leavitt Bowen—mutilated the dead, taking scalps and body parts as trophies and souvenirs. They confirm that a baby was placed in a wagon feedbox and later abandoned beside the road. They confirm that a soldier killed a pregnant woman and cut her unborn child from her body. They confirm that the officers of the Fort Lyon battalion reacted angrily to Major Anthony's decision to join Chivington's expedition to Black Kettle's village. They confirm that Charley Autobees, an important Arkansas Valley rancher, saved the life of interpreter John Smith during the fight. And the letters confirm Chivington's ambition and his threats directed against both Cramer and Soule.

The letters also provide critical new evidence and enlarge the understanding of Sand Creek.

First, they shed light on the exact site of Black Kettle's village. Cramer said the command "marched all night up Sand [Creek], to the big bend in Sanday ... and came on to Black Kettles village of 103 lodges. ... " This supports the accuracy of maps drawn by the Cheyenne mixed-blood George Bent, which place the village in the big bend of Sand Creek.[7] It also confirms Cheyenne oral tradition, which holds sacred the southernmost big bend of Big Sandy Creek, located in present Kiowa County, Colorado. Moreover, Soule's letter provides information on the fight's logistics. Most historical studies have placed Black Kettle's village immediately on the bank of Big Sandy, but Soule makes it clear that the Fort Lyon battalion, which approached the village from the high bluffs south and west of the village, opened fire while they were still a hundred yards from camp. This suggests that the village lay farther away from the creek bank than commonly supposed.

Second, the letters reveal that the officers and men of the Fort Lyon battalion united in their condemnation of the Sand Creek action. They not only establish that Soule and his entire company did not fire during the fight, but they also reveal for the first time that Cramer refused to fire, and they imply that Lieutenant Cossit held his fire as well. The letters further establish that Lieutenant James D. Cannon, backed by twenty men of the First Colorado, saved John Smith's life after the fight. They also point to an armed "face off" between the veteran First and the "Hundred Dayzers." The letters reveal, too, that Colonel Samuel Tappan intervened to save the lives of William Bent and his family at Bent's ranch after the fight, backed by a detachment of the First led by Cramer. The

The Cheyenne and Arapaho delegation at Camp Weld in Denver, September 28, 1864. Kneeling in front, from left, are Major Edward W. Wynkoop and Captain Silas S. Soule. Seated are, from left: White Antelope, Bull Bear, Black Kettle, Neva, and Notanee. Standing, from left, are: unidentified soldier, unidentified, John Smith, Heaps of Buffalo, Bosse, Dexter Colley, and unidentified. Several weeks before this conference, Wynkoop, Soule, and 120 soldiers gathered at Smoky Hill with the chiefs. There, Wynkoop convinced the Indians to meet in Denver with Territorial Governor John Evans and Colonel John Chivington to discuss peace. Chivington directed the chiefs to surrender to Wynkoop at Fort Lyon, but Chivington instead effected a double-cross and attacked the unsuspecting Indians at nearby Sand Creek.

newfound letters additionally show that the officers of the First held Major Anthony in utter contempt for his eagerness to join Chivington's expedition.[8]

The letters contain other previously unknown information. They indicate that both John Smith and Private Louderback waved white flags to stop the advancing troops and establish the peaceful character of the village. And they indicate that Black Kettle and other chiefs initially thought the approaching soldiers had come not to war but to confirm the peace established at Fort Lyon and Camp Weld by Chivington, Evans, and Wynkoop.

Beyond providing graphic detail of the massacre and its aftermath, the Soule-Cramer letters are important because they became the cornerstone of the government's investigation into Sand Creek.

For two weeks following the massacre, Chivington kept his expedition in the field in a fruitless attempt to locate Little Raven's Arapahos. When he finally abandoned the search on December 6, Chivington left his troops and hurried to Fort Lyon where he bragged that Sand Creek would bring him a brigadier general's star. The column reached Fort Lyon four days later. Cramer accompanied the Third as far as Bent's ranch, where the Third again threatened the old trader and his family. Here, Cramer told Captain Theodore Cree—a strong Chivington supporter—that he intended to expose Sand Creek for the massacre it was.

At the same time, others began efforts to effect an investigation. Indian agent Samuel Colley and his son, Dexter, and John Smith, father of Jack Smith murdered at Sand Creek, prepared evidence to present to the Commissioner of Indian Affairs in Washington. On December 9, two days after news of Sand Creek reached Denver, Stephen S. Harding, the territory's chief justice, wrote Secretary of the Interior John P. Usher warning that Chivington's victory might be tainted. These reports and others reached important Republican officials, but without confirmation from the military itself, they remained purely rumor and speculation.

Then came the Soule-Cramer letters.

To be sure, junior officers carried little influence outside their own regiments. But both men knew Major Wynkoop, their former commander, who now had close ties to district and department headquarters. Their real conduit, however, was Colonel Tappan, a witness to the November 28 Fort Lyon confrontation between Soule-Cramer and Chivington. Tappan exerted great influence through his friend General John P. Slough, the former commander of the First Colorado now stationed in Alexandria, Virginia, and who was a favorite of Secretary of War Edwin M. Stanton.

Soule wrote his letter to Wynkoop on December 14, noting that Tappan would leave for Denver the following day. Two days later, an unidentified officer of the First wrote to General Slough declaring Sand Creek to be a massacre. The letter with a Denver postmark was apparently—but not conclusively—written by Tappan. Cramer composed his letter to Wynkoop on December 19, saying he was preparing a detailed report for Slough.

Wynkoop's movements at mid-December are unclear. After his recall from Fort Lyon he had been assigned to command at Fort Riley, Kansas—Upper Arkansas district headquarters—but he left there sometime in December to go over to Fort Leavenworth and defend his actions before departmental commander General Samuel R. Curtis. When he returned to Fort Riley he received word of the Sand Creek affair and became enraged. The Soule-Cramer letters had arrived by then, along with official reports, and Wynkoop immediately forwarded a copy of Cramer's letter to Hiram P. Bennet, Colorado's delegate to Congress. On December 31, the new district commander, General James Ford, doubtlessly influenced by the Soule-Cramer letters, ordered Wynkoop back to Fort Lyon to assume command and investigate the "Chivington Massacre."

Wynkoop's report on Sand Creek, combined with supporting affidavits, pushed both Congress and the military to act. On January 10, 1865, the House of Representatives passed a resolution calling on the Joint Committee on the Conduct of the [Civil] War to investigate the Sand Creek affair. The Senate followed with a resolution withholding the pay of the Third until hearings had been held on Sand Creek. And on January 30, Delegate Bennet wrote to General Slough, asking him for a copy of Cramer's report, and specifically mentioning Cramer's letter to Wynkoop, which he had received. "I propose to show Chivington in his true colors," Bennet said.

When the military commission convened in February, Soule was called as the first witness and his testimony provided the basis for the case against Chivington and the Third. Cramer, who followed Soule on the stand, methodically and carefully gave damning testimony concerning Chivington's actions at Sand Creek. More testimony corroborated the claims made by Soule and Cramer.

On April 20, the commission adjourned to allow Chivington time to prepare his case. Three days later Soule was murdered on the streets of Denver.

When the military commission reconvened, Chivington presented a series of depositions, including one which accused Soule of theft, drunkenness, and cowardice. In Soule's defense, documents were placed into the record confirming that Soule believed he would be killed because of his anti-Chivington testimony.

At this point in the hearing, the military captured one of Soule's killers, Charles A. Squier. Squier quickly escaped, however, and the arresting officer, Lieutenant James D. Cannon—who had also testified against Chivington—was found dead in his hotel room, a victim of poison.

Soule's killers disappeared and never faced prosecution.

As to Joseph Cramer, despite testimony designed to portray him as a vindictive subordinate out to discredit his commander, his steadiness and integrity proved too great for the charges to be believed. Yet Cramer's life—like Soule's—was tragically short. In August 1864, he had been thrown from his horse. The injuries he sustained to his liver and stomach plagued him for the rest of his life; indeed, complications from the fall forced him to interrupt his testimony before the Sand Creek military commission. He continued, however, to serve in the First Colorado until November 19, 1865, when he mustered out in Denver. Soon he left Colorado and with his wife settled in Solomon, Kansas, a farming community in Dickinson County. In 1870 voters elected him sheriff, but he served only briefly. He died December 16, 1870, age thirty-one.

The remarkable Soule-Cramer letters never became part of the public record of the original investigations, and after the two congressional committees and the Judge Advocate General's Office released their reports, the letters disappeared to history. The sole evidence pointing to their existence was in Hiram Bennet's letter to Slough.

Their reappearance in the year 2000 caused a sensation. That July, U.S. Senator Ben Nighthorse Campbell of Colorado, an enrolled member of the Northern Cheyenne Tribe and a Sand Creek Massacre descendant, introduced a congressional bill to authorize the Secretary of the Interior to establish the Sand Creek Massacre National Historic Site in Colorado. Senate Bill 2950 was referred to the Committee on Energy and Natural Resources Subcommittee on National Parks, Historic Preservation, and Recreation.

Two weeks before the scheduled hearing on September 14, Linda Rebeck of Evergreen, Colorado, brought to the Colorado Historical Society letters written by her great-grandfather, Marl L. Blunt, who settled in Colorado in 1859. Included in the packet were materials related to Sand Creek, including manuscript copies of the Soule-Cramer letters. Rebeck had recently discovered the letters packed away in a trunk in her mother's attic. Society officials immediately recognized their importance and with Rebeck's permission contacted Senator Campbell, who read excerpts from the letters during the Senate hearing and entered their full contents into the Congressional Record. The effect was immediate. Senator John Warner of Virginia, who attended the hearing, rose to say that never in his tenure in public office had he heard such moving—and disturbing—testimony. *The Denver Post, Rocky Mountain News*, and newspapers across the country ran front-page stories on the Sand Creek letters.

The Soule-Cramer letters suddenly were the subject of a fast-breaking news story. But even more importantly, they helped push the Sand Creek bill through the Senate and House. On November 7, President Clinton signed the bill into law.

In the winter of 1864–65, the Soule-Cramer letters helped to launch investigations which exposed the Sand Creek affair as a massacre. One-hundred and thirty-five years later, those same letters helped ensure that Americans would never forget the horror and crime of what occurred on the Big Sandy that bleak November dawn of 1864. The power of the letters, then and now, lies in their simple honesty, their moral outrage, and the determination of two young men who wanted to see justice done.

Colorado Heritage, Winter 2001

Endnotes

1 Captain Soule wrote Colonel Chivington on October 11 and October 17, 1864, advising him of the situation at Fort Lyon.

2 When Wynkoop departed Fort Lyon, he carried two letters praising his course of action with the Cheyennes and Arapahos, one signed by the officers under his command and the other signed by prominent ranchers and citizens in the Arkansas Valley.

3 George Bent, the son of William Bent and his Cheyenne wife, Owl Woman, suffered a wound at Sand Creek but did not die. He escaped to the Smoky Hill with other survivors. A month later, he joined the Dog Soldiers and fought with them in the full-scale war against the whites that followed Sand Creek.

4 This episode apparently occurred after the Sand Creek expedition was over.

Colonel Samuel F. Tappan chanced to be at Fort Lyon when Chivington's command arrived on November 28. He had just returned from a trip to Washington, D.C., where he had met General Ulysses S. Grant. Tappan was Chivington's old foe, dating back to the early days of regimental organization. He took careful notes of all conversations between Chivington and the Fort Lyon officers.

5 Chivington clearly hoped to win a brigadier general's star from the engagement. He boasted about it at Fort Lyon after Sand Creek. Actually, his commission in the Army had expired before the massacre. Upon his return to Denver, he asked to be relieved as commander of the Colorado Military District. The Army acquiesced, which ironically removed him from the reach of the military when charges were brought against him concerning his actions at Sand Creek.

6 Chivington's troops killed many chiefs at Sand Creek, including White Antelope, War Bonnet, Standing-in-the-Water, Yellow Wolf, Old Little Robe, and One Eye. However, Black Kettle and Minimic escaped. Left Hand, the Arapaho chief, suffered a mortal wound at Sand Creek but died in the Smoky Hill villages.

7 See David Fridtjof Halaas, "'All the Camp was Weeping': George Bent and the Sand Creek Massacre," *Colorado Heritage*, summer 1995.

8 Anthony would himself become a critic of the Sand Creek affair. He justified himself on grounds that Chivington had deceived him, and that he joined the expedition believing that it would move against the villages on the Smoky Hill Trail. Later in life, he would defend his role and insist that the village at Sand Creek included hostiles.

T he rags-to-riches-to-rags story of Horace A. W. Tabor, his ever-loyal first wife, Augusta, and his much younger second wife, the golden-curled Elizabeth "Baby Doe" Tabor, has held its appeal for generations. Thousands of words have been written about how Horace and Baby Doe lost their fortune but not their love; about how Horace accepted a political patronage job to survive; about how Baby Doe had to move into a shack at their Matchless mine in Leadville; and about the tragic end of their younger daughter, Silver Dollar.

But for decades no researcher confronted all of the 50,000 rambling, perplexing, and sometimes frightening writings that the elderly, haggard, and impoverished Baby Doe scribbled in her Leadville shack as her mind and body disintegrated. Judy Nolte Temple decided to try her hand at figuring them out. Temple had performed other diary analyses: Her *A Secret Be Burried* [sic]: *The Diary and Life of Emily Hawley Gillespie, 1858–1888* was an outgrowth of her doctoral dissertation (as Judy Nolte Lensink) and was published in 1989 by the University of Iowa Press.

During the Tabor project, Temple found she could work for only limited periods of time before she found Baby Doe's writings so "depressing and haunting" that she had to step back for a while. Even after a decade of researching Baby Doe's dreams and visions, Temple is still trying to understand Baby Doe—whom she describes not as insane, but rather "eccentric; as close to being a true mystic as anybody I have studied." Temple came away from the project with "an incredible empathy for how she suffered."

Temple is associate professor of women's studies and English at the University of Arizona at Tucson. Her book-in-progress, from which this article was drawn, is titled *The Madwoman in the Cabin: The Dream Worlds of Baby Doe Tabor.*

The Demons of Elizabeth Tabor: Mining "Dreams and Visions" from the Matchless

—Judy Nolte Temple

The love triangle and ensuing tragedies surrounding Horace Austin Warner Tabor, Augusta Pierce Tabor, and Elizabeth Bonduel McCourt Doe constitute the most famous romance story of Colorado history, and maybe even of the West. Few people are fully aware, however, of the torments endured by Elizabeth "Baby" Doe Tabor in the decades following the collapse of Tabor's fortune. Indeed, she left a written record—albeit a peculiar and often frightening one—that has largely gone unexamined until today, despite the numerous books and articles that have been presented over the past century-plus on the Tabor topic.

H. A. W. Tabor was born near Holland, Vermont, on November 26, 1830, and learned the stonecutter's trade. In January 1857, he married Augusta Pierce, his employer's daughter, and the couple embarked for Kansas and Colorado Territories.

Difficult years followed, as the Tabors—and their fellow adventurers—discovered that gold nuggets were not strewn about the ground, free for the picking up, as they had been told. As others returned disgustedly to the Midwest or East, however, Horace and Augusta remained in Colorado. With the unwavering support of the ever-devoted Augusta (who cooked for the prospectors and took in washing to help earn money), Horace Tabor variously was a postmaster and storekeeper in Buckskin Joe and Leadville.

One day, two prospectors whom Tabor had grubstaked struck it rich, and part of the fortune became his. Other mining ventures, such as his famed Matchless mine east of Leadville, followed, and soon the unrefined

Horace Tabor was a Silver King, constructing opera houses in Denver and Leadville, a Denver office building, and moving into an elegant home in the capital city. Soon he would even become lieutenant governor and—for twenty-six days—a U.S. senator from Colorado.

Augusta's presence, however—perhaps because of her plainness and lack of verve—was wearing on Tabor, and his name became increasingly linked with that of the pouty-faced, blonde, divorcée-about-town Elizabeth McCourt "Baby" Doe. On January 2, 1883, Horace and Augusta dissolved their marriage. The divorce was not of her wish, and when it finally was issued, she asked the judge to enter in the official record: "Not willingly asked for." On the following March 1, Senator Tabor and Baby Doe were married at the Willard Hotel, Washington D.C.'s finest, with President Chester A. Arthur and congressmen in attendance. He was fifty-two; she was twenty-eight. Tabor gave Baby Doe a $75,000 diamond necklace as a gift. Tabor's riches would disintegrate, but the marriage would not. Neither would the peculiar bond between Horace and Baby Doe, which endured long after his death.

"Not willingly asked for." That moving statement by the first Mrs. Tabor doomed the social fate of Baby Doe and dampened the political prospects of Horace. It was one thing for a wealthy man to keep a woman on the side and quite another for him to jettison a long-suffering and devoted wife and openly take up with a woman "from the mining camps." Newspapers from throughout the nation detailed the ostentatious nuptials between Horace and "Lizzie," as he called her. When the Catholic priest who wed the couple later discovered they were each divorced, he did not record their marriage.

Horace and "the second Mrs. Tabor"—still called "Baby Doe," her mining-town moniker—returned to Denver. When they went out for the evening at the splendid Tabor Grand Opera House, the attention they drew upstaged the unfortunate actors. On July 13, 1884, they had a daughter, Elizabeth Bonduel Lily Tabor, called "Cupid" by her parents; and in 1889 the couple had another baby, ostentatiously named Rose Mary Echo Silver Dollar Tabor ("Honeymaid"). Despite the interest generated by the well-dressed Baby Doe, by the grandly outfitted little girls, and by their mansion at the foot of what became Denver's Capitol Hill, the Tabors were never accepted in Denver's social circles.

Silver Dollar Tabor during her days as a "dancer" in Chicago.
There she died under the name "Ruth Norman,"
scalded to death at age thirty-six.

By 1893, due to poor investments and his unwise faith in the permanent monetary value of the silver ore that had made him a multi-millionaire, Horace Tabor was on the road to bankruptcy. People expected Baby Doe to leave Horace and again use her beauty to find a third husband for financial security, but she stayed by his side as he sold off her jewels and their home. In 1899, Tabor, who by now out of charity had been given the political job of Denver postmaster, died at age sixty-nine from complications of appendicitis. According to the legend, his parting words to Baby Doe were "Hold onto the Matchless mine, it will make millions." Eventually Baby Doe Tabor moved to Leadville with her young daughters, and ultimately into a shack at the Matchless in order to work the mine herself in hopes of returning it and the Tabor name to their glory.

Daughter Lily abandoned Leadville for a more conventional life among Elizabeth's relatives in Milwaukee, Wisconsin, while the errant Silver, as she was known, remained in Leadville and became notorious for her high spirits. Silver tried careers as a journalist in Denver, a film actress in Colorado Springs, a novelist in Chicago, and ultimately a "dancer" in various midwestern cities. In 1925, she was found dead at age thirty-six in a Chicago boarding house, drunkenly scalded, according to the legend. It was a body that Elizabeth never publicly claimed as that of her beloved daughter. Declaring that her Silver was still alive in a convent somewhere, Elizabeth continued to live at the Matchless on Fryer's Hill, becoming eccentric and increasingly fixated upon religion.

When Elizabeth ventured down to Denver, her eclectic clothing—men's mining work clothes, a veiled driving cap, old boots, and a large crucifix—made her seem to old-timers as a ghost of faded mining days, and as a crazy woman to young people unfamiliar with her saga. Her name occasionally appeared in Colorado newspapers as she fought creditors and lessees in her indefatigable battles over ownership of the Matchless. Her frozen body, dressed in tatters and feet wrapped in newspapers, was found at the Matchless on March 7, 1935.

News of the sad end to her lonely vigil was circulated throughout the world. The tiny, eighty-year-old woman described in one account as "a small, bent figure trudging over the snow-covered road from Fryer's Hill wearing an old overshoe on one foot and the other wrapped in burlap" proved *in extremis* to a new generation what it meant to be faithful to an ideal. Belated homage was paid to the formerly-scorned Baby Doe, now affectionately honored in newspapers as one of the last links to the mining heydays of the Old West.

At the time of her death and since, writers have recounted and illustrated the Tabor story, with headlines such as "Once-Glamorous Beauty Soon Became Just Weary Wrinkled Woman Dressed in Shabby Garments Long Outmoded." Such notions, of course, ignore the three decades that the widow Tabor spent, day by day, in virtual isolation and poverty. ...

Up in that cabin she religiously, obsessively, wrote thousands of accounts—her "Dreams and Visions"—during her thirty-six years of widowhood. Elizabeth Tabor also kept an occasional diary that she perhaps hoped to combine with her descriptions of religious visitations, omens, and "devils" (who sometimes bore the names of real-life Coloradans) with

342

the intent of eventually making them public. Shortly after Elizabeth's death, *The Denver Post* printed an interview with a Mrs. Boehmer who had recently visited the elderly recluse at the Matchless mine. According to Boehmer, Elizabeth pointed to two paper bags on her cabin shelf and said, "In those sacks are my notes of the past, little stories and explanations of countless visions I have experienced. They are truly my memoirs. Some day I hope to publish them." Feisty to the end, the eccentric and perhaps mad Elizabeth Tabor at age eighty still hoped to tell her side of the family saga as an attempt to speak back to the hurtful legend of "Baby Doe." Elizabeth had been outraged in 1932 by the publication of David Karsner's sensationalized book about her, *Silver Dollar*, which was followed by a Hollywood film that drew huge crowds to its Denver premiere. She wrote to friends: "I am now as for a long time alone. I am breaking my heart over that Book and that Picture Show."

Elizabeth's autobiographical memoir was never published and probably never written, given her age and precarious health. In fact, her varied life writings were not available to the public and scholars for more than three decades after her death. Because of the personal nature of the Tabor correspondence that included the names of still-living prominent Coloradans, the papers had been sealed by a Leadville judge in 1935. Then a conflict over access to the papers developed between the most popular Tabor biographer, Caroline Bancroft, and the secretary of the State Historical Society of Colorado, Edgar McMechen, who was the administrator of Elizabeth's estate and considered himself a potential Tabor biographer. When that was settled with McMechen's retirement in 1953, some of the papers were briefly made public in a *Denver Post* series which in turn intrigued a new generation with the story of Baby Doe. Then the huge task of processing and organizing the enormous collection of more than 50,000 items kept Elizabeth's notes from the public eye until 1967. This long absence of Elizabeth Tabor's authentic voice only fueled the growth of the Baby Doe legend. ...

Elizabeth's Dreams and Visions suggest answers to questions which the pat legend leaves unsatisfied: How could a beautiful and once-wealthy woman survive her voluntary exile in a humble cabin? How could a mother deny her own daughter's death? How mad was Baby Doe? Buried deep within Elizabeth's papers are spirits and the "living dead" with whom Elizabeth lived at the Matchless for all those years.

Memoirs—or Morass?

Despite Elizabeth Tabor's best intentions, no genuine memoir or remotely coherent narrative has been found among the thousands of Tabor papers housed at the Colorado Historical Society library. Instead, patient archivists and potential biographers encounter scribbled, misspelled, rambling renditions of troubling dreams; frightening spirits; and crudely illustrated visions that seem to come from the disintegrating mind of an isolated old woman. Yet within this daunting morass exists the unique, poignant, and intimate voice of "Lizzie" Tabor that draws us into a dream world she inhabited for thirty years. Like the Ancient Mariner, Elizabeth Tabor speaks with the power of the tormenting story she was irresistibly compelled to tell and re-tell. In life writings that float between diary, diatribe, and the divine, there is a rich lode of information about recurring themes in Elizabeth Tabor's life: her relationship with her children, especially with her troubled daughter Silver; her ambivalent relationship to husband Horace ("Papa") Tabor; and her tortured quest to preserve the Matchless mine.

While Elizabeth Tabor was not a conventional autobiographer, she was a dedicated collector of family papers, clearly driven by an "itch to record" that characterizes many people with historical instincts. After her death, seventeen trunks whose forty years' storage Elizabeth paid in a Denver warehouse, and other mementoes she stored at St. Vincent's Hospital in Leadville, were discovered, yielding hundreds of items and a wealth of writings. This rich mine of memorabilia bequeathed by her to future scholars fulfilled a pledge of fidelity which Elizabeth made in her 1894 diary as the Tabor wealth was evaporating: " ... all I can bequeth [sic] to my little ones is my good name ["good name" is then crossed out and the word "Honor" written above it], my fidelity as a daughter-sister-mother & wife such as I have tried to be. ... " By saving the Tabor family papers and her personal scrapbooks at great financial sacrifice, the destitute widow indeed proved her fidelity to her family, even if her good name was forever gone. She thus joined a long lineage of "compensatory diarists" (such as Charles Lindbergh) who felt misunderstood in their own times and thus created—for future readers who they hoped would be more empathetic—records of their innermost thoughts.

Within the Tabor trunks were several forms of life-writing by Elizabeth: scrapbooks sometimes annotated in code, diary notes, and sacks containing thousands of Dreams and Visions. In the fourteen scrap-books, some of which by now have been microfilmed, are hints of Elizabeth's world view that also influenced her dream narratives: events that occurred two decades apart appear next to each other in the scrap-books; obituaries of her two stillborn sons and of her large beloved natal McCourt family compete with glowing newspaper articles about Horace's rise to fame. We see "correct" linear chronology discarded, and stories of life competing in the scrapbooks with the accounts of death that was ever-threatening to nineteenth-century families.

The diary notes reveal Elizabeth Tabor to be an irregular journalist who turned to this form of life-writing when she was most upset. During the Tabors' 1894 financial crisis she reviews her past and laments that her brother Peter McCourt, at that time the business manager for Horace, who would soon desert him, was among her "living dead," a term she used for enemies who had hurt her. The diaries, written on neat stationery, paper scraps, and the backs of calendars, pick up with vehe-mence during troubled times. One occasion was in 1914–15, when her twenty-four-year-old daughter, Silver, whom she intimately called Honeymaid, was rebelling. On Christmas Day 1914, Elizabeth used a piece of newsprint from *The Denver Post* as her "stationery" to comment on her sadness and perhaps its insensitive joviality. Atop its banner headline which read "There Is Not Anybody In Denver Who Has Not Had a Merry Christmas," she wrote her own observation: "O my Blessed Lord this is not true. I only wish it were/many are with broken-hearts like poor lonley [sic] me alone alone alone. Not one soul came to me to-day or last Eve and where is my darling child Honeymaid. God watch over her her mind has gone. God will save her for us. O darling Lily & the Babies."

While the poignant diary shows how isolated Elizabeth had become at the Matchless, in the world of her Dreams and Visions she was never alone or idle. In fact, she relied on portents from her dreams to guide her daily interactions. Also found within her diary narratives are accounts of her dreams, suggesting that Elizabeth saw a strong relationship between her diminishing "real" world that was circumscribed by poverty and death, and her expanding "dream world." It becomes difficult for a reader to ascertain what is a dream and what is reality, a reflection perhaps of Elizabeth's own hybrid dance between the two.

Entering the Dream World

Friday January 24–1919—about 3-30 A.M. I had just got in
bed for the night. I could not sleep, in a moment I knew our
Tabor was close to me on my right, my husband Mr. H. A. W.
Tabor who died on April 10–1899. He had his arms around
my shoulders, his left arm around my shoulder in the back
and his right arm acrost the front of my shoulders holding me
tight his face was close to my face and his mustache long am
[sic] beautiful as it was moved over my face. I could feel its
hairs on my face and his breath only his same warm sweet
breath with that same odor that only his breath had pleasing
and sweet no one had that same breath. ... I knew God had
sent our Tabor to me. So I spoke out very loud, thus:
  In the name of Jesus is this Tabor?
  In the name of Jesus is this Tabor?
  In the name of Jesus Christ Who was Crucified and Died
on the Cross for us is this Tabor? Then I was certain it was
Tabor then I asked Tabor in a loud voice thus—Will our
Child Silver soon come back to me? Quickly Tabor in a
strong clear voice—"Yes"—then in a moment he said "Keep
awake" in his own natural firm kind voice. ... Where my
Spine meets my head a strong current made my head bend
down on my neck. ...

By the time Elizabeth wrote the above narrative, she was recording
more than 350 Dreams and Visions a year and placing them in her trunks
for safekeeping. Within those complex writings is evidence that she tried
to organize them, but it is unclear whether they were intended for her
own autobiographical use or for some future biographer. In either case,
they demonstrate that she clearly anticipated they would reach future
readers. One wishes that Elizabeth had shorn up the mine of her papers
with better timbers, for the Dreams and Visions are disconcerting. Some
are scrawled in horrible handwriting that circles around brown paper the
size of a grocery bag; others are in daunting yet tantalizing code; many
contain seemingly disjointed words such as "spirits, the devil, No. 6" with
no connecting verbs, while others contain no helpful punctuation. The
disorder of the "memoir" may reflect the psychological chaos Elizabeth

was experiencing as she was dunned by creditors, harassed by mine lessees, and haunted by pleading letters from her daughter Silver.

Yet textual clues within the Dreams and Visions clearly indicate that Elizabeth was demanding that attention must be paid to her writings, and that she intended her disjointed autobiographical writings to be understood. Within this "madness" of fragmented scraps is a method. There are clues within the papers that Elizabeth took her dream world seriously, that she developed a recurring set of symbols and characters that guided her, that she increasingly relied on her night specters to guide her waking actions and to foretell the future, and that she had several stories she intended to tell for posterity. One sees the hand—albeit a shaky one— of the would-be editor of a "memoir." For example, Elizabeth paid assiduous attention to the dates of her various Dreams and Visions, sometimes correcting herself in order to record the exact hour of an apparition's appearance. She also took pains to clarify some items, such as a character's relationship to herself: "Nealie (my dead sister)." She would reiterate a particularly strong dream's content: "I had a glorious dream to-day of Jesus Christ The Everliving God Talking to me 4 times (four times) I was so happy. ... " She signed her most vivid accounts, such as the one just cited, with her two full names—"Mrs. H. A. W. Tabor" and "Mrs. Elizabeth B. Tabor"—in an apparent effort to make them "official." She illustrated particularly strong visions with crude drawings to perhaps help a future audience "see" what she had experienced. All of these tactics would be unnecessary for a purely private writer; they show her attempts to guide a reader through the labyrinth of her dream world.

Some of the most choppily incomprehensible scraps of paper in the worst handwriting turn out to be notes or rough drafts of dream descriptions Elizabeth perhaps scrawled upon waking in the middle of the night. Rather than light a lamp that would disrupt her direct experience of the dream, she may have chosen scribbled immediacy in the dark. Later, she would copy the dream account onto better paper in neat handwriting and sometimes mark the scrap "copied and filed," serving as a meticulous Scribe of the Self. Usually the recopied dream would be a longer and clearer version of the original notes. The faithful Elizabeth then saved the rough draft, so that its terse lines became a reiteration of the dream's theme. But closer examination of the subtle differences between one quite good draft that Elizabeth marked "I must keep this to show" and its resulting improved version reveals subtle attempts to make the dream more "literary" and therefore worthy of a memoir. Elizabeth was serving as writer and editor of her body of writing. Notice in the following how Elizabeth elaborates on the setting, accentuates the sense of action with more verbs and adverbs, and adds descriptive words to help us visualize her terror:

> *Version one:* Monday morning about 2-30 A.M. while kneeling close to bed saying my prayers I heard outside my window from low down 2 terrible heartbreaking very loud cries one right after the other very pearcing & sharp from no living person it was a spirit crying it was the Banchee ...

> *Version two:* Sept 13–1920—Monday morning about 2-30 I was kneeling down by the bed praying—and all at once I heard down outside of my window as if low down—and all was so still not anything stirring I heard a loud pearcing heart-rendering shreaking cry so sad and awful, then in a few seconds about a minute it gave out the very same loud terrible cry so sharp so agonizing pearcing the night & so mournfull only twice It cried I got to the open window before the 2nd cry was finished O it was unearthly like the Banchee-Cry. ...

Searching for Silver

A predominant theme in the scraps is the Tabors' younger daughter, Silver. She represented to her mother the dream of re-establishing the Tabor name, especially when in 1910 Silver—then a striking twenty-one-year-old—was photographed presenting Theodore Roosevelt with a copy of a song she had written. But by 1914, rumors in Leadville said that Silver was fond of liquor and men, which sent Elizabeth into frenzied action to rescue her daughter, who in turn was mortified when her mother followed her at midnight to confront her boyfriends. Soon the darling Silver, who in the happy days had reported her own dreams for her mother to record, was becoming her mother's worst nightmare. Silver then moved to Denver for more freedom and opportunity. Now totally alone, Elizabeth Tabor processed the trouble with Silver in her Dreams and Visions, which served the agonized mother on several levels.

Some dreams simply relive in concentrated form the mother-daughter duels that Elizabeth had probably encountered. The rumors about Silver fuel the dream's plot as the dreamer witnesses the growing defiance and danger her daughter embodies. By recording her agony, Elizabeth acknowledges it so that she can deal with it by giving her load to her heavenly Counselor:

> June 2—1915 I dreamed this terrible thing I was walking on a Denver St[reet] Phil [her brother Phil McCourt] was standing on the edge of the sidewalk several people were standing near him as I passed he jeered at me & said "your daughter your daughter" & sneered at me. ... Then I ... saw my poor darling child Silver all bent over drest in light with a white cloth tied over her head her face was O so white & her eyes were the blackest & she was so drunk she was unconscious she was talking to trying to to some men that stood in a door way she was looking so hard at me O I thought I would die of grief in this terrible dream. ... I gave it to God when I woke up.

Other dreams make concrete the battle between good and evil that Elizabeth felt was going on within her daughter, whom she characterized as "hypnotized" by bad people rather than being intrinsically bad. This battle is waged in the dream world between those visitations featuring a "bad" Silver and those with her "good" counterpart. The war is often symbolized by Silver's eyes—healthy versus sick yellow—or Silver's gaze which either turns lovingly toward the dreamer or avoids the mother's frantic searching face. These tortured dreams remind us that Elizabeth was a mother much like those of today who look deeply into their children's eyes for confirmation of the truth, for signs of drug use, for connection. They reveal a mother crazed by her daughter's deterioration rather than the Crazy Mother of the Baby Doe legend. In 1914 when Silver was first being what writer David Karsner aptly referred to as "tarnished," Elizabeth tried to break up Silver's relationship with an Ed Brown, which infuriated the willful Silver. Elizabeth feared Ed was after not only her daughter but also after Elizabeth's "other silver"—the Matchless mine. In her dream world, Elizabeth dresses her child in the white of innocence and sees her as a victim of rape—a crime that occurs symbolically on the grounds of the beloved mine:

> Sunday May 3 or Monday May 4 1914 I had a Vision first I heard Silver say "Wait I want to bid you good by, then I saw

349

her in the whitest dress O so white and the front of it was all covered with blood very red then I saw her face then I saw her on the Matchless Mine near the water boxes & I saw a tall young man the form & size of Ed Brown throw her hard & terrible down on the ground & he stood over her his hand pushing as hurting her & he was leaning over her it was terrible. ...

By 1921, correspondence from Silver to her mother documented the painful descent of an ambitious young woman thwarted by poverty, irregular jobs, and several operations, at least one of which was a "miscarriage." Silver often wrote to her mother (who was desperately praying to God to provide a piece of bread for dinner at the Matchless) to send money. Silver explained over the years that she had to pay doctors for a "miscarriage" in Indianapolis and at least two other gynecological operations by 1921. Even the most doting and denying mother could not avoid her daughter's wandering sexuality or render it totally passive in the dream world:

July 15—1921 I dreamed a sad & terrible dream of my darling child Silver—she was sitting down she had I think white wrapper on and she looked sad and on her knee sat a small long black snake with its body standed (part of it) straight up & its terrible head up high the snake was sticking out its terrible tongue and (O my God save her) for she was putting out her finger and touching that snakes tongue every time he stuck it out & that was all the time quickly it was the devil & the snake showed it was the devil My heart was broken I should die of grief to see my precious child touching a snakes tongue & it sitting up on her lap. O she is in trouble O Blessed God let me get to her. ...

Sometimes the dreams show Elizabeth's ability to place her deepest sorrows onto more neutral objects such as animals in her attempts to cope. She often dreamed happily of a dapple horse, reminiscent of her favorite carriage animal during the wealthy Denver days, or had troubling visions of Silver's favorite cat, which had died in an accident. Did the following dream project Silver's "miscarriage" onto the figure of a dog? In it, the mother-dreamer realizes her inability to save the "dog"— her own child—and foresees an inevitable farewell:

On Holy Saturday, April 19, 1919, Baby Doe depicted a foot-long black-and-grey striped "Snake Viper" which tried to "sting my heart." The snake rested in her hand, meaning that "it is some one of my own blood and close to my aching agonized heart [Silver Dollar?]." The snake's colors, she wrote, signified that its human counterpart was "possessed of an evil spirit; the black stripe is the devil, the grey is the real person but sick not normal because the color is grey—if it were white the person would be normal. O Blessed Saviour Jesus spare them."

Aug 7–1916 I dreamed I had a little all white Poodle dog on my lap & its front leg was bent to its back & I did not pull it around to the front soon enough & it was dying & blood was on it & I could see its stomache swell out & see the dark red blood bulged out in the stomache through the skin it died & its face was calm & lovely & I kissed it and Silver was with us & she kissed it. I am sad over this dream.

The image of Silver associated with a baby or babies recurs often in the dream world—and then sadly in the real world. Diary entries scribbled on one of Elizabeth's calendars combine to suggest a mystifying story that utilizes the numerical code Elizabeth had devised in the 1870s to obscure embarrassing words in her scrapbooks. She assigned each vowel a number so that 1 equaled "a," 2 was "e," 3 was "i," and so on. Atop the calendar page is written "20th b1by S36v2r," which when decoded is "20th baby Silver." The calendar sheet also contains code at the February 20, 1915, date: "9:30 A.M. B1by" ("baby"). Two days before that, February 18, in a circled entry is the puzzling "Loan Fantz paid Foster," which could be read left to right, up and down, or in a circular direction.[1] In Elizabeth's case, the fact that she "told" the story on her calendar and then coded the core of the tale on the top of the paper almost like a banner headline, teases the line between what was secret and what is almost a scream for attention.

This cryptic coded calendar, combined with some of Elizabeth's correspondence, leads to a question that may ever be unanswered: Was a child born out of wedlock to Silver on February 20, 1915, and taken to a foster home with the assistance of Dr. Theresa Fantz, a Denver physician friend of the Elizabeth Tabor? Or did the marked day and time indicate when Silver's would-be baby was aborted by Dr. Fantz, the latter who in a cryptic letter written on May 28, 1915, observed to Elizabeth: "Saw Silver on the street yesterday. ... She of course did not recognize me. I am here simply for people's convenience when I'm of no more use they toss me aside." Or did Elizabeth first learn from a letter she received on that date about Silver's early stages of a pregnancy—one that ended in October of that year by what her daughter called a "miscarriage" in Indianapolis? The fact that at the bottom of the calendar Elizabeth notes "Silver told me she wants 15000" (probably $150.00) adds to the confusion and sense of Silver's desperation. On the back of the diary-calendar is a notation by Elizabeth that mysteriously shows how her desperate daughter inhabited the dream world as well:

> [February] 9. I had a vision of Silver coming to door with a
> black vale over her face to hide her identity to go to have it. ...

An unsuccessful search of baptismal records at the Denver Catholic Archdiocese suggests that answers about an actual child may never emerge. It may not even matter whether a baby was born, for in her dream world Elizabeth often saw babies and young children who were real to her. Sometimes they are happy and laughing, sometimes Silver tries to hide them from her mother, sometimes they match the age of a child born in 1915, and on occasion mother and daughter together hold "our" baby:

> February 27–1919 ... I dreamed again I was with Silver &
> another woman in a cheap house bare new pine floor, Silver
> came & handed me 2 (two) small babies in white swaddling
> clothes as Indians wrap up their babies & their heads had little
> close white hoods on she said here are your babies the dark
> one is your little boy who died long ago I dug him up the
> other is your new baby who just died I said O yes & kissed its
> little face & laid them both down on the lounge & Silver & the
> woman all danced around. ... Now this is the second time I
> have dreamed lately of Silver and I digging up the grave of
> my baby boy who died 26 years ago. ...

The babies Silver holds may represent Elizabeth's own two stillborn sons, one born when Elizabeth was married to Harvey Doe and the other by Horace Tabor, for in numerous dreams Elizabeth created a large family that sometimes combined both of her husbands, her Wisconsin kin, her daughters, the two stillborn sons, and those perplexing unidentified babies. Or the dead babies Silver holds could represent an actual "buried child"— or children—of Silver's. The happy children who often inhabit the dream world could represent Silver's potential fertility and a brighter future. Or the children hidden downstairs or under covers in repeated dreams could be the potential re-birth deep within the earth of Elizabeth's dearest "child"—the Matchless mine, a beloved topic over which she and Silver had often dreamed together back in their harmonious days on Fryer Hill.

God showed me this lovely Vision of the little girl who he so often sends me in Visions dressed most always in Plaid bright

During her occasional visits from Leadville to Denver, Elizabeth stayed at the second-class Hotel Milo (two and one-half dollars a week; bath down the hall). "O Blessed Jesus, God I love you," she wrote on the hotel's letter paper, "O how I suffer, I hope no one will ever suffer as I do for my poor Silver. ... "

colored gingham & this time Good Friday 1922 She came
twice quickly one after the other & second time brought her
Hat made of same goods as her dress all plaid gingham & she
took a hat pin & pinned her hat on her head to tell me soon
No 6 [mine]shaft would be started. O how merciful Jesus God
our Blessed Saviour is to us. I-we adore Thee Jesus

Elizabeth was interested in analyzing her own dreams and often
noted that a little girl in gingham symbolized the Matchless mine. In her
dream world, Elizabeth sees the little girl on the property; the little girl
is endangered, and the little girl is befriending or warning her. In one
vivid dream, both the potential fertility of the Matchless mine and perhaps the buried fertility of Silver merge:

Nov 30–1920 at [the Matchless] No. 6 shaft bucket-full of
children it looked like a bouqet of flowers going down 6 &
when it got down the baby got frozhen & cryied & they
brought baby right up & all the rest of children stayed down
it looked lovely like a boquet of bright flowers

This may be the ultimate clue to the myriad dreams of Silver, babies,
and the little Matchless girl: If the mine could only give birth to wealth
again, the family's former fame would be reborn. Then the other Silver
would also return home—as she hinted in her letters asking that "a private room with running water" be added to the mine shack—and new life
would emerge from the Matchless.

As Silver approached the nadir of her life, her letters about liquor,
drugs, and her own lost hopes must have tortured Elizabeth, causing
nightmares which she also religiously recorded. But just when her
despair seemed overwhelming, Elizabeth experienced a rare ecstatic
dream to resurrect her daughter, rendering her into a "dream child" in
both senses of the word:

Easter Sunday April 16–1922—I dreamed Jesus Blessed me to
ease my sorrow. I saw my darling Silver come she had on a
table the most wonderful, most beautiful Marvelous
Magnificent snowy Pure White Marble Statue a Bust of her
Father H.A.W. Tabor—her darling papa. ... She had made all

> by herself it was her Masterpiece hers alone, she stood close
> to the Statue her hand resting on it she was in a long blue &
> white large plaid gingham apron which she wore while making
> the wonderful Statue—O Bless Jesus our Divine Saviour

By the awesome power of her deluded mind, Elizabeth Tabor drew together her dead husband and dying daughter in one monumental moment. Ironically, as Elizabeth was dreaming of a marble statue to commemorate her husband, Horace's beloved Grand Opera House in Denver was being converted into a movie theater. Silver by 1922 was wearing scant costumes as a dancer, but in the mother's dream world Silver was dressed like the beneficent Matchless mine girl, symbolizing to Elizabeth that both of her silvers would be redeemed. ...

At the time of Elizabeth Tabor's death, much was written about the "little bundle" that she often carried. Journalists speculated that she hid ore samples, silver, or money in a bag that formed an integral part of her costume. Given her obsessive care for the Matchless mine, others surmised that she stored contracts or mining stock in that bag. Elizabeth herself often dreamed of losing, hiding, or retrieving her beloved bundle. Her laboriously accumulated personal papers reveal that what she most dreaded relinquishing in that bundle—a bundle often resembling a baby—was her own writing, especially her cherished Dreams and Visions. And when the aged guardian of the Matchless mine died, her final bundles of papers were indeed stolen from the cabin. In the waning years, Elizabeth Tabor's task of transcribing her Dreams and Visions may have helped preserve her last and most valuable treasure of all: her matchless mind.

> Excerpted from "The Demons of Elizabeth Tabor: Mining
> 'Dreams and Visions' from the Matchless"
> *Colorado Heritage*, Winter 2001

Endnotes

[1] Diarists such as Samuel Pepys of the seventeenth century and adolescent girls into the twenty-first century have employed codes to obscure what they nonetheless seem compelled to record. Yet codes serve to actually arrest another reader's eye, to highlight the very item the diarist most wishes to hide.

L arry Borowsky has an uncanny ability to distill the essential story from complex historical themes. As the principal writer for the Colorado Historical Society's Roadside Interpretation Program, he regularly condensed piles of photocopied research material into concise blocks of text for historical marker panels. These short narratives engage readers on a personal level while communicating broad subjects about the state's past. Borowsky called upon this ability for a *Colorado Heritage* article highlighting the State Historical Fund, a grant program that fosters historic preservation projects statewide.

Borowsky, currently editor of the Society's *Colorado History* journal, knew that not many readers would make it through a long article about a grant program, however noble its purpose. So he incorporated his assignment's themes into a compelling true story about a national phenomenon that started with one man and one theater in a small Western Slope town during the Great Depression.

Borowsky pulled his story idea from research compiled by Brooke Cleary for *High Stakes Preservation*, a Colorado History Museum exhibit that explored several of the 2,000 statewide preservation projects made possible by the State Historical Fund. Administered by the Colorado Historical Society, this grant program was established by the passage of the 1990 constitutional amendment that legalized gambling in Central City, Black Hawk, and Cripple Creek. The Fund allocates a portion of the tax revenues from gaming to public or nonprofit groups for historic preservation activities throughout the state. The program's leveraged effect on Colorado's economy has been calculated in dollars—billions of them. But comments from main street business owners, local historical societies, schoolchildren, and tourists indicate another, less tangible benefit of the program.

Borowsky's article speaks to that benefit. When an organization preserves a part of its heritage—whether a Depression-era theater, a courthouse, or a school—the community gains a direct connection to the stories of its own past.

Delta's King of Kings:
The Egyptian Theatre and the Bank Night Craze

—Larry Borowsky

A Hollywood executive once described Bank Night as the "iron lung" that nursed the motion-picture industry through the Great Depression. Attendance sagged badly at movie houses in those belt-tightening times; even a ten-cent seat in the balcony lay beyond the means of many families. Theater owners tried everything to fill their empty seats: slashing prices, handing out door prizes, running double features, and doing whatever else they thought might work. But their losses continued to mount. Americans simply could not afford to waste precious pennies on entertainment—not while struggling to make their rent and put food on the table. The breaking point arrived in 1933, when fully one-third of the nation's movie theaters went out of business.

Bank Night was born in that desperate year, and it brought customers back with the only lure that mattered: cold, hard cash. This simple promotion worked in the manner of a raffle or lottery: The theater selected a patron at random and awarded him or her a wad of bills, usually fifty or one hundred dollars but sometimes a much higher sum.

Contestants entered by placing their names in a registration book in the theater lobby or box office. On the evening of the drawing, typically a Monday or Tuesday, patrons jammed the theater hoping to hear their registration number called. A child was called forth from the audience and led onto the stage, where he or she donned a blindfold, reached into a large drum, and withdrew the winning ticket. The victorious patron had to appear within a few minutes to claim his or her prize; failing that, the prize money rolled over to the following week. At that point, most of the audience got up and went home; by the time the house lights dimmed and the two-reeler began, the "sold-out" house might be three-fourths empty again. But the exhibitor's cash register was full—and stayed that way.

The losing contestants came back the following week, and then the week after, and the week after that, paying their way into the theater each time on the chance that their number might finally come up. Since the registered players often outnumbered the seats in the house, proprietors had to sell standing-room tickets or even run the public-address system out into the street, where the overflow waited in a densely packed mass.

Such scenes occurred all over the nation, in large cities and tiny burgs. By 1937, perhaps 6,000 of the nation's 15,000 movie houses held a weekly Bank Night drawing. The *Saturday Evening Post* hailed Bank Night as a national institution and gushed, "It has profoundly affected the social life of America. ... It's got to the point where nobody can schedule a basketball game, a church sociable, or a contract party on Tuesday night because everybody is down at The Gem hoping to cop a cash prize." The *Post* estimated the nation's aggregate Bank Night payoff for 1936 at a whopping $50 million.

This impressive industry sprang forth from a most unlikely source: a thirty-dollar giveaway promotion at the Egyptian Theatre in Delta, Colorado. Charles Urban Yaeger, a district manager for Fox Intermountain Theatres (the Egyptian's parent company), pioneered the idea in the spring of 1933, hoping to keep the Egyptian from going under. Yaeger came up with the idea out of desperation, after having run through every stale gimmick and stunt in his repertoire. "The most I hoped for," he would later confess, "was that it would hype the box office for two or three months."

But Yaeger had stumbled upon the ideal formula. Bank Night was perfect for Colorado, and perfect for the times. Its lucky-strike mechanism carried a whiff of the mining-rush spirit that had given birth to Colorado and remained part of the state's character. Moreover, Colorado—and the West in general—had always represented boundless opportunity; so, too, did Bank Night. Here were profits for the taking, and if one didn't win this week's drawing, well, there was always next week.

Opportunity had never been scarcer than it was during the Great Depression, and Americans' faith in it had never been so violently shaken. In 1933, the year Bank Night began, some 15 million adults (nearly one in four) could not find work. The jobless clustered in breadlines and

Hoovervilles, their prospects dim and their morale dimmer. Farm fore-closures numbered in the hundreds of thousands during the early 1930s, and more than 10,000 banks failed—including a staggering 4,000 in the first two months of 1933. The financial system stood in such a state of panic that every bank in America closed its doors on Friday, March 3.

That bankless day, ironically enough, came the very day after the Egyptian staged the first-ever Bank Night—and just one day before Franklin Delano Roosevelt took the oath for the first of his four presidential terms. The temptation exists to draw parallels between the Bank Night handouts and FDR's great relief programs: Was this a pop-culture prologue to the New Deal? Well, maybe in a symbolic sense. For Yaeger's idea seemed to tap the same vein of optimism that gave rise to Roosevelt's policies. From the very start, he hyped his promotion at the Egyptian as an antidote to economic despair, calling it a "great depression-dispelling event" and a "gold war on depression." The *Delta County Independent* echoed the theme in a short notice headlined "Egyptian Plans Big Prosperity Event for City." The accompanying article began: "Yellow gold is going to outshine any trace of depression."

That message seemed to hold the secret to Bank Night's appeal. Here, amid the flood of bad news, was a stubbornly upbeat enterprise, one guaranteed to send somebody home happy. Even the setting—the palatial Egyptian, built at the height of Jazz Age prosperity—buoyed the spirits, while reaffirming a cherished American ritual: the night at the movies. All of these factors made Bank Night a uniquely reassuring pastime and help explain the fervor with which Americans embraced it.

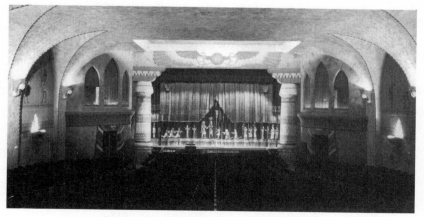

The Egyptian Theatre's Exotic Revival interior

"The value of Bank Night to the exhibitor is obvious," noted *Time*. "It helps fill his theatre on off nights and permits him to run cheap films to packed houses." But to the patrons who packed those houses, Bank Night clearly meant something more. It was, indeed, a "depression-dispelling event"—a promise that this week might bring better news than last week, and next week better news than this. And the millions of dollars it cycled back into the economy often made a real difference. Bank Night, observed the *Saturday Evening Post*, "has kissed dozens of prize winners off relief, has tilted hundreds of mortgages, paid for college courses, operations, and gin."

Even those who never won a dime at Bank Night seemed to reap some intangible payoff from it. For Bank Night wasn't really about winning.

It was about having a chance.

A similarly eager, hopeful spirit surrounded the opening of the Egyptian Theatre in 1928. It was Delta's first five-star facility, a quantum step forward for this hinterland town in far western Colorado. Founded in 1882, the community had thrived as an agricultural center, counting fruit, beans, and sugar beets among its profitable cash crops. Delta prospered mightily in the 1920s, adding a new cannery, a sugar factory, and more than three hundred new residents (a 15-percent increase). Construction boomed downtown, with a grand new Elks' Hall and an assortment of handsome brick storefronts; in 1926 the city paved Main Street and added sidewalks and electric streetlights.

The movie industry enjoyed an equally auspicious decade. The 1920s brought the first "talkies" and the first Academy Awards. More important, they witnessed a flourishing of theater construction. Large, ornate venues (commonly referred to as "cinemansions") rose in cities across the nation, signaling the movies' final conquest of vaudeville as the nation's top form of entertainment. The money sunk into these picture palaces testified to their importance; they served as signature landmarks that defined a neighborhood's or a community's identity, much as sports arenas help to shape cities' identities today.

The Egyptian Theatre was to be the diamond in downtown Delta's crown, a proud display of the town's success. Built at a cost of $75,000, it was every bit as gaudy as the finest theater in Denver, with every big-city amenity and convenience. It belonged to a big-city movie house chain, the Denver-based Dickson & Ricketson circuit, and it promised to deliver big-city stars such as Douglas Fairbanks, Greta Garbo, Lon Chaney, and Harold Lloyd. Delta's two existing theaters, the Colonial and the Rialto, lacked the budget and clout to book first-rate Hollywood features. But the Egyptian would give the town a venue worthy of such entertainments—and so, in a very literal sense, would lift Delta up from the B-list to the A-list.

The man who built the Egyptian, Frank Henry "Rick" Ricketson, was thoroughly big-city, too, having already forged and cast aside several successful careers—first as a sports editor at *The Denver Post*, then as a water-rights attorney, finally as an officer of the 312th Cavalry during

The year 1933 was another lean one for the five-year-old Egyptian Theatre, the pride of downtown Delta until the stock market crash left it struggling for survival. The solution was Bank Night, a straightforward cash giveaway meant to bring people back to the movies.

the Great War. He opened his first theater in 1923, using $600 in borrowed cash, and expanded to thirty venues during the flush years thereafter, with properties in Colorado, Wyoming, South Dakota, and Nebraska. In 1929, a year after the Egyptian opened (and just before the Crash), Ricketson sold the Dickson & Ricketson chain to the Hollywood-based Fox circuit for half a million dollars; he remained in charge of the company (renamed Fox Intermountain Theaters) and continued to work out of his office in Denver.

The Delta market was a natural fit for Dickson & Ricketson, which already owned a theater in Montrose (the Oriental). Local business leaders spent many months courting Rick Ricketson, optioning two lots on Main Street for his convenience and arranging for favorable financing. Frank Stearns, publisher of the *Independent*, helped package the deal and rally public support. The papers were signed in early 1928, and construction began right away.

To design the Egyptian, Ricketson hired one of Denver's finest architects, Montana Fallis, a protégé of the great Frank Edbrooke. Fallis had made his reputation twenty years earlier with the Ideal Cement Building, the first all-concrete structure in Denver. He went on to create many of the city's best-known Art Deco landmarks, including the Denver Chamber of Commerce Building, the Buerger Brothers Building, and the Mayan Theatre at 110 Broadway.

The Egyptian, designed two years before the Mayan, shared many of that venue's characteristics. Both were done in the Exotic Revival style, which enjoyed a brief vogue among theater designers in the mid-1920s. A large sun-disk relief dominated the Egyptian's stuccoed façade—a Winged Sun, or Scarab of Welcome, dating to the reign of Rameses XII. The hieroglyphic motif continued inside the lobby and along the walls of the auditorium, where stuccoed arch vaults, busts of the pharaohs, and painted figures enhanced the theme. Lotus-flower columns framed the stage, while the proscenium arch overhead featured the same Winged Sun scarab. A $3,000 curtain hung in front of the stage, while a $12,000 Robert Morton organ loomed in the orchestra pit. The theater's 750 air-cushioned seats boasted fine, color-coordinated leather upholstery. State-of-the-art heating and air-conditioning systems kept the auditorium at a constant, comfortable sixty-eight degrees.

To herald the opening of this great civic improvement, the *Independent* issued a special thirty-two-page "Progress Edition" on September 28,

1928. "Egyptian Theatre Reflects Age of Glorious Pageantry," the front-page headline read; the article beneath it overflowed with breathless praise in deathless prose:

> What a jewel box! Verily a treasure chest, studded with jewel lights that gleam and glow, all colors of the rainbow. ... At the Egyptian the divinest of arts has been welded to the universal language of a silver sheet in a new harmony—a symphony of sight and sound, which with its subtle alchemy can sway the soul and bear away on the wings of enchantment, the visitor to this temple of a thousand delights.

The grand opening took place on October 1, 1928. All the leading lights of Delta attended, along with visiting dignitaries from Montrose and Grand Junction and reporters from as far away as Cortez. The Paramount and MGM theater chains sent delegates, as did the giant Pathé distributorship—big-city, all the way.

The gala program began with an overture performed by Mary Upson, a young virtuoso from the Denver Conservatory of Music, upon the "silver voiced" orchestral organ. There followed a display of dancing and acrobatics by the Welch sisters of Gunnison; a comedic skit by the Coy Brothers, vaudevillians and radio performers; and a series of speeches and dedications, interspersed with more blasts from the organ. Then came a newsreel, an MGM short, and at last the feature attraction: a Paramount comedy called *The Fleet's In*, starring Clara Bow.

In the aftermath, the *Independent* crowed:

> No words can properly describe the beauty of this edifice. One must see it to appreciate its beauty. It is the last word in carefully blended colorings, the heavy padded carpets, draperies, lights, and hangings all blending in perfect harmony, while burning incense lends an Oriental touch to the whole scene.

Nobody knew, of course, that Delta's era of glorious pageantry had just about run its course. And had they known, would they have done anything differently? The Egyptian was, in some sense, the city's gift to itself, a celebration of past good fortune and a reward for hard work. "It's going to be a day," the *Independent* wrote, "that will go down in Delta's history as 'The Day of Days.'"

The high hopes the theater embodied would soon dissolve into Great Depression gloom, but so what? Delta had its jewel box, its treasure chest, and all the colors of the rainbow; and the pot of gold lay just around the corner, Great Depression or no.

Of all the thousands of Bank Night winners, none won bigger than the man who invented it, Charles Yaeger. Thirty-one years old when he launched the scheme, this large, gregarious man had previously distinguished himself only by his ability to plug away in obscurity. When Bank Night made him rich and famous overnight, nobody was more stunned than he. In the few interviews he granted, Yaeger discussed Bank Night dreamily, as if in awe of his sudden good fortune—and aware that it might desert him just as suddenly. Asked by a reporter how it felt to be wealthy, he replied shyly: "You know, it makes a fellow feel pretty good when he thinks he finally amounts to a little something."

A little something is exactly what Yaeger amounted to before Bank Night. He was born, fittingly enough, in Central City, Colorado's first great wheel-of-fortune town, and divided his boyhood between Denver and Raton, New Mexico. In early adolescence he dropped out of school to work

The Egyptian's marquee advertises the Cecil B. De Mille epic *The King of Kings* in October 1928, just a few days after the downtown theater opened.

364

alongside his parents, who operated a succession of small-town cinemas and vaudeville halls. The family toiled in places such as Creede and Del Norte and Las Cruces, New Mexico—about as far from Hollywood's bright lights as one could get. Yaeger's father managed the house and ran the film projector, while his mother provided the piano accompaniment (this being the silent-movie era). Young Charles collected tickets, served as an usher, swept the floors, and did other dirty work. This unglamorous apprenticeship carried him into early manhood and brought him back to Denver in the mid-1920s, where he took a job checking tickets at the Santa Fe Theatre.

He bounced from job to job until the late 1920s, when he worked his way into a position as a booker for Dickson & Ricketson. After Fox bought the chain in 1929, Yaeger drew a field assignment as the Western Slope district supervisor. The posting returned him to the same out-of-the-way circuit he'd grown up on. But Yaeger went cheerfully and, more than likely, with gratitude. Amiable and eager to please, he was the model middle manager—an organization man, a lifer. He weighed 250 fleshy pounds, stood a shade under six feet, and possessed an honest face and a disarming, toothy smile. Loyal, unassuming, and obedient, he was trustworthy with the cash box and able to get along with almost everyone he met. The big man's smallest attribute may have been his ego.

His territory included southern and western Colorado, plus New Mexico. Times were already hard: The Depression had begun to settle in, and theaters had started to feel the effects. By 1931 Yaeger was hustling hard to draw paying crowds to his venues. He trotted out all the tried-and-true gimmicks—beauty pageants, talent nights, cut-rate matinees, and the like—and teamed up with local merchants to give away poultry, bracelets, groceries, music lessons, and whatever other goods or services he could pry loose. A Christmas-tree promotion in the winter of 1932 helped shore up an otherwise deadly season. But the scramble never ended, and Yaeger was fast approaching the point of diminishing returns.

In early 1933 he initiated a program called "Prosperity Day" at the Egyptian Theatre. Patrons who presented special coupons at the box office could purchase Tuesday matinee tickets for just ten cents, or evening admissions for fifteen cents. It wasn't a moneymaker, but Yaeger still liked the idea. For prosperity, he sensed, was the main thing on everybody's mind, and it was what people really craved—not a dressed turkey dinner or a month's supply of pipe tobacco but something more lasting, something worth making an effort for.

"We'd given away everything under the sun," Yaeger told the *Rocky Mountain News* in 1936. "I used to wake up nights trying to think of a new angle, something that would keep people coming to the theater week after week. One day—I remember I was shaving at the time—it hit me, just like that. Cold hard cash. That's what people want. And not just five dollars either, but something big enough for them to want it."

Yaeger sat down with pen and paper and worked out the numbers. The purse he began with—thirty dollars—represented the equivalent of 120 admission tickets at twenty-five cents each. In the 725-seat Egyptian, that meant he had to fill one-sixth of the house to break even; anything beyond that would put him ahead for the night. To give his idea a chance to catch on, he slotted it for eleven weeks, with a seventy-five-dollar grand prize at stake the last week to sweeten the pot. Yaeger placed entry forms at half a dozen local businesses and took out ads in the *Independent*. He called the promotion "Gold Night."

The first drawing took place on March 2, 1933. That evening the Egyptian screened a lighthearted British mystery called *The Penguin Pool Murder*, the first feature in the popular Hildegarde Withers series. Edna May Oliver played Miss Withers, a sharp-tongued schoolteacher/sleuth; the cast also included James Gleason and Robert Armstrong, who a year later would play the bombastic promoter Carl Denham in *King Kong*.

Yaeger was not in the house to see the early returns; business had taken him to New Mexico that evening, so he phoned the Egyptian's manager, Harry Moore, for a progress report. Moore told him: The house is spilling over. We've grossed more tonight than we did all of last week. They're lining up at the door.

The news came as a pleasant surprise to Yaeger, who hadn't expected anything near a sellout. Obviously he'd underestimated his idea. But he still regarded Gold Night as a short-term promotion; despite the unexpectedly good start, it would probably lose its drawing power after a few months, just as every other promotion did.

Two weeks later, a Warner Bros. release called *Silver Dollar* began a three-day run at the Egyptian. It starred Edward G. Robinson as a prospector named Yates Martin, who struggles in a Colorado boomtown, finds a massive silver vein, builds a fabulously profitable mine, moves to Denver, builds an opera house, and leaves his wife for a showgirl named Lily. The character, obviously, was a thinly disguised version of Horace Tabor, the most famous of Leadville's silver kings.

But Yates Martin's story also foreshadowed the tale that was about to unfold for Charles Yaeger. Bank Night represented his lucky strike—his ticket to fame and fortune.

The Gold Night promotion continued at the Egyptian through the spring of 1933, and crowds remained heavy throughout the entire eleven-week run. When it ended, Yaeger simply rolled it over for another eleven weeks. He also added it to the schedule at the Oriental Theatre in Montrose and began testing the promotion on a one-time basis at other theaters under his supervision. That summer, outside the West Theatre in Trinidad, Yaeger saw a line of people standing two abreast in a driving rain, waiting to get inside for the prize drawing. It was the first time he'd attended a Gold Night in person, and what he saw floored him. No promotion he'd ever heard of had generated this kind of response. He began to take his idea more seriously, viewing it less as a quick shot in the arm and more as a marketing venture with long-term potential.

By the end of the year Gold Night had lost none of its appeal; ticket sales increased everywhere Yaeger tried it, and the crowds kept coming back week after week. The longer it ran at each venue, the more popular it got. Unsure of how to capitalize on his idea, Yaeger called his boss, Rick Ricketson, in Denver, and together they devised a plan to take the promotion nationwide.

Ricketson had the theater contacts, financing clout, and legal know-how to put Yaeger's idea into action. The two became partners in a firm called Affiliated Enterprises, and under that banner they copyrighted the promotion (now called "Bank Night") and began licensing it to movie houses on a royalty-fee basis. Participating theaters paid five dollars a week for the rights; in return they received a contest registration book, special tickets, advertising materials, and a giant hopper for the weekly prize drawings. Yaeger quit his job with Fox Intermountain and moved to Denver, setting up shop at 2165 Broadway, and he and Ricketson brought in a Warner Bros. executive named Claude Ezell to supervise sales.

Initially, they hoped to have a hundred theaters under contract by the end of 1934. They reached that milestone within a month. By the end of the year more than a thousand theaters (most in small towns) had jumped aboard, and the large national circuits had begun to take notice. Yaeger built up a far-flung sales organization, with representatives in twenty-six states, and began pulling down major clients. The Loew's theater chain signed up; so did the RKO, Fox, and Warner Bros. circuits. By 1936, some 250 theaters were holding Bank Nights in New York City alone. The fabled Strand in Los Angeles had a weekly Bank Night; Manhattan's Stork Club launched a spinoff.

As Bank Night began moving into the big cities, Affiliated raised its weekly licensing fee from five to fifty dollars. Within two years, the company was raking in (depending on whose estimate you believe) between $50,000 and $125,000 a week in royalties. Bank Night prize amounts rose accordingly. Where the Egyptian had dangled just thirty dollars a week for Gold Night, theaters now began offering $100, $500, even $1,000 awards. A Bank Night winner in Denver took home $2,400 in July 1936. A Chicago theater topped that, handing out $3,000, only to be surpassed by a New York movie house that gave away a $3,500 jackpot.

Within the span of two years, Affiliated Enterprises had become one of the biggest players in show business. Charles Yaeger, clearly unprepared for celebrity, struggled to keep himself out of public view. He stopped eating in restaurants, studiously avoided cameras, and turned down all but a handful of interview requests, spurring at least one national publication to refer to him as "Mister X." Ignoring advice to move his company to New York or Hollywood, he continued to live in a modest four-room apartment in Denver. "We're doing okay here," he shrugged. "Besides, I can't find a city as close to such swell trout fishing as Denver."

As the home base of Affiliated Enterprises, Denver not surprisingly became the nation's unofficial Bank Night capital. The Lucky Seven theater chain, largest in the city, alone had 92,000 Bank Night registrants—this in a municipality of 300,000. Some venues held two Bank Nights weekly, on Tuesdays and Thursdays. The Huffman chain began giving away an automobile a week at each of its seven cinemas; a rival chain, not to be outdone, decided to give away a house. Such exorbitant prizes helped push the city's overall Bank Night purse for 1936 to more than $250,000. Denverites took the pastime seriously enough that at least one local insurance company began selling special Bank Night policies to indemnify contestants against the chance that they might be absent when their number came up in the drawing.

Chicago ranked as another hot Bank Night town; so did Des Moines, Iowa, where movie-house crowds grew so large that police and fire departments had to post special units to keep them under control. And in New York, theaters handed out an estimated $3 million in prize money annually, according to *Motion Picture Daily*. But the most dedicated Bank Night loyalists resided in the small towns. There, for one evening every week, life virtually ground to a halt so everybody could assemble down at the local cinema—perhaps one of the very same rickety Main Street auditoriums in which Charles Yaeger had grown up. The prizes were smaller here than in the big-city chains, but the event loomed somehow larger.

About the only place in all of America that Bank Night didn't catch on was the nation's capital. Theaters there didn't need big-dollar promotions to lure an audience; the well-paid federal work force provided a reliable paying clientele. But even there, Bank Night seem to have made some sort of an impression: In 1938 Congress considered a bill to establish a national lottery.

That piece of legislation, in truth, was inspired less by Bank Night than by the illegal "numbers" lotteries, sports-betting pools, and pyramid schemes run by racketeers large and small. An editorialist in *Reader's Digest* assessed this illegal trade at $5 billion to $6 billion a year, and argued that letting the government in on the action might yield perhaps $1 billion in new revenues—at a time when the entire federal budget totaled less than $10 billion.

The bill never made it out of committee, however, thanks to a determined campaign of opposition. Detractors lambasted the proposal from the stump and the editorial pages as nothing more than state-sanctioned gambling, an affront to the nation's morals, an assault upon the work ethic. A national lottery, they argued, would exploit the suffering poor, dangling a get-rich-quick illusion before them to wring free their last few nickels and dimes. Advocates pointed out that almost every nation in Europe raised funds through a government-sanctioned lottery; even the famously fair-minded Nordic countries ran them. Moreover, public opinion polls showed that Americans favored a national lottery, 55 to 34 percent. But the nays echoed loudest in Congress, where the very word "lottery" seemed to carry illicit connotations.

Bank Night suffered from the same taint in certain quarters. As its popularity grew, so did the backlash against it. Commentators and politicians questioned its legality and, at times, tried to crush it under the blunt heel of anti-lottery laws. In Chicago, police interrupted Bank Night drawings at sixteen theaters and, as audiences booed, hauled the house managers off to jail in handcuffs. Four days later a court ordered the prisoners released and declared the drawings unequivocally legal. A judge's ruling halted Bank Night in Iowa for five months, until the state supreme court tossed out the decision. High-court jurists in New Hampshire, New York, Tennessee, Arkansas, Minnesota, and Massachusetts also found that Bank Night did not violate anti-lottery laws. The Kansas Supreme Court prohibited Bank Night as practiced in one specific chain of theaters but otherwise reserved comment.

Rick Ricketson, with his lawyerly mind, had foreseen such complaints and threaded the copyrighted Bank Night rules through various loopholes in the law. Contestants paid nothing to register for the prize, and the money they paid to attend the drawing was, strictly interpreted, merely the price of admission for a movie; Bank Night thus did not fit the technical definition of a "lottery." Enemies could deride it as a shell game all they wanted, but they didn't have a legal case—and so the practice continued.

Affiliated Enterprises' legal department stayed busy with another set of disputes: copyright infringement suits. The company filed these by the dozens against theater proprietors who conducted fly-by-night versions of Bank Night (under awful names such as "Buck Night," "Payday," and "Screeno") without paying the royalties due. According to Emmett Thurston, Affiliated's general counsel, the firm had several hundred lawsuits pending at any given time. "So far we've won every case," he boasted. "Every decision has been favorable."

But Bank Night continued to suffer from image problems. Hollywood studio heads abhorred it, believing it placed their lofty artistic creations in a cheap sideshow atmosphere. At first they denied their best releases to Bank Night theaters, until the practice became so widespread that the studios had to back off. The press, meanwhile, reported on a series of cases in which duly selected Bank Night winners had to go to court to claim prize money withheld by unscrupulous theater owners. *Literary Digest* noted a disturbing trend in some midwestern towns: Hoods began stalking theaters on Bank Night and jumping the prizewinner as he or she walked home with the loot.

All contributed to the growing perception of Bank Night as an unsavory or low-class activity. The deluxe Loew's and RKO chains ordered Bank Night halted at all their theaters nationwide. In New Orleans, the daily newspapers agreed to stop running Bank Night advertisements. In Pittsfield, Massachusetts, local authorities gave theater owners a choice: discontinue Bank Night or lose their Sunday exhibition privileges.

In an unguarded moment, even Rick Ricketson characterized Bank Night as an unfortunate but useful contingency:

> A few years ago the giveaway was not considered show business. And even now, it is a racket that every exhibitor dislikes to employ. The depression and poor pictures have made it a necessary adjunct in certain types of theaters. Whether an improvement in pictures will eliminate this type of box office stimulation is a matter that the future will have to decide. My hunch is the giveaway racket is here to stay, or at least until ended by legislation.

The future proved Ricketson's hunch wrong. Bank Night was *not* here to stay; indeed, by the late 1930s it had virtually run its course. With the Depression beginning to lift, theaters no longer had to work so hard to get patrons through the door. The minute their balance sheets allowed it, they dumped the Bank Night promotion and got back to business as usual. The iron lung was no longer needed; the patient could breathe on its own again.

Within a few years, the nation would be at war, and Bank Night no longer fit the times. In that era of sacrifice and duty, the pursuit of individual windfalls appeared unseemly, if not unpatriotic. Bank Night no longer possessed the magic ingredients that roused the public's ardor. But it had served its purpose. In 1933, the year Charles Yaeger began the first Bank Night experiments, movie attendance nationwide totaled 54 million. By 1936, at the height of the Bank Night mania, it had risen to 81 million—a 50-percent increase. Without question, stirrings in the economy helped drive the numbers upward. But Bank Night surely accounted for millions of those additional ticket sales.

It also made a big success of Charles Yaeger. In 1937 the young man who had worked so hard in small-town movie houses all over the West finally bought his own theater in downtown Denver. With additional purchases over time, he built up two Denver theater circuits, Atlas Theatres and Atoz Amusements. True to his gambling heart, Yaeger got into the horse-racing business and developed a stable of twenty thoroughbreds. He also became an early and devoted fan of Las Vegas, spending every New Year's Eve there for more than two decades. He died in Denver on January 25, 1977.

Rick Ricketson remained one of Colorado's most prominent show-business figures. From 1946 through the mid-1970s he served as head of the Central City Opera House Association, where he helped produce the original opera *The Ballad of Baby Doe* in 1956. Four years later he served as a producer on a Twentieth Century Fox feature called *For the Love of Mike*. It, too, possessed a bit of Bank Night's get-rich-quick spirit, telling the story of a Native American boy who races horses and uses the winnings to build a village shrine. Ricketson went on to become a trustee of the Kennedy Center for the Performing Arts in Washington, D.C., as well as president of the Denver Center for the Performing Arts. He eventually won a Citizen of the West award and was enshrined in the Colorado Business Hall of Fame. Ricketson died in Denver on June 18, 1987.

The Egyptian Theatre, like most small-town theaters, had its ups and downs over the ensuing years. Delta's population went into decline after 1950, costing the Egyptian patrons, and newer theaters in neighboring Montrose and Grand Junction stole many of the remaining customers. The grand building suffered accordingly. The curtains and organ were removed, along with the columns supporting the proscenium. The leather upholstery frayed, and the intricate hieroglyphic-style murals disappeared under layers of paint and wallpaper. By the 1990s the Egyptian appeared headed for the wreck heap, until local leaders and state historic preservationists stepped in to save it. One of only a handful of Egyptian Revival theaters left in the United States, the building gained a place in the National Register of Historic Places in 1993.

A three-year, $220,000 restoration ensued. Conservators painstakingly uncovered the lost murals and recreated the Egyptian busts; additional work to the foundation, walls, and roof helped stabilize the structure. To help celebrate the completion of that work, the Egyptian held a special screening on October 1, 1997—the sixty-ninth anniversary of the theater's opening. A silent 1927 classic called *The King of Kings* (one of the first movies ever shown at the Egyptian) topped the bill. Guests drove up in old Model T Fords and wore period attire, filling the newly refurbished auditorium with a genuine Roaring Twenties buzz. At intermission, a giant drum appeared on the middle of the stage, and an usher reached in and drew out a slip of paper and called out a patron's name. For one night, anyway, Bank Night had come home—and the Egyptian itself was the grand prize.

Colorado Heritage, Summer 2002

I n the winter 2002 issue of *Colorado Heritage*, William Wei profiled Ralph L. Carr, who served two wartime terms as Colorado's governor beginning in 1939. Wei focused on Carr's controversial stance against the relocation of Japanese American citizens away from the West Coast and into internment camps following the Imperial Japanese Navy's attack on Pearl Harbor. Carr's unpopular championing of the Japanese Americans' constitutional rights, Wei argued, cost the governor his political career.

Following publication of that provocative and well-received profile, *Heritage* editor Steve Grinstead began discussing the need for an authoritative look at Denver's early Chinatown neighborhood. Although the neighborhood had received many passing mentions—largely in reference to Denver's anti-Chinese race riot on Halloween Day of 1880—never had it enjoyed the kind of overview that would bring its history into the grasp of a broad audience.

Wei happily accepted the challenge.

For his unprecedented look at Denver's Chinatown, Wei delved into a wealth of published and unpublished sources, in the process interviewing descendants of Chin Lin Sou, Chinatown's original "mayor." Wei looks at the first laborers who came from China to work in the mines of Colorado, and he casts light on the perception of Chinatown's residents as dangerous, opium-smoking "Celestials" who practiced a heathen religion—a perception that led to the neighborhood's "Hop Alley" nickname.

Wei is a professor of history at the University of Colorado at Boulder, and he directs the school's Sewall Residential Academic Program in American Studies. Among his many publications are the 1985 book *Counterrevolution in China* and the 1993 work *The Asian American Movement*. A popular lecturer on Asian history and culture, he worked in 1997 as a journalist covering the historic handover of Hong Kong to China.

History and Memory:
The Story of Denver's Chinatown

—William Wei

He was the man with no name. The first Chinese to arrive in Denver was identified simply as "John Chinaman" and described in the pages of the June 29, 1869, *Colorado Tribune* as "a short, fat, round-faced, almond-eyed beauty, dressed in shirt, blue overalls, blouse and hat, with his pig-tail curled up on top of his cranium as nice as you please." Behind the stereotypical label, "John Chinaman," and the feminized portrayal, it is difficult to recognize the man whom other accounts portray as an individual around forty years old, who came from southern China (most likely Guangdong province), and who spoke a Cantonese dialect. "John" was part of the Chinese Diaspora, pushed out of China by dire poverty and pervasive strife, and drawn to frontier America by the opportunities it offered. He most likely came in the hopes of earning enough money to support his wife and family in China, with the dream of saving enough to buy land or open a business when he returned. As such, he was like many other immigrants (Italians and Greeks, for example) who came to America as temporary workers.

"John" was probably among the first generation of Chinese who came to America as part of the California gold rush. Like thousands of other immigrants, he discovered that the country was hardly a "Mountain of Gold," the name the early Chinese gave to America. After trying his hand at mining, he probably worked on one of the many railroads being built at the time, perhaps the famous Central Pacific portion of the Transcontinental Railroad. In all likelihood, "John" was one of the discharged laborers who had completed the Kansas Pacific Railroad and went to Denver seeking gainful employment—founding Chinatown in the process.

Almost from the moment he arrived in California, "John" found himself an unwelcome immigrant. Considered an economic competitor, he faced a virulent anti-Chinese movement that had as its slogan, "The Chinese must go!" This dislike expressed itself in a host of discriminatory laws, including national immigration laws designating Chinese as a people "ineligible to citizenship," denying them civil rights and protection—hence the derogatory expression, "Not a Chinaman's chance." These sentiments would hound "John" wherever he went, including Colorado. Still, in spite of the hostility, he stayed in America because his family depended on him for support. For that reason, he was willing to work for comparatively low wages and under the worst conditions, making him a formidable competitor in the emerging American capitalist economy. Indeed, he and other Chinese pioneers were prepared to venture forth to the Rocky Mountains to find work and new opportunities, establishing Chinatowns wherever they went. None of these Chinese communities was more prominent than Denver's Chinatown.

Historically speaking, there was only one Denver Chinatown. In memory, however, there were always two. First and foremost was "Hop Alley," a mysterious and vice-ridden place that captured people's imaginations. That

A woman, perhaps warming herself at the fire, rests while
tending a Chinatown tobacco store.

375

Chinatown was more of an idea than anything else, one that allowed people to play out their fantasies about Chinese. To the extent that Denver's Chinatown is remembered at all, it is likely to be as Hop Alley. Second and nearly forgotten is the ethnic ghetto where Chinese immigrants found refuge in the hostile milieu that was Colorado. It was a place they could call their own, a community that gave them moral support and physical security. It was there that they could eke out an existence and maintain their cultural identity, replicating the traditional Chinese social structure and modifying it when necessary to fit the state's frontier society and economy.

Both Chinatowns occupied the same physical space: The neighborhood was established around 1870 on Wazee Street between Fifteenth and Seventeenth Streets, next to the old "red light" district and near other ethnic enclaves where European immigrant workers lived. "Wazee" itself is a Chinese name, according to Gerald E. Rudolph, author of a study of the Chinese in Colorado. (If Rudolph is correct, it may mean "Street of the Chinese" in Cantonese.) From Wazee Street, Chinese residents spread out to five areas of lower downtown. By 1940, most ended up on the periphery of lower downtown in the area of Market and Twentieth Streets, near the site of today's Coors Field.

Remarkably, today there is no evidence that Chinatown ever existed in what is now the Lower Downtown (or LoDo) Historic District—apart from a small plaque placed by Lower Downtown District, Inc., on the side of a building at Twentieth Street between Market and Blake. Indeed, it would be difficult to imagine that LoDo, with its high-priced condominiums, upscale boutiques, and gentrified neighborhoods, once housed a thriving working-class Chinese-American community.

Both Chinatowns were perceived as alien places, inhabited by people whose racial and cultural characteristics set them apart from the dominant society. The Chinese were considered "strangers in the land" who were incapable of assimilating into American society. Until the very end, the Chinese who lived there were never able to break out of the various boundaries that confined them.

"Hop Alley," as Denver's Chinatown was known to the city's white residents, gave birth to a number of urban legends about itself and the Chinese who lived there. Its name was suggestive: "Hop" referred to the opium that had become synonymous with the Chinese and "Alley" to the locations of entrances to the buildings where Chinese lived. These entrances were probably situated in the back for greater security and privacy. It was rumored that tunnels and secret rooms accessible only by trap doors connected the buildings.

Denver's white population largely viewed Hop Alley with suspicion and a degree of fascination. Its inhabitants were branded "heathen Chinee" who presumably engaged in idolatrous behavior. Naturally, as "heathens"—that is, non-Christians—they were thought to indulge in every vice known, including opium smoking, gambling, and illicit sex, and presumably a few additional vices unknown to the general public. To many, Chinese were dangerous, every one of them a potential *boo how doy*—a "hatchetman" or "highbinder." As a group, Chinese were suspected of being thugs who protected the criminal activities of the "tongs" or Chinese secret societies that were rumored to run Hop Alley and to engage in wars between rival factions. Even though Denver's Chinatown never had a "Tong War," the Chinese served as a convenient "bogeyman" to frighten young Denverites. An 1896 *Visitor's Pocket Guide* to Denver recommended protection for any whites venturing into Chinatown: "Chinese quarters—Wazee, between Sixteenth and Seventeenth; Market, between Twentieth and Twenty-first. Visitors apply at Central Police Station for guides."

Hop Alley was considered a notorious place, replete with brothels serviced by exotic women, gambling halls frequented by glamorous people, and opium dens catering to drug addicts. Its unsavory reputation was to a large extent the work of "yellow journalism," an irresponsible press that published sensational stories to feed its readers' apparently insatiable appetites for information about the Chinese community. Typical was S. A. Meyer's December 1909 article in the *Denver Times* in which he describes Chinatown as "A dark, narrow alley, a series of dingy entrances, cubbyholes, underground passages, dismal, all-smelling places ... the much-discussed, much-feared rendezvous of the tongs." As if Chinese inhabitants were some sort of nocturnal creatures (vampires come to mind), Meyer goes on to say:

> It is only at night that you can see the Mongol quarter of Denver awaken into exotic life. Its people come into being with the dark and disappear with the dawn. Its acrid odors sting the nostrils. Fiery, contemptuous, bland, serene, foul

> smelling, your Oriental maintains that indefinable barrier that
> has kept the East and West apart since the centuries began.

Meyer's characterizations are typical of what is now recognized as "Orientalist" discourse: presenting Asians through a series of stereotyped images. According to Edward Said, the well-known critic of Orientalism, such views depict Asians as "irrational, aberrant, backward, crude, despotic, inferior, inauthentic, passive, feminine and sexually corrupt." Specifically, Meyer refers to the Chinese as Mongols, even though the Chinese and Mongols belong to different ethnic groups. By identifying them as one and the same, he implies that the Chinese are descendants of the fearsome "Mongol horde" who devastated Europe in the fourteenth century. He ends the passage with an allusion to Rudyard Kipling's "The Ballad of East and West," which begins with the separatist refrain, "Oh, East is East and West is West, and never the twain shall meet."

While the Chinese engaged in various vices (like the rest of American society), they hardly had a monopoly on them. Though much was made of the Chinese prostitutes, there were actually very few of them in Denver. According to the March 28, 1880, *Rocky Mountain News*, there were ten prostitutes in Chinatown. But except for the occasional story about the plight of certain Chinese prostitutes, there is little reliable information about them. Receiving even greater attention was the Chinese propensity for gambling. Indeed, Chinese were famous in the American West for their games of chance, such as the card games fan-tan and pi-gow (a.k.a. cowpie poker), and their willingness to risk their hard-earned money on them. Despite periodic raids on Chinese gambling halls, the problem persisted into the early twentieth century. By the end of Chinatown's existence, however, gambling had become little more than a social event for small stakes.

The vice most closely associated with the Chinese was the smoking of opium. Denver had seventeen opium dens, twelve of them in Chinatown. Citizens thought most Chinese were "opium fiends." Certainly there were Chinese who smoked opium, but they were mostly non-addicted social smokers. In fact, opium dens flourished in Chinatown because of the large number of white patrons. Before World War I, according to retired police captain Tom Russell, 60 percent of the dens' customers were addicts from uptown Denver. Presumably, they and the Chinese smoked opium to escape the drudgery of their daily lives.

While opium smoking was socially frowned upon, there was no law against it until the Harrison Narcotics Act of 1914.

Since most Chinese in America were "drug free," why were they portrayed as opium addicts? According to columnist Ed Quillen, it was part of a discernible pattern in the maligning of minority groups. In a *Denver Post* review of *Menace in the West: Colorado and the American Experience with Drugs, 1873–1963* (published by the Colorado Historical Society in 1997), Quillen outlines the process: "First create press hysteria over some substance. Tie that substance to a minority group, and fabricate fears that the plague is spreading into the majority population." In the case of the Chinese, Quillen says:

> During the formative years of Colorado Territory, the menace was opium. It or its derivatives were common ingredients in patent medicines then used by all classes of society, but the smoking of opium was portrayed as the peculiar vice of Chinese laborers, who were despised anyway because they worked hard and cheaply. ... Exposés of the opium dens or "hop joints" of Denver's Chinatown on lower Wazee Street were a periodic feature of the local press. Newspaper accounts worked the association of opium smoking with the Chinese to the mutual discredit of both. ... Then came published fears that white people were acquiring the vile habit, or as the headline put it: "Caucasian against Mongolian—the Survival of the Fittest."

In this way, the Chinese were portrayed as conveyors of a social disease.

Besides Hop Alley, there was the *other* Chinatown, a ghetto where Chinese gathered for mutual support in an unfamiliar and often hostile environment. In Denver's Chinatown, they were among countrymen who could help them find an abode and a job. There they could find goods and services denied them elsewhere. Perhaps most important, it was there that they found a refuge that offered spiritual solace, providing a meeting place where they could socialize and engage in traditional religious practices.

Despite the *Tribune's* mocking welcome to "John Chinaman," Colorado's territorial government initially sought to attract Chinese to the area in order to provide a reliable and inexpensive workforce. On February 11, 1870, less than a year after the arrival of the first Chinese, the Colorado Territorial Legislature adopted a joint resolution encouraging more Chinese to immigrate to the area. It did so in the belief that Chinese labor would "hasten the development and early prosperity of the territory, by supplying the demands of cheap labor." The resolution guaranteed them "security in their persons and property," though the subsequent persecution of and violence against the Chinese throughout the state proved that to be illusory. The motive behind the resolution was the need for laborers to do the hard physical work necessary to make Colorado economically viable. Except for the brief deluge of people during the 1859 gold rush, the territory suffered from a dearth of workers.

Resolution notwithstanding, few Chinese came to Colorado, preferring to go to places like Boise Basin, Idaho, where they found greater economic opportunity. In 1865, an overland route from California to Idaho had been established, facilitating the journey of Chinese miners. However, in 1876, when gold was discovered at Boulder Creek, an influx of independent Chinese miners came to try their luck. Others came to Gilpin and South Park Counties as members of labor gangs working the placer and gulch mines, six to seven days a week, for about thirty-five dollars per month without board. Utilizing their knowledge of water management, Chinese specialized in placer mining, which involved collecting surface gold from streambeds—a labor-intensive activity that most other workers avoided. Contrary to allegations made against Chinese miners, they were usually not in direct competition with native-born and European immigrant miners who preferred underground mining.

Like the larger city of which it was a part, Denver's Chinatown served as a base of operations for those working in the Rocky Mountain region, bringing together Chinese merchants, labor contractors, and workers into a pioneer community. For them, Chinatown served as a transit center for those taking on supplies before heading off to the mines and construction projects and as an entertainment center for those seeking rest and recreation.

The Chinese who moved to Denver did so just as the city was expanding in size and population. Their growth in numbers paralleled the city's: In 1870, there were only four Chinese in a city of 4,759; in 1880, only 238 of 35,629. Though the Chinese made up only a small fraction of the city's population, on March 16, 1871, a group of citizens living in the Wazee area presented a petition to the Denver Chamber of Commerce requesting their removal. Needless to say, this did not bode well for the fledgling Chinese community.

As with other Chinese communities in America, Denver's China-town was primarily a "bachelor society" that provided few opportunities for family life. Although a little over half of the men who lived in Chinatown were married, most had left their wives in China. This reflected the Chinese tradition of women staying at home to care for children and their husbands' parents while the men went away to work. The men remitted their earnings to support the family in China. Occasionally wives joined their husbands in America, but only after the husbands had established themselves and could support the family; it was usually merchants rather than laborers who could afford to do so. Few women lived in Denver's Chinatown. In 1880, there were only twenty-nine Chinese women; by 1885, their numbers had declined to twenty-two. This situation became more or less permanent with the passage of the Chinese Exclusion Act of 1882, which prohibited the entry of workers' wives. Meanwhile, anti-Chinese sentiment made intermarriage between Chinese and whites a very rare occurrence.

This gender imbalance prevented the establishment of stable families and the creation of a succeeding generation in Denver. The imbalance would begin to correct itself with the repeal of the Chinese Exclusion Act in 1943 and the influx of Chinese immigrants after the Immigration Act of 1965. But it was only in 1990 that the Chinese of Colorado attained a balanced ratio of male to female.

The early Denver Chinese also had limited employment prospects. As a frontier community, the city offered few occupational choices. The Chinese were unable to avail themselves of many of these, being excluded from those occupations that placed them in direct competition with whites. They were, however, able find work in service occupations that white workers avoided, notably as laundrymen.

Seeing the demand for laundry services, Chinese began opening hand laundries in the 1870s. Starting a hand laundry was comparatively easy, requiring no more than a scrub board, an iron and ironing board, and a small place in which to work. A hand laundry was easy to operate since it required little skill and little knowledge of the English language. And as a business that required little capital, a laundry allowed a common laborer to become a small businessman. As such, it gave a Chinese worker a modicum of status in his village in China, where it counted, even though being a laundryman was a low-prestige occupation equated with woman's work in America. But most important, laundry businesses allowed Chinese to earn enough to provide for their families back in China. In some instances, men even saved enough money to return to their family in China, where they bought land to farm or started another business.

Eventually, most Denver Chinese made their living as laundrymen. In 1870, Chinese ran only three of the forty-five laundries in the city. But by the end of the decade, the Chinese may have operated as many as 130 of the city's 262 laundries. The Chinese hand laundry became a common sight in Denver as in other American cities. Until steam laundries displaced the hand laundries at the end of the nineteenth century, the Chinese had a virtual monopoly on the Denver laundry business. As the Chinese were forced out of the business, they began opening what is now the ubiquitous Chinese restaurant that caters to the general population.

Nevertheless, not all Chinese were forced to engage in menial work to survive. A few did better than that and were even able to move in circles outside of Chinatown. Among these select few, none was more prominent than Chin Lin Sou—Chinatown's first mayor. But as his life illustrates, even he found it impossible to lead a completely independent existence beyond Chinatown.[1]

Like most Chinese pioneers, Chin Lin Sou was born and raised in southern China. Born in 1836, Chin (his surname) immigrated to America as a young man. At the age of nineteen, or twenty-two according to some sources, he went to work for the Central Pacific Railroad as a labor contractor to manage the Chinese building its portion of the Transcontinental Railroad. After finishing his work on the railroad, Chin was one of the first Chinese to immigrate to Colorado.

Among Chinese pioneers, however, Chin was atypical in his appearance and the way he lived. He was tall (over six feet) with blue-gray eyes: characteristics that suggest his family may have originated in northern China. Also unlike most Chinese in America, he was a naturalized citizen and was thus able to bring his wife to America. They had six children, all of whom were born and raised in America, making the Chins the first Chinese-American family raised in Colorado. Their fifth-generation descendants still live in the Denver area.

Chin Lin Sou, mayor of
Denver's Chinatown

Chin had a refined manner and learned to speak English fluently. In 1877 the *Central City Weekly Register* remarked that Chin spoke "English fluently as anyone and [was] a man of great executive ability and intelligence." In the eyes of mainstream society, he compared favorably to his countrymen. Later, in a 1919 article on frontiersmen in *Denver Farm and Field*, he was described as "more progressive than most of his sleepy race" and "as strong as a crowbar and as brave as a lion when it came to tackling the affairs of life."

For all of the above reasons, Chin became a leader in the Chinese community. He made his home in Denver's Chinatown and was considered its first mayor—that is, the spokesman for the Chinese community. He was a prominent member of the local branch of the Chee Kong Tong (Zhigong tang), a benevolent organization in Chinatown. The Chee Kong Tong was also a secret society that supported Dr. Sun Yat-sen, who led the revolution that overthrew the Qing Dynasty in 1911.

Though Chin owned a place on Blake Street, he never stayed in Denver for any appreciable length of time. Instead, he worked throughout the state, usually as a contractor supervising Chinese placer miners. Initially, he was in charge of some 300 miners working in Black Hawk. Later he worked for the Cameron brothers, overseeing Chinese workers at their mining site near Central City. Because of his reputation as an honest man, he was offered the office of Central City marshal. He turned down the offer, claiming that being Chinese gave him enough problems to manage. Such was the case on May 21, 1874, when Chinese were blamed for accidentally setting Central City afire while performing "a heathen worship or celebration of rites," as reported in the *Register*. Chin felt compelled to go to the newspaper office to defend his countrymen and set the record straight. On May 25, 1874, the newspaper reported his comments:

> Chinese are too frequently made the victims of circumstances which any other nationality would escape without censure, and they desire to have their side of the case represented as it is. [Chin] asserts in the most positive manner that the ... occupants of the house ... were not engaged in any religious or funeral rites or ceremonies; were not celebrating a holiday as has been asserted. ... [The Chinese] believe the accident was caused by a defective flue, or in an undiscovered parting of the pipe communicating with the chimney.

Because of the high regard with which he was held, the *Register* concluded, "we are bound to accept [Chin's] story as much more truthful than any which have been previously reported."

In addition to working as a labor contractor, Chin was an entrepreneur who owned and leased land, mainly abandoned mines that whites no longer considered profitable. Indeed, the *Farm and Field* article referred to him as "full of the unconquerable ambition to succeed where the Yankee spirit had laid down." However, when he undertook a business venture he found it prudent, if not absolutely necessary, to do so in partnership with a white friend or associate. He owned stores in Nevadaville and Smith's Hill, for example, in partnership with Edward L. Thayer.

After a protracted illness, Chin Lin Sou died on August 10, 1894. Both the Chinese community and mainstream society expressed their admiration for him. E. L. Harris, one of Chin's business friends, said he was a man of "fine personality, strictly honest in business, and respected by all who knew him." Presumably intending a compliment, the *Rocky Mountain News* obituary referred to him as the "White Chinaman" who had many white friends. On February 18, 1977, as part of the Colorado Centennial-Bicentennial observance, Chin Lin Sou was immortalized with a stained-glass portrait installed in one of the "Heritage Windows" in the old Supreme Court room in the State Capitol. Chin occupies the upper half of the window, while Naoichi Hokazano, a Japanese-American labor contractor, occupies the lower half.

Though intended to honor Chin Lin Sou as an early Colorado pioneer, the portrait conveys another idea. As Chin's great, great granddaughter Linda Jew observes, the window suffers from a distortion. In the photograph upon which the portrait is based, Chin wears a western-style suit, but in the stained-glass window he wears a red Chinese gown, presumably to make him appear more exotic. In doing so, the artist has reduced Chin to a public representation of "John Chinaman."

Admired though he was, Chin was never able to advance beyond the Chinese community. In spite of his acknowledged intelligence and long years of experience, it is telling that he never managed white employees nor occupied a leadership position outside of the Chinese community. He and his family resided in Chinatown rather than in the general Denver community, probably for the same reasons other Chinese did: It was simply safer. But as the infamous Denver race riot would prove, for Chin Lin Sou and other Chinese there was no safe haven anywhere in the state.

Among the ethnic enclaves that emerged in nineteenth-century Denver, Chinatown was the most visible. And because of that visibility, the Chinese who lived there were easily singled out for persecution—a situation that resulted in Denver's first recorded race riot.

Though there were few Chinese in Colorado and their work was too specialized to constitute competition, they were still perceived as an economic threat. The most agitated toward the Chinese were the European immigrant laborers who saw them as a potential peril to their livelihood and as willing puppets of the "capitalist" owners and managers. Ironically, both the European immigrant laborers and the Chinese suffered from conflicts with mainstream society because they belonged to an alien culture, practiced exotic customs, and had a relatively low standard of living. The essential difference is that the Chinese were characterized as such because of their race. Eventually, European workers subsumed their ethnic identity under the broader identity of "American." Perversely, they could affirm their Americanness through their opposition to the Chinese, deflecting anti-foreign prejudice away from themselves in the process.

Politicians exploited this antagonism toward the Chinese as a way of attracting political support. During the 1880 presidential election,

Republican Party candidate James A. Garfield was accused of wanting to import cheap Chinese labor as a way of supporting capitalists and opposing workers. As part of its own campaign, the Democratic Party organized an anti-Chinese parade in Denver, inflaming hostility toward the Chinese. Trapped between ethnic conflict and political-party competition, the Chinese became economic and political scapegoats. They were persecuted throughout the state, suffering a racial pogrom that culminated in the infamous Denver race riot.

On October 31, 1880, the riot began when an altercation broke out between several whites and two Chinese playing pool in a saloon. Thousands of rioters marched on Chinatown, some shouting "Stamp out the yellow plague!" and destroying everything in their path. The following day's *News* reported that Chinatown was "gutted as completely as though a cyclone had come in one door and passed ... out the rear." The only fatality was a laundryman, Look Young. According to the popular 1951 account by Forbes Parkhill in *The Wildest of the West*, Look was "lassoed and dragged to death, and his body was strung up on a lamppost." But an autopsy reported that Look had actually died from a "compression of the brain, caused by being beaten and kicked." Look left behind a wife, father, and mother in China, all of whom depended on him for support. His death served as an admonition to all Chinese in Denver's Chinatown. Dr. Harley Look (possibly one of Look Young's descendants) recalls that when he was a boy growing up in Denver in the 1930s, his mother often warned him to return home before nightfall lest white people lynch him.

Ch'en Lan-pin (Chen Lanpin), the first Chinese minister to the United States, ordered F. A. Bee, the Chinese Consul of San Francisco, to investigate the tragedy. Bee concluded that the property damage amounted to an estimated $53,655. He also observed that:

> There was but one opinion among all classes of good citizens—that the Chinese residents had given no cause for the outrage, but, on the contrary, were law abiding and peaceable. My attention was directed to the fact that not one of the 400 resident Chinese had ever been before the courts of Denver for the crime of theft; therefore the only object the mob had was rapine and murder.

Based on this information, Chen complained to William Evarts, American Secretary of State, requesting that the Chinese in Denver be protected, their losses be compensated, and those guilty of attacking them be punished. While expressing indignation over the outrage against the Chinese, Evarts noted that the U.S. Constitution prevented the federal government from interfering in the internal affairs of a state. It was Colorado's responsibility to provide redress. No Chinese, however, was ever paid for property or business losses. Twenty-four rioters were arrested but later released because of insufficient evidence. The four men accused of murdering Look Young were tried and acquitted, closing a shameful chapter in Colorado history.

After the riot, one might have expected the Chinese to abandon Denver. Instead, they chose to remain and rebuild. Five years later, the Chinese population had actually grown to 461, paralleling the growth of the city's general population, which had increased to 61,491. In both cases, the populations had nearly doubled in size. By 1890, the population of Chinatown had reached its apex at 980. The steady growth of Chinatown was a result of the anti-Chinese movement in Colorado. Almost from the moment the Chinese arrived in the territory, anti-Chinese incidents occurred throughout the state. In Nederland, Chinese were expelled from the Caribou mines; in Gregory Gulch, their queues (pigtails) were cut off and they were run out of town; in Leadville, instead of being coerced to leave, they were prevented from entering. Alpine, Aspen, Balfour, Black Hawk, Creede, Cripple Creek, Gothic, Ouray, Rico, and Silverton were scenes of anti-Chinese episodes. This racial antagonism and the loss of employment forced Chinese to flee to Denver's Chinatown for safety and work.

A growing population brought greater demand for and diversification of services within the Chinatown community. According to Xi Wang, in 1885 most of the 461 Chinatown residents continued to work as laundrymen; there were also three servants, six cooks, two porters, nine shopkeepers, two doctors, three clerks, seventeen cigarmakers, four grocers, a butcher, three barbers, and a restaurant worker. Many of them provided the community with ethnic-related goods and services. The shopkeepers, for example, carried goods directly from China, including herbs that the two doctors probably used as part of their traditional Chinese practice. With these additional services, Denver's Chinese could live in a more self-sufficient community. At the same time, they were essentially confined to Denver's Chinatown until World War II, with almost no opportunity to assimilate into the dominant culture or achieve social mobility.

As with other Chinatowns, then and now, Denver's Chinatown served as a tourist destination, attracting visitors in search of exotic sights and sounds—not the least of which were the Chinese people themselves. They were, of course, racially different from the whites who made up the majority of Coloradans. Accentuating the difference was their hairstyle, consisting of a shaven head and a queue. Other differences included their clothes: Except on special occasions, Chinese tended to wear shapeless black cotton pants and blouses, and umbrella-shaped hats made of split bamboo or grass.

Whites also found the ways of the Chinese strange. The custom they appreciated most was the Chinese New Year celebration, with the posting of colorful red paper banners conveying good wishes and invoking good luck for the coming year, a dragon parade, and, of course, fireworks. A custom found more suspect was Chinese religion. Wherever they went, Chinese established temples where they could pray, meditate, and hold meetings. Usually these temples were called "joss houses," a pejorative term that ridiculed the beliefs and religious rituals of the Chinese. (*Joss* supposedly derived from the Portuguese *deos*, meaning "God.") In 1884, the first temple in Denver's Chinatown was established on Wazee Street. An April 1884 *News* article described it as consisting of a small room painted in bright colors. At one end was a table upon which were placed candles and other ritual articles. Behind the table was a large picture of three Chinese, probably representing deities.

Perhaps the Chinese custom that whites found most esoteric was the reverence for the dead. In comparison to the solemn Christian funeral where mourners dress in black, Chinese funerals were raucous affairs where mourners wore white. A Chinese funeral procession usually included a brass band playing loud music and mourners providing food, drink, and the burning of "spirit money" to ease the deceased individual's departure to the spirit world. Whenever possible, the family sent the bones of the deceased back to China to be buried with those of their ancestors.

After reaching its peak in 1890, the Chinese population steadily declined. By the end of the century, it fell to 306. What sounded the

Chinatown community's death knell were the exclusion laws. Two years after the riot, Congress enacted the Chinese Exclusion Act, prohibiting the immigration of Chinese laborers for ten years and the naturalization of Chinese residents in the United States. It also denied the entry to wives of Chinese workers already in the country. Ten years later, the act was renewed for an additional ten years. In 1902, it was made "permanent." With the Exclusion Act, the Chinese have the dubious distinction of being the only national group to be identified in federal legislation as undesirable for immigration to the United States.

After the passage of the Chinese Exclusion Act, almost no Chinese entered Colorado for some sixty years. The population and economy of Denver's Chinatown declined. With so few Chinese women, there was no significant increase in population to replace those who died. The few young people raised there tended to leave, usually for California, in search of opportunities denied them in Colorado. Those who remained tried to survive the best they could, finding work mainly in local restaurants.

By 1940, when Denver's Chinatown was finally destroyed, the Chinese population had fallen to a mere 110. The residents consisted of three Chinese families—the Fongs, Looks, and Chins (lineal descendants of Chin Lin Sou)—and a group of elderly Chinese men. They lived in an area of abandoned and decaying buildings near other people of color who could not afford to live elsewhere. According to an official report on Chinese women:

> The living conditions are bad. There is no place for the children to play except on the street in a miserable neighborhood. Mexicans and Negroes with low ideals of life abound in this section of the city and make a bad situation worse.

The neighborhood was eventually designated a blighted area, subjected to urban renewal, and replaced by warehouses and small factories. Chinatown was no more.

World War II changed American immigration policy towards the Chinese. Since China was an ally of the United States in the war against Japan, Chinese were now acceptable members of American society and the exclusion laws became a public embarrassment. On December 17, 1943, the Magnuson Act ended an immigration policy that had blatantly discriminated against Chinese. Now, Chinese could immigrate to the United States (under a very limited annual quota of 105) and become naturalized citizens. The socioeconomic situation of the Chinese in America slowly began to change. Chinese-American veterans returning from the war found that in spite of their participation in the American armed forces, they continued to face discrimination. For example, William and Edward Chin, grandsons of Chin Lin Sou, served in the United States Army Air Corps during the war. William, a first lieutenant, fought with the famous Flying Tigers in China, and Edward, a sergeant, found himself in the European Theater, participating in the North African and Italian campaigns. Yet after returning home from the war, they were still unable to live where they wanted. They could, however, find jobs in Denver. William worked as a mechanic for the Bell Music Company, which made jukeboxes, and Edward as an electronics technician for Decimeter, a small firm making radar-receiving units for the Navy. Afterwards, they were able to move on to other, better-paying jobs.[2]

The Magnuson Act also served as a catalyst for reforming other immigration laws. The most significant of the new legislation was the Immigration Act of 1965—a liberal policy based on the principle of equality rather than an individual's national origin. With the passage of that act, Colorado's Chinese population grew. By 1980, it had reached 3,897; by 1990, it was 8,695; and by the end of the century, it was 15,658.

Along with the increase in the number of Chinese in Colorado, the character of the Chinese immigrants has changed significantly. Instead of coming mainly from southern China, Chinese have emigrated from Hong Kong, Taiwan, and elsewhere in the Chinese mainland, including the north. Instead of ordinary laborers, many of them are well-educated professionals who work in the state's "high tech" sector. There are now many women (and entire families), correcting the gender-ratio imbalance of previous years. Instead of living in a common neighborhood, the new Chinese immigrants can reside anywhere in the state, choosing mainly the cities and suburbs. Given the dispersal of the Chinese and the variety of their backgrounds, particularly linguistic, it is doubtful that they will ever come together to reestablish another Chinatown.

Excerpted from "History and Memory: The Story of Denver's Chinatown,"
Colorado Heritage, Autumn 2002

Endnotes

1 The original version of this article includes an extensive interview with the descendants of Chin Lin Sou, some of whom are fifth-generation Coloradans and vividly recall growing up in the final years of Denver's Chinatown.

2 William and Edward Chin are among the descendants of Chin Lin Sou who took part in the interview reproduced with the original version of this article. The two share memories of both their experiences in the armed services and their lives in Chinatown.

Ruth Chin, granddaughter of Chin Lin Sou

S ome of the best articles on Colorado history can be found in the Colorado Historical Society's monthly membership newsletter. Most state historical societies use their newsletters to inform members about upcoming exhibits, lectures, and tours. Some add brief features highlighting artifact donations or newly designated historic buildings or sites. The Colorado Historical Society newsletter offers something more.

Since 1997, *Colorado History NOW* has featured substantive and entertaining articles—including a cover story written by the Society's chief historian—in addition to the usual event calendar and exhibit announcements. The cover stories seldom promote Society programs; their sole purpose is to share new, interesting, and accessible historical scholarship.

When Modupe Labode joined the Society's staff as chief historian in 2002, she continued a tradition of providing members with diverse stories. Her first three articles covered a Salvation Army farm colony, a mountain summer camp for African American girls, and the Great Depression–era Unemployed Citizens League of Denver. These subjects not only reflect her passion for neglected topics, but speak to her ability to dig up seldom- or never-before-told stories. Labode's profile of Colorado's female cycling pioneers fits that mold. It also reinforces her conviction that short, entertaining essays can touch on larger themes, such as late-nineteenth-century gender issues.

Before coming to the Society, Labode earned her doctorate in history from Oxford University and taught at Iowa State University. In addition to writing for the Society's publications, she applies her talents to outreach programs, exhibit development, and mentoring the next generation of public historians. She also supervises the Society's Roadside Interpretation Program. Andy Stine, the program's assistant coordinator, found the references to Dora Rinehart that inspired this article.

Colorado's Cycliennes

—Modupe Labode

During the last quarter of the nineteenth century, the bicycle became enormously popular in Europe and the United States. Initially cyclists rode the "ordinary," a bicycle with a very large front wheel. More people took up the sport when the safety bicycle, which had front and rear wheels of roughly the same size, became widespread. Cycling was popular in Colorado, and Denver became one of the centers of the sport, supporting manufacturers, clubs, and in 1893, a magazine, *The Cycling West*, began publishing in Denver and San Francisco. By one estimate, four out of every ten Denver residents had a bicycle in 1900, making Denver the city with the most bicycles per capita in the United States. And unlike many other areas of the country, Colorado was friendly to women cyclists.

Women taking up the wheel—as aficionados called the bicycle—caused furious controversy. The strident tone of the debate can be explained, in part, because most people recognized that bicycles could change women's lives. Susan B. Anthony averred that the bicycle did "more to emancipate woman than anything else in the world." The controversy focused on whether or not it was healthy or proper for women to ride.

In 1893 *The Cycling West* reprinted an article from the *New York Mercury* in which a writer inveighed against women cyclists, mainly in order to mock such retrograde ideas. The journal asserted that the suggestion that women stick to the side saddle was simply absurd and that western women who cycled were healthy and ladylike. Over the years, *The Cycling West* carried numerous reports from physicians who asserted that bicycle riding provided especially good exercise for women.

The other aspect of riding that disturbed many commentators was that unchaperoned women could come and go as they pleased. Critics alluded to the dangerous activities that women could get into when they met men, of various classes, on bicycle paths. *The Cycling West* dismissed concerns about propriety and published poems and stories, such as "What Love and a Wheel Did" and "Proposal on Wheels," that playfully described the opportunities that cycling provided for flirting and assignations.

Coloradans in *The Cycling West* generally took a more liberal position on these matters than their counterparts in the eastern United States and Britain. This attitude probably related to the state's recent history. When women worked long and hard hours on farms and ranches, the assertion that cycling damaged women's health seemed without merit. Many critics of women cyclists saw the bicycle as the harbinger of the "new woman" who demanded the right to vote. But, women had been voting in Colorado since 1894, so the fear of women's suffrage held little power. *The Cycling West*'s editorialists had running feuds with their eastern counterparts over many issues in the politics of cycling; the difference in attitudes toward women cyclists in the West and East surely provided another issue of contention.

The Cycling West occasionally ran a column dedicated to women's issues. The column's central focus was finding clothes for women that were both practical and maintained a middle-class woman's respectability. The writers in *The Cycling West* deplored bloomers, but columnist Myrtle Reed urged her readers to dress sensibly for the sport. Reed advised women to abandon hip pads, corsets, and long skirts in favor of the "natural figure" and skirts that ended just above the ankle.

Organized cycling was exclusive. Some elite cycling clubs, such as the Denver Wheel Club, and the events they organized, were open only to well-off white men. However, one aspect of competitive cycling in which women could participate was the century ride—one hundred miles in one day—and Colorado's women appear to have been leaders in this event.

Dora Rinehart of Denver was one of the first women "centurions." Over the objections of her doctor, she took up bicycle riding in September 1895 to regain her strength after a bout of scarlet fever. She found cycling a pleasure and a challenge, and quickly began to ride centuries—over one hundred of them in 1896. She rode the popular circuits from Denver to Evans, Greeley, Platteville, and Colorado Springs. She and her husband took shorter rides together; Rinehart maintained, "I do not like to go on a hard run when my husband is with me, for you know it does take so much starch out of a man to ride a century." In 1896 she rode two hundred miles in sixteen hours and eighteen minutes, the fourth fastest time in the country. During that year, Rinehart logged 17,196 miles—a record for Colorado, the most of any woman in the United States, and the fourth highest mileage of any rider, man or woman, in the country.

The Cycling West praised the "petite but herculean" Dora Rinehart as "America's greatest cyclienne." She possessed "determination, grit, and firmness" as she rode through "rain, darkness, mud, snow, and slush" without complaint. She was one of the few women to endorse products: the Stearns bicycle, the Olive wheel, and the Samson tire. An enterprising Denver seamstress, Mrs. Baxter, even marketed the "Rinehart Skirt," modeled after the divided skirts that Dora Rinehart favored. In 1897, she had the honor of leading the cycle parade at the unveiling of Philadelphia's Washington Monument.

Dora Rinehart pioneered endurance bicycling in the 1890s
and became known as "America's greatest cyclienne."

Dora Rinehart's successes inspired other Colorado women to take up competitive riding. In the fall of 1897, Ida East attempted to beat Dora Rinehart's record for the number of centuries in thirty days, but she fell just short of her goal. Then twenty-six-year-old Katherine Wamsur came out of nowhere to take the Colorado century record for women. Wamsur, like so many others, started riding for health after she moved to Denver from St. Louis. During twenty-two days in the fall of 1897, she made twenty-two century rides.

Century rides were an outlet for women who wanted to participate in competitive, challenging events. *The Cycling West* opined that women excelled because the best distance riders were "small, wiry," and full of nervous energy. According to the beliefs of the time, women were more highly strung than most men, so it should be no surprise that a woman could keep riding past the point when "a sturdy, robust man will break down."

At the beginning of the twentieth century, the wheel abruptly fell out of favor. Working class people continued to use bicycles, but advertisements increasingly promoted bicycles as toys for children. The elite replaced bicycle clubs with automobile clubs. In 1900 *The Cycling West* renamed itself *Cycling West and Motor Field* and extended its coverage to matters concerning automobiles and motorcycles; the magazine eventually dropped coverage of cycling altogether. Cars took over the paved roads that cyclists had championed. And a new debate concerning women and wheels sprung up, this time over the propriety of women driving automobiles.

Colorado History NOW, August 2003

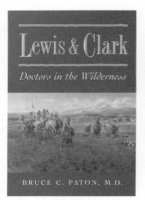
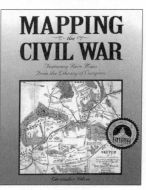